Blaze

— ♘ CORAL CANYON COWBOYS —

LIZ ISAACSON

ISBN-13: 978-1-63876-198-3

The Young Family

Welcome to Coral Canyon! The Young family is BIG, and sometimes it can be hard to keep track of everyone.

The graphic on the following page might help you keep track of everyone.

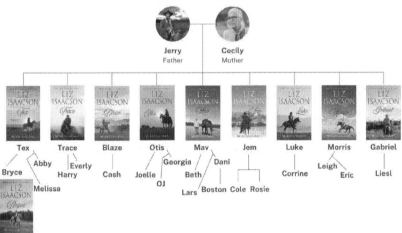

Young Family Tree
As of BLAZE, Jan 31, 2023

Jerry
Father

Cecily
Mother

Tex — Abby
Bryce
Melissa

Trace — Everly
Harry

Blaze
Cash

Otis
Joelle
OJ

Mav — Georgia — Dani
Beth
Lars — Boston Cole Rosie

Jem

Luke
Corrine

Morris — Leigh
Eric

Gabriel
Liesl

THIS IS UPDATED THROUGH BLAZE (JAN 31, 2023).

Here's how things are right now:

JERRY AND CECILY YOUNG, 9 SONS, IN AGE-ORDER:

1. TEX
   Wife: Abigail Ingalls
   Son: Bryce (20)
   Children he and Abby share: Melissa (9 months)

2. TRACE
   Engaged to: Everly Avery
   Son: Harry (14, turning 15)

3. BLAZE
   Dating: Faith Cromwell
   Son: Cash (11, turning 12)

4. OTIS
   Wife: Georgia Beck
   Daughter: Joelle (Joey / Roo, 10)
   Children he and Georgia share: OJ (Otis Judson, newborn)

. . .

5. MAV
   Wife: Danielle Simpson
   His daughter: Beth (8)
   Her son: Boston (9)
   Children he and Dani share: Lars (2)

6. JEM
   Son: Cole (6)
   Daughter: Rosie (4)

7. LUKE
   Daughter: Corrine (6)

8. MORRIS
   Wife: Leighann Drummond
   Children he and Leigh share: Eric (4)

9. GABRIEL (GABE)
   Daughter: Liesl (4)

1

Blaze Young left the family party while it was still in full swing. His son was not here with him this year for Thanksgiving, but he'd agreed to stop by his ex-wife's parents' house anyway. In truth, he'd done so just to be able to leave the Young family shindig early.

He paused outside, though the Wyoming winter had started early this year. Honestly, it started early every blasted year, and Blaze hated the cold. If he had a pretty redhead to keep him warm, he might not mind it too much.

He banished all thoughts of Faith Cromwell, noting that she marched out of his mind—with that gorgeous auburn hair and those unkissed lips—without much of a fight today. He disliked that too, but she'd broken up with him when they'd just been getting started, and he wasn't going to chase her.

That wasn't really Blaze's style and never had been.

"I thought you were leaving," one of his brothers said, and

Blaze glanced casually over his shoulder. It wasn't Jem, as his brother hadn't spoken to him since the night Faith had broken up with him.

Blaze had tried to apologize, but Jem wouldn't come out of his bedroom. He'd texted him, and Jem hadn't responded. He'd moved out the very next day, and he hadn't asked anyone for help.

But Blaze had put their momma on the job, and she'd organized the brothers and wives to go help him get his house set up. Blaze had not gone, so he only knew about Jem's new place and the conditions of it second-hand.

Since then, though, he did go with Mav in the morning to help with Rosie and Cole. Mav always went in first, and if Jem wasn't up yet, he gestured to Blaze from the front door, and Blaze would go in. And Jem was never up in time to help his children get off to school, get breakfast, or show them he cared about them.

Blaze worried about him constantly, but faced with Luke in the near darkness though it was only three-thirty, he managed a smile. "I am," he said. "Just taking a minute to enjoy the silence."

"Right?" Luke practically growled the word.

"You goin' to Tea's?"

Luke nodded, but a big sigh accompanied the action.

"Brother, that doesn't sound like you want to go to Tea's."

"Her family is as big as ours," Luke said. "Last time I was at her house, it was like her front door was one of those revolving ones. You know, how they never lock and anyone can walk in anytime?"

Blaze watched the dislike roll across Luke's face and tense up his shoulders.

"Not only that, but I haven't introduced her to Corrine yet." He glared at the gray sky above them. "I haven't even *told* her about my kid yet, and a couple of days ago, Tea said she didn't want kids."

"Mm." Blaze wasn't in the business of offering unwanted advice. If Luke wanted to talk, he'd listen, but he wasn't going to tell Luke what he should do.

"I love my daughter," Luke said fiercely. "I love all the kids in our family, and maybe I'm stupid, but seeing Tex with his new baby, and Mav, and even Otis and Georgia, even if it's not biologically theirs...I want another baby."

He didn't say that he'd missed out on most of Corrine's first three years of life, but he didn't have to. Blaze had missed eleven years, so he got it without words being said. He also didn't want to say he wanted to try being a father to a baby too. A toddler. A five-year-old who got to go to kindergarten for the first time.

Blaze smiled just thinking about it. "So what are you going to do?"

"I don't see how I can keep going out with her."

"Mm." Blaze fisted his hands in his coat pockets. "And yet, you're standing out here like you'll leave to go to her family party."

"I'm not a total jerk," Luke said. "I can't break up with her on Thanksgiving." He glared at Blaze, but Blaze had faced two-ton bulls, and Luke was nothing compared to them. He shook his head. "Besides, she just said it to a friend, and I overheard. Maybe she didn't mean it."

"Maybe she didn't," Blaze said. "Go. Have fun."

Luke frowned. "But what if she means it?"

"Then, brother, you figure out what to do." Blaze put his arm around Luke. "Do you like her?"

"Yeah." He didn't sound like he did though.

"Yeah, I'm convinced," Blaze said.

"There's...." Luke shook his head, a personal war marching across his features now. Like Blaze, he was dark in every way. He had good reason to go slow with women, but Blaze didn't pry into Luke's private life. He knew his brother's paternity had been up in the air for a while there, and Blaze wouldn't wish that kind of betrayal on anyone.

He may not be proud of what he'd done in the past, but he'd never cheated. Luke hadn't either, at least that Blaze knew of.

"There's what?" Blaze asked.

"Nothing." Luke took a deep breath and coughed. "Wow, it's too cold to do that." He smiled at Blaze, and a tiny bit of it went up into his eyes. "Where are you headed? Home?"

"Over to the Peters'," he said.

Luke's eyebrows went up. "Really? Isn't Cash in Utah?"

"Yeah." Blaze nodded. "Yep. But Fiona doesn't talk to her parents hardly at all, and they need the lifeline to their grandson." He spoke softly and slowly, not wanting to say anything too badly about his ex-wife. He knew the reasons she couldn't come back to Coral Canyon, and he didn't blame her. Not one bit.

He'd even enjoyed getting to know his ex-in-laws, as messed up as that sounded. Cash had too, and his son had a massive, amazing support network here in Coral Canyon that he desperately needed.

"You're a good man, Blaze." Luke put his arm around Blaze too.

"I'm trying to fix a lot of things I broke," Blaze said. "That's all."

Luke nodded. "Yeah, I get that." And he probably did.

They stood there for another few seconds, and then Luke dropped his arm so Blaze did too. "I should go," his brother said.

"What am I going to do about Jem?" Blaze asked.

Luke had taken a couple of steps away, but he turned back instantly. His eyes widened, and he searched Blaze's face. "I don't know, Blaze. None of us know what to do about Jem."

"He didn't drink like this in Vegas," Blaze said. "I'm worried I forced him into retirement when he wasn't ready."

Luke stepped back up onto the curb. "No," he said. "Blaze, this isn't on you at all."

"I humiliated him in public."

"No, he did that himself with how much he'd drank." Luke shook his head. "Blaze, Jem loved Chanel, even if their marriage wasn't perfect. He's drinking to erase her." He spoke with enough power to make Blaze think he had personal experience with such things.

So Blaze nodded too. "I've apologized a dozen times." More, even. "He won't talk to me, and he's my best friend." Blaze's chest collapsed again, just like it did every time he thought about Jem and the state of their relationship.

"Tex is talking about an intervention," Luke said. "Rehab.

Someone's gonna need to take his kids if he goes into an inpatient facility. Blaze, we all know that will be you."

"Could be Mav," he said. "He takes Rosie a lot."

"It'll be you." Luke was right, because Blaze didn't have a job, he didn't have a wife, and he didn't have small children the way Mav and Dani did.

"His house is a wreck," Blaze whispered. Every morning when he went inside, another layer of Blaze's heart shredded off. Honestly, someone should take Jem's kids right now, and the only reason Blaze hadn't done it yet was because he thought it would destroy his brother even further. At the very least, that directive couldn't come from Blaze.

Tex, maybe. Even Trace, who Jem loved and admired. Blaze had once thought Jem loved and admired him, but they weren't the same men they'd been on the rodeo circuit. Things changed. Too many hard truths had been spoken.

Regret lanced through Blaze, though he thought he'd done the right thing. Maybe just not at the right time.

"Yeah, I've been over there," Luke said. "We'll talk more at Tex's on Sunday, okay?" He clapped Blaze on the shoulder, which sent a shock along his back, where he'd had surgery earlier this year.

He grunted, and Luke yanked his hand back. "Sorry. Shoot, Blaze, I'm sorry."

"It's fine." The discomfort faded as quickly as it had come. "I have to get going too." He smiled at Luke, pulled him into a hug, and they went to their trucks. He made the quick drive to Carrie and Marion's, parked in the driveway, which only held one other vehicle, and reached for the loaf of chocolate sourdough bread his momma had made for them.

On the front stoop, he rang the doorbell, so unlike what a true family member would do. But when Carrie Peters opened the front door, she wore a smile as big as Jupiter. "It's Blaze," she called into the back of the house, and then she wrapped him up in a tight, motherly hug. "Oh, it's so good to see you."

"Sorry I don't have Cash this year," he said as he hugged her back.

"We'll take you alone." She stepped back and grinned at him, and Blaze saw all the fair features of his son in her face.

He smiled at her and offered the bread. "My momma made it."

"Thank you," she said. "Come in, come in. It's freezing out there." He entered and she closed the door behind him. "But it's a good thing you've got your coat."

He'd started to unzip it, because Carrie had the house heated to the level of Hades. Maybe hotter than that. He paused. "Why do I need a coat?"

"We're going to the food truck rally," Carrie said cheerfully. "They're taking donations if you can give it. Otherwise, you can eat anything out of any truck for free."

Blaze's heart sagged down to his stomach. "Oh, great," he said with zero enthusiasm. Marion came out of the kitchen, along with Fiona's brother and his wife, and Blaze hugged them all. "Ready?" Marion asked, and he reached for the winter coat that had been draped over the back of the couch.

"So ready," Blaze said, sweating already—and not only from the insane temperature inside this house.

"Do you want to ride with us?" Carrie positioned a scarf around the back of her neck and looked at him with raised eyebrows.

"I think the rally is downtown," he said. "That's almost back to the canyon, so I'll drive." That way, he could leave if he wanted to. When he wanted to. If he maybe ran into Faith.

Of course you're going to run into Faith, he told himself. She'd plastered all over the social media for Hole in One that she'd be at the free food truck rally today. Blaze might have gone otherwise, but he didn't need to make things awkward for either one of them. Not at a charity event.

He followed Carrie and Marion and McKenzie and Matt over to the food truck rally. Plenty of people had come out for this thing, and that lifted Blaze's spirits. Hopefully, this event would raise a lot of money for people in need. A voice in his head told him that he could help with that, and he should.

So after he parked, he reached over and opened the glove box to get out his checkbook. He quickly scrawled out a check, scribbled on his signature, and stuffed it in his back pocket as he slid from the truck.

He hadn't parked very close to the Peters', but he'd find them once he got to the massive circle of trucks. As he walked down the block toward the festivities, he scanned for the bright pink doughnut truck that would be covered in even more fluorescent sprinkles. He didn't see it.

Of course, there were more trucks on the other side. He approached the line to enter the big inner circle, and he found the Peters' waiting for him. He forced a smile to his face and joined them.

As they approached the donation box, he reached for his check.

"We're doing a raffle from the donation box," a man kept saying. "Checks will have the info, but if you're donating cash, be sure to get a ticket." Over and over he said it, and two women worked the line, handing out tickets.

At the box finally, Blaze shoved his check inside and flashed the man a tight smile.

"All right!" someone yelled into a microphone—which never needed to happen in Blaze's opinion. "It's time for our four o'clock drawing. Owen, bring that box up here, would you?"

Blaze kept moving, because he was in now. He scanned all the trucks now, left to right, right to left. There was no bright pink one. Maybe she wasn't here. Concern spiked inside him. Could her truck have broken down again?

After they'd broken up, she hadn't contacted him again, though he'd tried to pay for her truck one more time. When she'd ignored him, he'd dropped the subject.

Maybe she'd never gotten it fixed. *But she has two other trucks,* he thought. He didn't care about the raffle, and he thought he really needed to find another dessert truck to get his Thanksgiving Day pumpkin pie fix. He stepped over to Matt, who'd gotten a complete list of all the trucks there.

"All right, we've got the lovely mistress of Hole in One drawing this hour," the announcer said, and Blaze jerked his attention back to the stage.

"Hole in One?" he asked right out loud.

"Yeah, they're here," Matt said, completely unaware of the way Blaze's heart had turned into a giant bass drum and was beating, beating, beating at him to find Faith and demand another chance.

He didn't have to find her, because she walked up on stage in the next moment. Her lovely red hair had been tied back, and she wore an apron that looked like a big tom turkey. She smiled out at the crowd, made a big show of looking away as she reached into the donation box, and withdrew a check with a flourish.

A check.

Blaze's mind went into a frenzy, but he told himself lots of people still used checks.

No, they don't, his brain screamed at him. People over seventy-five and retired bull riders, apparently.

Faith grinned with all the happiness she possessed as she looked down at the check. He knew he'd won the moment all of her emotion slid behind a strong, tall, cement wall.

"Well?" the man on stage with her asked. "Who is it?" He peered over her forearm and let out a squeal. "My goodness!" He started searching the crowd. "Blaze Young, and he wrote a check for fifty thousand dollars!"

A collective gasp went through the crowd, and Blaze had never wanted the earth to open up and swallow him whole more than he did right now. *No,* he thought. *No, no, no.*

Had he really written a check for fifty grand? He honestly couldn't remember.

"Where's Blaze?" the man asked. "Let's get him up here!" He actually put his hand to his eyes as if he needed to shade them, when there wasn't a stitch of sunshine to be found.

Blaze stood at six-five and had shoulders like a linebacker.

He couldn't hide in a crowd even if he wanted to. Plenty of people knew who he and Jem were, and all of those eyes landed on him.

He lifted one hand as if to wave off the announcer, but he would not be swayed. He actually waved back. "There he is!" He looked over to Faith. "Come on, Mister Young! Get up here and collect your prize."

Blaze saw no other choice, and he told himself with every step that if Faith were the prize, he'd have run up and accepted gladly. As it was, he climbed the steps on the side of the stage and moved on wooden legs to stand next to her.

She stared at him, that wonder and wide-eyed look so perfect on her pretty features, and Blaze stared right on back.

"Well, isn't Faith and Hole in One the lucky one today?" the man said, and Blaze wanted to shove the mic down his throat. "She'll get half of the donation for her business, and the other half goes right to residents here in Coral Canyon! Let's all thank Blaze for supporting small businesses and the community. Come on! Put your hands together!"

He didn't have to ask more than once. The crowd there whooped and hollered, but Blaze felt like he'd been hollowed out.

Faith got half the money?

Oh, she was going to kill him, and as he stood there with a forced smile on his face, he was actually looking forward to it.

2

Faith Cromwell couldn't stay on this stage for much longer. The cameras kept going off, and she felt sure she and Blaze Young—blasted *Blaze Young*—would be on the front page of a dozen papers tomorrow. Online articles. Social media. The works.

So she kept her smile buttoned in place, and she even pinched the very tippy corner of the check on the right side of it while Blaze did the same on the left.

"All right!" Karl finally boomed into the microphone. "Wow, wasn't that exciting? Thank you for the donation, Mister Young, and those of you out there waiting for food? Don't forget to donate too!"

Faith needed to get off the stage. Now. She'd left Ricky and Walt in the truck alone, and while they were just fine, she was the one who sold the most doughnuts. They worked like dogs, though, and she hoped she could give them some of this money.

She didn't even know what twenty-five thousand dollars looked like. Her eyes dropped to the check—it looked like half of that. She couldn't even imagine writing numbers like this and then signing her name on the line, but Blaze had done it—and sloppily too.

Looking up, she figured he'd be gone. Out of the spotlight, where he claimed he didn't like to be—at least not anymore. But he hadn't left the stage. He hadn't looked away from her. Her mind blanked at the sight of that rugged jawline, those full lips, the dark and dreamy eyes.

He watched her without speaking, and she half-heartedly lifted the check. "You had no idea what you were doing when you wrote this, did you?"

He shook his head, and Faith wanted to rip the check to shreds. At the same time, she absolutely would not do that. Guilt gutted her, and she wished she could rewind time seventy-one days. Then she'd be sitting at dinner with Blaze, his brother making too much noise with his rodeo bunnies, and they'd get up and walk out together.

He'd hold her hand and drive her home. He'd walk her to the door and kiss her good-night. Oh, how Faith had dreamed of kissing Blaze good-night. And for the past seventy-one days, she wouldn't have been alone. She wouldn't have struggled to get her third truck back in the rotation. She wouldn't have thought of Blaze every day, wondering if she'd hurt him too much for him to take her back.

One look into those black-as-coal eyes, and she knew she'd hurt him...but not so much that he wouldn't give her a third chance. He'd probably strike her out if she failed with him again, and Faith wasn't going to take that swing.

He wasn't right for her, plain and simple. That was why she'd ended things before.

She herded him toward the steps, and he went silently. Once she'd joined him at the bottom of them, she grabbed onto his forearm and took him around the back of the stage so they could have some more privacy.

"We do a raffle drawing every thirty minutes," she said. "One of the food truck owners gets to draw out of the donation box. The donator gets a bunch of free coupons for our truck, and we get half of the amount of money we pull."

"Did it cost you anything to get to do that?"

She nodded. "Yeah, I had to donate a certain amount to the general fund for Hunger No More." The food truck committee had named them as their receiving charity this year. "You realize we didn't even raise twenty-five thousand dollars last year, total?"

"I wasn't around much last year," he said coolly.

Faith sighed and reached up to push her newly-cut bangs off her forehead. She hated them and regretted cutting them. But she'd needed something to make her feel different. She hated getting up in the morning and looking at herself in the mirror. Seeing the same woman who'd broken up with this fine specimen of a man, walked out on him, and then refused to respond to any of his texts or calls.

Her pulse thrummed in her veins, setting her entire blood-stream on fire. "Yeah, well, we didn't even raise twenty-five thousand dollars last year, and now, with this—" She waved the slip of paper. It was crazy that something so insignificant could mean so much. "You've exceeded it single-handedly."

He swallowed and nodded. "It would've been nice to get a memo on what people usually donate."

"For comparison," she said, glancing over her shoulder. "Tony from Chicken-Chicken pulled out a twenty dollar bill a half-hour ago."

"Congratulations, Faith," someone said, and she turned to smile at another food truck owner.

"Thanks," she said with a laugh. As she turned back to Blaze, the façade fell away. "You see why this is shocking."

"I do now, yes," he said. He shifted his feet in the dirt, and she noticed he'd gone full cowboy for Thanksgiving. Blue jeans. Black leather jacket that barely fell to his waist. Midnight-black cowboy boots. He even had a matching hat.

No wonder she was about to blurt out how stupid she'd been and beg him to take her to dinner tomorrow. She gritted her teeth and bit back the words.

"Well, I should go find my people," he said.

"Who did you come with?" she asked. "I didn't see any of your brothers."

"My ex's parents," he said.

That made Faith's eyebrows shoot up. "You hang out with them?"

"No." He smiled at her, and wow, he couldn't do that. Heat filled her face, and she had to look down so she wouldn't return the grin. "I visit them," he said. "They're my son's grandparents, so I try to stay in touch."

"That's...." Adorable. Perfect. Touching. Amazing.

Faith could've said all of those things. She didn't know how. Blaze himself was adorable, perfect, touching, and amazing, and she'd never felt so inadequate in her life.

Then his fingers stroked along the side of her neck to her jaw. Fire licked through her system, and she brought her eyes up as he gently nudged her to do the same with her head. "I miss you," he said quietly. "It's sure good to see you and talk to you."

Faith didn't know what to say. Nothing had changed between them. Had it?

They were still from two different worlds. He would always outshine her and be on another level than her. Always. She was his opposite in every way, including how he could say things so eloquently, and she stood there mute and unsure.

His gaze burned into hers. "Congratulations on winning the donation." He dropped his hand and moved by her to go back the way he'd come. Faith turned and watched him, go, every cell in her body urging her to call him back and tell him she missed him too.

Her mouth couldn't do it, and Blaze walked around the corner and past the steps that led up to the stage. Then he was gone.

"I miss you too," she whispered. "I may have been wrong to break up with you." A sigh fell from her lips, and she folded the check in half and put it in her front pocket. She had hours of work ahead of her, and her guys needed her in the truck.

Before she moved, though, Faith took her phone from the front of the turkey apron. She might not be able to say things right to Blaze's face, but she'd always been a pro at texting him. She hadn't erased any of his messages, and in fact, the man's name was still pinned to the top of her texting app.

That alone spoke how she really felt about him, and she quickly thumbed out a message and hit send.

I miss you too. I'm sorry I broke up with you in September. Do you think we could try again or am I insane?

She shoved her phone into the pocket again and told herself she would not check it until she made it to her truck. "Why can't you talk to him?" she muttered to herself. "What is this third try going to look like, Faith? You texting him day and night and never seeing him? You have to learn to *talk to him*."

She went around the corner of the stage, her stride as long as she could make it. Irritation at herself burned through her veins. Her complete ineptitude was just another reason she shouldn't ever go out with another man.

"No," she said to herself. "Just not Blaze Young."

"Why not Blaze Young?"

She froze at the sound of his voice. He stood on the fringes of the crowd, obviously having just pushed through them. He held up his phone. "You're not insane."

Faith wanted to run and hide. "I don't think it'll work."

"You just asked if we could go out again." He frowned. "I'll take you right now."

She shook her head. "You're here with your in-laws."

"Ex-in-laws." He came closer to her. "Explain this to me." He looked at his phone and back to her. "And tell me what's going on in your head."

"The same stuff as before," she blurted out. "You're like,

this mega-god of a man. You write checks for fifty thousand dollars, Blaze. You're like, perfect all the time. Perfectly dressed. You smell perfect. You say all the perfect things. And I don't know if you've noticed or not, but I'm a mess. A huge, hot mess, and perfection shouldn't get mixed up with hot mess."

Her chest ached because she'd spewed all of that in one breath. She wiped her hair back and drew in a deep breath. "I hate my bangs. I work fifteen hours a day. I think about you all the time and wonder if I did the right thing or if I was just scared."

He still said nothing, and Faith wasn't sure how long she should keep talking. "So I second-guess everything, you know? Everyone will look at us and go, 'wow, what's he doing with a loser like Faith Cromwell?' or 'Jeez, did she win him in some bachelor auction? That's the only reason a man like him would go out with her.'"

Blaze cocked his head and studied her, but blast him, he still said nothing.

"So then I focus on my truck and my employees, but I go home alone every night. No one texts me during the day. I'm *lonely*, and so then I wonder if I want to go out with you just so I won't be lonely, because you made me feel less lonely, and is that a good enough reason to want to go out with someone?" She shook her head. "I'm not making sense, I know."

She pressed her eyes closed and tried to think through the frenzy in her mind. It was impossible. "I'm not saying anything else until you say something."

"There's so many things wrong with what you just said."

Her eyes popped open. "How dare you?" She swatted at his chest with both hands.

Surprised filled his expression, and he stumbled backward. For one, two, three terrible moments, she thought he might fall, but he caught himself. Then he caught her around the wrists.

"I'm not wrong."

"Yes, you are," he growled at her. He brought his hands toward him, and hers went with them. She followed, and they stood nearly chest-to-chest, both of them breathing hard. "One, I'm not perfect. I'm about as far from that as a person can get. I've just been hiding it all from you. Two, you're not a loser. Never once have I thought that, and no one else is thinking that. Three, you're not a hot mess. You're a medium mess, and I happen to like it. It makes my hot mess of a life seem more...normal."

She blinked at him, pure surprise running through her.

"Four," he said. "I'm lonely too, and yes, it's okay to go out with me so we can both be less lonely."

"You have a million brothers," she said, finding her voice again. "You can't be lonely."

"Faith, sweetheart," he said, his voice grinding through his throat. "A man needs more than brothers." His gaze burned into hers. "You're feisty, and I love that about you. You didn't hesitate to talk to me the first time we met; it's only been recently that you've withdrawn, and I hate that. I don't want the scared-rabbit version of Faith Cromwell. I want that gorgeous, sexy, redhead who barked at me to get out of her truck, called me arrogant, and said she wouldn't go out with me."

Faith couldn't believe this man. She pulled her wrists out of his grip and then straightened her apron. "Fine," she said.

"Fine."

"You're still arrogant."

"At least I didn't tell you how much money I have this time."

"No, you wrote a check for fifty grand," she said dryly.

Blaze took a step closer to her. "Have you taken five seconds to think that you being the one on stage to pull that check from the donation box wasn't a coincidence?" he asked. "Because I have—just five seconds—and I'm not even that religious, full disclaimer. But I feel like God is telling me to try again with you. And blast it all, I want to shake Him and ask, 'Why? This woman doesn't even like me.'" He sucked in a breath, held it, and then exhaled.

Her eyes flashed between his, trying to read the emotion in the dark depths. "There's so many things wrong with what you just said."

"Enlighten me," he said.

Faith had to get back to her truck. She could not stand here and do this with him right now. "I will," she said. "At dinner tomorrow."

Blaze looked like she'd thrown ice water in his face. The expression only stayed for two seconds, and then he smoothed it away. "All right," he said. "I'll pick you up at six."

"Fine," she said.

"Fine." He reached up and smoothed her bangs back down. "I like the bangs," he said quietly, showing her that Dr. Jekyll and Mr. Hyde personality he had. She supposed she did too, going from silent and scared to demanding and flirty.

"I really do have to get back to my truck," she said.

"Right." Blaze dropped his hand again and fell back another step. "You have the same number?"

"Yes."

He tipped his hat at her and said, "See you tomorrow, Faith Cromwell." Then he turned and melted into the crowd again. Several of them stared at her, and Faith lifted her chin and set her sights on her ugliest food truck, which sat parked right in the middle across from the entrance to the circle.

She hadn't had the funds to paint it pink like the others, but it didn't matter. A huge line of people waited outside the truck, and Faith pushed Blaze and all of his perfect glory from her mind—at least for a moment.

He wouldn't go so easily, and she found she didn't even want him to. She was even less lonely when he lingered in her mind, and as she worked the rest of the food truck rally, she practiced over and over talking to Blaze the way she did her customers.

Lord, she thought. *He might not be religious, but I am. Could you make me less insecure, please? Less tongue-tied, just for one evening.*

Faith could admit she hadn't prayed much in the past year or so. It seemed like no matter what she asked of the Lord, she didn't get it. She'd been learning, however, that it wasn't about getting what she wanted. Prayer was about maintaining an open conversation with the Lord.

And she needed to do the same thing with Blaze.

You did it with God by praying no matter what, she thought, and the answer to her prayer appeared in her mind.

She had to talk to Blaze, no matter what. No matter if she was nervous or scared. Insecure or weak. Full of self-doubt or not.

She simply needed to keep talking to him. After that...well, Faith would start their third try off with dinner—a dinner full of conversation—and then she'd go from there.

3

Blaze pushed open the garage door, the emptiness of his huge mansion sinking into his chest. The silence here hurt him, and he thought he needed to get a dog. Maybe he could call that puppy rental place that Everly had used over the summer and get a canine to come stay with him until Cash got home.

As if summoned by his thoughts, his phone rang, and his son's name sat there. Blaze grinned as he swiped on the call. "Hey, buddy," he said. "How was dinner at your mom's?"

"She took us to a buffet," Cash said, and he sounded fairly enthused about it. Funny, when Blaze had done that for Thanksgiving one year in Vegas, Fiona had lectured him for an hour. He supposed a Thanksgiving buffet in small-town Southern Utah was different than the monsters in Vegas, but Blaze hadn't realized that then.

He did now. As Cash's primary caregiver, he was so much

more attuned to where his son went, with whom, and when he'd be back. He'd taken Cash to Salt Lake, where Fiona had met him for the hand-off, and she was driving their son all the way back to Coral Canyon to return him.

She'd stay for a couple of hours to see her folks, and then be on her way again. He'd text her later about his evening with them, and he'd keep it all light and fairy tale-like.

"It was so good, Dad," Cash said. "They had a whole station that was just pies."

"Wow." Blaze chuckled, his own oven woefully cold. He hadn't even had the foresight to buy a pie or two for tonight. "And your favorite kind was—" He hung on the word so he and Cash could say, "Apple," together.

Blaze grinned, mostly for himself. Mostly because he knew his son's favorite flavor of pie, something he hadn't known two Thanksgiving's ago. He'd come a long way in a short time, and that was his excuse for being tired all the time.

He sank onto the couch and reached for the remote control, smothering the sigh that threatened to leak out. "I had some great pie bites from a food truck at the rally," he said. "But it's too dang cold to be outside for very long."

"Has it snowed yet?" Cash asked.

"Not yet," Blaze said. He'd welcome the snow, because then this super-cold snap would break. As it was, the ultra-blue skies only meant his lungs would shrivel in the thirty seconds it took for him to take the trash out.

Something slammed on Cash's end of the line, and he said, "I have to go, Dad. Mister Foster from down the street just showed up with the rice crispy treats."

"Who's Mister Foster?" Blaze asked. Cash didn't answer, and Blaze pulled the phone away from his ear. His son had already ended the call. Blaze frowned and tossed the phone onto the ottoman in front of him. He didn't care if Fiona dated, not even a little bit. He found it surprising, sure. She hadn't really been out with anyone that he knew of, and he reminded himself that he didn't talk about his personal life with her either.

She was allowed to date, just like he was. He glanced over to his phone, wondering if he could text Faith. Probably not a good idea. She still had plenty of rabbit blood inside her veins, and the slightest movement on his end would send her fleeing.

That, plus, she had plenty keeping her busy at the rally tonight. Blaze had nothing to hold his attention but a lame crime drama he put on the television. He kicked off his boots and put up his feet, really slouching into the couch.

"Yeah," he said to himself as his eyes drifted closed. "The only thing better about tonight would be some of those rice crispy treats, my son, and a dog." He made no move to rectify two of those things, because the rent-a-puppy place surely wouldn't be open until Monday anyhow.

THE FOLLOWING MORNING, BLAZE DASHED DOWN HIS front steps, noting the maddening blue sky overhead as he strode toward Mav's truck. His brother lived a good fifteen minutes from Blaze, so at least the interior of the truck would be warm.

In fact, a blast of heated air struck Blaze in the face as he opened the passenger door. "I don't see why I'm comin' this morning," he grumbled as he boosted himself into the luxury pick-up truck.

"Get in the back, bud," Mav said without looking at Blaze. He was practically in the backseat himself, trying to wrangle his kids. When he did meet Blaze's eye, he looked ready to call it a day already. "I have all of them today," he said. "And they haven't stopped begging me for waffles since we left the house." His voice got louder and louder near the end of the sentence.

Blaze grinned as he turned to look at his niece and nephews. Mav had a daughter here with him for the holidays—Beth. His wife, Dani, had a son she'd brought to their marriage—Boston. And Mav and Dani had a boy together—Lars. He was almost two, and utterly aware of his rising power in the world. He did a half-scream, half-laugh, and Blaze pressed his eyes closed to make sure his brain didn't leak out of his ears.

"Yeah." Mav sighed and put the truck in drive again. He eased it around the corner of Blaze's rainbow driveway and turned back down the street the way he'd come. "You have to come, because I need help with the waffles."

"I have to come, because you think Jem is going to let me take his truck and his kids to get waffles."

"That too," Mav said easily though his fingers on the steering wheel tightened. They'd been going to Jem's on school days to make sure his son got out the door on time and his daughter got fed. Blaze had brought Rosie back to his house a time or two, but Mav always took her home to Jem.

On weekends, when their brother didn't surface for days, Tex, Otis, Morris, and Mav had been handling things so Blaze wouldn't have to come face-to-face with the brother who wouldn't talk to him.

Mav forwarded every text he got from Jem that expressed thanks. Tex and Morris did too. Blaze had never received one himself, and he told himself it was because Jem didn't think he'd been there to help. Why would he? Blaze never went inside in the morning until Mav cleared the coast. He didn't text and lecture his brother. He didn't talk to him at all—not since he'd apologized over and over and over for pushing Jem when Jem wasn't ready to be pushed.

Sadness threaded through Blaze now, the same way it did every time he thought about his best friend. He and Jem had shared *so much* in their lives. They'd lived together in Vegas, far from every other Young on the planet. They'd traveled together. Consulted together. Trained together.

Not once or twice. For years and years and years. When Blaze needed to make a decision, he went to Jem first. Losing him had been a huge blow Blaze had not anticipated. He hadn't known his actions from a couple of months ago could cause such a divide between them, and he hadn't realized how integral Jem was to his happiness.

"I miss him," Blaze whispered to his own reflection in the passenger window.

"He misses you too," Mav said. The man must have supersonic hearing to have heard Blaze, but he didn't question it. He was a father—and had always been a good one, unlike Blaze—so Mav had many years of practice to be able to hear someone when they spoke. He listened to others; he always had.

"Luke says there might be an intervention." Blaze swung his attention to Mav then.

"Family dinner at Tex's on Sunday." Mav's jaw kneaded as much as his fingers then.

"Jem won't be there?"

Mav gave him a dry, withering look. "When's the last time we've seen Jem on a weekend?"

"Fair point." Blaze enjoyed the mild arguing in the backseat, because it covered this conversation. "Momma invites him every week, though. Maybe this week, he'll come."

"If he does, then I'm sure someone will bring it up anyway," Mav said. "Luke and Gabe don't hold back things that need to be said."

"Sure," Blaze said.

"You usually don't either."

"It absolutely cannot come from me," Blaze said. "If you *don't* want Jem to do something, have me suggest it. Otherwise...." He left the word there, because it used to be the complete opposite. In fact, just a few summers ago, Mav had wanted everyone in the same room for a family reunion, and he'd texted Blaze to make sure Jem would come. Blaze was a few years older than Jem, and he could normally get his younger brother to do whatever he wanted him to do.

Not anymore.

"What are you doing tonight?" Mav asked. "Dani's making the creamed corn she forgot about yesterday, and Daddy gave us a whole smoked turkey."

Blaze shifted in his seat, hoping the movement was small

enough to go unnoticed. "Oh, uh." He cleared his throat. That wouldn't be. "I have a date tonight. I think."

"You think?"

"It's with Faith." Blaze looked over to his brother, and their eyes met. Enough was said for Mav to know that yeah, Blaze *thought* he had a date that night. With Faith, however, anything was possible.

"Well, if it doesn't happen tonight," Mav said. "It will soon, I'm sure, and you'd be welcome unannounced at our place."

"Thank you."

"How'd you get her to go out with you again?" Mav was one of the few people Blaze had kept updated on his love life, mostly because there wasn't a lot to update with, and also because Blaze would rather poke out his eyes with dull spoons than talk about a woman he liked with someone. Almost anyone.

For some reason, Mav was safe for him. He always had been.

Kind of like Jem, he thought.

"She was at the rally last night," Blaze said as he exhaled. "I went with the Peters', and I...ran into her."

"Sounds intriguing," Mav teased. His grin widened, and Blaze only shook his head as he allowed the tiniest of smiles to touch his lips.

"Not really," he said.

Mav made the last turn onto Jem's street, and his sad, nearly-falling-down rental came into view. His grin dried right up then, as did Blaze's. "I hate this road," Mav said as his truck hit one of the larger potholes.

"I hate it too," Blaze said, but not because of the physical characteristics of it. "I hate turning down it. I hate how sad it makes me feel. I hate how...dark it is."

"Yeah," Mav murmured. He pulled into Jem's driveway, their brother's truck parked there. So he was home. Of course, the truck was always parked there in the mornings; it was evening when no one could find Jem.

He put the truck in park and twisted to look at his children. "You guys stay here with Uncle Blaze, all right? I won't be gone but a minute."

"No," Blaze said. "I'm gonna come in with you this time." He eyed the front window, where the curtains fluttered. "Rosie's seen us."

"You sure?" Mav asked, his eyes heavy on the side of Blaze's face.

"Yeah." He didn't turn and look at Mav. "If I'm takin' his kids and his truck, I'll have to face him, won't I?" He opened the door, an icy blast of air nearly punching the life from his lungs. A choice word went through his head, but he didn't let it out in front of the kids. "Plus, I saw him at Thanksgiving yesterday, and we were fine."

They weren't fine. They'd played nice so they didn't ruin the holiday for Momma and everyone else. Blaze had gotten an earful from both Abby and Georgia, and he'd promised he wouldn't cause any drama for the holidays.

Mav's hurried footsteps came up behind him, and Blaze let Mav go up the steps to the front door first. He knocked and called, "Jem? It's Mav," before he opened the door. It wasn't locked, which irritated Blaze, and they went inside.

"Uncle Mav!" Rosie skipped toward him. "Uncle Blaze,

look at my new dress." She wore a pretty pink and white check-ered dress that Blaze knew had come from Georgia. She'd gotten a new shipment of clothes in with a set of dolls that apparently went with some books.... Blaze had gotten lost about there—but he knew the dress matched a doll. And Rosie picked up the doll and held it toward him too. "It's the same one as Gillian's."

"It sure is," Blaze said with a smile.

"Have you kids eaten breakfast?" Mav asked as Cole switched off the TV. "I'm taking my kids for waffles, and we thought you'd like to come."

"Yeah!" Rosie cheered, but Cole's gaze flickered toward the hallway.

"Daddy's asleep still," he said.

"So you haven't eaten." Mav rocked back on his heels, his expression neutral. How he did that, Blaze didn't know. He felt two seconds away from turning volcanic and erupting, but he'd kept himself dormant for the past few months while helping the kids. He could do it today too.

"No," Cole said. "I can go ask him."

"I will." Mav took a quick step in front of Cole. "Why don't you help Uncle Blaze find your daddy's car keys? My truck is full." He grinned at Cole and then Blaze, his eyes holding a sense of wariness for that single moment, and then he disappeared down the hall.

"The keys are in the kitchen somewhere," Cole said. "I think in the drawer by the stove." He led the way in there, and Blaze unconsciously started to clean up the fruit roll-up wrappers and cups that had been left on the tiny two-barstool peninsula. His brother didn't cook much, but the kids did eat breakfast here, so Blaze was well-versed with putting dishes in the decade-old dishwasher and cleaning up papers, boxes, and wrappers from the convenience foods they ate at other times. He'd become an expert at taking out the trash and throwing away his brother's leftovers. Jem had been like that in Vegas too, always wanting to take his food home...where he never ate it.

The sink didn't have too many dishes in it from yesterday, thankfully, and Blaze put the cups there that he was sure he'd load into the dishwasher come Monday morning. Cole opened the drawer and rummaged around, but he didn't find any keys.

"I don't know, Uncle Blaze."

"Can we not go?" Rosie asked.

Blaze faced her and swooped toward her, picking her up as her chin started to wobble. "I want to go, Uncle Blaze." She whimpered and wrapped her skinny arms around his neck.

"You can come," he soothed her. "We just have to find the keys." He should've driven his truck, but Mav hadn't said anything about bringing all the kids. Plans changed all the time, and Blaze knew that better than anyone. When it came to his family—as loud and as big as they were—he'd stopped making plans years ago. Then he never had to be disappointed or irritated when things changed.

He started looking in the drawer while Cole moved to another one. Blaze wasn't sure where Jem put his keys when he finally stumbled home. He could still have them in his pants pockets for all Blaze knew.

His coat.

He'd just turned toward the side entrance to the house

when voices came down the hall. Plural. Mav's *and* Jem's. Panic reared inside Blaze, but he couldn't very well throw his four-year-old niece to the floor and run out before his brother saw him.

In fact, all he could do was turn in that direction before Jem entered the kitchen. He cut off mid-sentence and stared at Blaze with Rosie in his arms. Blaze cleared his throat. "Morning, Jem."

"Morning," his brother said back automatically. Almost instantly after the second syllable came out, his features darkened. "What are you doin' here?" He took the few steps to Blaze and plucked Rosie away from him. "Why is my daughter crying?"

"She's not crying, Jem," Mav said.

Blaze inched backward, ready to fade into the peeling wallpaper if possible. Maybe he could reach the door and slip outside.

"I want to go get waffles, Daddy," Rosie said, and she was definitely crying.

"We just need the keys, Daddy," Cole said. "Then you can go back to bed." The boy would be seven in a few weeks, and Blaze wanted to shout that at Jem. Did he even remember? Was he planning anything for his son's birthday?

But Blaze couldn't ever say such things. For one, he'd barely been there for Cash for the first nine years of his life, so it would be like the pot calling the kettle black. For another, Jem didn't need Blaze's reminders right now.

"Waffles?" Jem asked as if he'd never heard of the breakfast food. "You guys don't need to take my kids for waffles."

"What do you have to eat?" Mav asked. If Blaze had voiced

the question, it would've sounded like a challenge. But with Mav, it didn't. "Because my kids are drivin' me bananas, and I'd love to squash their waffle dreams." He smiled at Jem, who still looked like he didn't know what planet he lived on.

"Here they are," Cole said, the distinct jingling of keys filling the space after Mav's statement. He stepped between Mav and Jem. "Can we go, Daddy? We don't have anything good here."

"Sure, we do," Jem said. He moved the few feet to the fridge and opened it. Even from where Blaze stood at the side entrance, he could see the fridge was almost bare. He exchanged a look with Mav and knew they'd be stopping by the grocery store sometime this weekend to replenish that.

Jem slammed the fridge closed almost as fast as he'd opened it. "You're right. We don't have anything good here." He slid Rosie to the floor, his expression dark, dark, dark. "I suppose you can go."

"Yay! Yay! Yay!" Rosie jumped up and down and yelled while Cole grinned and handed the keys to Blaze.

"Wait a second." Jem's fists balled up. "Kids, go get your shoes and coats." He waited while they did that, and he didn't look away from Blaze for a single moment in the interim. "You're driving?"

Blaze dropped his gaze to the ground. "Yes. I left my truck at home."

"You're taking *my* kids." He wasn't asking this time. "In *my* truck."

"Jem," Mav said, not gently, but not forcefully either. "If I didn't have my kids with me, it would be me taking them, and you wouldn't care."

Blaze looked up in time to see Jem flick his gaze to Mav and then focus on him again. Blaze held up the keys. "I'd love to take your kids, Jem. I used to take them to do things all the time."

"No." Jem advanced a step, but he wasn't menacing without spurs on. "We went together."

Blaze swallowed, his emotions so out of control right now. "Yeah," he agreed. "And it was awesome. I miss that. I miss *you*." He fisted the keys and held them out. "You could come if you wanted." It wouldn't be just like old times, but it would be a lot better than the months of silence between the two of them. Heck, this conversation was already more than Blaze had gotten since that fateful night when Faith had broken up with him and he'd ruined everything with Jem.

"Jem, I'm sorry," he said as Mav stepped between them.

"Hey, back up, Jem." He put one hand on Jem's chest. "And you can come, sure, but you'll ride with me. No matter what, Blaze is gonna have to drive your truck, because I'm not convinced you're sober."

All of the bravado inside Jem deflated. He backed up and turned around. "I'm not," he said. "You can go. Take 'em. Take the truck. Go." He started to leave the kitchen.

"Jem," Blaze and Mav said together.

He paused but didn't face either of them again. "Just...go."

Mav started to move forward, but Blaze put his hand on his brother's shoulder to stop him. Jem padded off down the hall, dropped to his knees to help Rosie with her zipper and give her a kiss, then said something to Cole that had the boy hugging his father tightly around the head.

Blaze's heart tore right out of his chest then. Jem had always adored his kids, and he would never neglect them on purpose. At the same time, he *was* definitely neglecting them because of his own pain and suffering.

The kids continued toward the kitchen, and Jem got to his feet. He looked back down the hall then, but Mav was already busy with herding the kids toward the front door. Blaze held Jem's eyes until his brother nodded—just once—and then he ducked out the side entrance too.

The air out here was far too cold to draw deeply into a man's lungs, but that was exactly what Blaze did. "Thank you, Lord," he exhaled, his breath fogging in front of him. The situation wasn't completely resolved, but there was now a crack somewhere one had not been before.

Blaze could work with a crack in his brother's armor. He'd done it before, and he could do so again. "All right," he said jovially to his niece and nephew. "Should we race Uncle Mav to get waffles?"

"Yeah!" Rosie cheered, but Mav just rolled his eyes.

"I'm parked behind you," he said to Blaze, who couldn't stop smiling anyway.

After helping the kids into the backseat, he got behind the wheel. "All right, guys," he said. "Seatbelts. And y'all can't eat too much, because then you'll be sick this afternoon." He looked at Cole and Rosie in the rearview mirror and adjusted Jem's seat so he could reach the pedals better.

"I can't eat too much either, because I have a big date

tonight, okay? Let's make a pact that we won't eat ourselves sick."

"All right," Rosie chirped, but Cole asked, "Can I get the chocolate chip pancakes, Uncle Blaze? I don't really like waffles."

"I don't see why not," Blaze said, his heart happier than it had been in weeks and weeks. "As long as you don't inhale them." The boy could eat fast, and the last thing Blaze needed was Cole getting sick on his watch. "Promise me now."

"I promise," the boy said, and with that, Blaze backed out of the driveway and followed Mav, in no hurry to try to beat his brother anywhere. After all, he didn't even know where they were going for breakfast.

He did know where he was going to take Faith for dinner that night—The Branding Iron. She loved steak and seafood, and it was Friday night. The premier steak house in Coral Canyon would have the best on their menu, and he'd already booked a reservation for two for six-thirty.

Now, all he could do was pray that she wouldn't stand him up. The way things had gone with Jem today made Blaze very hopeful for tonight. Very hopeful indeed.

4

Faith cursed under her breath as she pulled into her driveway.

"What?" Trinity asked. "I'm sure it's not your blouse. You can't even be home yet."

"It's not my blouse," Faith told her sister. "Though I feel like a clown in it." She'd been at her sister's house for the past three hours as the two of them worked through Faith's hair, makeup, and clothing choices for tonight's date with Blaze.

She'd been out with him before, yes. But something about tonight's dinner felt special. It felt like a lot hinged on how well it went, and she wanted to knock his socks off the moment she opened the door.

The cowboy billionaire wouldn't be late, she knew that. Blaze was nothing if not punctual, and he'd told her that the rodeo had taught him that. "Can't miss flights or call times," he'd said. "Or I wouldn't have a career."

She'd teased him that dates weren't quite as important as a billion-dollar rodeo career, and he'd disagreed with her. *A date with you is more important,* he'd said.

The man knew all the right things to say, that was for dang sure.

"So what's going on?" Trinity demanded.

Faith blinked as she brought her sedan to a stop. "Orion just texted."

"You will ignore him," Trinity said even as Faith picked up her phone to check the text from her employee. "Faith, do not look at that text!"

Faith didn't answer as she swiped over to the message. *This truck is out of juice, boss.*

A sigh slipped out of her mouth.

"I heard that," Trinity said. "I don't know why I'm still talking to someone who isn't *listening to me.*"

"One of my trucks is down," Faith said, her mood for the evening turning absolutely sour. She was already nervous as all get-out, and now she had to deal with a broken-down truck too? Couldn't God cut her a break for once?

He did, she told herself. *When you pulled a fifty-thousand-dollar check from a box.*

The very thought lifted her spirits. "It's fine," she said to the nighttime air. "I'm going inside, and I'm going to tell him to close down the truck and go home."

Trinity said nothing as Faith got out of the car. She'd made it up the steps and started to close her garage door before her sister said, "Who are you, and what have you done with Faith?"

Faith laughed, glad to be inside where her heater worked.

She didn't envy Orion or Joe out on the trucks tonight. "I got that money in the rally yesterday," she said. "I can fix the truck later."

"L-later?" Trinity repeated. "Faith, seriously. Is this you?"

Faith sighed again as she set her keys down on the built-in desk in her tiny kitchen. "You think I don't listen to you, Trin, but I clearly do. You're always telling me how I don't have to rush off and fix every problem the moment it happens, aren't you?"

"Yes, but—"

"And then I do it, and you're questioning me? I think I'm going to change out of this clown-blouse and go see if I can get under the hood of that truck and fix it myself."

"Don't you dare," her sister hissed.

Faith grinned, because she was definitely more sarcastic than Trinity. "Which part? Change out of the blouse or go fix the truck?"

"Either one," Trinity said. "One, you don't have time to change. Two, you can't even hold a wrench the right way."

"I can too," Faith said, though most of her skills with tools involved the kitchen type. "Maybe." They laughed together, but Faith didn't know how to let her giggles linger. "Trin, is this okay?"

"Oh, there you go again. Not listening." Her sister's chuckles faded. "Faith, if there's ever a time you listen to me, now is it. Do *not* stand in your own way tonight."

Faith nodded, her voice stuck behind a lump in her throat. Trinity had spent the afternoon with her, assuring and reassuring her that going out with Blaze again was indeed okay.

More than okay. Absolutely the right thing to do, because she couldn't let their relationship end with her running out of a restaurant while he dealt with his intoxicated brother. She hadn't even said goodbye to him properly.

"I know you're there," Trinity said. "Do not cry, either. I worked so hard on those wings!"

"I'm not going to cry," Faith whispered.

"Mm hm." Trinity didn't say anything else, giving Faith a few seconds to just be.

"I love you, Trinity."

"I love you too, Faith," she said. "I want to hear all about this date—but not tonight if you're out late. In the morning. Ty is killing me with his early-morning demands to be fed."

Faith grinned and agreed, then ended the call a moment later. Her nephew had recently turned three years old, and he loved to get up really early in the morning, let the dog out, and then demand breakfast. Trinity and her husband had curbed the toddler's ability to open the door and let their family pet go roaming the neighborhood, but the toddler still climbed in bed with them nearly every morning before six a.m.

Faith didn't serve doughnuts for breakfast, but she did work late into the evening sometimes. Now that winter had arrived, any time after four-thirty felt late, and her slumber parties with her nephew had dried up. Otherwise, she'd take Ty for Trinity and Corbin, and she'd let him wake her up early in the morning. Funny thing was, he never did.

She hadn't told Trinity that, though, and it was one secret Faith was willing to keep from her sister. How she felt about Blaze...she hadn't been able to keep that a secret, and she'd

48

texted the whole story about the check and her messages to him and what they'd talked about over the course of the evening last night.

Thus, Trinity had been waiting with the curlers, the makeup, and the clown-blouse this afternoon. Faith looked down at it, almost getting blinded by the bright yellow. "Oh, I have to change."

She'd taken two steps toward her master bedroom, her low heels clicking against the tile, before the doorbell rang.

Her stomach seized; her feet froze; she looked toward the front door as if she was a naughty cat and if only her eyes moved, whoever was there would simply go away.

Blaze wasn't going to go away, Faith knew that. He'd been texting her all day, almost like he'd been waiting for their communication doors to open up again, and then he could flood her with his thoughts and the happenings of his life.

She liked it, actually, and seeing him with his brother and nieces and nephews that morning had warmed her soul.

"He's a good man," she told herself as she pivoted on her toe and began the walk toward the front door. As her house was small, and her stride long, she arrived there after only a few steps. Blaze didn't ring the doorbell again, and Faith's fingers moved swiftly over the locks to get the door open.

He stood there in all his cowboy glory, the dark blue jeans slung low on his hips, the belt buckle not quite the size she'd seen in the pictures online but big enough. He wore a leather jacket, of course, because what else did super-rich, hot, former rodeo champions wear?

Black leather, duh.

Underneath that, the hint of a dark gray shirt peeked out. He wore black cowboy boots on his feet and a black cowboy hat, as if the rest of his features weren't already as dark as midnight too. They were. Oh, they were.

His nearly black hair matched his dark-as-coal eyes—which currently glittered at her. He might as well have whistled at her, but he didn't, because he had more manners than that.

His gaze did drop down the hideously yellow blouse to the black slacks she'd managed to get Trinity to let her borrow. Then to her heeled feet, where his eyes rebounded to hers. "You are gorgeous," he said, his voice a touch on the throaty side.

Of course.

Blaze didn't say she "looked" a certain way. She *was* gorgeous, as if she'd be just as pretty in sweats and slippers. And his voice couldn't just come out normal; it had to be husky and low, as if she stirred something inside him that churned up emotion and left it in the back of his throat.

"I'm gonna have a hard time not kissing you tonight," he said as he stepped inside. "I'm assuming I can come in? You don't have a coat on yet, and it's freezing out here." He closed the door behind him as she backed up to give him room.

He faced her again, everything about him so fluid and easy. Faith folded her arms. "You think you're going to kiss me tonight?"

"No, ma'am." He trailed his fingertips up her bare forearm. "I am not. I made a promise with myself not to kiss on the first date."

"We've been out before."

"Mm, yes, but not since we started again." Those delicious eyes met hers. "Unless you want me to kiss you tonight?"

She did...and she didn't. The very idea of kissing him sent a shiver of anticipation sliding up her spine. Fear took over about the base of her neck, and her stomach swooped.

Blaze only grinned at her, and she had no idea what he found on her face. He wrapped her in his arms and held her against his solid, warm chest. She held him back, every lonely piece of her heart mending and coming back together into a whole with a simple hug.

"Mm, you smell great. You look amazing. Do you need another minute, or can I get your coat?"

"You can get my coat." She stepped out of his arms, gave him a shy smile, and indicated her front entry closet.

He opened the door and studied the contents of it for only a moment before he plucked a coat from the hanger. "I think this one." He'd selected a black, puffy, bomber jacket, and it would've been the one Faith had chosen for herself. "I love this blouse, by the way. It's such a great color with your hair."

Faith dang near rolled her eyes, but she managed to slide her arm into one sleeve instead. "Trinity will be thrilled to hear it," she said.

"You don't like the blouse?" He circled her as she turned and slid on the other sleeve.

"I think it's a little bright."

"I think it's perfect." His hand slid along her waist as he came to her side. "Still love the bangs." He looked up at them and then back at her. "The Branding Iron okay? You never said."

"I didn't think I needed to state the obvious."

He grinned at her, and that smile should be illegal. "Sometimes you do."

"Well, then, I think you look rather dashing tonight, Mister Young." She flattened his jacket collar—which was already perfectly flat—and leaned into his chest a bit more. "Very tasty."

He chuckled and shook his head. "You're not going to make me break my promise."

He brought out a side of her Faith didn't know very well—a side that could tease and giggle and tuck her hair behind her ear. "If you say so," she said—another thing she didn't even know she *could* say.

She led him to the door, but he opened it. The night air was no joke, and they shelved the witty banter in favor of hurrying to his truck, which he'd left running. "Thank goodness," she said as the warm air flowed across her face. He steadied her as she hoisted herself into the truck, and he was all grins as he closed her door and then hurried to get behind the wheel.

Faith didn't detect any limp in his stride now, and the moment his door closed, she asked, "How's your back?"

"Just fine," he said smoothly.

She put her hand on his forearm. "Is it, Blaze?"

He paused and looked at her, and Faith thought *she* might be the one to kiss *him* that night.

"I've been worried about you," she whispered.

"Have you now?" His eyes danced with mischief. "Clearly not enough, or you'd have come by. Sent food. Something."

She pulled her hand away as he started chuckling. "Oh, come on." He grabbed her fingers and tucked his between them.

"Yeah." He sighed, his eyes down on their hands. "I've missed this." He raised those deep, dark eyes to meet hers. "I've missed you, Faith."

Faith swallowed, her sister's warning rotating in her head. *Do not stand in your own way tonight.* "I've missed you too, Blaze."

His grin was exquisite, and she wondered how many people told him that they missed him. In that moment, Faith realized that maybe not very many. She smiled and ducked her head too, his hands deliciously warm against hers.

"Oh, don't think I can't see what you're doin', Miss Cromwell." He flipped the truck into reverse with the wrong hand, so he didn't have to let go of hers.

"What?" she asked.

"Tucking your hair. Smiling like that. You're trying to make me kiss you before the date ends."

"The date hasn't even *begun*, Mister Young," she threw back at him.

"It most certainly has. I came to the door and picked you up already."

"Mm." She settled into her seat and let him drive. "Who has Cash tonight?"

"Cash is in Utah with his mother," Blaze said.

"Oh." Faith looked at him, but he didn't tear his gaze from the sleepy neighborhood road. "Really?"

"Yes, really," he said.

"Did he just go today?"

"No, he's been there all week." Blaze glanced over to her. "He comes home on Sunday night. Why?"

Faith reseated her fingers in his, getting all the pieces lined up. "You were at the food truck rally with—"

"Her parents, yes."

"Without him?"

"Yes."

Faith wasn't sure what to make of that. She blinked a couple of times, wondering why this news surprised her the way it did. "I—I suppose I assumed he was with you last night, so he could see his grandparents."

"He'll see them on Sunday," Blaze said. "Fiona will visit them for a little bit before she leaves for Utah again."

Fiona. She hadn't heard his ex's name before. "Does she come to Coral Canyon often?"

"No," Blaze said. "Hardly ever."

"Why is that?"

Blaze glanced over to her then. "It's really complicated, and not really my story to tell."

"Oh," Faith said again. "I—I'm sorry?"

Blaze sighed, rolling his head to his left, away from her. "It's nothing to apologize over. Sorry I was a little short there. It's just...her relationship with her parents is really delicate. There's a lot of bad blood there, and she makes the best of a difficult situation."

Faith nodded, reminding herself not to start talking so soon. If she gave Blaze time, he'd speak again. This time, though, he didn't. So she asked, "But you're okay with your son over there?"

"Yeah, sure," Blaze said. "They didn't lie to me for my entire life." He turned toward her, his face a mask of shock. "I mean—

they're not bad people. I'm fine if my son knows them. I *want* him to know them. Fiona does too."

Faith decided to let this wash away for now. She smiled and squeezed Blaze's hand. "All right. Tell me more about this rent-a-puppy you think you're going to get next week."

"Oh, I don't just *think* I'm going to get him," Blaze said, that genuine smile coming to his face. "I'm going to get him. Tuesday at ten a.m."

Faith liked his childlike exuberance. "I suppose you have time for a puppy in your life. It's just me who can't keep a goldfish alive."

"That's because your tank is saltwater," he shot back.

She burst out laughing at his quick wit. He grinned and grinned, but he didn't laugh. "I've missed that laugh, Faith Cromwell."

"I've missed the way you call me by my first and last name all the time." She beamed at him. "And you're right. I manage to keep eight saltwater fish alive just fine."

"You'd do great with a puppy too." He turned the truck onto Main Street, where far more streetlamps shone from above. "You don't even go to work until noon."

"Are you calling me lazy?"

"I would never." He grinned at her. "Besides, you just told me yesterday how you work fifteen hours every day. I'd have to be an idiot to think you're lazy."

"Working a lot of hours doesn't mean one isn't lazy," she said.

"Oh, boy," he teased. "Here we go."

"What?" she asked. "It doesn't. It might just mean I'm not very good at what I do."

"You don't really think that, do you?" He peered at her as he came to a stop at a red light.

She wasn't going to bring her food trucks on the date tonight. "I don't know. No? I'm a good baker, but Blaze, it would be easier to get up at three a.m. and go make doughnuts at the grocery store. I'd be off by noon, have a stable income, and get to take naps every day."

"Sounds totally boring," he said.

She smiled and shook her head, because she'd told him once that she couldn't imagine herself living that kind of life. "Maybe so." She didn't say anything else, but with Blaze, she'd never had to.

"Tell me what's plaguing you," he said quietly.

"No," she said. "Not tonight. Tonight isn't going to be about work."

"What's tonight going to be about then?"

"Something that's not work," she said.

"Well, if you don't have a topic, maybe I should take you home right now." He grinned at her as the traffic started moving again.

"How about *you* come up with a topic, Mister Smarty Pants?"

"Work," he said without missing a beat.

"No," Faith said. "Vetoed. Try again."

"Uh, goldfish?" he guessed.

"Wrong." She laughed for a moment and then tried to straighten out her lips. Unsuccessful, she let herself smile and feel it way down deep inside herself. Yes, being out with him was far better than sitting home alone, even if she had to wear the bright neon blouse to do it.

"I don't have a topic," he said.

"Hm, maybe we should end this now." She grinned at him, glad when he made no move to slow down the truck.

He smiled back and asked, "Did you spend any part of Thanksgiving with Trinity and her family?"

"Yep. I helped her make rolls in the morning, and we ate about one. Then I went to get the truck ready for the rally."

"The rally was good?"

"Yeah," she said. "I pulled this fifty-thousand-dollar check out of the raffle box, and it came with a really hot cowboy."

Blaze looked at her again, his eyebrows sky-high. "Really hot?"

"Or maybe he was really cold, I don't know." She grinned at him, her confidence falling with every moment where his smile stayed hidden. "I guess our signals—my signals—have been kind of...off lately."

Blaze returned his attention out the windshield. "You've been fine, Faith."

"I made a promise to myself too, you know."

"Oh? What was it?" He flipped on his blinker and eased into the middle lane so he could turn left into The Branding Iron.

Faith swallowed, her throat suddenly so dry when she'd been fine before. She watched the oncoming traffic continue to whiz by, not sure how to tell him the promise she'd made.

"Faith?"

"Do you ever feel like you're one breath away from getting in a head-on collision?" The lights stopped coming at her, but Faith continued to stare down the block. Blaze could easily turn now, but he didn't.

She blinked, blinked again, and looked at him. "You can turn."

"You're not getting out of telling me what you promised yourself." He made the turn. "But I'll give you a minute to organize your thoughts. I know you like that."

She did like that, and though a rush of cold fear washed over her, Faith did her best to combat it by telling herself she'd once held her own with Blaze Young. Before she'd known who he was and how much money he had, she'd stood up for herself. She'd turned him down flat.

She didn't want to do that again, but she didn't have to wilt in his presence either. He found a parking spot in silence, pulled in, and killed the engine.

"It's gonna get mighty cold out here pretty fast," he said. "You ready yet?"

5

Oh, Blaze could get burned by that fire in Faith's emerald eyes. "That sounds like a blackmail statement." She reached to unbuckle her seatbelt and then open her door.

Blaze flung out his hand to stop her. "Wait. Wait a minute. I'm gonna come get the door for you."

"I can open my own door, Blaze."

So no more teasing Mr. Young. He saw how it was—and he liked it. He liked her, and all of her gentleness and all of her sass and everything in between. Too much already, he knew, though he'd managed to keep that a secret until his kissing comments tonight. She was simply too scrumptious not to think about tasting.

Then *she'd* called *him* tasty, and dang if Blaze hadn't needed the icy air outside to cool off a little bit.

"You can tell me the promise whenever you'd like, okay? Let me come get the door for you, so I can pretend to be a proper gentleman?" He lifted his eyebrows, only releasing her arm when she nodded.

He got out and rounded the hood. He had her door open in record time, and he couldn't help touching her waist as she slid to the ground. "I'd say it's icy and to be careful, and then I'd hold onto you tightly as we cross the lot, but it hasn't even snowed yet." He grinned at her. "Any chance I can hold onto you tightly anyway?"

Faith softened and nodded. "I promised myself I wouldn't stop talking to you."

He let his surprise pour through him, covering it by moving out of the doorway and slamming her door closed. "Stop talking to me?"

"You make me kind of nervous," she said. "Then I can't say what I want to say, and I have to text it to you instead. Like yesterday."

He nodded, everything gelling. She had let him walk away and then texted him some very nice things. Things he'd needed to see and hear. "Ah, I see."

"So I promised myself I'd just...keep talking to you. Even if I'm nervous, or even if I think I sound stupid."

"You never sound stupid," he murmured. She did let him keep his arm around her, his hand on the far side of her waist, as they walked toward the entrance to the steakhouse. It was absolutely freezing, but neither of them hurried the way they had at her place.

She took a big breath several steps from the entrance, and Blaze glanced over to her. She did seem more nervous now than she had at her house and in the truck. He wanted to jump in and rescue her from her thoughts, but he didn't. He'd learned to let some silence hang in his life, mostly from his son, who needed some extra time to process things before he understood them.

"I've always wanted to be a baker," she said as he reached to open the door. "I loved baking growing up. Trying new recipes." She sounded much more relaxed, and then the whoosh of noise and heated air covered them as they entered The Branding Iron.

He took her hand and wove through the Friday night crowd to the hostess stand. "Blaze Young," he said to the woman there. "I had a reservation at six-thirty." He really wanted somewhere quiet for him and Faith to be able to talk, and he kicked himself for booking The Branding Iron.

"He's on four," a second woman said. "He called earlier."

"Four?" the first woman asked, peering at her tablet. "You sure? These are blocked off."

The second woman looked at him, and Blaze gazed back. He knew she recognized him—or at the very least, considered him a high-roller. Someone important. "One's for him." She picked up two menus. "You can come with me, sir."

"Perfect." He gave them both a smile and took Faith with him, leaving the crowd of people waiting for a table behind. Thankfully. He followed the woman in all black past noisier tables, through the whole restaurant to a set of double doors in the back.

She hipped her way through them, and relief pulsed through Blaze as the din got reduced to almost nothing. She indicated the cozy, circular booth against the wall. "Is this okay?"

"Yes, ma'am," he said, really laying on the drawl thick. "This is perfect."

He let Faith scoot in first, and as the woman opened her menu and handed it to her, Blaze took his spot on the other side of the table. The woman handed him a menu too and said, "There should only be one other couple back here while you two are. Thanks for being one of our premium guests tonight." She gave them a smile oozing with warmth and charm and added, "Marianne will be your waitress tonight, and she's assisted by Leon for a wide variety of alcoholic and specialty beverages."

"That sounds fun," Blaze said, though he wouldn't be drinking tonight.

"If you need anything, there's a button right behind you." She indicated the wall, and Blaze found the small, black button that almost blended into the upholstery on the booth's back seat. "Enjoy your evening." She turned and walked away, and Blaze drank in Faith's reaction.

She looked a little shell-shocked, to be honest. Blaze tilted his menu higher and looked at it. The words swam together, because he wasn't really reading them. "Now I know what it means when they ask me if I want to be a premium guest."

A soft scoff came from Faith. "You didn't know?"

"No," he said. "I called last night to get a reservation, and they asked if I wanted a premium one." He lowered the menu slightly. "I didn't know what that meant, and I wanted the reservation. So." He shrugged one shoulder and tried on a smile. "Now I know."

"Most people would ask that question before booking it." Faith gave him a pointed look. "But I forget—you're not like most people." She too looked down at her menu, but she wasn't as relaxed as she'd been when talking about her recipes.

Blaze wondered where she'd been going when she'd started to tell him that about herself. They'd been out before, and he'd learned things about her then too. Not that bit about always wanting to be a baker, though. "Did anyone teach you to bake?" he asked. "Momma? Grandmother?"

She looked at him, her eyes so open and vulnerable. Blaze wanted to freeze time, so he could see her like this whenever he wanted. Her surprise melted quickly, and she said, "My mother and grandmother were both excellent cooks. They taught all of us to cook and bake."

"All of us?" He didn't care about the menu right now. Marianne and Leon would give them as much time as they wanted. "I thought it was you and Trinity."

"We just both live here in Coral Canyon," Faith said. "I have an older brother in Montana, and a younger sister who moved with my parents when they went to Gilbert."

"To get out of the cold," he supplied, remembering that she'd told him her parents had moved to Arizona about five years ago.

She nodded. "Yes."

"Do you ever think you'll move south?"

She shook her head. "Not right now, no." She'd given up looking at her menu too, and a hint of playfulness returned to her expression. "What about you, Mister Young? You're already a big world traveler, I hear."

"You hear?" He blinked at her in an attempt to flirt. "From whom would you hear that from?"

"The Internet."

Blaze rolled his eyes, not thrilled she'd looked him up online. He knew what was out there, and not all of it portrayed him accurately. Or rather, it *did* portray the man he'd once been correctly, but Blaze wasn't that guy anymore.

She giggled, and Blaze scooted around the table a little more so he could be closer to her. She put her hand on his leg, and he covered it with both of his as she looked at him with those big, gorgeous eyes. "Did you always want to be in the rodeo?"

"Yes, ma'am," he said. "Since I was a little boy." He smiled at her. "My parents didn't have much money and a lot of boys. That meant anything we wanted to do, we had to earn ourselves. My daddy helped me and Jem with our training— driving us to the arena and back, getting us to competitions in junior high—but boy, we worked for it."

"Doing what?"

"We had a two-hundred-acre ranch," he said. "Tex bought it a couple of years ago. He works it now."

Their waitress arrived, along with their drink connoisseur, and Blaze paused the conversation there to listen to their selection of drinks and specialties. Once they'd gone, Blaze reached up and removed his cowboy hat. He hung it on the hook Marianne had pointed out and ran his hand through his hair.

"I think my brothers thought we got favored," he said. "Especially the younger ones. The twins."

"I still haven't met any of your brothers," Faith said. "Well, except for Jem." A worried edge entered her eye. "How is he? I know you said the two of you haven't...I don't really know. We haven't talked much since that night."

Blaze swallowed and nodded. "Yeah, we haven't." He didn't want to talk about Jem tonight, so he gave her another smile. "Can I tell you about him another time?"

"Of course."

Gladness swept through him. "Great. So tell me where I can find you tomorrow, and I'll bring the twins by. They're taking me to the movies tomorrow afternoon, and if you're available, I'd love to see you again in the evening."

"Hm, I don't think that's going to work." She gifted him with a brilliant smile that showed all of her straight, white teeth. "I'm working the evening shift tomorrow at the craft mall."

"Breakfast, then."

She shook her head, still smiling. "I don't eat breakfast, Blaze, remember?"

"You make doughnuts for a living," he said. "How can you not eat breakfast?"

"We do breakfast trucks on the weekend anyway," she said. "I'm afraid tomorrow and Sunday are out."

"You sure? Sunday evening? You close early on Sunday evenings, if I remember right."

"You're so persistent."

"When people call me that, it's usually a compliment." He watched her light continue to shine. "You make it sound like an infectious disease."

She laughed then, and Blaze really wanted to make her do that again and again and again. As she sobered, she met his gaze. He'd been grinning at her, but they both sobered. "Maybe Sunday evening," she conceded.

"I have to be out at my brother's in the afternoon," he said. "But you tell me what time you're done, and I'm happy to just crash at your place for a little bit."

The conversation paused while Leon delivered their drinks. Blaze started to chuckle at the Pineapple Party he'd ordered. The glass stood at least eight inches tall, filled with bright yellow slush, a real pineapple wedge hanging on the edge of the glass and a red powder rimming the glass.

"Enjoy," Leon said, and Blaze immediately reached for his straw so he could stir his drink. Faith had gotten a mojito, and she also reached for the fun drink.

"Isn't your son coming home on Sunday night?" she asked. "Who's going to take care of him?"

Blaze hadn't exactly forgotten about his son, but he'd failed to account for him in the equation of when he could see Faith again. He let a disgruntled sigh escape his lips. "Fine. It's feeling like Monday until I can see you again."

She grinned at him. "That it is."

A couple of hours later, Blaze pulled into Faith's driveway. More than half of him wanted to say, "Goodnight. I had a great time," and let her walk herself up to the door. If he went with her, he felt certain he'd break his promise to himself.

At the same time, he couldn't just kick her to the curb and drive off because he couldn't control his hormones. He got out of the truck and went to help her down. She'd boxed up her excess food—and his—and the Styrofoam made squeaking noises as she dropped to the ground.

Their breath steamed in front of them as they hurried to the door, and Faith opened the door she hadn't locked. She stepped inside, but Blaze didn't dare follow her. After setting down her leftovers, she turned back to him and said, "Blaze, this was a magical date. Thank you so much." She stood closer to his height now, as she'd stepped up to enter her house. She put both hands on his shoulders and leaned into him.

His hands knew exactly where to go, and he balanced her easily with his palms on her hips. "Thanks for goin' with me," he said.

She leaned toward him, and Blaze froze. His mind stopped working, despite his many and varied experiences with women. Faith's lips brushed his cheek and said, "Call me tomorrow, okay, cowboy?"

"Yes, ma'am," he murmured, and then she backed into the house, her hands leaving his body and his falling uselessly back to his sides. She grinned and ducked her head as she gently closed the door, and Blaze didn't move until he heard all the locks slide and click into place.

Only then did the cold reach him, and he spun around and hurried back to his truck before he froze to death standing on Faith Cromwell's front stoop. He was fairly sure he'd just had the best date of his life, and he couldn't wait to talk to Faith again.

"Two whole days," he muttered as he backed out of her driveway. His mind moved and maneuvered for another way to see her, even if she was working. With such a great meal in his belly, and Faith's lips burning into the skin on his face, he couldn't come up with something right now.

But he would. Oh, yes, he would, because he absolutely could not go two full days without seeing her again.

THE APP ON BLAZE'S PHONE ALERTED HIM TO SOMEONE walking up his front sidewalk before the doorbell sounded. He found Gabe there, dressed as he usually was—slacks, button-up shirt, shiny shoes. Today, because it was Saturday and he wouldn't be going to work in his law office, Gabe didn't wear a tie.

Blaze grinned at his brother, grabbed onto him, and hugged him. "Hey, brother."

"Don't break my back, Blaze," Gabe griped at him. Out of all the brothers, Gabe was by far the most proper. The fact that he couldn't even put on a pair of jeans on Thanksgiving weekend testified to that.

"Like I'm gonna break *your* back," Blaze shot back at him. "You're early, but c'mon in." He had a twitchy feeling in his gut as he stepped back and drank in Gabe's gaze. The twins were identical, and they both had the softer, rounder features of their mother. Blaze had gotten all angles and lines from their dad, but his hair color at least spoke of his inclusion in the Young family.

"Morris won't be here for an hour," Blaze said, turning away from Gabe. "I thought we said eleven."

Gabe entered the house and closed the door behind him. "We did."

So he had come early on purpose. Blaze would find out why whether he wanted to or not, he knew that. He wasn't sure he wanted to take on more drama or negativity in his life, but he'd always been that brother for his family. Heck, he'd noticed and felt the unrest in Bryce, his nephew, over the summer as the young man had kept coming around. It was almost like Blaze put off an air of acceptance, and all of his brothers knew they could tell him anything, and he wouldn't be shocked.

"Coffee?" he asked.

"I'd love some," Gabe said. "My favorite place in Jackson was closed this morning. They'd had a flood."

Blaze thought of Faith and what that would do to her business. "That's awful," he said, and he set about making the one thing he actually could. Gabe wasn't one to beat around the bush, but he also didn't immediately volunteer any information.

Once he had a steaming cup of coffee in front of him, along with a sugar bowl and a pint of cream, he sighed. "I need your help with something."

"Shoot." Blaze pulled out a barstool and sat beside his brother.

Gabe flicked a dark look in his direction, not really looking at him. Blaze hated that, and no one did it better than Gabe. "Did Morris tell you about how I pretended to be him over the summer?"

Blaze did his best not to go into rapid-blinking mode, but his eyelashes still fluttered a few times before he could slow them. He lifted his coffee mug to his lips and took a slow sip. "He did not."

Gabe rolled his eyes then. "I dated his press manager in the NFL briefly over the summer."

"Okay," Blaze said.

"She thought I was him, and well, I didn't correct her."

Blaze fought a smile, because the twins had often traded places in junior high and high school too. "Why not?"

Gabe shrugged and actually reached up as if he'd loosen his tie. It took his fingers a moment to realize it wasn't there, and he dropped his hand back to the counter. "I don't know. My life is so...boring. So vanilla. When she saw me at the grocery store, she just started gushing at me, and it was...."

"Exciting," Blaze said. "Not boring."

"Right." Gabe exhaled and lifted his mug too. "Not boring."

"She must not have met Liesl."

Gabe shook his head. "I never introduce my daughter to anyone."

"Ever?"

"Not women," Gabe said.

Blaze scoffed and stared at his brother. "That can't be true. If you're dating someone seriously, they're going to have to meet her."

"This wasn't serious." He finally brought his eyes to Blaze's for longer than half a millisecond. "I've never dated anyone seriously enough to introduce them to Liesl."

Blaze hadn't had Cash living with him for a decade, and Faith was the only woman he'd dated since moving to Coral

Canyon. He wasn't sure if it was serious or not, but he sure felt like it could become such pretty quickly. Or not, seeing as how Faith had made a promise to herself to keep talking to him.

"Fair enough," he said. "What would you have done if things had gotten serious with her?"

"They wouldn't have," Gabe said matter-of-factly. "She's not the type you get serious with."

"Gabriel," Blaze chastised. "So you were just in it for the fun?"

A smile touched Gabe's lips for a moment. There, then gone. "I kissed her a few times is all," he said. "Don't make me sound like a total player."

Blaze chuckled, because that would never be a word he'd use to describe Gabe. "So why are you telling me this?" he finally asked.

Gabe let out the sigh of the century. "Because," he said. "Now Morris thinks I'm unhappy, and he keeps trying to set me up with women."

"Just tell him no," Blaze said. He'd only had to do that a few times before everyone in his life had backed the heck off. Blaze had never had a problem getting his own dates, thank you very much.

"You've met Morris, right?" Gabe asked. "He's like an over-eager golden retriever."

Blaze laughed again, though he loved Morris deeply. "He cares about you," he said. "And maybe he doesn't want *his wife* to find out he's seeing someone he's not." He cocked his eyebrows at Gabe, who had the decency to duck his head and look ashamed.

"I'm not going to pretend to be him again," he muttered. "I just thought you could say something to him."

Blaze scoffed again. "I think you've mistaken me for Mav." He gestured with his coffee cup. "His place is down the road a little."

Gabe gave him another withering look. "No, I'm asking *you*. Morris listens to you."

"Since when?"

"Since always."

Blaze shook his head. "One, I'm barely getting to know you and Morris again, so I don't think that's true. Two, this has Mav written all over it. You might as well ask him, because if you ask me, all I'm going to do is text him and ask him what to do." He took a swallow of coffee. "Or, you can just tell Morris to knock it off. That you're sorry, and you won't impersonate him again, and PS, you can find your own dates."

"You make it sound so easy."

"Gabe, you're a terrifying man," Blaze said with a wide grin. "Don't tell me you can't handle your twin."

"What does that mean?" Gabe demanded. "I'm terrifying?"

"See?" Blaze said, still smiling for all he was worth. "That tone right there has me quaking."

"Yeah, really looks like it," Gabe said dryly.

Blaze chuckled and stood to clean up the cream and sugar. "Seriously, Gabe, just tell him." He put everything away, opening a drawer to stash the little packets of sugar substitute.

His eyes caught on the envelope he'd gotten at the food truck rally a couple of nights ago, and his fingers buzzed as he reached for it.

Until this very moment, he hadn't known how he'd see Faith today or tomorrow, but with this simple envelope, he suddenly did.

"Knock, knock," Morris called, and Blaze quickly swiped the envelope and shoved it in his back pocket. He should've known both of the twins would be early, and he was glad he'd gotten up and gotten ready when he had.

"Oh, hey," Morris said, and Blaze noted that he only looked at Gabe. "You're here already."

"Yeah."

Blaze looked back and forth between them. "All right," he said. "Intervention. Morris, he's not going to pretend to be you again, okay? Gabe, just tell him."

Gabe wore the fiercest glare Blaze had ever seen on his face. "It's fine, Blaze."

"Morris, he doesn't want you to set him up with anyone again," Blaze said, not about to spend the day with these two if they wouldn't even talk to each other. He already had a strained relationship like that. "Okay? So don't set him up. Gabe will find his own women and be his own self." He looked between the twins again. "Okay? So can we go to lunch and the movies, or do I need to keep talking?"

"You don't need to keep talking," Gabe bit out.

Morris looked truly surprised, and he took a step closer to Gabe. "You didn't like Melinda?"

"Oh my word," Blaze muttered under his breath. "You guys hash it out. I'm gonna go brush my teeth." He needed a minute to plan his visit with Faith, and maybe by the time he looked up where her trucks would be today, the twins would have worked through this.

Faith ran the social media for Hole In One, and as he saw the post saying she'd be at the craft mall all day today, he remembered she'd told him that.

"Craft mall, here I come," he murmured to himself, something he'd thought he'd literally never say out loud.

6

Faith stood in the parking lot, her hands buried deep in her coat pockets, and waited for the news. When Roxy emerged from the truck, she knew it wasn't good.

"I hate to say it," the woman said as she wiped her hands. "But this truck has bad wiring, Faith. That's why it keeps breaking down on you."

"Can you fix it?" she asked.

"I'd have to pull the whole thing apart." Roxy shook her head. "It's back in the walls, honey. I'm sorry."

Faith looked away from the mechanic. The Grand Tetons could barely be seen through today's storm clouds, and she thought of Blaze and how he'd said he wanted a storm to come through town and break up the bitterly cold blue skies.

"Can you do it?" she asked. "Or do I need a master electrician?"

75

"I can call Ellory," she said. "He'd have to come do a lot of it, and he's only down here from Dog Valley once a week now."

"Is he booked out?"

"I don't know," Roxy said. "I can call him right now?"

Faith nodded, her mouth set in a determined line. If she could get all three food trucks on a reliable rotation, she might be able to make a real living running her doughnut truck. If not, she could barely afford to pay her people, pay for supplies, and keep her heat on. She needed more than that, or it wouldn't matter if she had heat, because she wouldn't have a house.

"It won't be cheap," Roxy said. "Probably at least six thousand."

Faith gave another curt nod and said, "Please call him. I'll wait in my car."

"You got it." Roxy went inside her shop, and Faith retreated to her sedan so she could cry if she wanted to. She found her eyes dry, because she wouldn't have to put the repairs on a credit card. Not this time.

She had money in her account from the raffle drawing. Blaze's money. It would more than cover the cost of rewiring. She could paint the truck too, and still have more than half the money leftover.

Have you taken five seconds to think that you being the one on stage to pull that check from the donation box wasn't a coincidence?

She'd been thinking about exactly that since Blaze had said it to her on Thursday night. He'd meant that perhaps the Lord had brought them back together. She'd been ruminating on that too, but she also recognized the Lord's hand in bringing her the funds she needed to fix her truck—maybe for good.

She'd been fighting with this vehicle for months now, and she was so tired of it. Her eyes drifted closed, and her mind wandered, eventually coming back to a prayer.

"Lord," she whispered. "I'd really like to see if I can make Hole in One successful. I can't do it with two trucks. I need this third truck. Please."

She opened her eyes, but Roxy hadn't come back outside. "Thank You for Blaze Young and his ignorance of the donations at the rally. Thank You for putting me on stage to get that money. Help me to be a good steward of it, and bless me that it'll be exactly what I need to turn my business around."

Roxy appeared in the doorway, and Faith exhaled as she got out of the sedan. Her feet crunched over gravel as she walked toward the mechanic and her friend. Her prayer continued silently, but it had morphed into *please, please, please.* The words ran through her head in time with her footsteps.

She pushed into the shop. "What did he say?"

Roxy looked up from the counter. "He'll be here on Thursday, and he said he can do it."

"In one day?"

She shook her head. "Probably two or three, he said."

Which meant four. A month. She'd be down a truck for a month. That would probably eat up the rest of the money she'd gotten at the rally, but Faith refused to be upset about it. She had the money, and she'd have to use it even if she'd like to save it for another rainy day. Heaven knew she'd experienced some real downpours this year.

Maybe she could put Joe and Orion on the other two trucks, and she could do custom holiday orders from home. That would be a third arm of income without the need for a truck. "Thank you, Roxy," she said. "I can leave her here for him?"

"Yep," Roxy said. "I'll put it around the back."

"Thanks," Faith said again, and she left the mechanic shop. She had to be on truck one in a couple of hours, but she went home and started sketching out her ideas for holiday orders. If she did half-dozen boxes and dozen boxes for family parties, she could easily fulfill the orders.

The most popular varieties of doughnuts during the holidays were her peppermint chocolate bar, and the hot chocolate and cookie crumble old fashioned doughnut. She could offer just those two for holiday orders, and she could require people to come to her house to pick them up.

"Or charge a premium delivery fee," she murmured to herself.

She flipped the page in her ideas notebook and wrote at the top of the page. *Holiday parties.*

Perhaps she should do some catering in the next month. She'd worked in catering before founding Hole in One, and she'd hated it. But this was for one month, and she didn't hate catering as much as she'd hate losing her house.

An alarm went off, her signal to stop brainstorming and get over to truck one so she could start the dough she needed for today's business. After silencing the beeping, she took another five minutes to post online about the options.

Truck three is out of rotation this month for necessary repairs.

:(*Which would you rather see? Holiday catering for business and family parties? Or custom holiday orders for pick-up?*

She posted a picture of her hot chocolate and cookie crumble doughnut and got herself out the door. The craft mall opened at eleven and closed at seven, and she planned to be there all day long. It brought moms, dads, kids, families, couples, and singles, and everyone wanted a doughnut at some point.

Joe was working the truck with her today, and she wasn't surprised to find his car already in the lot where she parked her trucks. He drove them to the mall, and together, they set out making the dough and getting it rising.

Faith loved making doughnuts, and she loved interacting with people. The kitchen inside the truck kept her warm and toasty, and within the first hour, she'd pushed her sweater sleeves up to her elbows.

Finally, in the middle of the afternoon, the stream of doughnut-lovers slowed, and Faith looked over to Joe. "I'll go grab us some lunch. Do you want a burrito or those steak fries?"

"Steak fries." He flashed her a smile and went back to cleaning up the back station. He was a quick worker, and Faith thanked the Lord above that she'd found him. He was a single dad of two little girls, and he had another job he worked too. His mother lived here in town, which was why he'd moved back here after his devastating divorce.

Faith stepped out of the truck, her breath lilting out of her mouth in a long exhale. The craft mall housed several fast casual places to eat, and since she'd worked here plenty, she knew the best ones.

Carlito's Mexican had amazing nachos and burritos—but

she'd stay away from the churros from now on, thanks. And Kitchen 72 had the best steak fries on the planet. Not that Faith had traveled much to truly know that.

You'll have to bring Blaze here and ask him. The thought of him brought a smile to her face, and she joined the short line in front of the Kitchen 72 storefront so she could put in her order.

While she waited, she tapped to check on her social media post from that morning. Her eyebrows practically flew off her face when she saw how many comments there were.

"Fifty-four?"

That had to be the work of scammers, but as Faith tapped to get them to show, they weren't spam.

Redneckgirl: I'd hire you for my family party any day!

Horses4ever: We have a family party coming up next week-end. How can I have you come? 17 people.

GoingtoWY: Family parties would be awesome.

CoralCanyon_DryCleaning: Our company party is on December 11 – we'd love to have you cater it!

They went on and on *and on,* and numbness started to spread from inside Faith's body to the outside. "This is unbeliev-able," she whispered. Maybe she didn't need a third food truck. Maybe she'd been chasing the wrong things for months now. A year. Longer than that.

She had a dozen new messages too, and people had taken their public comments into her private inbox. They truly wanted to hire her. Faith's thumbs started flying back and forth across the screen as she answered them.

"Faith," someone said, and she looked up.

"Marti." She grinned at the woman in the order window. "You know what I want."

"Two steak fries, two Diet Cokes." Marti started tapping on her tablet.

"You got it." She handed over her credit card when Marti needed it, and she took her receipt, noted the number, and moved out of the way.

Ten minutes later, when her number got called, Faith had eight parties booked for the next three weeks, and she'd call an emergency staff meeting the moment she got back to the truck.

Unfortunately, a huddle of people waited outside Hole in One, so Faith stashed the food and her phone and got back to work. The rush ebbed, and she and Joe grabbed a bite to eat while they could.

"Did you see my post this morning?"

"Mm, yes." He nodded and put another forkful of steak and potato in his mouth. A groan followed it. "I love this sauce so much."

"Me too." Faith felt certain they sprinkled magic into the special sauce on the fries, because she couldn't get enough of it either. It was tangy and sweet, with a hint of spiciness at the tail end of it. It coated her tongue like cream, and she swiped a fry through it before eating it.

"Lots of people said parties," he said. "Are you going to do that?"

She nodded as she hurried to finish chewing. Once she'd swallowed, she said, "Yes, I booked eight while standing in line at Kitchen Seventy-Two."

Joe beamed at her. "That's great, Faith."

"I'll have to go over the schedule for December again," she said. "We need to have a staff meeting."

He nodded, the lines around his eyes drooping a little. He suddenly looked tired, and he said, "Just let me know when."

"I will." By some miracle, they were able to finish eating, and Faith had just turned to wash her hands so she'd be ready to take more orders when she heard a familiar voice.

She stuck her head out to the side so she could see through the window, the water coming from her faucet icy enough to make her flinch. Blaze stood there with two men who looked exactly like each other.

The twins.

"There she is," Blaze said when his eyes landed on hers. "Heya, Faith."

"Howdy," she said, slipping into her girlfriend persona. "Give me three seconds to wash up. We just had a long enough break to have something to eat."

"Sure." Blaze looked over to Joe, who'd just collected their trash. "Hey, Joe."

"Good to see you again, Blaze."

"You come here a lot?" one of the twins asked.

"Often enough to know Joe," the other one said.

"Not that often," Blaze barked at them.

Faith hid her smile and washed her hands as quickly as she could. When she stepped up to the counter again, she picked up her pen and ordering pad. "What'll you fine gentlemen have?" She looked at the three of them, and it was clear they were related. Tall, dark, handsome, each wearing a cowboy hat that looked like it cost more than her house. They probably did.

One of the twins gaped at her in surprise, and one scowled in her direction, as if her asking for his order wasn't the right thing to do.

Blaze grinned and took a small step toward her. He covered her hand and the pen and pad with both of his hands. "How many coupons can a single customer use in one trip?"

Faith blinked at him. "Coupons?"

"Yeah." He pulled an envelope from his back pocket. "See, I got all these coupons the other day, and my brothers and I...well, we like doughnuts, but I'm sure there are some rules to how many of these I can use."

He took out the wad of coupons she'd put in the envelope for the winner of the raffle drawing at the Thanksgiving Day rally. His eyes came up, and they held such hope that Faith wasn't sure what answer he wanted.

She also didn't want to make him and his twin brothers two dozen doughnuts for free. And if she told him he could only use one coupon...he'd have to come back another time to use another one. And then another one. And then another one....

"You can only use one at a time," she said, leaning into her elbows on the counter. "Sorry, cowboy."

"One?" He started shuffling through them like he'd spent some time in a casino in Vegas. "Uh, let's go with this one." He slapped a buy-one-get-one free coupon on the counter, though she'd seen him go by two or three of the exact same thing in his stack.

"You got it, Mister Young. What would you like?"

"I want the Elvis one," he said. "Boys?" He looked left and then right. "Oh, Faith, these are my brothers. Morris." He hooked his thumb to his left, to the man who'd been softly surprised at Faith. "And Gabe. Gabe is older, of course."

"Of course?" Gabe asked. "What does that mean?"

He was the grumpy one, and he turned his dark eyes on Faith. "I'll have the Strawberry Sunrise, please." He had manners, she'd give him that. "I can just pay for it, since I don't have a coupon." He dug in his back pocket for his wallet. "I mean, I'm not the one with a billion dollars in belt buckles in my closet, but whatever." He gave Blaze a glare, to which Blaze simply started to chuckle.

"And I didn't play professional football for five years and get an *astronomical* salary." Gabe tossed down his card as he looked at Faith. "But I'd love the Strawberry Sunrise, please."

"You got it," she said.

"I only played for four years, for the official record," Morris said. "And take the free doughnut if you want it. Jeez."

"Boys, boys," Blaze said, clearly enjoying himself. He was made of angles and jutted jaws while they were rounder, but Faith did like the way they interacted with one another.

"He's a big wig lawyer," Morris said, muscling his way in front of Blaze. "Don't let him fool you. He's loaded too."

"I am not," Gabe growled. "If you tell one more woman how rich I am, I swear I'm going to slash your tires."

Blaze burst out laughing, but Faith didn't think Gabe was kidding. She scribbled down his order and Gabe's and looked at Morris. "What would you like, sir?"

"Cookies and cream, please," he practically bit out. "Blaze is paying for making me come today."

"Oh, please," Blaze said easily, getting out his card too. "You two have been beggin' me for a movie date for a month."

Morris rolled his eyes but didn't otherwise argue.

"What did you guys see?" Faith asked. She ran Gabe's card first and waited for the receipt.

"The new Collin Girth film," Gabe said.

"It's an action movie," Morris said over his shoulder. "Not a film. I'm getting us a table over here."

"I'll get him a table in Oklahoma," Gabe muttered.

"Can you be nice for four seconds?" Blaze finally griped at him. "This is my girlfriend, and now she's going to think our family is dysfunctional." He pushed Gabe's receipt toward him. "Tip her good, bro."

"She's your girlfriend?"

"I told you we were coming here for a reason." Blaze rolled his eyes.

Gabe picked up the pen and wrote on the receipt. When he looked up at Faith again, his eyes had softened. "I'm so sorry, Faith. Really. Blaze sometimes doesn't say things the way he should. Had I known you were his *girlfriend*, I'd have been nicer. Really."

She collected his receipt and pushed Blaze's toward him. "It's fine," she said. "We've been out once. He wouldn't even kiss me goodnight."

Blaze's pen scratched as he dragged it across the counter. "I wouldn't what?"

"He made a promise to himself and everything." Faith grinned at him, feeling sparkly and like she had fizzing candy popping through her blood. "You didn't tell your brothers about your self-pact?"

"He's always making these stupid promises," Morris said as he re-arrived.

"She's his girlfriend," Gabe said.

That froze Morris too, and he once again gaped at Faith. He thawed quickly and snapped his mouth shut. "Well, I wish I'd have known that. I'd have been on better behavior." He smiled at Faith. "I'm Morris Young. It's great to meet *Blaze's girlfriend*. I'm not sure—"

"Stop talking," Blaze said. "Whatever you're about to say, don't."

"Oh, I'd like to hear it," Faith teased as she shook Morris's hand.

Blaze gave her a glare. "And I was going to give you a big tip, but now...." He wrote on his receipt and shoved it back at her. "Maybe I won't."

"The tips get split," she said. "And Joe needs the money."

"I'm fine," Joe said from behind her, and she quickly ripped off the cowboys' order and stuck it up for him. He'd already started on two of the doughnuts, and she didn't dare meet his eye. She wouldn't be able to keep herself from laughing then.

She beamed down at Blaze. "I can't wait to hear about your other promises, Mister Young."

His stoic face cracked, and he shook his head. "Well, if I could get you to go out with me again, I'd tell you."

"I said Monday," she said.

"Yeah, but we have nothing calendared." He pulled out his

phone, looked at it and then her. "Should I just stop by with another coupon and another brother?"

She grinned at him. "That's up to you, cowboy."

"Oh, boy," Gabe muttered. "Lovely to meet you, Faith." He clapped Blaze on the shoulder. "I see why you like her. She's as quick as you." He left with Morris, the two of them with their heads bent together the way she imagined twins would be.

"They're interesting," she said to Blaze.

He glanced over his shoulder to them and then focused on her again. "Breakfast? I know some of my brother's wives like Breakfast Brothers, and they open early."

"Joe works there in the mornings." Faith chin-nodded to him as he put Gabe's doughnut on the counter. "I bet he could get you some coupons."

Joe burst out laughing, and that caused Faith to do the same. Even Blaze laughed, and since there was no one in line behind him, she picked up Gabe's doughnut and took it down the steps and around the corner to Blaze.

"You know I didn't come just to use a coupon." He took her free hand in his and leaned in close. His lips didn't make true contact with her skin, but the promise of his kiss against the side of her throat had her trembling.

"I know," she said. "You wanted me to meet your brothers."

"They're at each other's throats today." He turned toward them, but they seemed to be getting along just fine now. "Until they have a common enemy. Then they're thick as thieves." He cleared his throat and took her toward the table Morris had reserved.

She put Gabe's doughnut in front of him. "Strawberry Sunrise."

He looked at it, at the perfectly round hole-doughnut with the pale pink strawberry glaze. A mango cream dotted the ring, and Joe had put delicate strawberry wedges into each dollop. "This is the prettiest doughnut I've ever seen." Gabe looked up at her in wonder.

"We're on social media," she said. "Tag us, and I draw a winner every week for a free doughnut."

"He lives in Jackson Hole," Blaze said.

"Well, if he wins, Morris could come get it and I wouldn't know." She smiled at the identical twins, but Blaze made a squeaking noise no man as tall and as broad as him should ever make, and then he started laughing and laughing and laughing.

Morris and Gabe did not, and Faith wasn't sure what inside joke she'd missed.

"Elvis," Joe called, and she turned to get the other two doughnuts. She delivered them to the table, which only had three chairs, and Blaze had sat down with his brothers.

"What?" he said to the twins. "That was funny." He looked up at Faith. "Can you sit with me for a minute?"

She checked the truck; still no line. "There's not a chair," she said.

He patted his lap, his midnight eyes glittering at her with hopeful danger. She swatted at his shoulder. "You're a menace to society," she said. "No, I have to get back to work." She walked away while he laughed again, and she maybe added a little sway to her hips just for him.

Maybe.

"He's back," Joe said quietly.

"Yeah," Faith said as she joined him at the back counter. "We're dating again."

"Good for you, Faith." His voice sounded sincere and friendly. "He sure seems to like you."

"Yeah," she murmured. She liked him too, and she hoped he'd stop by her truck every day with a different coupon until he'd used them all. At the same time, she couldn't help wondering *why* he liked her, and if Gabe could really see why Blaze did.

"I can handle the truck if you want to take off early," he said.

Faith shook her head and twisted to get the receipts and put them in the cash box. "No," she said. "I'll see him on Monday." She glanced up and out the window of the truck, but none of the Youngs looked in her direction.

She glanced at the receipt and gasped. "Joe." She spun back to him and showed him Gabe Young's receipt.

"Is that a hundred-dollar tip?"

She put Blaze's receipt in his hand. "And that's a thousand." Her blood started to boil, and she grabbed both slips of paper from him. "I'm going to give him a piece of my mind."

"Faith, wait," Joe said, but she marched away from him.

Back down the steps and into the cold, but it didn't clear Faith's head. She marched right over to Blaze, who glanced up, the joviality disappearing from his face. He got to his feet as she said, "You can't tip us a thousand dollars."

"Why not?"

"You gave her a thousand?" Gabe asked. "Show off."

Blaze didn't even look at him. Faith stared at him, trying to find a reason why he couldn't do that. She didn't want his charity?

As the seconds ticked from one to two to three, she saw he hadn't done it out of charity. He'd done it because he wanted to. Tears welled in her eyes, but she pressed them back. Away.

Then she grabbed his face with both of her hands, and with the receipts sandwiched between her palm and his right cheek, she matched her mouth to his and kissed him.

7

Blaze grabbed onto Faith and tried to keep up with her. Gabe and Morris catcalled around him, and other voices joined into the fray. Maybe. Blaze wasn't sure of much in this moment, other than Faith tasted like salt and steak, and he wanted a lot more of that in his mouth.

She let him take control of the kiss, and he slowed it and deepened it at the same time, his pulse kicking into a new gear as he settled his hands along her waist and held her flush against his body.

He finally ended the kiss, a sigh slipping between his lips as he did. He opened his eyes, expecting to be all alone with Faith —but he wasn't.

It was dark, sure. But the lights outside the craft mall shone brightly, and every eye within fifty feet had been trained on the two of them. He didn't care, but he did want to know what in the world Faith had been thinking.

He met her eye, and she ducked her head further. "Tell me what time you get off," he said, his voice full of frogs and shards, making it husky and hoarse.

"Not until nine-thirty," she whispered. "And I was up at six."

He knew what that was code for, and it was *I'll be tired, Blaze. Too tired to talk. Too tired to kiss you like that again.*

"I'll be at your place," he said anyway, an idea popping into his head. "With some minty hot chocolate and that scented lotion you like. I can rub your feet."

"Blaze." She fiddled with the zipper on his jacket, her eyes trained there too.

"If you say no, I'm going to make a scene," he whispered. "Worse than the one you just made by kissing me in front of everyone." He grinned at her, glad when her lips tipped up into a tiny smile too.

She finally looked up and met his eye, and dang, if an arc of electricity didn't curve through his body, setting every cell on fire.

"Fine," she said. "It's a free country. I can't tell you where you can't park your truck."

"No, you can't." He slipped his hands off her hips, and she backed up.

She cleared her throat and nodded at him as she slipped back into the hot librarian mode she used on him sometimes. "Thank you for the generous tip, Mister Young." She looked at Gabe. "You too, Mister Young. Thank you." With that, she turned and walked back to her truck. Blaze watched her every move until a couple of women stepped up to the window to order and he couldn't see Faith any longer.

Only then did he sit down, the air finally entering his lungs properly again. He looked at Morris, who stared back. Then Gabe, who gave him a warm smile. "She's nice," Gabe said. "I like her."

"Yeah." Blaze rubbed his mouth. "I like her too. Too much."

"Yes, that kiss was *quite* scandalous," Morris said. "I bet it ends up online." His eyebrows rose suggestively.

"Who cares?" Blaze asked. "I don't have a career anymore. They can't take back my money or my belt buckles because I kissed a woman in public." He glanced over to Faith again. "That was a *good* kiss." He looked at Gabe. "Right?"

"You looked like you were enjoying yourself, yes." His brother grinned and started to chuckle. "And holy cow, Blaze, can you tell me how you got her to go out with you?" He looked over to Hole in One too. "Because every woman I go out with is more boring than me, and she has...."

"Fire," the three of them said together. Blaze wanted to get burned by it badly, but he kept that to himself. She'd kissed him first, and he'd have to do something about that later. What, he didn't know, but he felt confident he'd think of something.

BLAZE APPROACHED TEX'S FARM SLOWLY, HIS FOOT ALL THE way off the accelerator as he took in the mess of trucks. He grumbled to himself about being fifteen minutes late and they'd probably served dessert already.

It was his fault he was late. He'd been on a call with Cash, and he hadn't wanted to get up. It was that simple, really. He didn't want any more conflict in his life, not after spending the majority of yesterday with the twins at each other's throats. He'd found it comical by the time he'd taken them to the craft mall to meet Faith and get doughnuts.

"And you told them you were taking them to see your girl-friend," he muttered as he pulled into the driveway next door. Abby's brother lived there, and the Youngs often took over their driveway too when they held big family gatherings at the farm.

Cheryl and Wade would likely be next door anyway, as Blaze had seen them at all major Young family functions in the past. Minor functions too. Abby still helped her brother a lot, and Wade and Cheryl had just had their first baby a month or so ago.

Blaze couldn't recall the name of the child right now, nor if it was a boy or a girl, but he was sure Abby would have the infant cradled in her arms in the house. Her, or Georgia, or Momma. All the women loved babies, and Blaze could admit that a tiny, helpless human was something special.

Having Cash had changed him, that was for sure. Not enough in the beginning, but he'd been trying to make amends for that lately.

He parked and headed next door, glad it hadn't snowed yet now. Otherwise, he'd have had to trek through the stuff to get to the steps that led up and into the side of the house. He went that way, expecting a wall of noise to hit him in the face when he opened the door.

It was loud inside, but not as vibrant as Blaze had expected.

He'd forgotten to look for Jem's truck, and it would be a miracle if his brother were here. He found himself hoping for that miracle as he shrugged out of his coat and hung it on one of the hooks that already held a garment.

Then he paused for a moment and said, "Lord, bless this evening and this family." Where the words had come from, Blaze didn't know. Honestly, he didn't. He wasn't a praying man. Of course, he'd prayed before. His parents had taught all the boys to pray growing up. They took all eight of them to church every week. Even now, most of his brothers went to church with their families on the Sabbath Day.

Momma and Daddy had never wavered in their faith, just like they'd never wavered in their love for him. No matter how far he strayed, they loved him, and he realized as he stood alone, just out of sight around the corner from everyone else, how God felt about His children.

He loved them too. Each of them individually. He loved Blaze.

His throat narrowed, and Blaze squared his shoulders and shook them, trying to find the brave part of himself he needed to get around the corner.

If Jem was here, Blaze would have to remain scarce. If he wasn't...everyone would fawn over him instead. It was like they could scent the weakest of them, and they piled around that man, trying to find out where he lacked so they could shore him up.

He supposed that wasn't a bad thing, but he didn't want any eyes on him tonight. He'd had plenty yesterday afternoon at the craft mall, and he suspected everyone talking and eating in the kitchen, dining room, and living room of this house had heard about his kisscapade with Faith Cromwell.

He'd asked Morris and Gabe not to say anything, but this was small-town Wyoming, and people talked. Even if his brothers didn't tell, the scorching hot kiss between him and Faith at the craft mall had to be on the gossip circuit here in Coral Canyon.

"I'm just going to call him," Tex said, his voice coming nearer. "He said he was coming."

Blaze moved around the corner then, almost running into Tex as his oldest brother approached. "I'm right here, Tex."

"Oh." Tex shoved his phone in his back pocket and drew Blaze into a hug. "Hey. I didn't hear you come in."

"I'm like a ninja," Blaze teased. He hugged Tex back, because it felt good to be missed. It felt nice to have a place to belong after being gone for so long. It was wonderful to be in a family who thought about him, took care of him, and wanted him around.

He'd lived a lot of his life believing they didn't—or at the very least, he hadn't wanted to be around them. That was really it, and Blaze swallowed as he stepped away from Tex. "Listen," he said. "I appreciate you including me."

Tex peered at him, obviously confused. "Of course. You're our brother."

"I know." Blaze didn't know how to right all the wrongs in his life. He'd sent a lot of emails in the past year, and he'd rebuilt a lot of bridges. Some people he never heard back from, and his counselor told him he had to be okay with that. People were fragile, and while the medical community could fix a lot of things, hurt feelings and broken relationships were two things that took the longest.

Not only that, but both parties had to *want* to be healed and fixed, so Blaze could send all the emails he wanted. He could apologize all he wanted. If the other people didn't care to hear it or accept it, things couldn't be fixed.

That wasn't on him, though. Not anymore.

"There was a time when I would've rather died than come to a family dinner," Blaze said. "I didn't want to be here, because I thought y'all didn't want me here. I know that's not true, and now, I want to be here. That's all I'm saying."

Tex nodded, though Blaze was sure he didn't understand. Everyone loved Tex and they always had. When he had a problem, the troops that rallied around him got into three digits. He was well-loved, the best son out of all of them, and a really, really good man.

Blaze was nothing like him. Nothing at all.

"Well, I'm glad you're here." He grinned at Blaze and turned back to the party. "Did you get ahold of Bryce?"

"No," Blaze said as he followed Tex. "Was I supposed to?"

"He said he was trying to call you last night and couldn't get through."

"Oh." Blaze had discovered the dead zone in Faith's house when all of the texts on the brothers' string had sounded the moment he'd walked out onto her front porch. But he hadn't realized he'd missed calls. "I'll call him after this."

"He'll be home in three weeks." Tex sounded utterly enthused about that, but Blaze knew what happened then.

Bailey had Bryce's baby, and they gave it to Otis and Georgia. Tex would surely have a knot of emotions to undo then, but he loved his son, and Blaze couldn't fault him for that.

"Blaze," Morris said as he turned with a plate full of food. "You made it."

"I was talkin' to Cash," he said by way of explanation. "Sorry I'm late." He glanced around, and sure enough, Jem stood on the fringes of the party, near the mouth of the hallway that led back to the bedrooms.

In the past, Blaze would get over to his side as quickly as possible. The two of them had always been paired up, and Blaze had always been the most comfortable with Jem. Something told him to do that now, and he moved past everyone as they said hello, only stopping to lean down and kiss Momma on the top of the head.

"Hey, Momma," he said quietly, and she patted his hand with hers as he continued by.

Blaze met Jem's eyes at the corner of the table, but he kept on going. By the time he stood next to his brother, the silence in the room had become complete. "Can I stand by you?" he asked in a near-whisper.

"I don't own the ground." Jem flicked his eyes back to the dining room table.

Blaze turned around and tucked his hands in his pockets. All of the adults stared at him, and he stared right on back.

Abby came down the hall, and she said, "Oh, Blaze, excuse me."

He side-stepped to let her pass, but she moved right in front of him. "I need you to hold her, please. I have to run next door and help Wade and Cheryl."

"Abs?" Tex asked.

She didn't answer as she shoved Melissa, her and Tex's little girl, into Blaze's arms. The baby had been crying, and she looked at Blaze like he was the Boogie Man.

"Hey, baby," he cooed at her. He balanced her on his hip and bounced her a little. "Have you had dinner? Maybe if we go sit by Gramma, she'll give you a cherry." He smiled at Melissa, and the little girl had tears clinging to her eyelashes.

"I'll go with you," Tex was saying, and Momma started pointing and directing people to move down so Blaze could sit by her with Melissa. "What's going on with them?"

"They just need help with the baby," Abby said. "And Wade's prosthetics." She seemed nervous and in a hurry, and the two of them left in the next moment.

Blaze brushed Melissa's tears from her eyelashes. "You hungry?"

She nodded and then laid her head against his shoulder, molding her soft body to his. His whole heart melted, and a smile filled his soul and his face. He looked over to Jem, who'd forgotten to be Mister Tough Guy, because he was smiling at the little girl too.

"Uncle Bwaze," Eric said. "Come sit. Sit by me." He went around Blaze and started pushing him from behind. Blaze laughed as he did what the boy wanted, as Momma had cleared him a spot between her and Eric.

With everyone settled, Eric put a piece of a buttered roll on the table in front of Blaze. "Here you go, baby," he said to Melissa, and she reached one chubby handful of fingers toward the bread.

Blaze now sat at the heart of the table, and he couldn't believe how well he fit there. Georgia put a plate of food in front of him, and he fed bits of it to Melissa as he ate, the conversation picking up and flowing around him.

"So," someone said in a lull a few minutes later. "Blaze. I heard you have a new girlfriend."

He looked down the table to Otis, who'd spoken.

"Yeah," Everly said. "I heard that too." She grinned at Blaze.

He finished chewing, swallowed, and cleared his throat. "Where'd you hear that?" Everly might know simply because of social media in town. She was very connected digitally, as was Faith. They had to be for their businesses. In fact, Everly and Faith were pretty good friends, and Blaze had asked Everly for advice regarding Faith in the past.

He met her eye, trying to read more in her expression than he could in the few seconds he held her gaze. Gabe said, "I was there. He definitely has a new girlfriend."

"It's not really new," Blaze said.

"First kiss last night," Morris said.

"Stop it," he growled at him. He glared over Eric's head at the boy's father. Morris simply smiled and dug back into his dinner.

"I saw it online," Jem said, and that once again made every voice box in the family go mute. He held up his phone. "In fact, there's a video of that kiss right here." He turned the screen toward them. His dark eyes danced with a dangerous fire Blaze didn't like. He needed this spotlight off of him. Now.

"It's nothing," Blaze said. "It's new."

"You just said it wasn't new," Momma said.

"Blaze," Georgia chastised, her eyes glued to her phone. "Do not let your son see this."

He hadn't seen a video of himself kissing Faith, and he didn't want to. "Can we talk about something else?"

"Is it new or not?" Daddy asked, and that again made several people clam up. Daddy didn't say much, and when he chose to talk, everyone listened.

"It's Faith, Daddy," Blaze said. "Remember, she broke up with me over the summer and then again last fall? We're just... tryin' again."

"Well." Otis cleared his throat. "The kissing looks like you're—it's, uh, going really, really well."

"Otis." Georgia elbowed him, but his brother grinned and grinned.

"*She* kissed *me*," Blaze said. Which really bothered him. He'd rubbed her feet until she'd fallen asleep last night, and then he'd carried her to bed, pressed a chaste kiss to her forehead, and slipped out like a thief in the night.

She'd texted him that morning, horrified that she'd woken up in bed and didn't know how she'd gotten there. He assured her nothing had happened, and that he was glad she hadn't woken once in the night.

"He left her a thousand-dollar tip," Gabe said.

Blaze growled, but Gabe only glared back. "Dear Lord." He looked up to the ceiling. "Help me. This family is driving me to madness."

The door opened and a screaming infant filled the silence that had ensued after Blaze's mock prayer. Abby, Tex, Cheryl,

101

and Wade entered in a rush of voices and cold air, and that thankfully took the spotlight from Blaze.

Abby quieted the baby, which was a boy if the pale blue blanket meant anything, and when Tex joined the group again, he glanced around and asked, "Did you start without me?" He looked at Jem. "Are you going to do the rehab?"

Jem's eyes widened and widened, and Blaze actually felt bad for him. "Excuse me?" he asked, and Blaze didn't think a hundred screaming babies could derail this conversation now.

8

Jem Young's heartbeat scattered through his whole body.
He'd lost his anchor in the family—Blaze—and he had no
idea where to look now.

He'd lost Chanel too, and he honestly felt like
someone had tied him to the tallest flagpole in the world,
hoisted him up, and told him to survive on his own in bitter,
cold winds. For days. Weeks. Months now.

Well, Jem couldn't do it. He wasn't built to be alone, and he
looked at Blaze helplessly. Blaze, who'd called him out in public.
Jem had moved out as soon as he could after that, which had
been a huge mistake. He couldn't take care of himself, a house,
his kids, none of it.

He absolutely wouldn't call Chanel, though. He'd been
untethered from her, and that hurt so much he couldn't see the
bottom of that pain. Sometimes, he felt like his heart would

simply stop beating, because surely he couldn't keep living like this.

It never did, so Jem had to find other ways to dull the hurt festering inside him. He found relief in the bottom of a bottle. In really loud, large groups at restaurants, sports bars, and clubs. In having a lot of women around him, as if he needed them to prove to himself that Chanel was the one missing out. To prove to himself that he was still wanted and desirable.

"I'm not going into rehab," he said as Trace stood to join Tex. The two of them together could take on the world, Jem knew that. Tex, the king, and Trace, the prince. They exchanged a glance, and then Blaze stood up too. He wasn't nearly as menacing with a child in his arms, but his eyes still flashed with concern.

Concern Jem didn't want. It was the concern that irritated him the most.

"Honey," Momma said. She wiped her mouth and stood up. "The boys are concerned about you."

"I'm fine," Jem said. He glanced at the kids table in the living room, where both Cole and Rosie sat with their cousins. "I'm not talking about this in front of my kids."

"Why not?" Mav asked quietly. He kept his seat, and in fact, he didn't even look at Jem. He sat nearest to him, and his voice had always been one of power in the Young family. He was the hinge, and he played the role very, very well.

"They already see you as you are, Jem," he said. "They know Blaze and I come over every morning to feed them and get them to school, because you can't." He did turn and look at Jem then.

Blaze had been coming all this time?

Jem sought out his best friend to see if that was really true. *Former best friend,* his mind whispered at him, a total lie.

Blaze was still his best friend. He had been for years and years, and one fight hadn't changed that. Mav brought the kids back in the evening, once Jem had stumbled home. He tucked them in, and Jem had assumed he'd been the only one to come in the mornings. Of course, he'd seen Otis and Tex a few times. Luke too. So Mav wasn't the only one helping. He just hadn't realized Blaze had been.

"You're going to lose those kids," he said quietly. "And that will ruin you, Jem. Please."

Tears filled Jem's eyes. "I can't...." His throat clogged, and he couldn't talk. He turned toward the front door, desperate to escape. He ran to it, yanked it open, and stormed out.

People said things behind him that didn't register in his ears, and he made it to the edge of the porch before a terrible yell ripped through his throat and filled the sky with the agonizing sound of a man in a great deal of pain.

Children began to cry behind him, and then the door closed. He really hoped he'd be alone, but he knew better. A single pair of boots sounded against the wooden porch as a man approached, and he wasn't surprised to find Blaze at his side a moment later.

He said nothing, and Jem worked his fingers open from the fists he'd curled them into. "Blaze," he said. "I can't go into rehab. Chanel will take those kids from me permanently, and I'll never see them again."

His older brother nodded a couple of times. "Probably."

"She works so much." Hot tears splashed his cheeks, but he didn't care. Blaze had seen him at his all-time worst, the lowest of lows, and he was the only one Jem could cry in front of. "I don't want nannies and babysitters raising my kids."

Blaze nodded again and kept gazing out at the horizon. After one more breath, he looked over at Jem. His bottom lip wobbled once before he cuffed Jem behind the head and hauled him into his chest. "Okay," he said roughly. "It's okay."

Jem sobbed and sobbed as he clung to Blaze. He didn't know what to do, but Blaze would.

"Breathe with me," Blaze said. "You've got to slow down." He took in a long, slow breath, and Jem tried to match it. As frantic as he felt, he couldn't, but on the next one, he did.

They inhaled and exhaled a few more times, and then Blaze stepped back. He held Jem with both hands now, right around the ears, and bent his head toward him. "Jem, I know why you're doin' what you're doin'. I do."

Jem nodded, only a hair away from breaking down again.

"But we have to find a way for you to deal with your losses that don't include you drinking yourself to death." Blaze's gaze turned fierce. "Okay?"

"Okay," Jem agreed.

"Because you will lose those kids if you keep goin' the way you're goin'." Blaze dropped one hand, but not the other. "Either to Chanel or the state of Wyoming. We've done what we can for you, brother. It's time to step up and be a man. Be their dad. Find yourself, and be him."

"Find yourself," Jem repeated, a fresh round of tears flowing out of his eyes. "I don't know how to do that, Blaze. Who are we without the rodeo?"

"For one, you're a Young," Blaze said, his voice echoing something Daddy had said so many times to his boys as they grew up. "And Youngs aren't quitters. We don't give up because things are hard. We don't run from a challenge. What do we do?"

Jem closed his eyes, the heat inside them too much for him to keep them open.

"Jem," Blaze said kindly. "What do you do?"

Jem swallowed and tried to think clearly. "You call on the powers of heaven," he whispered. "You ask your family for help. You find a way to fix whatever you've broken." He opened his eyes. "I'm so sorry, Blaze. I shouldn't have moved out the way I did. I need you." He broke down again and dove back into his brother's chest. "I need you, I need you, I need you."

"Sh," Blaze murmured. "I'm right here, and you can move back in tonight. It's fine. It's okay. Everything is going to be okay."

Jem quieted again, and the two of them sank to the top step. Neither of them wore a coat, but Blaze didn't complain, and Jem couldn't imagine going back inside. He couldn't face his family again. Ever.

Of course, he'd have to do that, and as Jem sat there, he had a vision of all of his brothers, and all of their wives, and all of the kids in the Young family opening their arms and receiving him right into the center of them.

They loved him, and Jem hung his head, more crying on the horizon. "What do I do now?" he asked Blaze in a whisper.

"You do what you've always done," Blaze said without missing a beat. "You take care of those kids, and that means you have to be their dad. Starting now."

Jem looked over to Blaze, and his brother's eyes softened the moment they met Jem's. "They need you, Jem. Not Mav, and certainly not me."

"Rosie can't stop talking about you," Jem said, a hint of bitterness in his voice as he gazed out at the lawn again. It was crisp and white, stiff already with frost. "I was about to tell her to ask you to go live with you, because she was drivin' me nuts."

"She can only come if you come," Blaze said. "And Jem, you don't want nannies and babysitters raising your kids, right?"

Jem nodded, the very thought of that making his jaw clench.

"Then you don't want me doin' it either," Blaze said. "Not sure if you've noticed, but I'm barely keeping my own life together here. I'm no good for those kids without you."

Jem shook his head. "You're doin' something right to have a gorgeous woman like Faith kissin' you the way she was."

Blaze said nothing then, and Jem didn't look at him. He'd spent almost his entire life at Blaze's side, and he could imagine the tight, jumping muscle in his jaw. It actually made him smile slightly.

"I'm going to freeze to death," Blaze said. He stood and then he offered Jem a hand up. Jem looked at it, and then up the arm to his brother. He took Blaze's hand and stood, coming chest-to-chest with his best friend.

"I love you, Blaze." Jem gripped him in another hug. "I'm sorry for ruining things between us with liquor and women."

"It's nothing I've not done too," Blaze said back, his voice thick with emotion. "We all have to find our own way, Jem."

Jem stepped back and took in his brother's rugged features. He had little scars in various places on his body, including one right along the top of his right eyebrow. It couldn't be seen unless he moved the hair there a little, which he never did. But Jem knew it was there, because he'd gone to the emergency room with Blaze after the bar fight that had caused the injury.

"How did you find your way, Blaze?"

His brother started toward the house, and it was only a few steps to the door. "Therapy, for one," he said. "Two, I actually want to change, Jem. I don't want to be the man who rode in the rodeo." He looked straight at Jem, right into him. Straight into his soul, his very center. "If you want to go back to the rodeo, go. If you don't, you have to decide who you want to be now, and start working on becoming him."

He opened the door and went inside. "He's comin' in, everyone. Get ready to give him a big hug."

Jem took a deep breath, because his vision was about to come true. He entered Tex's house—his childhood home too— and found Blaze standing with Rosie in his arms. His baby girl beamed at him, her skinny arms outstretched, and Jem rushed at her and held her in his arms as tightly as he dared.

"I love you, baby," he whispered. "Okay?"

"I love you too, Daddy." She wept against his chest, and Jem looked at all the Youngs gathered in the small house. Tex and Abby had pushed out the back of the house to make it a little bigger, but with all of them there, it still barely held them.

He closed his eyes against all of their compassion, their

concern, their love for him and his kids. How he'd missed it previous to this, he didn't know. It streamed through him now, coming at him from all sides, and he felt it changing him.

He knelt down and put Rosie on his knee so he could open his arm for Cole. The boy flew into his chest, crying too. "It's okay," he whispered to him. "I'm gonna be the dad you guys need and deserve, okay? I am."

He needed something and someone to be, and what nobler cause was there than that of a father? He couldn't think of one, and with renewed purpose, he passed his crying kids to Blaze and stepped into his daddy.

"I'm so sorry, Daddy," he whispered.

"Nothing to be done about it," Daddy said gruffly. "But to move forward, Jem. It's time to move forward."

Jem nodded against his dad's shoulder, and then he faced Tex. "I'm sorry I fumbled that all up," Tex said sincerely. "I should've known they wouldn't start without me. None of them can say anything." He raised his voice on the last few words. "About anything."

"Tex," Abby admonished. She smiled widely at Jem. "We love you, Jem." She gave him a quick hug, as she still tended to her fussy nephew. She gazed at the baby fondly, and Jem looked for his own mother.

She'd been telling him for weeks to make things right with Blaze, and Jem hadn't done it. Every day had fractured him more and more until he stood in the farmhouse, a completely broken man. He embraced his mother, said, "I'm sorry, Momma," and began his journey to fix and heal all of the things that he'd broken.

He knew it wouldn't happen in one day, or one week. He'd seen the effort Blaze had put in over the past year, and while Jem was afraid of the work, he wanted to be the man Blaze was.

He wanted to be someone else, and to do that, he had to change—and he was finally ready to do that.

9

Blaze had no emotional capacity left. Dinner at Tex's had utterly ruined him, but he pulled into his ex-in-law's driveway, Fiona's SUV already there. She'd been texting him for a half-hour before he felt like he could leave Jem at the farmhouse, so he quickly got out and jogged up the front sidewalk to the door.

Cash opened it before he could ring the bell, and Blaze laughed as he lifted his boy into his arms. "Oh, I missed you so much." He hugged his son tightly against his chest, this reunion so unlike the others they'd had over the years.

"Blaze," Marion said. "Come in, come in."

"Did you bring Grandpa a gift?" Blaze asked as he set Cash on his feet. The older gentleman held a pioneer toy in his hand —a ball attached to a string that he was trying to get into the center of the paddle.

"Yep," Cash said. "We stopped at Cove Fort yesterday, and we got some souvenirs for everyone."

"Wow." He chuckled as Marion practically threw the ball. It was a good thing it was attached to the paddle, or Blaze thought there'd be some broken vases and windows soon enough.

"There you are," Fiona said. She rushed out of the kitchen, pure panic on her face.

"What's wrong?" He took her into his arms, feeling her tremble. "Are you okay?" He kept his voice low so as to not alarm her father or their son. The two of them laughed, and Blaze stepped back from Fiona. He kept his hands on her shoulders as he peered at her. "Fi, talk to me."

"I just hate being here." She glanced over to her dad. "It feels so fake."

"Fi, if you're not going to say anything to them, then you have to play the game."

She glared at him with all her blue-eyed power. "I've been here for an hour. How long do I have to stay?"

"I don't know." He wasn't her father, and he wasn't in charge of her. His heart bled for her, but the only reason he was here was because of Cash. Without him, and Blaze would've never seen Fiona or her parents again.

He tamped down his impatience with his ex-wife and her family. His family drama was enough for him, and he honestly felt like he couldn't take on more. "It smells like brownies."

"Of course," Fi bit out. "My mother thinks chocolate baked goods fix decades of lies."

Blaze shot her another look that said, *Either say it or don't, but don't act put out if you're not going to say it.*

She watched Cash and Marion for a few moments, and then she said, "He loves him too much. I can't ruin that for him." She folded her arms and retreated to the kitchen. Blaze sighed in relief as she went, because he seriously couldn't console his son tonight. Being the shoulder for Jem to cry on had drained him completely.

He'd texted Faith about everything that had happened at the farmhouse, and he'd called her on the drive here. *You're a good brother*, she'd told him, and for the first time in his life, Blaze felt like he was a good brother.

He hadn't spoken any more to Jem about moving back in, but he suspected he would very soon. Tomorrow, even, because he needed help with the kids—and he'd need Blaze to help him stay home and away from the bars in town.

Blaze would gladly do it, too, because he wanted Jem to keep his kids and find his happiness. As he listened to the conversation float back to him from the kitchen, he realized he wanted Fiona to find her happiness too.

She'd left Coral Canyon because of some deceit and lies in her family, and that preserved her from having to face them. But had it made her happy?

He gave his son a smile and went into the kitchen.

"Oh, Blaze is here." Carrie bustled over to him and swept a kiss across his cheek. "How was your weekend, Mister Rodeo Star?"

She was in fine form today, and Blaze caught Fiona rolling her eyes as she turned her back on her mother.

"I retired from the rodeo, Carrie," he said. "Years ago." He smelled a bit of alcohol on her breath, and he once again glanced over to Fiona. Her brother and sister-in-law were still here, and thankfully, they provided a good buffer between Fi and her mother.

"I know that." Carrie giggled and turned her attention to the brownie scooping happening. "Are you staying for dessert, Blaze?"

"Oh, no, ma'am." He rocked back onto his heels. "My momma made cake and pie for dessert tonight, and I am stuffed full."

Fiona looked at him, then dug into the carton of vanilla ice cream again. She nodded to the bowl in front of her. "You can take that to Cash. His suitcase is in the back of my car."

"I'll move it." Blaze took the bowl of brownies and ice cream out into the living room and said, "Cash, your momma dished you some dessert. Sit down to eat it now, okay?"

His son cheered, and Blaze handed him the bowl. "Bud, we can't stay for much longer, okay? I'm gonna go move your bag, and when you're done there, we have to get going." He smiled at his son and pushed the flop of hair off his forehead.

"Okay, Dad."

He watched his son for a moment. "You feelin' okay, son?"

"Yeah." Cash held red spots in his cheeks. "It's just hot in here, and I was showing Grandpa how to get the ball in the dent." He smiled and took a bite of his ice cream.

Blaze nodded, because the Peters always kept their house hotter than anyplace he'd ever been before. He went outside and moved Cash's bag from Fiona's car to his truck, and he found he didn't want to go back in.

He stood in the dark night, the cheery lights pouring from the windows creating a sense of serenity and calmness he knew didn't actually exist inside the house. It just proved to him how deceiving some things could be, and he sighed out a long breath.

The front door opened, and Fiona came outside with a paper plate in her hand. "My mom won't let you leave without taking these." She handed him the plate, which held four brownie squares on it.

He smiled at them and then her. He didn't know what to say, so Blaze lifted his arm and pulled his ex-wife into his side. "I'm sorry, Fi."

She was a strong woman, and she'd never relied on him for much more than money. Even then, she'd told him years ago she didn't need it. He'd kept sending it anyway, because that was the only way to soothe his conscience. He knew now that money didn't solve anything. He had to be present if he wanted to be a father, and relationships were worth far more than any currency.

But they had to be cultivated. They took a lot of work, and Blaze honestly wasn't sure he could've been in the rodeo and maintained any relationship at all. The only person he'd been able to do that with was Jem.

Fiona sniffled and wrapped her arms around Blaze, the two of them standing in the driveway in the darkness, the moon overhead dimming as clouds drifted by in front of it from time to time.

She cried quietly for a few minutes and then straightened. "I'm okay."

"Where you stayin' tonight?" he asked gently.

"A hotel in town. Not far."

"Tomorrow?"

"Salt Lake."

"Home on Tuesday?"

Fiona didn't answer, which meant no. Blaze didn't ask another question, because she didn't have to give him an accounting of her life. He'd simply wanted to ground her in something easy and simple, and her travel schedule was something she'd know forward and backward.

"I'm actually stopping in Salt Lake for a few days," she finally said. "My biological father lives there, and I've been emailing with him."

Shock coursed through Blaze, and he turned and looked fully at his ex. "Really?"

She nodded, anxiety pouring from her now. "I've given all the information to Jessie, so if I end up dead somewhere, she'll know who I was with."

"I want that information," Blaze said instantly.

"Blaze." She huffed out her breath. "I can take care of myself."

"You're the mother of our son," he said. "I want to know who you're meeting and where, so if something happens, I don't have to rely on your best friend to fill me in." He glared at her. "You know what you're doing, yes. I trust you, of course. You're a grown woman, but Fi...." He shook his head. "Just because he's your biological father doesn't mean you can trust him."

"You're right." She nodded. "I know. I'll send you all the info too."

"Thank you," he murmured. "I once again find myself outside in this absolutely frigid weather." He drew in a breath that hurt his nostrils and his lungs. "Why do I live here?" He turned back to the house, the answer to that question right in front of his face.

He lived in Coral Canyon so he could go to the farmhouse for family dinners on the Sabbath. He needed the support network, and he liked the small town feel after many years of lights, noise, partying all night, and oppressive activities twenty-four hours each day.

Coral Canyon was slower. Sweeter. Better than anywhere he'd ever lived, and he wanted to give his son a calm, quiet place to finish growing up.

"I'll get Cash," Fi said. "Thank you for...." She gestured to him. "Letting me cry. And vent."

"You can do either anytime, sweetheart." He reached up and brushed her blonde bangs off her forehead. "I'm seein' someone again. Someone good."

Fiona smiled at him. "That's great, Blaze."

"You?" he asked. "This Mister Foster from down the street?"

Fiona dropped her chin, her smile still stuck to her face. "Maybe."

"He better be good to you," Blaze said.

She looked up at him, the challenge in her eyes glinting in the moonlight. "I was a complete failure to you," he said. "And I see you in there, and you're not happy. I just want you to be happy."

Fiona blinked, all the hardness in her gaze disappearing. "Thank you, Blaze. I want you to be happy too."

"I'm working on it," he said as he tipped his head back to gaze up to the stars. "I sure appreciate you forgiving me for all I did wrong with you and Cash."

"Blaze," she said. "You were never a bad father."

"You'd have to be around to be bad," he murmured.

"When are you going to stop beating yourself up for that?" she asked.

He looked at her, the answer to her question nowhere in his head. "I don't know."

"You should stop tonight," she said. "You took care of us the way you knew how, and now you're doing things differently. He adores you, you know, and I know the two of you had a rough first year together." She brought back the smile. "But anyone can feel how much you love him, and how you would literally do anything for him. So stop, okay?"

Fiona put her hand on his forearm. "Promise me you'll stop beating yourself up for things you've already fixed."

He nodded a couple of times. "I'll try."

"Okay." She backed up a step. "I'll send Cash out."

"'Bye, Fi."

His son came out a couple of minutes later, and Blaze grinned at him, took his hand, and loaded him in the truck. They made the drive back to the mansion on the lake as Cash prattled on and on about his trip to Utah, the road trip back, and all the things he'd done.

Blaze loved listening to him talk, and he loved that he hadn't come home to an empty, quiet house tonight. After he'd parked in the basement garage and they'd gone into the kitchen, he paused.

Someone had been here. His nose knew, and his gaze swept the dining room table and then the huge kitchen island to find the source of the maple he could smell.

He found the culprit sitting on a plastic tray next to the in-counter stove he never used. Four perfectly iced and decorated Salty Cowboy doughnuts—his favorite—sat there, and that meant Faith had been in his house.

A card lay next to them, and Blaze picked it up as Cash asked, "Do I have to go to bed right now?"

"Yes," Blaze murmured. "It's already eight-thirty, and you have school in the morning." He tore his gaze from the white envelope with his name scrawled delicately on it and looked at his son. "When's the last time you showered?"

"Yesterday," Cash said. He rolled his eyes. "I'll go get ready for bed."

"I'll be in soon," Blaze said. "Make sure you use toothpaste to brush your teeth," he called after his son, who did not answer.

He opened the envelope and pulled out the card inside. It had a bright-pink-frosted doughnut on the front, with plenty of sprinkles on the pastry and off of it. He smiled at it, because it was so Faith, and then he opened it.

I'm sorry I missed you, but my sister called and said her son had fallen and his mouth was bleeding, so I had to leave the doughnuts and go.

I know your family wore you out tonight, and I thought a treat and a hug might help. The hug will have to be virtual. #hug

She'd drawn a heart and then signed her name, and Blaze sighed as he finished the card and started reading it again.

A treat and a hug. Those two things did fix a lot of problems, usually, and he hugged the card to his chest and pressed his eyes closed. He swore he could feel Faith in the fibers of the paper, smell her perfume, and hear her voice.

The sensation only lasted a few moments, and then it all disappeared. He set down the card and picked up his phone. Exhaustion tugged at him to go get ready for bed, but he dialed Faith on the way to the master bedroom.

"Hey," she whispered after she'd picked up. "I'm holding my sleeping nephew, so I can't talk loud."

"Okay." He kept his voice low too. "Thank you for the doughnuts, love." His throat narrowed, because while Blaze had the experience with women, it was all fake. This was so much more than anything he'd ever had with a woman before, and he didn't know how to speak true feelings. "They mean a lot to me."

She let a few beats of silence pass. "Why is that, Blaze?"

He entered his bedroom and put his keys on top of the dresser. "I don't know," he said, but he did.

"Oh, someone's lying." A whimper came through the line, and she shushed her nephew back to sleep.

"Maybe I am," Blaze whispered. "I think—it means a lot to me that you were thinking about me, Faith. That's what it is. It's touching. I don't—I've never had anyone thinking about me and hoping I was okay."

"I'm sure that is not true," she whispered back. "Your momma for sure has been praying over you for years."

"Yeah." Of course his momma had been. "It's different when it's not your momma," he said. He switched the phone to speaker and removed his jacket and started to pull his shirt over his head.

"Mm."

He pictured her rocking back and forth, a little boy snug and content in her arms, and Blaze sure did like that image in his head. "Do you want little boys and girls to hold while they sleep?"

"Yes, sir," she whispered. "I'd love to be a mom."

He nodded, though she couldn't see him. "What about a step-mom?"

Faith once again didn't jump right in with an answer. "I could try," she finally said. "I should probably meet Cash at some point."

"Yeah," Blaze said. He tossed his clothes on the recliner in the corner of the huge bedroom and stepped into a pair of gym shorts. "He'll be at school tomorrow, but sometime."

"Can I text you with the time tomorrow?" she asked.

"You think you're going to sleep in?"

"I think I'd like the option."

Blaze smiled and said, "Of course, sweetheart. Text me when you're ready. I'm ten minutes away."

She yawned, the sound of it peaceful and serene. It triggered a yawn in his body too, and she said, "Goodnight, Blaze," near the tail end of it.

"'Night, Faith. See you tomorrow."

The call ended, and Blaze plugged in his phone and went to brush his own teeth before continuing down the hall and around the corner to Cash's room. The boy sat at his desk, an anime playing on his phone as he worked on one of his coloring books. It was such a normal, nice scene, and that made Blaze smile.

"Time for bed, bud," he said.

His son had changed into his pajamas, and he set down the red-orange crayon. "I'm barely tired."

"Well, I'm bushed," Blaze said. Cash never made his bed, so Blaze shook out the blanket and pulled the sheet up tight. "You can leave your anime on while you lie down, okay? You've got an alarm set?"

"Yes," Cash said. "I forgot to turn the stupid thing off over the break, and I got up every day at six-thirty."

Blaze chuckled and tucked his son in tight. He leaned down, marveling that his back didn't sting and pull and shoot lightning down his leg and up to his ears. "I love you, son. I'm so glad you're back."

"Love you too, Daddy." Cash smiled as he hugged Blaze, and Blaze left the lamp on for now. He'd go shut down the house, locking everything and turning off the lights, and he wouldn't be one ounce surprised if, when he returned in ten minutes, Cash was sound asleep.

With the house ready for bed, Blaze detoured into the front office and sat in front of his computer. The Santa's Stocking Stuffers meeting was on Tuesday, and he needed to get in touch with the department store manager before then.

He quickly made a list of things he needed to get done

tomorrow, including a few items for his charity work, and then he switched off the lamp. He sat in the dark for a moment and simply let the silence and stillness fill him.

In quiet moments like this, Blaze could feel and hear things he normally couldn't. "Lord?" He phrased it as a question, because while he'd prayed here and there since returning to Coral Canyon, he'd felt a bigger presence in his life today.

It hadn't been all him comforting Jem. He'd had words given to him, and he'd been strengthened beyond his own capacity so he could hold his brother while he sobbed.

That had to come from...God, and Blaze wanted—he *needed* —to know if the Lord was even listening to him. If He even saw what Blaze was trying to do. If He even cared.

He couldn't write an email to heaven, so he sat in the dark, his eyes closed, and whispered, "I'm sorry for all the things I've done that have led me away from You."

His mind started to get loud, and he paused, snuffing out the clamoring guilt and negative voices that told him how he'd never be able to be forgiven for *every*thing.

"Please forgive me," he said next. "I'm trying, and if Thou wilt lead me, I will follow."

He had nothing more to say, and the heavens didn't open. A sense of safety and peace Blaze had never, ever felt before crept into his heart, and Blaze's eyes flew open.

He knew.

He *could* be forgiven for everything, and God was very, very aware of him and his efforts.

Now, he just had to keep trying, and sometimes that was harder than anything else.

10

Faith's nerves bounced through her veins as she carried a bin of supplies toward a house she'd never been inside before. She felt like she possessed some muscles in her arms from years of kneading dough, but she'd overpacked this bin. Badly.

She nearly dropped it on the stoop and then went up the few steps after it to ring the doorbell. Her chest heaved with anxiety combined with the physical effort of carrying the bin, and she had no idea what to expect on the other side of the door.

Heat rushed out ahead of anyone or anything, and Faith came face-to-face with someone old enough to be her grandmother. "You must be Faith," she said.

"Yes, ma'am." Faith smiled at her with as much professionalism as she could. "Seems like I found the right house."

The white-haired woman stepped back. "That you did.

Come in. I know Shirley hasn't stopped talking about these doughnuts."

Faith bent to get her bin, and she kept her smile hitched in place as she entered the house. It smelled like cinnamon and pine were having a war for the dominant scent, and Faith very nearly gagged. She disliked that fake cinnamon smell almost more than anything.

"In here?" She went into the kitchen without waiting for confirmation. Thankfully, the countertops were clear, and she slid her bin right onto the nearest one. She exhaled heavily, pulled down her jacket, and turned to face the woman. "I have more in the car."

"Just come in and out as you need to." She smiled again. "My daughter will be home in about thirty minutes." She shook her head, though she had a good air about her. "She always cuts everything so close."

Faith only smiled, because it wasn't her place to comment on how a stranger got ready for her holiday party. Shirley Rice was paying her to be here and serve up to sixty mini festive doughnuts and thirty-six full-size doughnuts of the Elvis Presley and the Red Velvet Revival.

All of the doughnuts had been made already, and Faith had frozen them last night. They reheated very well in a very hot oven, and she turned to get that started. Once they were hot, she'd decorate them and tier them up on the brand new party-ware she'd purchased this week.

"I'll be right back," she said to the woman, who didn't respond. Faith went back and forth two more times, bringing in her carefully crafted pastries. She opened the first bin, which

Blaze had helped her pack after his Stocking Stuffer meeting, and Faith took out the baking sheets she'd also bought only a few days ago.

She'd gone through every step of this party prep herself, making note cards of how long everything took. Then she went over it with Blaze while he sat at her bar on Wednesday night. Last night, he'd taken her cards and made her tell him her strategy without them, and now that Faith had everything in front of her, her hands knew exactly what to do.

She laid out all the miniature doughnuts on two trays and put them in the oven. They'd take longer to glaze, frost, and decorate, and she could reheat the bigger doughnuts while she did that. She only had one tray left, but she got it ready with the larger doughnuts, and then she lifted her stand mixer out of the bin.

"No wonder I almost died carrying this in," she muttered. Next time, she'd ask Blaze to come help her get set up. He wouldn't be able to stay for the duration of the party, but he sure as heck could use the muscles God gave him to help her get her supplies into the venue.

Faith had done this so many times in her life, she barely had to think at all about dropping in the deep red food-grade coloring to make the holly berries on the festive doughnut bites. She'd already made the sculpted green leaves, and she was using gold candy balls for the center. She'd sculpted gnomes and trees, cardinals and reindeer, already too, and having so much done in advance allowed her to focus on decorating.

It also allowed her to think shamelessly about Blaze. She'd seen him every day this week, because he refused to let a day go by where he didn't get to be in her presence. Just thinking about him made her warm, and she sure did like spending time with him.

He'd gone over some of his Stocking Stuffer items with her, and he said his office was filling with presents he had to figure out what to do with. She'd asked him if they needed to be wrapped, and he'd said vaguely, "Some of them. I've gotta figure that out too." Then he'd sighed mightily, and she had asked him why he'd signed up to do the Santa's Stocking Stuffers event if he didn't like it.

"Service isn't about doing something you love," he'd said, giving her a curious look. She knew that, because she hadn't wanted to leave his house last weekend to go help Trinity with her son. But she'd done it, because her sister needed her.

She'd told him she'd come help him sort the gifts and wrap them, and he'd said he was going to take her up on that offer.

The back door of the house opened, and a harried woman entered with shopping bags draped over both arms. "Oh, good," she said, completely out of breath. "You're here."

"Shirley." Faith abandoned her accessories and went to help the woman she'd only spoken to on the phone.

"I'm fine, I'm fine." She dumped everything unceremoniously on the dining room table and pushed her hair out of her face. Only then did she give Faith a smile. "It smells amazing in here."

She dove into the bags while Faith stood there. "You sure you don't need any help?"

"Nope. I'm going to get this table set and then go change,

and I'll be ready." She started to work around the table, which had a double-leaf in it and could seat eighteen people.

"Where would you like me to put the doughnuts?" Faith asked as she returned to the kitchen. This house wasn't brand new and huge like Blaze's, but it was easily twice as big as Faith's. She'd never be able to even get a table in her house as big as the one Shirley had here.

"We're going to mingle in the living room," she said. "So out there. I'll clear you some room on the credenza, okay?"

"Thank you." Faith flashed a smile in Shirley's direction, but the woman had all of her attention on the work at hand. She set a table for sixteen faster than Faith had ever seen it done, and then all the bags and items she'd brought got whisked away.

Some she took into the living room, where Faith could hear the two women talking. She kept her head down, the clock ticking now. The large doughnuts came out of the oven, and Faith dunked them in the glaze they needed—a caramel one for the Elvis Presley—and set them aside.

The red velvet cakes needed frosting only before the final decoration, and Faith started whipping that. The salted peanuts got applied to the still-wet caramel, and Faith got the bananas out too. She wouldn't do those until moments before the party began, because she didn't want them to turn brown and gross. The only thing worse than a brown banana was a cold egg, in her opinion.

She finished with the festive minis, trayed them, and took the box with her tiered display stand out into the living room. Shirley and her mother had disappeared, but Faith could clearly see where to put the doughnuts. The living room had been magically transformed into a Christmas wonderland too, with three flocked-white trees that had not been there when she'd arrived. Or so she thought, but she'd been pretty focused on getting the bin to the kitchen.

She quickly set up the display stand and brought out the mini doughnuts. They filled it, as she'd practiced this menu twice this week since booking this party. Blaze had a lot of brothers willing to eat miniature doughnuts, and she'd taken several to her truck the next morning too.

After piping the frosting on the red velvet doughnuts, they got a sprinkling of "snow," which was large flake sugar Faith had sprayed with food-grade gold glitter. She sighed as the perfection of the Red Velvet Revival doughnuts smiled back at her.

"They're perfect," she murmured. They got placed on a festive tray with greenery and boughs to compliment the red and white already in the doughnut, and once Faith had them displayed and she'd returned to the kitchen, all she had left were the bananas.

She checked the clock and got slicing.

"All right," Shirley said with a heavy sigh as she returned. "How are we doing? Almost done?"

"Yep." Faith placed the slices between the peanuts, and once the last one had been stuck in the caramel, she looked up with a smile. She froze, because Shirley had turned from harried housewife into glamorous supermodel. "Wow," Faith said. "You look great."

"I hope so." Shirley reached up and touched the back of her hair, which had been swept up into an elegant up-do. "My boss is coming tonight, and if he doesn't ask me out...." She shook her head, her eyes glittering with holiday cheer. "This dress ought to do it, don't you think?"

She wore a deep navy blue gown with more sequins and sparkles than Faith had ever seen in real life. "Yes." She cleared her throat. "Yes, that dress is magnificent." It scooped toward Shirley's ample chest, and it only went over her shoulders with spaghetti straps. It clung to her curves all the way to her knees, and the thick fabric dragged on the floor despite the silver heels on her feet.

Faith couldn't even imagine wearing a dress like that, and she wondered if Shirley's boss was blind.

She quickly got back to work, her face heating. The Elvis Presley doughnuts found their home on the credenza, and Faith took quick pictures of the holiday feast for her social media. She looked up and found Shirley doing the same thing with her holiday table décor.

"Can we get one?" Faith asked. "I'll only post it if you want me to, but you're my first catering client."

"Of course." Shirley smiled for all she was worth as Faith took the selfie, and then she started cleaning up.

"I'll come get the trays later," she said.

"Tomorrow's fine," Shirley said. "Thank you, Faith. These look divine." She clicked photos of the doughnuts too, and a bit of pride swelled in Faith's chest. Her concoctions *were* beautiful, and part of her wanted to stay so she could hear Shirley's party guests exclaim over them.

But Blaze waited for her, and Faith suddenly wanted to see him more than ever. She lugged her bins back to the car—two of them lighter than before—and drew in a deep breath.

"Thank you," she whispered as her car started to blow warm air. "That went so well, and I needed it to. Thank you." She flipped the car into reverse and backed out of the driveway just as another car approached.

She couldn't help pausing to watch as a man parked on the street and got out of his sleek, black SUV. He wore expensive clothes with a costly coat, and he walked like someone who was used to having things done for them.

He was handsome, for sure, and he didn't seem blind as he made his way up the driveway and sidewalk to Shirley's front door. Faith smiled to herself as she drove away. "Bless them to have a great party."

She didn't pray for her and Blaze to have an amazing evening, because Faith already believed they would. The ornery cowboy had softened for her, and she wasn't so tongue-tied around him anymore.

They'd been getting to know one another again, and he'd asked her a few really personal questions—like if she wanted kids and how she felt about her parents living so far away. Other than that, they spent time together in an easy, casual way.

He hadn't kissed her again, and Faith's heartbeat trembled as she thought about that. Why hadn't he?

They hadn't talked about her impromptu and completely wild kiss at the craft mall last weekend, and Faith suddenly wanted to. So it was a good thing she'd be seeing Blaze in only a half-hour.

Right?

"Look." She showed him her phone with all the pictures she'd taken. "Aren't they the cutest things ever?"

"Yes," he murmured, his hand snaking along her waist and keeping her close. "They're perfect." He leaned into her, as if he might press a kiss to her cheek. But he didn't. "Mm, you smell like sugar."

She turned toward him and found those dark, dangerous eyes glinting at her with desire. Faith put her phone down and turned into his arms. "Blaze."

"Hm?" He closed his eyes and held her in the circle of his arms effortlessly. They swayed together, and if Faith closed her eyes, she could easily see how the world would narrow to just the two of them, dancing in the slow circle in his kitchen.

Cash was here in the house somewhere, but Blaze was just waiting for Trace, Everly, and Harry to arrive before they could leave to go get a late dinner.

Her pulse quivered, but Faith took a breath to steady herself. "I wanted to ask you something," she whispered.

"Go ahead."

"You haven't kissed me again," she said.

He tensed, and then pulled back, his eyes open now. "I haven't kissed you at all."

She blinked. "Yes, you did."

"No." He stepped away from her completely, leaving her cold and wondering what she'd done wrong. "You kissed me— and you know what? I really liked it, but I wish I'd have initiated it."

Faith held very still, trying to make sense of his statement. "You're mad about the kiss?"

"Yeah," he said. "I'm mad about the kiss."

"Well—" She cut off, because she hadn't expected him to say that. He hadn't *acted* mad about the kiss—he'd kissed her back quite passionately, in fact.

"I—" She lifted one hand in a flapping gesture and then let it fall back to her side. She stared at him, and he stared right on back, those eyes brewing a storm that Faith simply knew would drench her.

11

Blaze couldn't quite believe he'd told Faith he was upset about the kiss. She didn't have anything to say about that, and he wasn't sure what he wanted her to say.

"You didn't like it?" she finally asked. Her voice sounded like someone had pinched her airway between their thumb and forefinger.

The last thing he wanted was to make her feel bad. "I liked it," he admitted, but she'd started to turn toward the living room, as the front door had been opened.

The puppy he'd rented barked, covering his words, and the security system said, "Front door, open."

"Front door, open," Harry imitated as he came through the foyer and into the living room. He wore a smile the size of the Tetons, his hand secured in that of a pretty blonde girl about his same age. "Howdy, Uncle Blaze."

"Howdy, Harry," Blaze growled. He reached for his own

cowboy hat, which he had not been wearing as he danced and swayed with Faith. He hadn't formally introduced her to Cash, and he wouldn't be doing that tonight either.

"It's snowing out there," Trace said as he came into the back of the house. "You sure you want to go ice skating tonight?"

Blaze looked at Faith, and she lifted her eyebrows at him. "We'll think of something," he said.

Everly Avery, Trace's fiancé, smiled her way right over to him. She balanced herself against him by lightly resting her hands on his shoulders as she leaned up to kiss his cheek. "Evening, Blaze."

"Hey, Everly." He couldn't help smiling at her, because she brought so much sunshine with her. Trace sure was lucky to have her in his life, and she returned to his side, both of them smiling like they owned the world.

And they did, because they were going to be married in the spring, and then the band would do their summer tour, and Trace was taking his whole family with him. *Unicorns and roses and cotton candy*, Blaze thought.

Immediately, he knew he wasn't being fair to Trace, the brother who had come to live with him for a few weeks after his major back surgery. That hadn't been easy for Trace, and Blaze shouldn't be having such poisonous thoughts about his brother.

"Hey, brother." He stepped into Trace and hugged him. "How's life?"

"Good." Trace sighed. "Luke is killing us at the gym, but good." He smiled over to Faith. "Howdy, Faith."

"Oh, you haven't met Trace." Foolishness ran through Blaze. His family knew he was dating, but that didn't mean she'd met them all. "Faith, this is my older brother. He's just older than me; just younger than Tex. Trace, and you already know his fiancé, Everly. His son, Harry."

Harry currently played with the little black puppy Blaze had had for a few days, and he looked up from the floor and raised his hand.

"You got Monster," Everly said. "Blaze, why didn't you tell me?" She dropped to the ground to play with the puppy too, and it jumped up and started licking her face. She giggled and scrubbed the dog's body with both hands.

Blaze looked at Trace, who wore a mildly horrified expression on his face. "Trace," he said. "My girlfriend, Faith Cromwell." He slid his arm around her, glad when she melted into his side. They hadn't been in the middle of a good conversation, but Faith knew how to put on appearances—at least for a few minutes.

"So great to meet you," she gushed, and Trace repeated the sentiment as he shook her hand. Everly, of course, hugged Faith, because they were already friends.

Blaze decided that was a good time to go. "You ready, baby?"

"Yes."

He helped Faith back into her coat, and she picked up her phone from where she'd set it on the kitchen counter. "Cash is downstairs playing video games," Blaze said. "If you're so inclined, you can go through the bedrooms down there. Jem's moving back in next weekend."

Trace's eyebrows flew off his face. "Is he now?"

Blaze nodded, his jaw already tight. He had a lot going on in his life right now, but he'd decided he wouldn't have it any other way. His brother needed him. He'd signed up for the Stocking Stuffers. He adored his son—and his family.

And now he had Faith to consider, and to be honest, she was the easiest part of his life. He didn't want to lose her, so he took her with him toward the garage door and out it. He helped her into his truck, and after he got behind the wheel, he started the vehicle but didn't put it in gear.

"I'm not mad about the kiss, Faith."

"You said you were, and you haven't kissed me again."

"Stop saying *again*," he said. "*You* kissed *me*. I haven't kissed you at all."

"That is just the most ridiculous thing I've ever heard," she said. "You kissed me back, Blaze. I wasn't imagining that."

"I've imagined kissing you again," he said. "But—"

"Aha! You just said again." Faith smiled at him in triumph, and Blaze shook his head though a smile threatened to curve his lips.

"I'm mad at myself I didn't kiss you first," he said. "I'm upset you didn't warn me it was coming. I'm desperate to do it again." He glanced over to her, trying to judge her reaction to all he'd said.

She wore fear and vulnerability on her face, and she reached for his hand. "I'm sorry, Blaze. I didn't know it was that important to you for *you* to kiss *me*."

"I've been thinking of some ways I could—I don't know. Teach you a lesson."

Faith half-laughed and half-scoffed. "Teach me a lesson for kissing you?"

"Yeah," he said gruffly. He finally put the truck in reverse and backed out of his garage. It sat tucked under the deck, so there wasn't any falling snow here, but as he went up the road and around his house, he had to flip on the windshield wipers.

"It's snowing," Faith said, her voice filled with wonder and magic. "I love the snow."

"Do you really?" he asked. He wasn't sure if they'd come back to the conversation where he "taught her a lesson" for kissing him first, but he half-hoped they wouldn't. He'd been thinking about kissing her tonight—really kissing her—and he hadn't lied.

He was desperate to do it.

So you will, he told himself as Faith started talking about how much she loved the winter. "My daddy used to take us ice skating and ice fishing." Her voice held plenty of nostalgia and love. "We went skiing in Jackson Hole, and my uncle had a snowmobile. Winter was fun."

"It's too dang cold," Blaze grumbled, apparently determined to be a complete grump tonight.

She laughed lightly, oblivious to his dark mood. He didn't want to go ice skating, but he pulled up to the rink anyway, where a semi-circle of food trucks had gathered and plenty of people were still lined up to get on the rink.

"You want to do this?" he asked, watching the mob of people out on the ice. It didn't seem fun to him at all. The rink sat in one of the downtown parks, with lots of bare-branched trees surrounding it. Walking paths wove through the park, but Blaze had never done much here. He didn't have a permanent dog to throw a ball to, nor a loved one to wander through the trees with.

He glanced over to her. "We could just take a walk in the snow."

Her face glowed and she nodded. "The rink is really full right now."

He nodded and got out of the truck. She waited for him to get her door, which he did, and then he slipped his gloved hand in hers. Blaze led her away from the ice skating rink, away from all the people, away from the noise.

She sighed once they'd started down the path, and some of the unease inside Blaze dissipated too. "I printed the list of things that need to be wrapped," he said into the snowy stillness.

"That's great," she said. "I can come over tomorrow or Sunday after church." She glanced over to him. "If that works."

"I have to have them to the Army Recruitment office in town by the fifteenth," he said. "So we've still got a week and a half."

"Okay," she said lightly. "I have two parties next week, but I don't think I need to practice so much."

"It does cost money in ingredients and decorations if you do everything three times."

"Right?" She looked over to him and brushed something off the brim of his cowboy hat. "Blaze, I'm really sorry about kissing you the way I did."

He didn't look at her. "It went all over the Internet, you know."

"It did?"

"My manager called me and everything."

"What did you tell him?"

"I told him that it wasn't a big deal. We're dating. Whatever." They walked on for several paces, the night getting darker and darker the further from the rink they went.

"What were people saying?"

Blaze had listened to Roger's voice for over an hour at the beginning of the week. "I don't know," he said. "Mostly speculation about who you were, and if we were together or if it was a stunt." He swallowed. "I, uh, well, I used to do a lot of stupid stuff, mostly for publicity." His chest felt too small to hold his heart. "You know that, Faith? Right? That I did a lot of stupid things while I lived in Vegas."

"You've said as much," she said.

"I can give you as many or as few details as you want."

She watched him for a moment, finally removing her arm from his and stepping in front of him. "Blaze, look at me for a second."

He did, but it took more from him than he'd thought it would. She was so beautiful, and so good, and so kind, and he had done so much wrong. How could someone like her ever want to be with him?

"I partied," he said. "A lot. I went home with women whose names I didn't even know. I—" He cut off when she put her finger against his lips.

"I don't care," she whispered. "That was a different man than who's standing here in front of me right now." Her eyebrows went up, and with her bangs the only part of her hair out of that dark pink hat, she was the prettiest picture of a small-town woman Blaze had ever seen. "Right? You're not that man anymore."

"No," he said. "I'm not."

"Then I don't care."

The snow fell softly around them, muting everything. Blaze wished he wasn't wearing gloves, but he was afraid he'd lose some fingers if he took them off. "Faith, I think you're the most amazing woman I've ever met."

With that, he brought her flush against him, tipped his head down, and kissed her. It wasn't the wild abandon with harsh strokes that she'd first kissed him with. This was a slow, sensual, explorative kiss that sent pleasure spiraling through his body.

"Blaze," she whispered as she pulled away. He claimed her mouth again, and she had no complaints about that.

He kissed her until he felt sure they were steaming in the cold weather, and then he pulled back. The earth had just been knocked off its axis, and Blaze honestly wasn't sure if he was coming or going. Faith had mixed up his life so completely, and in the very best way.

"You know what?" he asked, his voice low as if he spoke too loud, it would disturb the branches.

"What?" she whispered, still tucked against his chest, her breath falling across his collarbone.

"I think I like the snow too," he said.

She lifted her head and looked at him, and Blaze smiled at her. "I'm not mad about that kiss."

She smiled back. "You're a possessive man, Blaze."

"Yes, I am." He pressed his hand into her back, keeping her

tightly against him. "I don't want anyone to kiss you, ever again, but me."

"Mm, that sounds like something a husband would say to a wife."

Blaze said nothing, because he knew the endgame here, and it was different than in Las Vegas or any of the other cities where he'd traveled and lived. He observed the trees here, the park through them, trying to picture himself as a small-town husband and father. It was a nice picture, but he was still a little too dark to truly fit the image.

"And the words of someone who needs to introduce me to their son," she continued.

He pressed his teeth together then, because she wasn't wrong. "Yep," he said. "Let's figure that out sooner rather than later, yeah?"

"Yeah," she said.

He gazed down at her again. "We're okay, right?"

"We're great if you're great," she said. "Because that was the best kiss of my life." She grinned at him. "You know how to charm a woman, Mister Young."

Blaze pressed a kiss to her forehead, glad for her words. He didn't want to charm her though. Part of him did want to charm her completely. Never let her know about all of his faults and shortcomings; he could hide them forever, couldn't he?

He absolutely knew he couldn't. He wanted to be himself with someone, without any secrets or shame.

He couldn't do that unless he was able to reveal some of the uglier parts of himself, and he'd certainly done that tonight.

"Let's go get some pizza or something," he said, and he gave her a smile as he turned around to go back the way they'd come. Pizza wouldn't fix everything, but his stomach wouldn't be so empty, and Faith wouldn't expect him to say too much more.

BLAZE FOLLOWED CASH INTO THE FARMHOUSE, HIS SON skipping ahead of him. Today, there hadn't been any trucks in the driveway here, except for Tex's. "Hey, hey," Tex said, and Blaze hung his coat and went around the corner to see Tex hugging Cash, the boy seemingly tiny in his brother's arms.

Tex looked at Blaze, the happiness in his face as real as Blaze had seen it in recent months. "Hey," he said.

"Hey." Blaze walked along the long kitchen counter and embraced his brother. "Bryce is home."

"Yeah." Tex clapped him on the back. "For now."

Blaze fell back a step. "Is he returning to Montana for winter semester?"

"He's registered for classes, yeah." Tex's smile had faltered, but he brought it back with renewed gusto when he met Blaze's eye. "I guess we'll see what happens."

Blaze nodded, because as much as someone tried to prepare to give their baby away, he didn't think that anyone could truly predict how they'd feel. Blaze had made a lot of mistakes in his life, and he'd never been able to truly know how he'd feel about one thing or another until he was living it.

He figured Bryce would have to deal with all of that as it came to him. Planning how he'd feel certainly wouldn't work, but Blaze knew Bryce, and the young man had most likely gone through every scenario and had a plan for all of it.

"Where is he?"

"Where do you think he is?" Tex nodded out the wide double doors made of glass. Blaze looked outside, a sigh filling his body. He didn't let it out, but he didn't want to go back outside. It was almost dark, and that meant the temperature was still falling.

"Can I go out?"

"At your own peril." Tex smiled, his eyes filled with apprehension and sadness. "I'll stay here with Cash, because Melissa should be getting up any minute."

"Abby's on the Bookmobile?"

Tex nodded and turned his back on Blaze. He looked out the windows, the dusk turning to twilight right in front of his eyes. He might as well get out there quickly, and he told himself it wouldn't be as cold in the barn as it was outside.

He retraced his steps and went back outside, turning left at the bottom of the steps and heading toward the barn. Bryce had four horses here that his father had been taking care of in his absence. He hadn't been attending school this past semester, but he'd been talking about going come January.

Blaze didn't think for a moment his nephew would resume his classes. The boy would be in an incredible amount of pain, and Blaze found himself silently praying for Bryce.

Inside the barn, the scent of straw and horses filled his nose, and Bryce looked over from where he stood next to a black horse. "Uncle Blaze." His voice sounded upbeat; a smile filled his face. He moved away from the horse and into Blaze's arms. "Mm, it's so good to see you."

"You too, son." Blaze held him for as long as Bryce wanted, and when he moved to step away, Blaze released him. He simply watched the young man as he ducked his head and swung back to the horses.

"Just getting my chores done."

"I bet your daddy is glad he's not out here doing it."

Bryce gave a light laugh. "I'm sure that's true."

Blaze let him retreat for several moments, and then he followed him. "You're talkin' to your daddy, right? Keeping him up-to-date with what's happening with you?"

"Yes." The quietness in Bryce's voice suggested otherwise, but Blaze didn't call him on it yet.

"It's important to talk to someone," he said. "It could be me, or a counselor, or your daddy."

Bryce tossed him a look that Blaze knew very well. He was annoyed at the things coming out of Blaze's mouth, but someone had to say them. Tex couldn't, and Blaze had some experience with similar things that Bryce was dealing with.

He didn't need to tell the boy everything, and Tex had asked him not to reveal any of the more devastating details. Blaze didn't need Bryce to know all of those things anyway.

He stopped at the stall beside the one where Bryce stood, and he simply stayed in the barn.

"I suppose you want to know how I'm feeling."

"I can probably guess," Blaze said.

"Good," Bryce said. "Because I don't want to talk about it."

"Your feelings? Or the fact that Bailey's due in two weeks and you'll be givin' that baby to Otis and Georgia?"

Bryce gave him a sharp glare. "All of it."

"How do you think it's going to go?"

He kept his head low as the seconds ticked by. "I think it's going to be terrible."

Blaze nodded, because at least Bryce had reached the point of honesty. "What are you going to do afterward?"

"I don't know."

"You been telling your daddy you're going back to Montana?"

"Yeah."

"Are you?"

"I still have an apartment there," Bryce said.

Blaze knew that didn't mean anything, but he didn't vocalize that. His nose started to run with the cold, and he reached up and stroked his hand down the horse's nose. He didn't know what to say to his nephew, and in the past couple of weeks since Blaze had truly felt the spirit of God in his life, he'd been seeking for it again.

He didn't know what to do a lot of the time. He wanted to be led, but the Lord wouldn't provide for him every step. Sometimes he had to take a leap of faith, step off the edge and into the darkness, before God would light the next portion of his path.

"Bryce, you know how Jem and I weren't getting along?"

"Yes," Bryce said quietly.

"He's moving back in with me tomorrow," Blaze said. "Because he needs the extra support. I don't know how or why

I'm the one to give it to him, because most days I'm treading water. But my house is huge, and I love him and his kids."

He wasn't sure what he was trying to say or where he was driving. But he felt like he just needed to open his mouth and the Lord would do the rest.

"You're welcome at my place any time," he said. "Day or night. Rain or shine." He looked over to his nephew. "You hearin' me?"

"Yes, sir." Bryce wouldn't look at him, and Blaze wasn't sure what he was hearing and what was simply bouncing off at this point.

"I don't ask as many questions as your daddy," Blaze said. "But I won't lie to him or keep secrets from him either."

"I wouldn't ask you to." Bryce did look up then, and now he broadcasted his fear plainly. "Is it bad that I just want it all to be over?"

Blaze's heart broke a little bit for Bryce. "Not at all."

Bryce nodded and stepped away from the horse. "Come on, then. We can't hide out here forever."

"We can't?" Blaze grinned at his nephew and slung his arm around him. "You're a good man, Bryce. Don't let one thing, even a really big thing, take you down."

His nephew nodded, but Blaze once again wondered how much of what people were saying to him actually got where it needed to go.

Doesn't matter, he told himself. The boy would have a thousand voices in his head, and all Blaze could do was pray that when Bryce needed to hear his, it would come forward and stir his memory.

"My dad says you're wrapping presents tomorrow night."

"Yep," Blaze said. "I have to drop everything off on Saturday."

"I can come help."

"Sure," Blaze said. "But my girlfriend will be there." He swallowed. "I'm introducing her to Cash for the first time."

Bryce looked at him, his eyebrows up and all the fear and worry gone. "Is that right?"

"That's right." Blaze grinned at him. "What? You don't think I can handle my girlfriend meeting my son?"

Bryce grinned on back. "I think that's a big step for you, Uncle Blaze." They laughed together, but Bryce wasn't wrong, and Blaze started a steady stream of prayer that tomorrow night would go as well as it could go.

12

Faith carried a covered tray of reindeer cupcakes as she headed for the front door. It opened before she got there, and her handsome cowboy entered her house, his expression searching and anxious. A smile touched her face, and he relaxed visibly as he straightened.

"Hey," he said. "I told you the cupcakes weren't necessary."

"I'm meeting your eleven-year-old son for the first time. Cupcakes are necessary." She put the tray to the side and leaned toward Blaze so he could kiss her cheek.

He slid his arm around her and held her close. "Mm, you smell nice."

"Sugary?"

"Not so much." He took a deep breath of her hair, and Faith felt more cherished than she had in a long, long time. "I'm getting this soft, flowery, soapy scent."

"Hm." She liked the weight of his hand on the small of her

back, and the way the warmth of his body wove through her own. "He's home alone right now, isn't he?"

"He probably doesn't even know I left." But Blaze stepped back, the desire swimming in those dark eyes. "Can I take those for you?" He relieved her of the cupcakes so she could slip into her coat.

It had snowed several times since that night in the park when Blaze had kissed her so completely that Faith didn't think any other man on the planet would ever be able to match up to him. She threw him a few little glances as she fixed her collar and wrapped a scarf Trinity had made for her for her last birthday.

She brightened and met his eyes. "When's your birthday, Blaze?"

He blinked a couple of times. "May. Cash will be twelve at the beginning of February."

She grinned and slid her hands inside his open coat, the tray of cupcakes between them. So maybe they weren't necessary right now. They certainly were making it more difficult to lean into him and kiss him.

"May—what date?"

"May sixth," he said. "I'll be thirty-nine." Those lips that knew exactly how to kiss her curved upward. "Dare I ask when your birthday is?"

"You dare." She giggled and pulled her hands back to zip her own coat. "My birthday was over the summer. July thirtieth. Trin made me this scarf." She smiled at the purple and blue yarn. "She knows I hate being cold in the winter."

"I feel like I hit the mark with my Christmas gifts then." He turned toward the door. "We better get going, so you can meet Cash before everyone else comes."

"Who ended up confirming?" She darted in front of him to get the door, and he went past her once it was open.

"Denzel's bringing his dog. Cash and I are real excited about that."

Faith smiled at his back, because Blaze wasn't lying. He adored dogs, and he'd been in a foul mood the day he'd had to return his rental puppy.

"Everly and Trace and Harry," he continued. "Bryce said he might come, and Todd Christopherson will be there with all of his gifts and his family. He's got a few kids, and I think they're all in town."

Blaze wasn't one to hold names and ages of people he barely interacted with in his head, Faith knew. "Sounds like a lot of help." She wondered if she'd made enough cupcakes.

"We have a lot of presents to wrap," he said. "And keep track of. I printed off the checklist you helped me make." He reached the truck and looked back at her. "Thank you for that."

She very nearly rolled her eyes. "You've thanked me ten times. It's a checklist. Stop it." She smiled so he'd know she wasn't really mad and opened her own door to get in the truck while he put the cupcakes in the back.

With him behind the wheel and driving, he asked, "How's the truck coming?"

Faith drew in a big breath. "Good. Really good. He should be done next week, but I have so many parties leading into Christmas, I don't have anyone to work it." She looked over to him, her eyes feeling so big and round. "Do you think I should hire more employees?"

He glanced at her long enough for her to see the surprise on his face. "I don't know."

"Blaze." She reached over and took his hand. His fingers curled through hers, tightening until they were well-seated—as if he never wanted to let go. Her blood fizzled in her veins, and she was glad his touch still excited her.

"I'm asking you what you think," she said gently. "It's not an answer to the world's problems."

"I don't know how to run a business," he said.

"The parties have been really successful. I'm charging a lot for them, and I'm working about the same amount. Maybe even less—but I'm making more. I could hire someone to run the third truck and keep doing the parties...." She let the idea hang there, because it had only existed inside her head previously.

Now that she'd spoken it out loud, she might have to actually consider it. Make plans for it. Take action to accomplish it.

"Would you rather be on the truck or doing parties?" he asked.

"Parties," she said. "Right now. I mean, they're inside." She smiled out the windshield, though darkness had covered everything, and the wintery landscape couldn't be seen. "In the summer, it'd be air conditioned. In the winter, it's warm."

"You could do the festivals as if they were parties," he said. "And still have your trucks running."

"Yeah." She clasped her right hand over his, holding onto him with everything she had. "I think I'm going to look for more employees. Joe and Orion are great, but it's hard to run the truck alone. They've been doing it, but I should get them more help." She'd been filling in around her parties too, so each of them only had to work solo a couple of times a week.

Blaze pulled up to his house and went down the dirt road and around to the back of it. Lights from his back deck glinted off the water of the lake, and Faith felt the vastness of the universe for a brief moment. Then he turned and they entered the garage, and the world didn't seem so big.

"Blaze?" she asked quietly.

"Yeah, baby?" He put the truck in park and looked at her. Really looked.

"Would you—I mean." She exhaled. "This is going to sound a little insane."

"I like a little insane." He grinned at her and leaned toward her, inhaling the scent of her skin, and skimming his lips along her neck. "Go on, love."

"If we...make it. If we end up married or whatever, will you care if I go to church and you don't?"

He pulled away, and Faith's pulse kicked up a notch. She studied his face, trying to iron out the emotions she saw there. They flickered and paraded quickly, and she couldn't make any of them stay long enough to decipher.

"No," he said finally. "I know you go to church."

"And you don't think you'll ever go?"

"I think...." He tore his gaze away and looked out the windshield. "I know God is there. I know it. Church muddles things for me. I'm not sure why." He faced her again, pure fear streaming from him now. "I'd like to try it again. Do you want to go with me on Christmas Eve?"

Pure joy burst through her. "Of course. With Cash?"

"Yeah." Blaze's slow, sexy smile appeared. "With Cash. Me, you, and Cash." He leaned toward her, his free hand sliding up the column of her neck, and his fingers curling around the back of it to hold her steady while he kissed her.

Sometimes Blaze kissed her quickly, and sometimes the passion pouring from him had him moving fast. Tonight, he held back, the restraint in his stroke almost as passionate as when he fisted his fingers in her hair and gasped when he finally released her lips.

Tonight, he simply pulled away, the feeling in the truck only able to be described one way. Faith met Blaze's eyes and ducked her head, the emotion too powerful.

He slid from the truck silently, and Faith watched him walk around to open her door.

"Love," she whispered. She was falling in love with Blaze Young—and falling fast and hard.

The door opened, and the emotion fled. Blaze's eyes danced with danger as he reached for her, and she didn't doubt for a single second that he'd missed the emotions of that kiss. "You're making me a better man," he whispered roughly in her ear. "I sure want to be the man you deserve."

He didn't wait for her to answer before he released her and moved to get the cupcakes. She followed him into the house, where warmth and bright lights in the kitchen greeted her. A boy with lighter brown hair than his father looked up from the dining room table, and he put down his colored pencil.

He wore jeans—pressed and clean and the deep, dark denim color Blaze always wore—and a black T-shirt with a huge, cream-colored horseshoe on the front of it. A logo sat over the left arm of the horseshoe, and Faith felt like she'd seen this design before.

She couldn't identify it before Blaze slid the cupcakes on the counter and Cash stood up. "Son." He reached for him, threading his fingers through Cash's on his right hand and Faith's on his left. "This is Faith Cromwell. We're seein' each other."

Cash nodded, his eyes so somber. "It's a real pleasure to meet you, ma'am."

Faith looked at him, her smile gathering in her chest and expanding upward. She glanced over to Blaze, who beamed like he'd just been crowned king. She started to laugh, and she took Cash's free hand in hers and pumped it.

"It's great to meet you too, Cash." She glanced past him to the book on the table. "Your daddy says you like to color."

"I have some temperature coloring books."

Faith released Blaze's hand. "I have no idea what that means. Will you show me?"

"Sure." He moved back to the seat he'd been in. "So see, this here's a winter one. It has temperature ranges in the picture, and you color it based on the temperature of that day." He tilted the book toward her, and it took Faith's eyes a moment to make out the picture among all the blues, pinks, purples, and blacks.

"Oh, I see it," she said. "It's a farm, with a cabin back there." She pointed. "Looks like you still have a lot of the foreground to do."

"Only if the temperature fits," he said. "So you work on more than one picture at a time." He flipped through the pages, and he had several partially-finished pictures. "It takes a while to get one done."

He looked over to Blaze and then back to Faith, who couldn't help noticing the way his eyes fired—that mirrored the way his father's did. "My counselor thought it would be good for me to have something that takes a long time to finish. I can learn patience and feel accomplished once it's finally done."

"He's gotten several done," Blaze said, and he pulled out the chair on the other side of Cash. "Do you want to show her these?" He slid a stack of papers in front of Cash.

He lit up like the sun. "You kept these?"

"Every one." Blaze grinned at his son, and this was a new grin Faith hadn't seen before. This was a soft, parental grin. Love and adoration oozed from the tough, rough cowboy, and made him seem soft from head to toe.

He flicked his eyes to Faith's, and her chest tightened against the enlarging of her heart. She was definitely falling for him, and watching him interact with his son was the most dangerous activity she'd done with him yet.

"This one is a warm temperature picture," he said. "It's one of the first I did over the summer after I started seeing Doctor Chelsea."

"It's a sailboat," Faith said. "I love it."

Before Cash could show her all of the pictures, the doorbell rang. Blaze got to his feet and said, "That'll probably be Todd. Everyone else would just walk in." He hustled off to let the people in, and Faith stood too.

"I made cupcakes for everyone. Do you guys have paper plates or anything we should use?"

"Yeah." Cash tucked his completed drawings into the book and closed it. He went into the kitchen proper and got out a stack of paper plates while Faith uncovered the cupcakes. "Wow." He leaned in close. "You made these?"

"Yes, sir." A hint of pride filled her with his reaction. "They're reindeers, see? And I made the heads with doughnuts. Body is cupcake. Head, doughnut." She'd piped on eyes and glued pretzels together with festive red frosting to make the antlers.

Cash looked up at her with wonder. "Could you teach me to do something like this?"

Faith didn't know how to answer, and several voices filled the vaulted ceilings with laughter and chatter. "Maybe," she said as Blaze came back into the kitchen with another cowboy who stood as tall as him.

And an Everett sister.

Faith gaped at the beautiful woman, who had two equally as gorgeous young women with her, neither of them older than twenty. She turned toward them fully, completely star-struck.

"Faith," Blaze said. "This is Todd Christopherson. The other rodeo champion I've been telling you about."

"Of course," she said with a smile. "He does talk about you constantly." She shook his hand while he laughed.

"He's the one who keeps us organized," Todd said, throwing a happy smile at Blaze. "This is my wife, Vi, and our daughters Mary and Daisy. Our son isn't home for the holidays yet."

"So great to meet you," Faith gushed, shaking hands all around.

"We're here," someone called, and Faith recognized the voice as Harry's.

"What are these?" Vi asked. "They're beautiful. Mary, look at these pastries." She gaped at them, and even reached out and delicately touched one of the antlers as if it might poof into dust when she did.

The three women looked at Faith. "Did you make these?'

"Faith is a master baker." Blaze came to her side, his arm around her waist and his chin almost on her shoulder. He pressed in so close, despite the enormity of his house. "They're cupcakes."

"And doughnuts," Cash said. "Right, Faith? I can have one, right?"

"Everyone can have one," Faith said. "They are two treats in one."

"She owns Hole in One," Blaze said, obviously bragging about her. "Best specialty doughnuts in town."

A pause filled the house, and then Everly said, "Holy Christmas crackers, Faith. These are the cutest things I've ever seen. Is this what you're doing for your holiday parties?" She picked up a cupcake too, and Faith could only smile as she bit right into the reindeer's nose. A moan filled her mouth, and Faith laughed with Todd and Blaze.

Trace rolled his eyes, and Harry grabbed a cupcake and went to sit with Cash at the table.

"Mary's interested in culinary school," Vi said. "I'm sure she'd love to talk to you more about what you do."

Faith looked at the dark-haired girl with her big, beautiful, nearly hazel eyes. They still harbored a bit too much brown to truly be hazel, but they were unique nonetheless. "I'd love to have you work with me," she said. "Are you looking for a job, or a one-time thing...?"

"Do you have a job available?" Mary asked, her tone beyond hopeful.

"I sure do," Faith said with more gusto than she'd felt about her work in ages. "It's—"

"You have to cater our wedding," Everly interrupted. "I want doughnuts everywhere."

"My Ev," Trace said. "We're feeding people at the wedding." He looked at Faith. "No offense, Faith."

She shook her head. "Dessert is not the same as a meal."

"We can do both." Everly turned to Trace with earnest pleading on her face. "Baby, we *have* to have a doughnut wall. Just try this." She picked up another cupcake and handed it to him, but Faith got distracted once again as more people entered the house.

Tex led in Abby, Bryce, and Melissa, who was being carried on her half-brother's hip. "Did y'all know there's about fifty bins of...stuff on the front porch?"

"What?" Blaze asked.

"Oh, yeah," Todd said. "That's all our stuff that needs to be wrapped."

Faith suddenly felt the weight of what this party was, and it wasn't for her to stand around hiring more help or taking compliments on her doughnuts. They had wrapping to do—a lot of wrapping to do.

Cash leapt from the table and said, "Dad, Scout's here!" He ran toward the front of the house, and Faith moved along the back wall so she could see all the way to the front door. Denzel Drummond limped into the house, with Morris and his wife and their son.

Faith hadn't met his wife or Denzel yet, and she glanced around the chaos to find Blaze. He came easily to her side, anchoring her, and she pressed her hip into him. "Thanks for inviting me to this."

"It's going to be insane," he said. "I didn't know Morris was bringing his family."

"Dad," Cash called again, this time from the foyer, where he knelt on the floor with a pretty German shepherd.

"You're going to get a dog, aren't you?" she asked as he stepped away from her.

His whole face glowed. "For Christmas." Then he walked away to go play with the canine and his son. She watched him, experiencing the life and joy this house held. She'd been here before, but it was different this time.

The life and joy came from the owner, and that was Blaze. A door opened, and another cowboy emerged.

Jem.

Faith pulled in a breath and started walking toward him without expressly telling her legs to move. "Jem," she said, and he turned toward her.

He'd moved back in a week or so ago, and Blaze hadn't had anything negative to say about him. He looked a bit rumpled, if Faith were being honest, and his two kids joined the activity on the main floor of the house with smiles and laughter.

Faith moved right into him and hugged him. He grunted, his

hands slow to come up and embrace her back. "It's good to see you," she whispered.

Jem tightened his hold on her then, said nothing, and simply clung to her. When he started to pull away, Faith did too. She wasn't sure why she'd done that, but Jem brushed at his eyes and said, "Good to see you too, Faith. I'm glad I didn't ruin anything between you and Blaze too badly."

"Jem." Blaze approached, his eyes moving back and forth between Faith and his brother. "I told you we're good."

Jem's forced smile said he was working on believing that.

"Faith, have you met my wife?" Morris asked. "Leigh, this is Faith Cromwell. She's Blaze's girlfriend."

"You made those cupcakes?" Leigh asked.

"Yes, ma'am." Faith shook her hand, noting the keen interest in Leigh's eyes.

"I owned a bakery in California," Leigh said. "I was going to open one here until I got pregnant again." She put one hand on her noticeable belly. "But I'd love to help you if you ever need it. I miss baking a lot more than I thought I would."

"I'd love that." Faith's throat narrowed at the goodness of people. At the amazing way the Lord put the right people in her life, right when she needed them.

"All right," Blaze yelled into the fray. "I've got my lists, and we need to get started. Let's all gather over here, please. Over here."

While everyone did that, Faith took a moment to watch him. He may be dark and dangerous. He might even be a little naughty. But inside his core, where his heart beat, he was made of pure gold.

165

They might not have much in common. They probably existed on two different ends of the spectrum when it came to interests, skills, and how they'd parent a child or train a dog.

Faith had once thought that meant she couldn't be with Blaze, that a relationship between them would never work out.

Now, watching him struggle with his pencil and paper to make an assignment, Faith believed that with work, sacrifice, and open communication, she could make this relationship with him work—and work well.

"Baby?" She stepped over to him and gently took the pencil from his hand. "Should I?"

"Yes," he said with plenty of relief in his voice. "Please. I have no clue what I'm doing."

Faith smiled at him and then faced the crowd. "Okay. I need Bryce, Tex, Morris, and Jem to bring in all of Todd's items. Those will go in the living room, okay? Not the office."

"I have a list for Todd," Vi called, waving the paper over her head.

"Perfect," Faith said, not missing a beat. "Cash, Harry, and Cole are in charge of the wrapping supplies for both groups. Boys, get half the stuff out of the office and take it to Mary or Daisy." They still stood near their mother, and the Young boys went to do as Faith said.

"Blaze, you'll hand out the tags with the gifts to be wrapped. When you finish one, the tag goes on it *immediately*. No exceptions. Okay?"

Several people nodded their assent, and Faith continued. "Okay. You'll bring it back to me or Vi, we'll check it off, and Blaze or Todd will put it back in their bins. Now." She drew a deep breath. "There are enough cupcakes for everyone." She'd made extra, so Morris, Leigh and Eric could still have one. "We bought a million tape dispensers and miles of wrapping paper. Let's see if we can do this without having to unwrap any presents tonight."

A cheer went up, though Faith didn't know why, and she turned to go into the office with Blaze.

"You're incredible," he murmured just before sweeping a kiss along her cheek. "Thank you."

She thought he was incredible too, but she didn't have time to tell him before he started handing out the first gifts to be wrapped to Abby and Leigh. They both looked at her with a knowing edge in their eyes, and she raised her eyebrows at them.

Abby only smiled and shook her head, but Leigh said, "Welcome to the family, Faith. I think you'll fit right in here."

13

Bryce Young rolled over as his phone started to ring. His heartbeat ricocheted from the top of his head to the bottom of his stomach. He reached for his phone, which he'd been leaving on all night long, in case Bailey went into labor.

Laney Whittaker's name sat there, and Bryce was immediately awake and swiping on the call. "Laney." Bailey's mother wouldn't call him in the early morning hours of Christmas Eve to wish him Happy Holidays.

"Good morning, Bryce," she said. Her voice held a sense of urgency Bryce had never heard before. "Her contractions are four and a half minutes apart. We're taking her to the hospital now."

Bryce reached for his jeans, which he'd draped over the back of his desk chair in the old farmhouse where he'd been staying with his parents for the past couple of weeks. Bailey had finished this semester of internship at the same time, and they'd returned to Coral Canyon together.

He spoke to her everyday, but he hadn't seen her in a couple now, and his pulse pounced all over his body, sending prickles along his skin. "I'm on the way. I'll call Otis."

Bryce could barely say his uncle's name, and he had no idea how he was going to make it through the next twenty-four hours. *One moment at a time,* he told himself, repeating something Abby had said to him a few days ago, when Bailey had come for dinner. When she'd left, Bryce had broken down, and he'd begged Abby and his dad to tell him how to survive this.

One moment at a time.

He'd been seeing a therapist in Montana, but the sessions were obviously on hiatus as he wasn't living there right now. For some reason, his thoughts lingered on the apartment in Butte he'd left behind. He'd nearly emptied the fridge, and he'd set the heat in the mid-fifties. He'd packed a couple of bags of clothes, grabbed his guitars, and left everything else.

As he left his bedroom, he told himself that of course he was going to return to Butte. Bailey had to go back to her internship, and he could admit he loved the woman. On some level, he loved her.

Maybe not enough to marry her and raise their baby together, but he didn't see how he could go through this pregnancy with her, deliver a baby, and hand it over to his aunt and uncle without some major emotional bonding between the two of them.

He knocked on his father's bedroom door and pushed it open with a couple of fingers. "Dad?"

His dad groaned and said, "Yeah?"

"Bailey's in labor."

His father sat up in the next instant. "I'll get dressed."

Abby started to say something, but Bryce backed into the hallway. He grabbed the keys to his daddy's truck and went outside into the bitter morning air. The moon shone with a full orb in the sky, lighting his way to the vehicle so Bryce could start it.

Someone would have to feed his horses in the morning, as they were divas and wanted breakfast at the same time every day, whether it was his son's birthday or not. He told himself he could text Wade when a few more hours had passed, and that they were just horses. They'd be okay without him today.

He dashed back up the steps to find his daddy reaching inside the fridge for something. He was fully dressed, right down to his cowboy boots, and Bryce paused. His dad moved in slow motion as he straightened, two bottles of water in his hand. He walked toward Bryce, his gaze heavy and blitzing with energy. "Here we go."

Bryce couldn't speak, so he just took the water, turned, and headed back outside. The drive to the hospital seemed to take forever and no time at all. The lamps in the parking lot shone with bright white light that actually hurt Bryce's eyes.

"Daddy," he said, the way he had as a little boy. He couldn't look at his father—who was becoming a grandfather today—and instead, focused out the window. "I didn't call Otis."

He'd completely forgotten, and another stream of guilt pulled through Bryce.

"I will," Tex said as he pulled up to the front doors. "Go on, son. I'll park, call him, and be right in."

His dad wouldn't come into the delivery room anyway, and Bryce wasn't sure he wanted to be there either. At the same time, he absolutely had to be in the room as Bailey gave birth to their son. He had so many warring emotions inside him, and Bryce had no idea what to do with any of them.

Anger simmered just beneath the surface, but he slid from the truck just as his daddy had said to do. He entered the hospital, completely disoriented. Thankfully, a Help Desk sat there, and while it wasn't manned, it did have a single sheet of paper with all the major departments at the hospital, including Labor and Delivery.

Bryce followed all the signs, his legs growing weaker and weaker with every step he took. He rounded a corner and came to a complete standstill when he saw Graham and Laney Whittaker. Bailey was not with them.

Graham caught sight of him first and got to his feet. Laney twisted, saw him, and quickly did the same. "Morning, Bryce," Graham said as if they were meeting for a quick bite to eat. Laney wrapped him in a hug, her tears slowly weeping down her face.

"Come on," she whispered. "I'll take you back." She did, and Bryce was so glad she was there. But she didn't enter the room with him; she only indicated it.

"I just go in?" he asked.

She nodded, and Bryce drew in the biggest breath he could hold. His shoulders boxed up, and he told himself to simply take the first step. He did, and before he knew it, he'd entered the room. He met Bailey's gaze from where she lay in the hospital bed, already gowned and ready. Her belly still protruded up, so she hadn't delivered the baby yet.

"Hey." He rushed toward her and took her face in his hands. He kissed her forehead and looked at all the machines nearby the bed. She already wore an IV, and he glanced at the two nurses in the room. "Do they know we're not keeping the baby?"

"Yes," Bailey whispered. "All the paperwork is in order."

Bryce moved around to the other side of the bed. "Have you decided what you want?"

"No," she said. "You?"

Bryce watched the nurses getting everything ready to keep a baby warm, wrap him in blankets, and more he couldn't even imagine. "I don't think I want to see him," he said. Which made no sense. The boy was literally going to be his cousin.

It was so messed up to think about it like that, but any child of Otis's and Georgia's would be his cousin. So his son was going to be his cousin, at least as far as the boy knew. Every time he'd look at the boy, he'd know who he really was, and he'd surely be able to see a mirror image of himself in the child's face.

"I think you'll regret that," she said.

"Then it sounds like you've decided." He put his hand on her shoulder, and Bailey wrapped her fingers around his. She didn't look up at him, but they were still connected in so many ways.

She groaned, and the machine started to beep, drawing the attention of the nurses. Bryce wasn't sure how to track time.

White light bathed everything in the hospital, obscuring the rising or setting of the sun.

Before he knew it, the doctor entered, his cheery smile so wrong for this situation. He talked to Bailey, who managed to answer his questions, and then he positioned himself at the end of the bed. "Oh, yes," he said. "It's time to have this baby." He looked up to Bailey and Bryce. "Ready?"

"Yes," Bailey said through clenched teeth. Bryce stood immediately behind her, and he did his best to support the mother of his baby as she gave it life. With one final push, the scream of a baby filled the air, and Bryce experienced an instant rush of relief.

"It's a boy," the doctor boomed, and he held up the patchy, red-skinned infant, who was still wailing like they'd all done something terrible to him. Bryce loved the baby with the first look, and then the nurse wrapped the boy in a blue-patterned blanket and took him from the doctor.

Bryce wanted to go over to the counter in the back of the room to be with his baby, but he stayed right where he was. That baby was not his.

Biologically, yes. But Bryce couldn't be the father that baby deserved. He knew it, and he'd known it for almost Bailey's entire pregnancy.

"Bryce," she wept, and he bent over and pressed a kiss to her temple.

"He's okay," he whispered.

"I want to hold him," she whispered back. "Just for a minute. Then they can have him." She looked up at him, tears streaking down her face. "We have to hold him and make sure he knows we love him."

That baby was going to be so loved in the Young family, but Bryce simply nodded. "I'll go ask if we can have a few minutes with him." He stepped away from the bed while Bailey delivered the afterbirth, and he simply stood next to the nurses as they bundled up the baby.

"Can she hold him for a minute?" he finally asked.

The nurse picked up the baby and turned toward him. She cradled the infant right against her chest, her smile kind and soft. "Of course." She tried to pass the baby to him, but Bryce backed up a step.

"I can't."

"Yes, you can, Mister Young." The nurse put the baby in his arms. "Hold him right against your chest. Yep, like that. Now." She nodded over to the bed. "Take him over there, so you two can say goodbye."

Say goodbye.

Bryce's emotions surged, and his chest hitched. He couldn't breathe, and the first thing he thought of to do was run. But he currently carried a baby—his baby—and he couldn't make a break for the exit.

He faced Bailey, and she wore such hope on her face that he found enough strength to walk over to her. He laid the baby in her arms, and she gazed down at him with love shining through her eyes. The baby grunted and squirmed, his eyes closed. He was a beautiful, beautiful baby, and Bryce couldn't tell if he had much hair, because the nurse had put a pale blue hat on his head.

"He's so perfect," Bailey whispered.

Bryce almost felt like he'd been removed from his body. Bailey wept, and her voice sounded too thick and too high as she said, "You are the best baby in the whole world. I love you so much." She bent over and kissed the baby gently. "You'll have the best momma and daddy ever, and we'll see you all the time, okay? We love you."

Her voice broke, and she shook her head. "Bryce." She lifted the baby, and he had no choice but to take him. He wanted to say all the same things to the perfect little human who'd just arrived on earth. He kissed the baby too and whispered, "I love you so much," before he made the trek back to the nursing station.

"All done?"

He nodded as he passed the baby back to her. "Thank you." His voice sounded like it had been raked through glass, and he turned back to Bailey and went to her side. He took her hand, and they gripped each other.

One moment.

In this moment, he wanted to be strong when he felt very, very weak. The nurse left the room, and it was like she took all the air with her.

The doctor patted Bailey's knee and said, "Good job, Momma," before leaving. Then it was just the two of them in the room, and Bryce turned away from her and toward the window. Tears flowed down his face, and he only let himself rage and sob for a few seconds. Then he boxed it all up, cinched it all tight, wiped his face, and returned to Bailey's side.

"I'm going to go get your mom, okay?"

Bailey had laid down in the bed, and she wiped her eyes as she nodded. "I'm sorry, Bryce."

"This is not your fault." They looked at one another, so much moving between them. Another sob wrenched in his chest, and he pulled back the sheet and slid into the bed with Bailey. "It's going to be okay. He's going to have the best life ever with Otis and Georgia and all those dogs and cats."

Bailey sob-laughed, and Bryce stroked her hair. "You gave him life," he said. "He knows we love him, and he'll know we wanted him to have a better life than we could give him. Otis and Georgia will tell him, I'm sure of it."

She nodded against his chest, and Bryce pressed his eyes closed. "I'm sorry, Bay. I'm sorry, I'm sorry, I'm sorry."

14

"Mister Young? Do you want to come with me?"

Otis Young leapt to his feet without even fully taking in the figure in the doorway. Georgia stood too, and they faced the nurse with a baby wrapped tightly in a blue blanket clenched to her chest.

"Oh." Georgia put her hand in his and squeezed.

"We need to give him a bath. You can both come." The nurse, Joyce, who'd already come to let them know a couple of times where Bailey was in the delivery, wore such kindness in her eyes and her voice. Otis thought pediatric nurses deserved a special place in heaven. She turned and left the doorway, and Otis hurried to follow her.

She said, "He was born only about twenty minutes ago." She allowed Otis and Georgia to catch up to her. "He's a good little boy, hardly crying at all while I got him dressed. He'll be ready to eat soon enough, but we can get him bathed and into his first pair of pajamas first." She beamed over to Georgia. "You have those, right?"

"Yes, ma'am," Georgia whispered.

The nurse walked them into the nursery, where the scent of formula, powder, and babies filled the air. Otis smiled, taking a moment to commit this to memory. He didn't want to walk through today in a blur, and he forced himself to slow down and experience every sensation.

His hand got tugged as Georgia continued on, and she glanced over her shoulder to him. "This is a good day, hon," he said. "Let's enjoy it."

"I will."

"You look like you might throw up."

"That's because she has our baby." Georgia nodded to the nurse who'd gotten ahead of them. "Come on. I want to give him his first bath."

Otis went with her, and the nurse let her wipe the warm water along the tiny baby's body. "We're going to need a name," she said. "Should we let his daddy diaper him?" She grinned at Otis, and he smiled back.

"I have a daughter already, Joyce."

"Yes, I know." She shook her head. "But it's been a while, I understand. Go on then."

The baby kicked, a cat-like wail raising up. Georgia picked him up, naked as he was, and shushed him. He pulled his skinny little legs up under his huge torso, and Otis couldn't stop smiling.

"Oh, no." Georgia held the baby out from her body, gently supporting his head. "He peed on me."

"I told his daddy to get him diapered," Joyce teased. She handed Otis the tiny diaper, and Georgia laid the baby back on the pad.

Otis stepped in front of the infant, and he got the diaper on the baby in only a few seconds. He didn't pull the tape too tight, but he secured it so the diaper wouldn't come off either. "Done."

He started to wrap the baby in a new blanket, as the other one had gotten whisked away somewhere. He didn't do it as tightly as the nurse could've, but he got the job done, and he lifted his new baby to his shoulder.

"We need to name him," Georgia said.

"Go on, then." He smiled softly at his wife.

"You're okay with it?"

"We decided on it."

She nodded, her dark eyes still harboring some anxiety he wished he could erase. Today was Christmas Eve, and they were getting everything they wanted. This was a joyous day, not a time to be upset or worried.

Georgia faced Joyce and said, "We'd like to name him Otis Judson Young, please."

"We've got all the adoption paperwork in place too," Joyce said. "I'll get the name going, and when you guys are ready, we can get started on all the signing. Once that's done, you'll be able to take your baby boy home."

"Really?" Georgia asked. "We don't have to stay? He doesn't have to stay?"

"Nope." Joyce's name got called, and she glanced over to another nurse. "Bailey and Bryce aren't requiring that the baby stay here until she goes home, so once baby Otis is cleared medically, he can go home." She gave them a quick smile. "Excuse me. Stay here as long as you want."

Otis slipped the baby into Georgia's arms. "Let's find you a rocking chair."

"I don't think we're really supposed to be in here, Otis." Georgia looked around. "No other parents are in there. Just babies and nurses."

He took in the nursery, seeing her point. "Joyce said we could stay here."

"That can't be true," Georgia argued. "There aren't any chairs in here." She took baby OJ with her toward another nurse. "Excuse me." She spoke brightly. "Is there somewhere we can sit with our new baby?"

"Sure." She turned and pointed toward the door they'd come in. "Go back outside, and then go to the very next one on the right. There's a quiet room there."

"Thank you." Georgia glanced over her shoulder, but Otis was already on his way to her side. He guided her toward the exit, and then into the quiet room.

The lights in here were far dimmer, and a row of rocking recliners faced the wall. Someone sat in the one just inside the door, but they didn't turn to look at Otis and Georgia. He indicated the last one in the corner, and Georgia went to sit down with their new baby.

He crouched against the wall and whispered, "Right here, hon. Then I'll go call everyone."

Georgia smiled for the camera, and he snapped a quick

picture without using the flash on his phone. Then he kissed Georgia and OJ and he made a quick exit.

He breathed out in the hallway and simply stood still for a moment, taking in the glory of God and allowing his gratitude to flow freely through him. "Thank you, Lord," he whispered.

A new weight settled on him then, and Otis looked down the hall. "Bless Bryce and Bailey at this time, and help me to...do and say the right thing so as to not make this harder for anyone."

He could sometimes say the wrong thing, and he didn't want to upset Tex or Abby, Graham or Laney Whittaker, or Bryce and Bailey. He already loved that little boy more than he'd anticipated, but that didn't mean he had to toss that in someone's face.

"Bless us all."

GEORGIA TOED HERSELF AND HER NEW BABY BACK AND forth gently. A low song hummed in her throat as she fed her son, and she kept her eyes closed as he learned how to eat. She hadn't had to give birth to him today, but she knew she still wouldn't be getting a lot of sleep in the coming weeks.

Otis's entire family would likely be out in the waiting room, as would hers. It was the holidays, and her brother had come to Coral Canyon for the festivities. She and Otis had Joey with them this year, and she hoped today's Christmas Eve dinner wouldn't be called off on account of OJ's birth.

She couldn't imagine Bryce attending Christmas Eve dinner at the rented barn where the Youngs had also celebrated

Thanksgiving. She wanted to hug him and Bailey, but she didn't want to cause them any more unrest.

She and Otis hadn't spent much time with the couple in the past few months since they'd moved back to Montana. Bailey would send pictures of her pregnancy every so often, but those had stopped in the past month. Bryce had only been in Coral Canyon for a couple of days over Thanksgiving, and he'd avoided both Otis and Georgia.

Even this morning, it had been Tex who'd called to say Bailey was in labor, not Bryce.

Tears gathered in her eyes, and she let them out slowly to paint lines down her face. Her baby squeaked, and Georgia opened her eyes to check on him. She'd not been a mother before, but she adored children. She did her best to cater to every child who came into her bookshop, and she adored Joey, Otis's daughter.

"You ate the whole thing," she cooed to the little boy. She worked the bottle away from him, and she smiled as his face scrunched up. "It's all gone, buddy." She lifted him to her shoulder to give him a pat, to get him to burp.

She rubbed his back and gave him short little bumps. "Your mama and daddy love you so much, OJ." She hummed again, a song she'd been singing since she was a little girl. "You'll have so many people who love you."

Time passed, but Georgia didn't know how much. OJ slept, and she did too, only waking when Otis whispered her name and put his hand on her shoulder. Her eyelids fluttered, and she opened them to see her handsome husband smiling at her.

"You can stay here and rest," he said. "I want to take him out to meet his grandparents."

Georgia's grip on the baby tightened for a moment, and then she handed him over to Otis, supporting his head until he slipped to Otis's bicep. "I'll come." She got to her feet, but she was tired. Still, she went with him, and they went out into the waiting room together.

Sure enough, quite a few Youngs had gathered, and Georgia was glad she wasn't the one holding the baby. Otis took OJ over to his mother and father while Georgia noticed that Tex and Abby hung near the back of the crowd with Graham and Laney Whittaker.

Her heart bled for all of them, and while she knew everyone was okay with the adoption happening, that didn't make it easy. She averted her eyes, only looking up when her mom hugged her.

"He's beautiful, dear," her mom said.

Georgia nodded, because she'd had no part in creating him. She'd lectured her mom over and over about what she could and couldn't say in front of any of the Youngs. The last thing she needed was her in-laws thinking Georgia wasn't grateful to be adopting this baby, or that she wasn't sensitive to the hurt an adoption could cause.

She'd been praying for weeks that she'd know what to say and do on this day, but she still felt just as lost in this moment as she had been over the past few months.

Trailing in Otis's wake, she hugged his brothers and their wives or fiancés, and when they got to the Whittakers, Georgia hugged Graham hard and for a long time, and she whispered, "You can see him any time you want."

Laney held the baby, her lovely smile filled with adoration as she gazed at the baby. "He's so perfect."

Georgia didn't have anything to soothe her with, so she stood with Otis and prayed, and prayed, and prayed.

"You haven't seen Bryce or Bailey, have you?" Otis finally asked.

Laney passed OJ to Graham and faced Otis and Georgia. "I went back and saw her, yes." She drew in a deep breath. "She's doing okay. They're going to be okay."

"Bryce has texted with me a little bit," Tex said. "But I haven't seen him."

Otis nodded, and Georgia had no idea what to say. In situations like this, she tended to shut down, and she gave herself a little shake and told herself not to do that. Otis would sometimes have to remind her to keep talking to him, to stay in the moment, but she did that herself this time.

She hugged Tex, because it couldn't be easy to see Otis and Georgia loving on his grandson. He did hold OJ after Graham, and he completely transformed as he held the baby boy. "He's wonderful," he whispered. He looked up at Otis, who sniffled.

Her strong, steady Otis. Georgia very nearly collapsed under the weight of her emotions, but she decided she could be the strong one for a moment where Otis needed to be vulnerable.

"You guys are going to raise him right," Tex said. "I'm so glad he's yours."

Georgia once again didn't know what to say, and Otis

embraced his brother, the baby between them, and whispered something. They separated, and then Otis took the infant from his brother.

"We love you," Georgia finally said, about the only words she could come up with that could even remotely describe how she felt.

"We love you too," Laney said, and Georgia took her hand and squeezed it.

"Come on, hon." Otis put his arm around Georgia and kept cradling OJ in his other. "Let's see if we can get him cleared to take home."

15

"Haven't seen him yet?"

Tex Young turned toward his wife as she came into the kitchen, their baby girl in her arms. She passed Melissa to Tex, and he grinned at his daughter. "Morning, baby." Her hair flew in all directions, and he made an attempt to smooth it down while Abby went to get coffee.

She poured a mug full and glanced over to him. "Tex? You haven't seen Bryce this morning?"

Tex turned back to the wide, tall windows that overlooked the backyard, the stable where Bryce's horses lived, and the recording studio in the shape of a big, white barn. "No," he said. "I know he's out there, because his bedroom door is open." And he wasn't in there. His bed had been slept in, and the boy never made it in the morning.

His son had stayed away almost all day yesterday, and he'd skipped the Christmas Eve dinner at the big red barn they'd started renting for family functions. He'd finally come home a couple of hours after dark, and he'd showered and gone into his bedroom after saying how tired he was.

He'd hugged Tex and Abby; his eyes had stayed dry; he simply wasn't talking yet.

It was Christmas morning, and Tex had no plans to get together with anyone in his family today. Abby's brother and his wife would come over for breakfast soon, and her parents would be here before then too.

They wanted to see Melissa open her presents for her first Christmas, and Tex had invited his momma and daddy too, but they were going to Otis's.

He and Georgia were settling in with their new baby, and they had Joey with them this holiday. Her parents and brother would celebrate Christmas with them too, as her brother didn't live in town and had come to meet OJ.

Trace had plans with his fiancé, Everly, and her brothers, and Morris was hosting Leigh's brother as well as Gabe and Liesl. In fact, Gabe had been staying with Morris for the past several days, and Tex had enjoyed having Gabe here in Coral Canyon instead of an hour away in Jackson Hole.

Mav had the biggest, busiest family, and they were spending it with one another—and Dani's mother, who also lived in town. Luke was joining Jem and Blaze at Blaze's lakeside mansion, where they'd picked up Christmas dinner on their way home from the family party last night, as none of them could do much more than boil water.

Tex couldn't speak too much about cooking, as it wasn't his strongest suit either. Abby came to his side and lifted her mug to her lips, taking a sip of her coffee. "You're worried about him."

"Yes, I am." Tex didn't know how to stop worrying about his son. Bryce would be twenty years old in a couple of days, and Tex felt like all of his ties to his son were being undone one by one. "He hardly said two words when he finally got home last night."

"He's processing," Abby said.

Tex nodded, because it did take Bryce some time to work through things. He'd always been a thoughtful kid, with a larger than life personality that sometimes got him in trouble. Tex had gotten full custody of him only a couple of years ago, and he hadn't had a single problem with the teenager until this summer. Until this pregnancy.

"I hardly recognize him," he whispered. "He's lost himself."

"He'll find himself again." Abby leaned into his side, and Tex put his arm around her. "He's still in there. He's just...."

Different, Tex thought. *Alone. Afraid. Drifting.*

Any of those word would've worked.

"I just want him to get his life back." Tex himself needed to find his way through the confusing path that now existed in his family, because he absolutely adored his grandson—and Otis and Georgia were going to raise him as their child.

"He doesn't know what he wants that life to be," Abby said. "You remember what that's like." She gave him a smile and turned back to the kitchen. "I'm going to start the sausage."

"Should I call him?"

"Leave him for another half-hour," Abby said. "Then he'll have to come in to get ready for breakfast."

Tex nodded, and Melissa started to fuss. He held her solidly against him as she flailed her arms and whined. "You hungry, baby?" He joined his wife in the kitchen and started making a bottle for Melissa. She'd hold it herself, and once it was ready, he laid her in the playpen in the living room, the soft white Christmas lights making her seem even more angelic than she already was.

She settled into the blankets and drank, and Tex decided he was going to go find Bryce. He'd barely gone into the bedroom to pull on a sweatshirt and then his boots when his son returned to the house.

He heard his low voice talking to Abby, and Tex paused just out of sight in the hallway. He couldn't make out what they were saying, but their voices seemed pleasant and low-key. Perhaps Tex was the only one worried about how today would go. And tomorrow. And then the next week, and moving into the New Year.

Bryce had said Bailey would return to Butte for the second half of her internship, and she'd graduate in the spring.

"Hello!"

Franny barked at the introduction of someone new to the house, especially someone coming in through the front door. Most people used the side door that came from the driveway.

"Hush, Franny," Abby admonished the door. "It's Grandma and Grandpa."

"I brought the artichoke dip." Abby's mother's voice filled the house, and Tex couldn't hide out in the hallway forever.

"Mom, we're having breakfast. We don't need artichoke dip."

"For later," her mom said.

Tex entered the main area of the farmhouse, smiling at Paul and Maxine, though Abby's mother had already bypassed the mouth of the hallway and gone into the kitchen with Abby.

"Merry Christmas," Paul said, and Tex moved into him for a holiday hug.

"Merry Christmas," he repeated.

"We've got a few presents," he said.

"You didn't need to do that." Tex watched him turn back for the front door. Abby's parents were kind, good people, but they didn't have a lot of money. The last thing he needed to carry on his conscience was that they'd spent money they didn't have on Christmas presents for him and his family.

Lord knew Tex had more money than he could ever spend in this life.

Paul returned almost immediately with a laundry basket full of red, green, gold, and white-wrapped presents.

"Paul," Tex chastised. "This is too much." He knew Abby had purchased some gifts for her parents and her brother's family, and he wouldn't be shocked if Cheryl and Wade arrived with their son and a basket full of gifts just like this.

"Oh, they're little things for the kids," Paul said. He started putting the presents under the tree, which stood right in front of the windows.

Melissa started babbling, and she pulled herself to a stand in her play pen. She screeched for someone to get her out, and Franny trotted over to stand beside her. She fell to her bottom and pressed one chubby hand against the netting on the play pen. Franny sat and leaned into her touch, and Tex loved seeing the two of them interact.

"Merry Christmas." Cheryl's voice came from the kitchen, and Tex turned that way. He came face-to-face with his son, and their eyes locked.

Bryce didn't look happy. The light Tex normally saw in his eyes and which shone all around him didn't exist at all right now. He didn't look miserable either, not like he had yesterday evening when he'd come home.

Tex didn't know what to say, so he grabbed onto his son and held him tightly. "I love you, Bryce," he whispered. "Merry Christmas."

"I love you too, Dad." His voice stayed steady, but Tex didn't detect any emotion at all. Bryce was an emotional person, and the lack of it bothered Tex. He pulled away and looked at his son, searching, searching, searching.

"Stop it," Bryce said. "I'm fine." He stepped back, and Tex let his hands drop to his sides. "I'm going to shower. I'll be out fast so I don't delay breakfast." He walked away, and Tex did his very best not to turn and watch his son's every move.

Wade walked toward him, and Tex grinned at him. "Merry Christmas, Wade." He carried his son, but he still gave Tex a quick hug.

"Can I put him in with Melissa?"

"She'd love that." Tex glanced over to his daughter. "I think she'd like Franny to get in there with her too." He smiled as Wade walked in his somewhat stilted way with his prosthetics and gently set his two-month-old in the play pen.

"Ba-ba-ba-by," Melissa babbled, clearly thrilled to have a friend her size.

"Dad?" Bryce asked, and Tex turned. Perhaps the best place to stand was in the mouth of this hallway, because all the traffic moved past this spot, and he could see nearly the whole house from here.

Bryce gestured to him from the doorway, and Tex went that way. He went into Bryce's room, and his son closed the door. Tex's nerves sizzled, and he watched his son now unabashedly. "What's goin' on?"

"When's the soonest I can leave Coral Canyon?" Bryce asked.

Tex's eyebrows drew down. "What do you mean?"

"I mean, are you and Abby planning a birthday party for me or anything? I haven't heard anything." He seemed agitated, almost angry, that he had to stand here and have this conversation.

"Yeah," Tex said. "We'd like to celebrate your birthday with you, but we didn't plan a party. We weren't sure if...." Bailey had been due on December twenty-seventh, and with Bryce's birthday the following day, Tex and Abby had decided not to complicate things by adding another party. "We thought we'd just go to dinner together as a family."

Bryce's jaw jumped as he clenched his teeth. "Okay. So I can leave the next day?"

"I guess," Tex said. "Are you going back to Montana?"

Bryce shrugged and turned toward the end of his bed. He started folding some clean laundry that sat there. "I don't know."

Tex prayed with everything he had, hoping the Lord would fill his mouth with the right words. He had in the past, but Tex's mind stayed blank. "Son," he said. "You don't have to leave at all."

"I do, Dad."

"Your horses are here," he said. "They need you."

"I'll ask Wade to take care of them again."

"I can do it," Tex said. They were done with recording now, and all he had to do all day was work out. Luke was adamant they work out and follow the same schedule they would have had they lived in Nashville, and he spent a couple of hours every morning at the gym.

Tex humored him and showed up for some cardio, and he did have some free weights in the basement he used a few times each week.

"As long as someone does," Bryce said.

"What—?"

"I don't know, Dad." Bryce finally tossed the unfolded jeans to the bed. He glared at Tex. "I just know I can't stay here. I can't, okay? I see all the questions in everyone's eyes, even if they don't say them out loud. I'll have to see all of the uncles, and Otis, and the baby, and I can't."

Still no tears, but the amount of agony and anger in his son punched Tex in the throat. "Okay," he managed to say, the last tie to his son starting to unravel. "We'll help you however we can."

Bryce clenched his jaw, his chin jutting out, and nodded.

Tex wasn't sure if the conversation was over or not, but his son didn't say anything else, and the tension in the room choked him. "I'll tell Abs you need a few more minutes."

Bryce nodded now, and Tex twisted the doorknob and left the room. Abby had just started to come down the hall, and she met Tex's eyes. "What's happening?" she asked.

He shook his head and instead of joining everyone in the living room or kitchen, he went into the master bedroom. Bryce hadn't cried, but Tex sure felt like shedding a tear or two. Or more.

Abby followed him and closed the door. "Tex, baby." She spoke with such compassion that Tex's hold on his emotions collapsed.

He sank onto the bed and cradled his head in his hands. His wife flew to the spot in front of him, pressing her palms against his knees as he started to weep.

"What is happening?" she asked. "What were you doing in Bryce's room?"

Tex looked at her, the anxiety and concern in her face for his son so real and so amazing. "He's leaving, Abs. As soon as he can, because he can't stand to be here."

She moved into him and held him tightly. "It's okay."

It really wasn't. "We're losing him," Tex murmured, his voice too high. "We've lost him. He's already gone."

The truthfulness of his words rang throughout the room, and Tex said, "He's already gone," again, his heart cracking so suddenly that he gasped in pain. Surely he wouldn't be able to take another breath, because he couldn't lose Bryce. It was too much, and he couldn't live through it.

And yet, he took another breath, and then another one.

Abby didn't tell him it was okay this time, because it wasn't. She loved Bryce too, and they'd talked and talked about what he might do and where he might go after the baby was born.

This was the worst-case scenario, and they wept together on that Christmas morning despite the usual cheerfulness of the holiday.

16

Bryce loaded his second bag into his truck and turned to find his family standing at the bottom of the steps. He'd heard them as they'd followed him outside, and he couldn't deny his father his goodbye.

"Daddy." He stepped into his father's strong arms, wishing he had even half of his father's bravery. A fraction of his good sense and intellect. A piece of his charm and wit.

Dad didn't say anything, and Bryce's emotions pitched left and right, up and down, as he hugged him. He stepped back and took Abby into a hug. "I love you," he whispered.

"You come home anytime," she whispered back. "You belong here, and you always will."

He appreciated her words, but he didn't believe them. He didn't belong here. Maybe at this farm, but Otis came here almost every day, and he brought Joey all the time. He'd be bringing the baby—Bryce couldn't even think the boy's name; it made him too human, and it was easier if Bryce simply kept calling him "the baby"—all the time too.

After stepping out of the hug with Abby, he kissed his half-sister and whispered, "I love you, baby girl." Then he bent down and scratched behind Franny's ears.

When he straightened again, he looked at his dad again. "I'm sorry about the horses. Once I get a job, I'll send you some money to keep them."

"That's insane," Tex said. "You don't need to pay us to take care of them."

His dad wore questions in his eyes all the time, and Bryce would never tell him that he was also a major reason Bryce had to leave town. He couldn't carry the weight of his father's questions, even if Bryce knew a lot of them.

Was he going back to Montana?

If not, where was he going?

Where would he live?

Did he have enough money?

What jobs could he get?

Would he come on tour with Country Quad this summer?

On and on, and Bryce didn't want to answer the questions. He didn't know the answers, as his current plan was to meet Bailey for lunch and tell her he was leaving town too.

And he wasn't going back to Montana.

Seeing Bailey was painful now, and Bryce hated that more than he hated the way his father looked at him.

"You call and tell me where you are tonight," he said, no room for argument in his tone.

"Yes, sir." Bryce hugged him again, and Dad followed him to the truck. He held onto the door as Bryce got behind the wheel.

"Drive safe," he said.

"I will."

"You have money?"

Bryce nodded, because his father had given him a credit card last night. He'd have to use it too, even if he didn't want to. He'd called his landlord and said he wouldn't be returning in January. He'd asked a buddy in Butte to go move everything into a storage unit.

After lunch...Bryce had no idea where he'd go. West? South? East? North?

He didn't know, and a thrill ran through him for the first time in the past ten months.

"Love you," Dad said, and he closed the door. He returned to Abby's side, and then they both stood there and waved. Abby grinned and grinned and even got Melissa to wave goodbye to Bryce.

That was a beautiful picture, and he committed it to memory as he backed out of the driveway and left the farmhouse he'd loved the moment he and his father had moved into it.

A weight lifted off his shoulders, and he even rolled them to make sure they were lighter than normal. They were.

"Dear Lord," he said aloud. "Guide me this day." He'd been praying for months, and his prayers and requests of the Lord had changed often. Right now, he simply wanted God to guide him.

Sometimes he still felt like God didn't hear him at all. He didn't answer, almost like He didn't know the answers to Bryce's problems the way Bryce didn't know the answers to his father's questions.

Every time Bryce thought that, he shook it out of his head. Of course God knew the answers to everything. He could see the world and all its inhabitants from beginning to end, and Bryce just wanted a little bit of that light.

He hated not knowing what was ahead for him, and the past year and a half had been day after day of him thinking, *I don't know.*

What do you want to do with your life, Bryce?

"I don't know," he said out loud.

Do you want to build and run a horse ranch, Bryce?

"I don't know."

Do you want to join the band? Be a solo artist?

"I don't know."

He did have his guitars with him, and he'd need to get a fresh supply of toiletries in a couple of days. And somewhere to stay tonight.

He'd done some research online, and he could get to Jackson Hole easily. Stay there and then decide where to go.

If he went south, he could get to Rock Springs or Laramie, depending on how far east he went at the same time.

After lunch, he thought. *You'll decide after lunch where you're going to go.*

17

Blaze laughed as Cash got the Irish setter they'd brought home for Christmas to stand up on its hind legs, putting his front paws on the boy's shoulders as if hugging him.

"Look at him, Dad."

"I see him," Blaze said, still chuckling. The dog had a gorgeous auburn coat that shone like red gold in the kitchen lights. He was a re-homed dog who'd just turned one a few weeks ago, and he'd come with his name—Hollis.

Blaze believed the Lord had led him to Hollis, as his owners were quite desperate to find a new home for him, and Blaze hadn't wanted a puppy. It had been serendipitous, and the couple had brought Hollis over on their way out of town for a sudden, immediate overseas move.

Cash had insisted they go to the pet store in town and buy anything and everything that caught their fancy, and Blaze hadn't objected. Everyone who came within fifty yards of Hollis adored the dog, because he was sweet, gentle, and intelligent.

Rosie and Cole begged to have Hollis sleep with them every night, but Hollis preferred Blaze and slept at his feet.

Christmas had been a great day with Jem and his kids here. Luke had come with Corrine, and since they'd ordered the food, they'd eaten like kings.

Candied ham and scalloped potatoes. Homemade rolls. And the pies. Pies for days, as Blaze had, in fact, eaten warmed apple pie with cream for breakfast a few hours ago.

"Uncle Blaze," Cole asked, and Blaze looked away from the show in the kitchen.

"What's up, buddy?" He reached down and tapped the boy's cowboy hat. He'd gotten it for Christmas from his father, and Blaze would bet a lot of money that the boy had been sleeping in it since. He certainly never took it off while he was awake.

"My daddy says you're leaving to go to town, and I was wondering if you might be going to the store?"

"I can," Blaze said. He hadn't been planning on doing any shopping. He was meeting Faith for an early dinner, and then they were doing their Christmas gift exchange though Christmas had come and gone five days ago.

Tomorrow night, he'd have her over to the house for a New Year's party, and he'd invited everyone in his family. His house was the biggest, no barn rental needed. Not everyone would come anyway, as some of his brothers had little children, and Otis had a brand-new baby.

"What do you need?" he asked Cash.

"Just some crackers," he said. "The wheat kind that are shaped like ovals. My dad lets me make peanut butter sandwiches with them, and we're out."

Blaze grinned at his nephew. "I can get you some crackers."

His front door opened, and Blaze didn't even flinch at the security system voice, nor the little girl skipping inside. Rosie carried her jump rope and a healthy flush in her cheeks. She used all of her strength to push the heavy front door closed, and then she turned back to the house.

"Uncle Blaze." She ran toward him. "That black cat is back."

"Is it?" He picked up the little girl and grinned at her, barely recognizing his life. Or himself. "Did you shoo it away?" Hollis had started a war with one of the neighborhood cats, and it was the only time Blaze had heard the dog bark.

"It just went by," Rosie said, playing with his beard. "I didn't do nothin' with it."

"Well, that's probably good," he said. "We'll let Hollis deal with the cat."

"Yeah."

Blaze put Rosie on her feet. "Is your daddy coming in?" Jem had gone outside with Rosie, as it was below freezing, and she was only four-years-old. Blaze lived on a safe street, in a great community, in a small Wyoming town. But Rosie still shouldn't wander the neighborhood alone.

"He was on the phone," Rosie said as she ran toward Hollis. She joined in with Cash and Cole as they played with the dog, and Blaze looked toward the front door.

Who was Jem talking to?

"Why do you care?" he muttered to himself. It wasn't like Jem was a reformed drug dealer, and he might be calling on his dangerous past contacts in secret. He didn't have to account to Blaze about who he spoke to, but Blaze still wanted to know.

His brother had been back in the basement for a little over two weeks now, and Blaze loved having him there. He didn't go out at night anymore, and Blaze had tried to keep him busy at the house.

That didn't always work, because Blaze had Faith to consider, and he wanted to spend time with her on evenings she wasn't working. Jem had said he was fine to babysit, and that taking care of three kids alone kept him hopping.

Blaze needed to get going in the next few minutes, so he went into his bedroom to change his clothes. He patted cologne onto his neck, plucked his cowboy hat from the rack beside his door, and went back into the main areas of the house.

"I'm headed out," he said to the kids, who'd moved their play to the living room. "Cole, did your dad come back in?"

"I don't know," Cole said.

"Front door, open," the cool female voice said, and Blaze turned that way. Darkness had fallen, and Jem moved from black to light as he entered the house. He brought a storm with him, and Blaze moved in his direction to put some distance between them and the kids.

"What's wrong?" he asked. He didn't want to be the older brother mother hen, but he had been these past couple of weeks.

"Chanel wants the kids tomorrow."

Blaze's surprise shot his eyebrows up. "What? That's not happening."

"That's what I told her. She can't just demand I bring the kids to Vegas whenever she wants. I don't live there, and in fact, I live quite far from there, and arrangements have to be made."

Blaze nodded, because he agreed. "I thought she was working this week."

"I guess her boss's wife had emergency surgery, so he said to take the next week off. She found out this afternoon and wants the kids." He looked past Blaze to where his children played with Cash and Hollis. "I feel like it's uprooting them right when we've started thriving again."

"It's a week," Blaze said. "When's the last time they saw their mother?"

Jem brought his gaze back to Blaze. "I don't know. Summer?"

Blaze didn't want to tell him what to do, so he just asked, "What are you going to do?"

"I told her I'd check flights tonight, but that Jackson isn't the same as a big major hub." He started to move past Blaze. "I'm going to ask them what they want to do."

"I'm headed out," he said. "Remember?"

Jem turned back to him. "Oh, right. Yes. Go. Have fun."

"Mav's on his way," Blaze said.

Jem's face turned dark again. "I can watch the kids on my own. I've done it before."

"I know," Blaze said, though he didn't like leaving Jem with the kids alone. Luke had come a couple of times, because his daughter was close to Rosie's age, and that helped him too.

"Mav wanted to come tonight, because Beth is going back to Jackson this weekend. That's all."

That wasn't a lie either.

Jem didn't answer, and Blaze told himself he was just annoyed with his ex-wife. He sat on the couch, his attention right back on his phone while the kids played around him. Blaze checked the time, and he could delay picking up Faith, because they didn't have a reservation at a fancy restaurant tonight.

In the end, he decided he didn't need to babysit Jem. He hadn't been drinking since he'd moved back in, and the first week or so was incredibly hard. He was doing better now, without the insomnia, the shaking in his hands, and the nausea that plagued him after every bite of food he took.

He'd been on a roller coaster of emotions, and Blaze had put up with anger, crying, and anxiety. Jem had started to settle into a more even version of himself. He was definitely more like the brother Blaze had traveled the rodeo circuit with.

His biggest symptom now seemed to be emotional fatigue, and Jem had been taking a nap every morning and afternoon since Christmas. Blaze had done a bit of research on how to deal with someone who quits drinking cold turkey the way Jem had, and he'd been at his brother's side every step of the way.

"Not tonight," he muttered as he walked through the house to get his keys and go into the garage. He paused at the door. "Jem? You sure it's okay if I go out tonight?"

His brother looked up from his phone, his dark eyes filled with irritation. "Yes. Go."

"Dad." Cash got to his feet and ran to him. "Are you going

out with Faith?" He wrapped his arms around Blaze's waist and hugged him.

Blaze grinned at his son. "Yep. You be good for your uncle. Help with your cousins, okay?"

"Yes, sir," Cash said.

"Uncle Mav is bringing Boston and Beth too."

Cash cheered and galloped through the kitchen, and Blaze grinned at him as he went back to Hollis and his cousins. He'd transform back into a more sullen version of himself once he had to return to school, but they had a few more days of the winter break to enjoy.

He left the house and texted Faith from the truck. *On my way, beautiful. See you soon.*

He hadn't been able to find a pet name for her that he liked. She didn't seem to mind any that he'd used in the past, but he hated calling her *sweetheart*. It almost felt condescending to him, as he'd used that term as such in the past.

This new version of himself never would, but Blaze hadn't been this man for very long. He still needed to find the right footholds and things he was willing to say and things he wasn't.

His phone rang, and he expected it to be Faith, but the truck told him it was Tex. He hesitated, because this wouldn't be an easy or short conversation. Blaze swiped on the call, telling himself he had ten minutes, and arriving at Faith's would be a good reason to get off the phone with his oldest brother.

"Hey," he said.

"You haven't talked to Bryce, have you?" Tex asked, bypassing the greeting entirely.

"No," Blaze said. "Not since yesterday afternoon."

Tex had called last night too. Blaze had told him everything he'd said to his son then. He sighed mightily, and Blaze could feel the grief in it. "He deactivated his pin while he was at lunch with Bailey."

That was new information for Blaze. "I'm sorry, Tex," he said, and he meant it.

"She doesn't know where he went either. He wouldn't tell her."

"Maybe he just needs some time to cool off," Blaze said, coming to a stop at the end of his street. He could make a joke about how Bryce didn't need to leave Coral Canyon to do that, as Mother Nature had arrived with all of her sub-zero temperatures. But he didn't. This situation with Bryce didn't have room for jokes.

"He promised me he'd call last night, and he didn't. He's not picking up today either."

That did surprise Blaze. "At all? You haven't spoken to him at all today?"

"Not one text or call." Tex wasn't grief-stricken; Blaze could feel the worry in his tone.

"Okay," Blaze said. "I'll call him right now. Just see how he's doing. Make it casual."

"Would you?"

"Sure."

"I didn't call to ask you to do that. I just thought he might have called you."

"He didn't, but if he was going to call someone besides you, it might've been me."

"I know you won't, but don't make it a big deal, okay? I don't want Otis or Georgia feeling bad." Tex mumbled the last sentence, and Blaze's heart went out to his brother.

"How are you feeling?" he asked.

"I'm okay," Tex said, another sigh filling the line. "I mean, I'm feeding my son's finicky horses, because he's on the lam, but I'm okay."

Blaze chuckled, because Tex was always okay. "Okay" meant "bad" for him, but Blaze didn't know what to do about it. He'd never been the brother to cater to how someone else felt, and he'd argued plenty of times with Morris and Gabe to get over themselves when it came to their hurt feelings about being left out of the family band.

For a lot of years there, Blaze didn't have time for emotions. He couldn't be thinking about something he'd said or done that might've hurt someone else while he rode a two-ton bull. He didn't have room for the injustices others had done to him in the saddle.

Now that he was retired, he could see that life had a lot more gray in it than he'd previously allowed.

"I'm on my way to Faith's," he said, an idea boiling in his mind. "I'll call Bryce now and get back to you, okay?"

"Okay," Tex said. "I'm sorry I'm bothering you about this."

"He's your son," Abby said on their end of the line. "You're not bothering him."

"Listen to your wife," Blaze said. "You're not bothering me."

"Thanks, Blaze." Tex hung up then, already talking to Abby, and Blaze let himself smile. They loved each other, and he remembered Tex dating her as a teenager. The fact that she'd still been living next door to the farm when Tex had come back to town had been serendipitous indeed.

"Or the Lord," Blaze murmured. "Making sure they got together." He came to the highway, and all he had to do was turn left, and then make the next left, and he'd curve around the road to Faith's. He pulled over so he could call Bryce first, and as the line rang, he thumbed out a quick text for her.

Got a phone call from Tex. Be there in another ten.

She'd answered his first text while he'd been on the phone with Tex, and it was a simple, *Okay. See you soon.* She wouldn't care about another ten minutes, as they were eating dinner at her place. She said she left her tree up through New Year's anyway, and they could have a quiet, romantic dinner in private.

All of that had sounded like a gold mine to Blaze, and he'd agreed easily. She knew what was going on with Tex and Bryce —it seemed the whole town did—and she wouldn't fault him for talking to his brother or nephew.

"Hey," Bryce said, surprising him. He looked up from the screen of his phone, as Bryce's voice had come through the speakers.

"Hey, son," Blaze said. "I'm just callin' to see how you're gettin' on."

"Good." Bryce sighed exactly the way his daddy had. "I mean, good enough."

Blaze wanted to ask him where he'd landed, but he didn't want to be too forward. "You've got enough to eat at your place?"

"I didn't go back to Montana," Bryce said.

"Oh." Blaze's eyebrows went up to match the surprise in his voice. He wasn't truly surprised, but he wanted Bryce to think he was. "I thought you would, what with Bailey goin' back there for her internship."

"Yeah...I couldn't. I, ahem, went south."

"South, huh?" Blaze's curiosity could've punched a hole in the sky. "Like, my south to Vegas? Or your daddy's south to Nashville?" He chuckled, noting that Bryce didn't jump right in to say where he was. "Both would be better than here. The high this afternoon was negative ten degrees."

"Seems like I got out just in time," Bryce said, his voice definitely a bit less guarded now.

"You did," Blaze said. "I'm thinkin' of goin' south too. It's too dang cold here. But not Vegas. It's not even super warm there in the winter."

"It's not?"

"No, sir," Blaze said, wondering how long they'd play this game. "Florida. Morris said Florida was nice in the winter."

Bryce cleared his throat. "I bet it is."

Blaze sighed, and he didn't try to hide it. "I'm worried about you, Bryce."

"Why's that?" The attitude had flown right back into place.

"Because no one knows where you are, that's why." Blaze could put plenty of bite into his voice too, and he wasn't surprised when Bryce gave another epic sigh.

"I know," he said. "I'm gonna call my dad in a minute, I swear."

"Yeah?" Blaze challenged. "Is my romantic date with my girlfriend going to get interrupted if you don't actually do that?"

"He called you, didn't he?"

"He did."

"I knew he'd ask someone to check in with me."

"No," Blaze said. "He didn't ask me to do that. I'm doing it, because I care about you, and I care about him, and you're both hurting right now." He took a big breath, the words he wanted to say right there in the back of his throat. He simply wasn't sure he should say them. He waited for God to stop him, and when He didn't, he continued. "You're causing him a lot of worry right now, son. It's fine wherever you are. He's not going to care. You can tell him you don't want any questions, and he won't ask them. But he deserves to know where you are. That you're alive and safe and warm and fed. He's your father."

Bryce sniffled. "I'm going to call him right now."

"Be sure you do," Blaze said, not letting up yet. "I've been waiting for my Christmas with Faith for days now, and I don't want another call from your daddy in a half-hour, askin' me if I've heard from you."

"No, sir," Bryce said, all the bravado gone from his voice now.

Blaze softened too. "Now, tell your favorite uncle where you are, so I can sleep tonight too. Your daddy is real tight-lipped about things concerning you, and I love you too."

Bryce didn't speak for a moment, and Blaze agonized over what he might be thinking. He honestly had no idea, but he hoped the boy wasn't too deep in his self-loathing. Finally, Bryce said, "Nashville, Uncle Blaze. I drove to Nashville."

"I—wow." Blaze had not been expecting that. "You're warm and safe and have enough to eat?"

"Yes, sir," Bryce said. "I'm in a hotel, and I ate a cheeseburger and fries about an hour ago."

"All right, then," Blaze said, wondering how Tex would take this news. "You call me if there's anything you need. I won't keep secrets from your daddy for long, but I bet I can manage it for a day or two if you need the time."

Bryce once again took several long seconds to respond, and his voice sounded like he'd inhaled helium when he said, "Thank you, Uncle Blaze. I love you too."

The call ended, and Blaze's heart felt heavier than ever. He hated that he knew where Bryce was when Tex didn't, but he couldn't help that. Sometimes he was easier to talk to. He thumbed out a quick text to Tex.

Talked to him. He's alive and well. He promised me he'd call you within the next thirty minutes.

Then he set his headlights in the direction of Faith's house. Tex wouldn't send updates to the brothers for a while yet anyway, and Blaze could set his family drama on the shelf for now.

He really wanted his Christmas celebration with Faith to be the quiet, romantic thing he'd imagined, and as he walked up her front sidewalk to the door, he actually turned off his phone.

Then maybe nothing would disturb them.

18

Faith watched her handsome cowboy come up the steps, shove his phone in his back pocket, and lift his head. His eyes seemed to meet hers through the peephole, but that couldn't be. Still, Faith's heartbeat skittered and scattered through her body, and she backed up a couple of steps at the intensity in Blaze's gaze.

He held so much power inside himself, and he didn't even seem to know it. She knew it. She felt it. It screamed from him and dove deep into her, no matter how hard she'd tried to keep him out, keep him back.

This time, she'd stopped trying to keep him at arm's length. This time, she kissed him every time she saw him. She'd bought Christmas presents for the man, after she'd consulted with her sister. Trinity had even helped her wrap them, and they'd talked about Blaze while the kids ate caramel corn and drank hot chocolate.

Faith couldn't remember a day this year when she'd felt as happy as she did today, with Blaze standing on her front stoop and the scent of dinner hanging in the air. He hadn't rung the doorbell yet, and she didn't want him to know she'd been watching for him since he'd texted last.

"Tex," she whispered. She'd met Blaze's oldest brother, and he'd had a crinkly-eyed smile and a strong handshake for her. He'd masked the cares he carried easily, but Blaze had told her about them all. They weighed on him too.

A moment later, the doorbell rang, and Blaze called, "It's me, Faith."

She wiped her hands down the front of her dress, feeling the bumps of the sequins. She looked down at herself, wishing she hadn't let Trin talk her into wearing the gown.

This was supposed to be a relaxing, at-home dinner and gift exchange between her and Blaze, not a night out at a city theater. She was no supermodel either, and she felt the extra weight around her midsection as it pressed against the restrictive fabric of the dress.

She wore a pair of simple red heels to go with the black dress, and she was now second-guessing the color of her garment. Black wasn't fit for Christmas.

Trinity's voice whispered in her head. *He's not there for Christmas, Faith.*

That got her to move toward the door, her footwear making sharp noises against the floor. She opened the door, a blast of the arctic air that had settled in Coral Canyon this week hitting her delicate skin.

Blaze's eyes immediately turned into pools. Hot, liquid pools of fire, and he licked his lips. "Well. Aren't you the most beautiful woman in the world?"

A smile sprang to her face, and she instantly tried to conceal it. "No," she said quietly, ducking her head. She tucked her hair, which she'd curled slightly and left to fall over her shoulders, and looked up at him through her eyelashes.

"I feel woefully underdressed," he said as he stepped into the house.

Faith didn't back up and give him much room to close the door, which he did with one hand. The other moved along her waist to her lower back. "Mm." He took a deep breath of her hair as Faith leaned into his broad chest. "I'm wearing jeans and you're wearing a dress. If you'd have told me to dress nicely, I'd have worn something better."

"You look fantastic," she said. "A little troubled, maybe." She tipped her head back and met his eyes. "Tex called?"

His expression changed, but Faith didn't draw back or quickly say he didn't have to talk about it. "If we talk about it now, then it stays here," she said. "At the doorway." She twisted and pointed to her lit Christmas tree behind her. She'd positioned it so that any visitors to her house would be greeted by it upon the first opening of the door. "Then we can exchange our gifts, enjoy our dinner, and ultimately, our evening."

She gave him a smile, and his gaze dropped to her mouth. "You just have all the answers, don't you?"

"Not all of them, Mister Young. Just this one." She rose onto her toes and touched her mouth to his. He latched onto hers instantly, but she pulled away. He growled, which made her giggle. She sobered quickly, mostly because Blaze's hand against her back was so insistent. "Just give me the short version of Tex's call," she said. "Then I'll kiss you properly."

He took another moment before he relaxed. "He hasn't heard from Bryce since he left yesterday morning. I said I'd call him, so then I had to do that."

Faith's eyes widened, and she drank in Blaze's face. "You got in touch with him."

"Yeah, he picked up for me." He looked at her, the darkness in him now not pleasant. "Don't tell Tex that, okay?"

"I'm going to call him right away," she teased.

He cracked a small smile. "Bryce told me he's in Nashville. I told him he better call his daddy and tell him, because I wasn't having my night interrupted." He took a step toward the back of the house, where the kitchen and living room sat.

"That's all?"

"That's all." Blaze's hand dropped to take hers, and he definitely didn't want to say anymore. "It smells great in here."

"Like sugar and roast beef," she said at the same time as him. "That's because I made doughnuts and beef roast." Her fingers on his tightened. "I didn't get my kiss."

"Oh, now you want your kiss?"

"Yes," she said. "Now I want my kiss."

Blaze turned back to her when they'd reached the heart of the house and took her face in his hands. He kissed her the way he wanted—the way she wanted him to—when he'd gotten a bit wound up by something in his life.

The unrest in him almost always traced back to one of his brothers—lately, it was Jem or Tex—but he worried about Cash returning to school, and he hated the cold weather, a fact which he'd complained about several times this month as the weather had continued to worsen.

They'd had several big snowstorms, but the plows in Wyoming knew how to clear the roads in a timely manner, so folks could get to school and work without too many delays.

His mouth finally softened against hers, and Faith hoped she gave back as much as she took from him. He pulled away and whispered, "Satisfied?" against her lips.

"No," she whispered. "You didn't leave it all at the front door. Started out a little frustrated."

His mouth curved upward, and Faith's did too, so she could kiss him smiling too, should she want to. She did, but her stomach growled, and she'd already waited an extra ten minutes for him. Dinner had been ready for about twenty minutes early as it was, but Faith wouldn't tell him that.

He chuckled and dropped his hands from her face. "You're something special, my Christmas dove." He gave her that sexy smile and stepped back. "I'm as hungry as you are, so let's eat first, yes?"

"Yes." She moved past him and into the kitchen.

With her back turned, he asked, "Why are there still so many presents under your tree?"

"They're for you." She twisted to look over her shoulder.

Blaze turned to look at her, alarm pulling across his face. "What? All of these?"

She smiled at him. "Yes." She turned back to take the lid off the slow cooker. "I didn't see you carrying in a basket of gifts."

"I got you one," he said. Crossness hid in the few words he'd spoken, and Faith tossed him another look. He'd crouched in front of the tree now, and he placed a single gift underneath it.

"Don't get excited," she said as she continued to line up the dishes that would make their complete dinner. "Some of them are quite boring."

"I'm sure that's not true." His voice came closer, and the heat from his body as he sidled up to her was very welcome indeed. She smiled and leaned into his side. If time could pause right here, she'd be filled with more joy than she'd ever thought possible.

"I like this dress," he murmured. His fingers ran up and down her bare upper arm as she sliced open a bagged salad she hadn't made yet so it wouldn't get soggy while she waited for him. "I like your hair." He moved his hand up to it. "I like those shoes."

"Behave yourself, Mister Young." She shrugged his hand away from her arm. "We're eating first. Then presents. Then dessert."

"And do I get to taste you for dessert?"

"No," she said with a smile. "I made doughnuts for that, Mister Young."

"I like it when you call me Mister Young," he murmured next, and he did touch his lips to her neck despite the way she stirred the green salad together.

"Blaze," she warned, though her legs felt one breath away from collapse.

He pulled away and gave her a knowing smile. "I don't like that nearly as much."

"About like your many and varied pet names for me," she quipped.

He chuckled and finally shrugged out of his black leather jacket. Even as cold as it was, he didn't wear a winter coat, something he'd told her he absolutely wouldn't buy. He'd suffer, but he wouldn't buy a winter coat.

When she'd teased him about that, he'd tickled her and then kissed her until she couldn't breathe.

"I rather liked dove." He flashed a quick smile in her direction.

"You do? Why?"

"Feels like a fresh start," he said. "A good luck symbol."

"The light after a dark flood," she said.

"Yes."

They'd gone to church together on Christmas Eve, and Blaze had held her hand quite painfully for the first half. She'd not brought it up with him, and there had been no other Sunday classes that day due to the holiday.

He hadn't exactly run out, but he'd only stayed until the last note of the final hymn had been played, and then he'd strode out of the chapel. She'd grabbed her purse and hurried to follow him, and she hadn't spoken to the pastor, because they'd beat him out of the building.

Blaze had said, "I'm sorry," once they'd gotten in his truck, but no other explanation had been given. She wondered if she could bring up anything religious now, or if she shouldn't.

She took a deep breath, still deciding when he looked up

and met her eye. She wanted tonight to be lighter than religious conversations that might turn south, so she gazed over the feast she'd put together. "I made a beef roast," she said. "Because my aunt used to make one every year for Christmas dinner."

"Did you visit her often?"

"Every few years," Faith said. "She was my mother's only sister, so we went often enough." She fixed the tongs in the slow cooker. "Mashed potatoes. Creamed peas. Caesar salad, and Trinity sent along some of her strawberry-pineapple frappe." She turned to the freezer to get out the frappe. "I almost forgot about the frappe."

With the cardboard container of it on the counter to thaw, she handed him a plate. "Ready?"

"Did you want to say grace?"

Faith lifted her eyes to his, suddenly feeling very self-conscious with him in her home. He'd been here before, of course. But they'd never eaten in like this. She'd never cooked for him before, at least not anything beyond doughnuts.

"Faith?"

"Hmm?"

"You've stopped talking." He set the plate back on the counter and reached up to remove his cowboy hat. "I'll say it." He offered her a kind smile and bowed his head. "Lord, we're grateful to be together tonight, Faith and I. I'm glad she's invited me to her house for dinner, and bless this food to strengthen and heal us. Bless my brother and his son, then my other brother, and all the brothers." A soft chuckle came out, but it only lasted a moment.

Faith kept her eyes pressed closed, because she didn't want to risk giggling too.

"Bless Trinity and her family, and help Faith not to be too nervous tonight, because she bought me too many presents. Amen."

Faith's eyes flew open, but no laughter threatened to follow. Her pulse did fly through her body with the speed of humming-bird wings, and she didn't know why. Yes, she did. Blaze knew she was nervous. How had he known?

"You stopped talking," he said. "I don't like it when you stop talking."

"I'm talking," she said as she picked up the only remaining plate. She didn't imagine for a single second Blaze would serve himself first, so she started filling her plate with food. She didn't say anything more, and neither did he.

Once he sat down kitty-corner to her, she looked at him. "I was thinking about how small my place is compared to yours." She moved her creamed peas around. "Okay? I can admit it."

"I love your house."

"It's cozy," she admitted. "And you've been here before, but I haven't fed you. I was just...suddenly nervous about making this meal and having you here and—all of it."

"I've eaten far worse than this, my dove." He took his first bite of meat and potatoes, his smile absolutely gorgeous. "Mm, yes. See? This is fantastic."

Faith did like the way he called her "my dove." It was far better than *sweetheart, baby, beautiful,* or even plain *dove. My dove* was far, far better.

Her smile felt timid on her own face, but she managed to take a bite of her peas.

"And I like *dove*," he said. "I'm sticking to that for now, unless you have any objections?"

"I don't need a pet name," she said.

"But I do." He smiled at her again. "I wish you wouldn't be so nervous around me."

"I wish you weren't quite so perfect." She regretted her words the moment she said them, as his face changed instantly. "I'm sorry, Blaze. I'm—" She swallowed, wishing she could take her tongue with the food. "Sorry."

He nodded at her, and the conversation stalled completely. Faith didn't like this any more than talking to him, and she put her fork down. "I'm sorry, okay? I won't stop talking."

Blaze's eyebrows rose, and he gestured with his fork for her to keep talking.

"I bought lame gifts," she said. "So I don't want you acting like they're fantastic, okay?"

"I wouldn't dream of it."

"You can speak freely about the food."

"It's great," he said. "Really, Faith."

She nodded, her chest still storming. "I actually like dove too." His smile widened then, and Faith wanted to swat it away. "Stop it."

"Stop what?"

"Smiling."

"I can't smile?"

"No." She couldn't stop her own smile either, and Blaze laughed outright. That alleviated the tension, and by the time, they moved over to the Christmas tree, Faith felt like the night might be able to be salvaged.

Of course, her gifts were quite lame, but she pushed against the nerves and inadequacy and picked up her first one. "Here you go." She joined him on the couch, allowing her joy to seep back into herself again. "Remember, no acting when you open it."

Blaze looked at her, and for how close they sat together on the couch, she could practically see the lighter flecks in his dark eyes. "I promise I'm a terrible actor." He tore the paper off the small box, his eyes trained down on it the entire time. His face lit up when he saw the writing, and he lifted his gaze to hers. "You got me the heated gloves."

"Totally utilitarian," she said, which was a direct quote from something he'd said about some of the gifts he'd purchased for his son. She expected him to laugh, but he didn't.

His eyes flickered between hers, something fond there. "Thank you, dove." He leaned forward and kissed her, and this held none of the irritation and frustration as their earlier kiss.

He then opened a new single-serve coffee maker, a box of the coffee mini-cups he'd said he loved, a new hooded sweatshirt with her logo on it, and finally, he held the last gift in his lap. She'd offered to open his, but he said he wanted her to do it last.

She sank onto the couch again, ready to be done getting up and down. He finished pulling the hem of the sweatshirt down, and she beamed at him.

"I love this," he said. "I didn't know you sold merchandise."

"I don't," she said. "I order things for me and my employees. That's it."

"So this is a limited-edition sweatshirt."

She shook her head, his ability to make her feel seen and special out of this world. "It's a sweatshirt, Blaze."

"Okay." He started into the largest package, his eyes as fiery as his name. "I'm so excited for this one. When I was a little boy, I thought the size of the present meant it was better."

"So bigger is better."

"Yeah." He grinned at her. "Always."

"Maybe not," she said. "My gift is really small."

"It's pretty terrible," he said, the happiness in his eyes going nowhere. He finished unwrapping the present and looked at the plain, brown box without any writing on it. She only smiled at him when he raised his eyebrows, and then he opened the flaps. He peered inside and said, "I don't believe it."

"It's really hard to buy for a billionaire," she said.

He pulled out the black winter coat she'd stuffed inside. "You bought me a coat."

"You said you wouldn't under any circumstance, and I couldn't stand the thought of you getting caught in a blizzard without a coat." She smiled as he leaned toward her, easily fisting her fingers along the hood of his shirt near his neck.

He kissed her, murmuring, "I love this. Thank you."

"It is hard to buy for you," she said.

He sat back and looked at his loot. "And yet, you got me quite a few things I'm thrilled about." He set them all aside then and got to his feet. "All right, Miss Faith Cromwell. It's your turn." He retrieved his single gift from beneath the tree, and quiet excitement built in Faith's chest.

He handed her the box he clearly had not wrapped, the

bright red bow nearly as big as the container itself. Right as she started to take it, he pulled it back. "I just want to give a caveat."

Surprise darted through her. "Okay."

"It's not as serious as you think." He handed her the box then and sat back down.

It had to be jewelry, and Faith's pulse pumped harder and harder. Her mouth felt far too dry, and she wanted to escape down the hall to brush her teeth so her breath would be fresher than it currently was.

Instead, she undid the bow and lifted the lid of the box. Sure enough, a black jewelry bag sat there, something concealed inside. She glanced up to him, but he had a plastic smile stuck in place.

"What is it?" she asked.

"Open it."

She lifted the bag from the box, noting that it was almost certainly a bracelet. She opened the bunched-closed top and sure enough, a bangle sat inside. The diamonds came into view immediately, and Faith's breath caught in her throat.

"Blaze," she breathed.

"I said it's not serious."

"It's diamonds." She removed the bracelet and sure enough, they glinted in the lights from the tree, which only sat a few feet from her. "Lots of diamonds." The bangle shone with white and red gems, and she knew none of them were fake.

She looked at him for an explanation as to how this wasn't serious.

"They're rubies," he said. "It's your birthstone. July."

"I know when I was born," she said.

He took the bracelet from her, and she somehow knew subconsciously he wanted her to hold out her hand. She did, and he slid it onto her wrist. "It's a close fit," he said. "I did that so you could wear it to parties, or on the truck, or you know, as you do dishes."

She couldn't believe him. "You don't do dishes with diamonds and rubies on your wrist, Blaze." She held her arm out, still not quite believing the piece of exquisite jewelry on her body. "This is—"

"Do not say too much."

She met his eyes, noting how dark his fire was now. "I wasn't going to," she said. "I was going to say, this is fantastic. Thank you so much." She wrapped her arms around him and held him tightly.

He did the same for her. "You really like it?"

"I love it."

"It matches those shoes," he whispered. "This whole outfit."

She could only smile as wave after wave of happiness washed over her. Faith had just pulled away when her phone rang.

"Leave it," Blaze said, so she did. He kissed her, and she lifted her braceleted hand to his face. He covered the jewelry with his fingers too, and Faith could lose a lot of time with this man, doing exactly this.

Her phone stopped ringing and immediately started again. "Blaze," she whispered.

"Fine," he whispered back.

Faith got up and hurried into the kitchen, where she'd left

her device. She didn't recognize the number on the screen, and that made her hesitate long enough to miss the call.

"You didn't answer," he said.

"I didn't know the number," she said, frowning at the phone. "But they did call twice." As she watched her phone, trying to see if the numbers meant anything to her, it started ringing again. Her heartbeat jolted, and she said, "It's the same number."

Blaze got to his feet. "Answer it."

She swiped on the call, buoyed by his courage. "Hello?"

"Faith," a man said. "Yes, she answered this time."

"Yes," she said slowly, because the voice sounded familiar. "Who is this?"

"It's Maverik Young," he said. "We've been trying to get in touch with Blaze, but he's not answering."

Alarm pulled through her, and Faith quickly lowered the phone and jabbed at the speaker button. "He's here with me. Is everything okay? Is Cash all right?" She tilted the phone toward him, as if he'd have Mav's number memorized. She didn't truly think for a moment that he would. "It's Mav," she whispered.

"Mav?"

"Cash is fine," Mav said, clearly not caring about their conversation. "You two haven't been watching the weather or the news, have you?"

"Now why would I be doing that?" Blaze asked. "Mav-who-should-not-be-bothering-me-tonight?"

"Because the storm arrived early, and the town has shut down everything," Mav shot back. "I'm stuck at your house, in fact, because they closed the canyon. So I can't get home, and there's no way you'll be able to."

Faith blinked as waves of a new emotion—shock—coursed through her. Over and over, while Blaze went to the window above her kitchen sink and looked out. There was no way he could actually see anything, and he turned back to her, a perplexed look on his face. "Cash?" he asked.

"In the tub," Mav said. "We're fine here, but brother...you'll have to stay there tonight."

19

Blaze blinked and then double-blinked. He swiped Faith's phone out of her hand, because she'd frozen completely. He tapped the button to get Mav off speaker and said, "Tell me what's going on," as he walked away from his stricken girlfriend.

"One, let's talk about how Jem, Cash, and I have all called you a handful of times each, and you didn't answer." He probably thought it was because Blaze had been snuggling with Faith, ignoring his phone. He wished it was more snuggling and more ignoring too.

"I turned my phone off on the way here," Blaze said.

"Are you serious?"

"Do I have to answer that?" Blaze headed down the hall toward the front door.

Mav certainly pressed his sigh out twice as hard as he needed to. "Word is that there was an avalanche that covered the highway heading to Jackson. So all emergency crews are on that, and everyone's been advised to stay wherever they are tonight."

"How'd you hear that?" Blaze asked. In the next moment, Faith's phone made an ungodly noise twice as loud as the ringing had been. He yelped and pulled it away from his ear to check it. His chest felt twice as small as it should've when he saw the winter storm warning.

Shelter in place – Thursday December 29 – until further notice. Emergency crews are out of town and will not be able to help immediately. Do not travel. Severe winter storm sheltering in place until noon on Friday, December 30.

He took a screenshot of it while it continued to blare, then tapped *Acknowledge* and thankfully, got the noise to stop.

"That's how," Mav said as Blaze brought the phone back to his ear. "We got that about ten minutes ago, but with your phone off...."

"The storm wasn't supposed to come in until tomorrow," Blaze said.

"The wind blew harder," Mav said dryly. "Listen, can you... can you stay there?"

"Yeah, I'm sure I can," Blaze said. He made his voice as light and as casual as possible. Faith had a couch. He dropped his chin to his chest and closed his eyes. "Cash?"

"We'll be fine here with Cash," Mav said. "Jem and I will keep the kids alive."

"Dani?" Blaze didn't open his eyes. The last thing he wanted was for his brother's wife to be dealing with things on her own.

"She's only home with Lars, and she was giving him a bath when the warning went off. He'll be in bed soon, and she's fine."

Blaze nodded and finally opened his eyes. "Okay, then I guess I'll stay here."

"They've got cops at the canyon entrance," Jem called.

"You can't get home anyway," Mav said. "Stay there. Stay safe."

"You too."

"Love you, brother."

"Love you too, Mav. Love you, Jem. Thanks for helping with Cash."

"We've got this," Jem said.

Blaze saw no other options, though his skin itched to kiss Faith quickly and head out. Head for home.

A home you can't get to.

"I'll turn my phone back on," he said.

"Good idea," Mav said. "'Bye."

"'Bye." The call ended, and Blaze faced Faith's closed front door. He hadn't been able to see out her kitchen window, and he had to know for himself. He opened her front door and looked outside. The snow fell in thick, fat flakes. So fast that he couldn't see more than a couple of inches. As if on cue, the wind howled, pressing the flakes sideways.

He slammed the door closed.

"Blaze?"

Spinning, he found Faith at the end of the hall, her arms folded across her chest. He returned to her and held out her phone. "Mav's right. I'm not going anywhere."

She took her phone without a word, and if she'd shut down

on him once already tonight over the type and size of her house, this would make her mute for the rest of his time here.

"I took a screenshot on your phone of the emergency warning you got."

She looked at her phone, tapping and swiping. Her face came up, more surprise there.

He smiled and reached to tuck her hair. "You have a couch. I'll be fine there."

"Blaze, you are not sleeping on the couch." She rolled her eyes and started down the hall that branched into the more private parts of her house. "I'm changing my clothes, and then we'll talk about who's sleeping where."

"I'm fine on the couch, Faith."

She spun on one of those sexy heels and marched back to him. "You had major back surgery only six months ago." She came chest-to-chest with him. "You are *not* sleeping on the couch."

His blood ran hotter than ever. "I can do it for one night."

"I would never be able to live with myself if it hurt you for even one minute." She shook her head, some of that attitude he loved so much fading. "I only have a one-bedroom house, but I'm sure we can work something out." She patted his chest, turned, and went down the hall.

He stood frozen to the spot while the bedroom door closed. "This is a one-bedroom house?" he wondered aloud. That couldn't be right. No, it wasn't a big house. He'd known that from the moment he'd pulled up to drop her off after Everly's dance event months and months ago.

But one bedroom? Just one?

He glanced over to the couch, because he'd been joking when he said he could sleep there. He'd simply not wanted to make more work for her by having her scurry around and get her guest bedroom set up for him.

Now he'd learned she didn't have one.

And no, he couldn't sleep on the couch. It did hurt his back too much, and while he'd go through a lot for Faith, he didn't want to injure himself needlessly.

He wasn't sure how long it took a woman to change out of a slinky ballgown, heels, her jewelry, and her makeup, but Faith returned before he'd moved a muscle.

"You're still standing here?" She gave him a smile that made him reach for her. As he drew her into his chest, the lights around them flickered.

"Oh, boy," he muttered as they both looked up to the ceiling. "Why do people do that?" he asked. "Look up whenever the power surges?"

"I don't know," Faith said.

He found her smiling when he looked down again. "So, you have a one-bedroom house? Funny, it looks bigger from the outside."

"It's two bedrooms," she said. "But I use one as an office. I just have the one...bed."

Blaze needed to see this office. "Just down here?"

"First left."

Blaze nodded once and stepped past her. He didn't have to go all the way into the office to know it wasn't going to work. For one, it wasn't very big, and for another, her desk took up almost all the space. She didn't have a recliner or anything to sit in other than the office chair behind the desk.

This wasn't an option, and he sagged into the doorway as Faith came to his side. "Nice office," he murmured.

"Want to see the bedroom?"

He only moved his eyes to look down at her, and shockingly, she didn't seem nervous now. "I suppose I better."

"The couch is out, then." She wasn't asking.

"The couch is not ideal," he admitted.

"Mm hm." She gave him a knowing look and ducked around behind him. "Come on, then."

He turned and watched her recede further into her house, turning into the last door on the right. For some reason, his feet felt like lead, and he could barely lift them. Shock coursed through him that Faith was being so cool about this, and he was suddenly the one who'd had his tongue tied in a knot.

He once again paused in the doorway, committing to entering the room a bit too much for him right now. Faith's house wasn't big, and she didn't have the cavernous master suite he enjoyed at the lakeside mansion.

Rather, her bedroom spoke of home to him, with a beautiful king-size bed draped in blues and whites and greens. She'd told him about her passion for pillows, and that showed on the mountain of them on the bed. There wasn't room for a couch, but she did have a recliner in the corner in front of the window, with a bookcase beside that.

"You read?" he asked.

"Not usually," she said. "If I have time, and I never have time." She stood beside a nightstand on the side of the bed closest to him, obviously the side where she slept. Blaze's throat had never been so dry as he peered further left and saw only wall.

"Bathroom there." She indicated a door leading out of the room only a few feet in front of him, and his gaze naturally followed that direction. "I actually just cleaned it, so it's the perfect time for a sleepover."

His eyes flew back to hers. "Do you have sleepovers a lot?"

"Not a lot." She took a step toward him, her smile genuine and oh-so-soft. "But my nephew came a couple of weeks ago. Remember, you came by for breakfast the next day?"

"Yeah." Blaze remembered, because both Faith and her nephew, Ty, had been in their pajamas when he'd arrived, and he'd enjoyed seeing her in a more rumpled state.

If he slept over, he'd definitely get to see her like that again.

He swallowed and cleared his throat. "Faith."

"It's okay." She ran her hands up his arms to his shoulders, then back down and around his body. She settled her head against his chest, and it was the easiest thing in the world to take her into his arms and dance with her.

They swayed slightly, or perhaps that was Blaze's frenzied mind. He had no idea what to say, though he felt like he should say something.

"I'm going to build a pillow wall," she whispered. "Okay? We're not going to sleep together-sleep together. But you'll be able to be in the bed, and I'll stay on my side, and you'll stay on yours."

"Yeah." His voice scratched his throat. "You know...." He cleared the giant lump in his chest, and it sounded painful to his own ears. "You know I've been with other women, right? I've told you that."

"I know that," she said, slightly stepping out of his arms. "But we're not going to do that until we get married. You know that, right?"

"Yes." He couldn't look away from her, despite the awkwardness he felt streaming through him. "I've done my best to repent, Faith. I swear I have, and I know I'm okay with God now."

She didn't smile the way he expected her to. Instead, she reached up and trailed her hand down the side of his face. "How do you know?"

"I asked Him." Blaze closed his eyes and leaned into her touch. "I've been writing emails and letters and making phone calls." The story simply poured out of his mouth, and while he'd told Faith parts of it, she hadn't heard it all so linearly. Blaze hadn't even articulated it as such before. "I've been rectifying what I can. Apologizing as I go. I've just been...working so hard to set all the toppled bricks in my life right, you know? And after the thing with Jem, I really felt like I wanted to email the Lord and lay it all out for Him, but I can't do that. I can't tell Him how sorry I am for the stupid things I've done. The only way we have to talk to Him is through prayer, and I'm not real good at that."

"You are," she whispered. "You prayed tonight, and it was beautiful."

Blaze barely heard her, and he didn't want to be reassured besides. "But I prayed, and I just—just had this overwhelming sense that I'm okay. That He knows about me; He's forgiven me; and He doesn't want me to backtrack and mess up again."

He opened his eyes and looked at Faith. "This is a real temptation for me, Miss Cromwell. I like you so, so much, and I'd be lying if I haven't thought about bein' with you."

She looked surprised, and Blaze felt instant shame at admitting such a thing. "Sorry," he murmured. He dropped his head again, but she brought it up gently.

"It's okay," she said.

"I don't dwell on it," he muttered. "It's a fleeting thought, and I push it out and move on."

"We all have thoughts," she said. "It's what you do about them that matters."

"Does it?" Blaze challenged. "Because I remember learning that I needed to keep my thoughts pure. And that's a challenge for me, and I'm still working on it."

"So there's the imperfection you're always telling me about," she teased.

But Blaze didn't want to be teased. "Faith."

"Okay," she said quickly as he started to pull away. "Okay, I get it. But this isn't going to be anything you'll need to repent of. I promise."

He regarded her for a moment. A quick glance over to the bed had his heartbeat thrumming. "All right. Let's go eat dessert. I think I'm hungry enough for a doughnut now." With his last word, a loud *pop!* filled the air, and Faith's power went out.

Darkness bathed them on all sides, and Blaze wasn't sure if his eyes were open or closed. Faith moved in front of him, and then the flashlight on her phone illuminated the small area between them.

"I have candles in the office," she said. "Follow me." She led the way out of her bedroom and into the office, where she loaded him up with another of her obsessions—scented candles. When he carried all he could, he followed her into the kitchen.

They hadn't cleaned up after dinner, but he managed to find a spot for the half-dozen candles, and Faith lit them.

He stood on one side of the peninsula, with her on the other, and their eyes met. He smiled; so did she, and Blaze swore he felt the earth disappear from under his feet.

And then he was falling. Falling, falling, falling in love with Faith Cromwell.

"I was going to heat the chocolate dipping sauce," she said, her voice loud in the silence of the world. He'd never stopped to think about how many things made noise around him, from the hum of the refrigerator to the whirring of the furnace. Without any of that, it was stunningly quiet.

Blaze felt that silence way down deep inside himself, and he wanted to lasso it and hold onto it for a long, long time.

"We can eat it cold," he said.

"Or we can heat it by the teaspoon." She kept her grin in place and turned to the fridge. It didn't light up the way he expected, and Blaze marveled at how much he relied on electricity.

"It's going to get cold in here," he said.

"I have a gas fireplace," she said. "We can huddle in front of that."

"You do?" He glanced into the living room, but the tree took up a large part of it. "Where? I've never seen a gas fireplace."

"In the bedroom," she said.

Of course. Blaze's pulse skipped and jumped at the thought of eating sexy chocolate desserts by the light of the fire...in her *bedroom*.

She opened a drawer and took out two spoons. After handing him one, she said, "You've gone quiet, Mister Young."

"I'm nervous," he admitted.

She opened the lid on the homemade chocolate sauce and dug in her spoon. She took his back and filled it with some of the sauce. "Hold it over the flame of one of those candles." Their eyes barely met before she went back to the bowl to get more chocolate sauce for herself.

"Then," she continued. "You can drizzle it over any doughnut you want. I didn't make any fruity ones, because I know you don't like the chocolate and fruit combination."

Blaze only liked chocolate with savory things, like peanut butter or pretzels. Bananas were tolerable, but strawberries? No, thank you.

His smile returned, and he said, "You're too good to me, Faith."

"No," she said. "You tell people how you feel." She grinned at him again. "I make doughnuts, so they know I care about them."

He rounded the peninsula so he could stand beside her. "You just care about me?"

"Yeah." She nudged him with her shoulder. "I care about you...a lot."

"Mm." He kept his smile to himself, because the word *care* here sounded a lot like *love*. "I've never been in love."

"Even with your ex-wife?" She paused in her heating of her chocolate sauce, her eyes wide, with the flames flickering in them.

Blaze shook his head and broke off part of a doughnut. He put the whole thing on his spoon and then slid the entire bite into his mouth.

Faith watched him for a moment, and then she burst out laughing. "I think you just bit off more than you can chew, cowboy."

There was a lot of dessert in his mouth, but Blaze kept on chewing. That way, he didn't have to talk. After he finally swallowed, he said, "You've said precious little about your dating history. Have you ever been in love?"

She kept her head down, her eyes trained on the candle in front of her. Her lovely auburn hair swung as she shook her head. "No," she murmured. "I dated here and there before I started Hole in One. Since then, though, I've been too busy to have a serious relationship."

"Until me," he clarified. "Right? I mean, we're pretty serious."

That got her to look up. "Are we?"

He wasn't sure if she was kidding or not—until that teasing smile filled her face.

"Funny," he said dryly. "Real funny."

She took a much more delicate bite of her after-dinner treat, swiping it through her spoonful of heated chocolate sauce before lifting it to her lips. He went back to his doughnut, telling himself not to ruin things by being too grumpy.

"Blaze."

He looked at her again, and hope filled him from head to toe at the vulnerable, eager look on her face. "I think we're pretty serious too."

A smile threatened to burst onto his face, but he didn't allow it to. He pictured himself having just ridden the biggest, nastiest bull in the rodeo—and he'd won. He never let that euphoria show on his face. Never.

Tonight, he didn't either. He did nod, and Faith enjoyed her treat while Blaze got some more chocolate sauce to heat. He'd finished his first doughnut when he felt the inklings of cold air against his nose.

"It's already starting to get cold."

"I agree." Faith set down her spoon and went behind him. "I'm going to go get the bedroom ready." She walked away, and Blaze wanted to call after her and ask what that meant. She returned in only a few seconds, a smile fixed in place.

"What did you do?"

"Turned on the fireplace and closed the doors," she said. "It'll heat up fast in there, and we can have a little picnic if you want to move this party in there." Her eyebrows went up, and before he could even fathom sitting in front of a warm, romantic fire, with chocolate sauce and doughnuts—and Faith—she started packing up the desserts to do exactly that.

20

Faith looked at herself in the mirror, the iridescent, white light from her phone flashlight casting her face into scary shadows. Fear ran through her the way a freight train would once it had lost its brakes.

She couldn't stop it, and yet, she couldn't hide out in her bathroom for much longer. Blaze didn't have anything to change into for bed, but she had pajamas she wore every night. She'd put those on, brushed her teeth, washed her face, and paced back and forth a few times. She'd used the bathroom twice now, and she literally had nothing left to do but go into her bedroom and face her boyfriend.

Blaze had been wearing jeans and a short-sleeved polo in red, white, and green under his leather jacket. He'd left that draped over the back of her couch, and the doughnuts she'd eaten rolled in her stomach.

"Shouldn't have eaten two," she murmured to her ghastly

reflection. Blaze had eaten more than that, and the fireside dessert picnic had actually been really nice. One, it was warm in the bedroom, and two, there had been doughnuts. Three, Blaze had been there, and everything in her life was better with Blaze in it.

"You don't love him," she told herself next, but for all she knew that could be a lie. She'd never been in love before, and the only comfort she had was that he hadn't either.

Reaching for her last bit of bravery, Faith picked up her phone and turned to leave the bathroom. She'd run out of battery soon, and she tapped off the flashlight as she re-entered the bedroom.

The fire still flickered, but Blaze had cleaned up the chocolate sauce, the doughnuts, and their plates and utensils, just the way he'd said he would. He'd rolled a blanket and laid it along the seam of the door, so the warm air wouldn't leak into the rest of the house.

She expected him to still be in front of the fire, but he didn't sit easily on the floor, so he hadn't lasted long there anyway. The dining chair he'd brought in stood against the wall, but Blaze had gotten in bed.

Her bed.

Faith swallowed and forced herself to close the bathroom door before she moved forward. She'd told herself to *be cool, play it cool*, over the past hour or so since Mav had called. They'd gotten another notification about the power, and the city of Coral Canyon had said they had crews out to work on the problem, but the wet, heavy snow had taken down a big pine tree, and that had landed on one of their major transformers.

Power was out throughout Coral Canyon, and Faith was actually glad she wasn't here alone. She'd lived so much of her life alone, and there was something about not having power that set her teeth on edge.

She'd assured Trinity she was okay, and she wasn't sure what her sister would've done if Faith hadn't been. She hadn't mentioned her sleepover with Blaze, because she didn't want to spend time texting her sister when she could be eating doughnuts with Blaze in front of a romantic fire.

Faith plugged in her phone, so when the power returned, it would start to charge. She took a deep breath and peeled back her covers. The wall of pillows stared at her, but Faith ignored their accusing cases and settled in bed with her back to Blaze.

The sound of his breathing mingled with the faint crackling of the fire, and Faith watched the flames, her eyes wide open. She felt like she existed on a planet of her own, and she could say and do anything she wanted.

"Do you ever doubt yourself?" she asked. She hadn't spoken very loud, but her question landed like a shout.

"All the time," Blaze said, his voice as equally powerful yet soft. "When I rode the rodeo circuit, I doubted myself every time I got on a bull."

"You did?" She didn't see how that was possible. "But you were a champion. You were so good."

"There's always the fear that *this time* will be the one that ends your career," he said. "Because that can happen with bull riding."

Faith absorbed what he'd said, her mind coming up with all kinds of things to say to this cowboy beside her. "Blaze?"

"Yeah, Faith?" He spoke with kindness, and Faith's shoulders finally relaxed into the mattress.

"You changed my life with that check at the food truck rally."

"I'm sure that's not true."

"It is," she insisted quietly. "Having that money made it possible for me to fix my third truck. It made it so my December wasn't so stressful. I was able to think outside the box and start doing catering and parties, because if it didn't work out, okay. I had this wad of money to count on."

"I'm glad."

"I know it probably was nothing to you, but it sure meant a lot to me." She actually loved talking to him in the dark, and she sighed. "So thank you. I don't think I've said thank you properly."

"You have," he said.

Faith rolled over and adjusted the blanket over herself. He'd taken the extra one she'd pulled out of the hall closet, and she was using her comforter. She closed her eyes and hugged one of the pillows to her chest.

A minute went by. Maybe two. His breathing stayed steady and deep and even. Perhaps he'd fallen asleep already.

"I sure do like you," she whispered. "I'm falling in love with you."

"I'm falling in love with you too, Faith," he murmured, and her heart leapfrogged over itself. "And it terrifies me. I don't want this to be too fast, okay?"

"Okay," she said. "It doesn't have to be fast."

"I just want to be sure of things," he said. "I have Cash, and I don't trust myself quite yet."

She nodded before she realized he wouldn't be able to see that. A hint of foolishness ran through her. "If you hadn't been a bull rider, what would you have done?"

A few seconds of silence came over the pillow wall. "I don't know, Faith."

"You've got nothing? No back-up plan?"

"I never needed a back-up plan."

"Hmm, that sounds a little arrogant," she teased.

He chuckled quietly, and then she sensed something. Movement and rustling, and then she yelped when his warm hand touched hers. "Maybe I'm a little arrogant," he said. "But I like to think of it as confidence."

His fingers wrapped around hers, and Faith sank into the feel of them. She didn't want to fall too fast either. She needed to know Blaze in every month of the year, and she needed a lot more time with his son if they were truly going to try being a family.

And try, she did want to do.

Faith looked up from her phone when someone sat beside her on the bench. "Cash," she said right out loud. She put her arm around him and smiled. "Where's your daddy?"

"Parking," the boy said. He gave her a smile too, and Faith wasn't sure what emotions marched through her. Nervous energy for sure. She'd met Cash a little over a week ago. Blaze told her he knew they were dating; he didn't hold things back from his son.

Faith had been around him several times since then, but she and Blaze hadn't merged their Christmas celebrations. She'd spent time with her family; he'd done the same with his.

Their forced sleepover was a few nights ago, and he'd stopped by her doughnut truck twice in the two days since then. They had party plans tonight at his mansion, with his entire family. He said he wasn't sure if they'd all come, but they'd all been invited.

The church service started, but Blaze had not come in yet.

Faith leaned over and whispered, "Was it snowing hard?"

"Not bad," Cash whispered back. "But the lot was really full, and my boots are new, so Dad dropped me off." He lifted his foot slightly, and Faith admired his new cowboy boots.

"Those are amazing," she said.

Cash grinned. "Dad got them for me." He sure did seem to love his father, and Faith's heart grew a size. She glanced up to the pulpit and then at her phone. Blaze had texted, but because she kept her phone on silent during church, she hadn't heard or felt the vibration.

I'm here, but I'm just gonna hang out in the back.

She frowned, immediately rejecting that idea. Her thumbs waited above the phone, poised to respond. If only she could think of what she should say to him.

Is Cash okay with you? I can have him go sit by my momma.

Faith knew how to answer that. *He's fine,* she sent.

"This New Year holds so many possibilities," Pastor Carmichael said, and Faith lifted her head. "Some of you are ready to move forward quickly." He smiled kindly, and Faith relaxed into the bench beneath her. She did love Pastor Carmichael's messages. "You're ready to leave this year behind and see what the Lord has in store for you. But some of you are moving a little more slowly. You need time to examine the things you did this year and either leave them or take them with you into the new year."

The woman in front of her started nodding, and Faith felt a glimmer of truth in the pastor's words. She was ready to move forward. This past year had been hard for her in several ways. Hole in One had challenged her greatly, though this past month had started improving.

Blaze had come into her life, and she'd battled so much self-doubt in the past six months. She was ready to leave that behind and see if she and Blaze could build something truly lasting and wonderful.

"Both are okay," the pastor said. "If you have someone in your life who's moving slower than you, support them. If you have someone in your life who's a jet plane, let them fly. The end destination is all the same, and the journey we take to get there doesn't really matter. Does it?"

Faith wasn't sure if it did or not. She'd been taught there was a right way and a wrong way to do things. Was the pastor saying that any path was okay as long as someone...what?

She cocked her head and peered at him.

"Some people don't make too many mistakes in their life," he said. "Some do. Does God love them less? Doesn't He want us all to return to Him? Some have a long journey. Some journeys are short. Some have a lot of potholes. Some are smooth waters. If you're feeling like you're on a stormy sea, in a boat without a radio or a raft, I urge you to go to the Lord. Now. Today. He will walk over the water to rescue you."

The more he spoke, the more Faith understood. Of course every journey home to the Lord was different from another. She felt outside herself as she came to understand that her experiences this year were completely different than someone else's.

This year could've been the best year of their life. Perhaps they'd gotten married and bought a beautiful new home. Maybe they'd started a very successful business, without broken down trucks and challenges around every corner.

Her experience was not *everyone's* experience.

She looked over to Cash, who glanced at her too. She smiled at him and leaned closer. "Do you like coming to church?" she asked.

He nodded. "It's not so bad. My grandma usually brings me, and then I get to have lunch at her house after."

"Your dad doesn't like it."

Cash wore an edge in his eyes now. "He says it's not that big of a deal if you don't go to church. He can believe in God and not go to church."

"Sure," Faith whispered. She pushed Cash's hair off his forehead. "If you like it, I can bring you."

Cash simply looked at her. "You like my dad a lot."

Faith wasn't sure what to say, but she wouldn't lie about it. "Yeah," she said. "I do."

Cash had the same hard mask on his face she'd seen on Blaze's before. He was lighter than his father, but the stone in his gaze was the same. "He likes you too."

"He seems to," Faith said. She leaned closer though the pastor was probably saying things she'd like to hear. "Does that bother you?"

"I don't know," Cash said. He looked back to the pastor, and Faith straightened to do the same thing. Her phone brightened in her lap, and she looked at it.

Everly had texted, and Faith picked up her phone and smoothed down her skirt. Her friend had said, *Look at you with Blaze's son. How cute.* :)

Faith's face heated. His son didn't really like her. He didn't want his dad to be dating her. They weren't having a wonderful bonding moment.

I need to talk to you, she sent.

Anytime, Everly said. *Want to go to lunch this week?*

Yes, Faith said.

Just us? Everly asked. *I guess the wives of the brothers go out every so often. I can invite Dani, Abby, Georgia, Leigh....*

Faith could only stare at the text. She didn't belong with those women. Did she?

Abigail Ingalls—now a Young—used to run the library. Dani had moved to Coral Canyon when she married Mav, and she'd done a lot of volunteer work in the community. Georgia had a brand-new baby and owned a popular bookshop on Main Street. Leigh worked at Whiskey Mountain Lodge, and she was one who'd gotten married and moved into a big, beautiful new home this year. Oh, and she was pregnant too.

A surge of jealousy raged through Faith. Leigh Young had everything Faith wanted—and what did she have?

What could she possibly offer those women?

I can see your face, and you're freaking out, Everly said. *I won't invite them.*

Faith looked up and to her right. Everly sat one row up on the side, and their eyes met. Ev smiled, because she was the kindest person on the planet. Her long, blonde hair spilled over her shoulders, and she sat next to the formidable Trace Young. His son sat on his other side, and Faith blinked, the images of Everly, Trace, and Harry becoming her, Blaze, and Cash.

When she focused again, it wasn't her, Blaze, and Cash.

Her heartbeat flapped like a flag in a stiff wind as her mind whirred. *You don't belong.*

The voice in her head started out quiet, but it grew, and grew, and grew.

Movement on her left caught her attention, and she looked away from Everly, who'd blurred in Faith's eyes.

A strong, warm arm slid along her shoulders, and Blaze pulled her to his side. Faith melted into him, this strong, safe place where she absolutely did belong.

He pressed a kiss to her temple and looked at her. "You okay, dove?"

She couldn't speak, so she simply nodded. Everything in her head burned, and she fought tears as she leaned into him. Cash settled on his other side, and she wondered how Blaze had known when to come sit with her.

He kept his head low and his voice nearly silent as he said, "My momma asked if you wanted to come to lunch at her place today."

That made her tense. "Should I?"

"It's just her and Daddy," he said. "She's not hosting a big meal, because I'm doing that tonight for New Year's Eve."

Just Blaze's parents. She'd met several of his brothers at the wrapping party, and that had gone well enough. There were just *so many* of them.

"Okay," she said. "And I'd love for you to meet Heather and Marc too."

He nodded and focused back on the pulpit. Faith did too, but the pastor's voice washed through her head, going in one ear and out the other without any comprehension on her part. She left her phone under her leg, on silent, because she didn't need the negative voices in her head to return.

One stayed, and it wasn't exactly negative. It definitely felt like a warning though. *If you marry Blaze, you'll be one of them. A Young. And then what will you do? How will you feel?*

She didn't know the answers, and she thought of Blaze on his side of the pillow wall a couple of nights ago.

It terrifies me. I don't want this to be too fast, okay?

The sermon ended, and they stood to sing the hymn. She expected Blaze to leave, but he held his ground. She took his hand in hers, and he looked at her. In that moment, she knew she had time to get to know his family members too. Even if she was scared, she could do it—because he stood at her side.

21

Blaze didn't know what to say as Cash ran ahead to the condo door. Faith had been quiet after church, and they'd left her car in the parking lot there so she could ride in the truck with him and Cash.

Cash hadn't said much either, and overall, the day felt somber and gray—much like the sky. It had stopped snowing, and what had come down had been a skiff of flakes.

Blaze squeezed Faith's hand and looked over to her. She slowed her step in time with his. "What were you and Cash whispering about during the sermon?" He hoped he didn't sound accusatory. He wasn't trying to be. "Just curious."

"I asked him if he liked coming to church." Faith swallowed. "He said he does, and we talked a little about how you don't." She glanced down the sidewalk, where Cash waited with both hands against his grandparents' door.

"They might not be here yet, bud," he called to his son. "He's so eager all the time."

"He's eleven," Faith said with a smile. "You don't remember being eleven years old?"

"As a matter of fact," Blaze said darkly. "I don't." He didn't want to eat lunch with his parents this afternoon. He didn't want a whole mess of people in his house tonight either.

"They love doughnuts," she said fondly. "I don't think he likes me much, though."

"What?" Blaze's eyes flew back to hers. "Why not?"

"I asked him how he felt about us dating, and he said he didn't know." They came to a complete stop, and she covered his hand with her other one. "I need to, I don't know. Warm him up or something."

"Warm him up?"

"To the idea of us dating. Or maybe it's just me."

"Honey." Blaze shook his head. He'd initially thought he'd stand against the back wall for the entire sermon, but he'd seen a change in Faith's shoulders after talking to Cash. She'd been putting off some strong vibes when he'd made his son scoot over so he could sit beside her, and he hadn't been imagining that.

"What?" she challenged. "I barely know him. He barely knows me. It makes sense that he doesn't like me; he doesn't know me."

Blaze studied her, that delicious fire in her eyes, the way her freckles stuck out a little more when she got upset. Not that he wanted her to be upset. "Cash has some needs," he said slowly. "I'm doing my best with him, but I'm sure he'd love to spend more time with you."

"He would?" Faith gave a little scoff that turned into a light laugh. "What would we do?" She jerked her attention back to him, her eyes as wide as the full moon.

"What?" he asked.

"He asked me to teach him how to cook," she said. "The night we did the Stocking Stuffer wrapping. I completely forgot about it." She turned toward him as if she'd start right now.

"We both could use that lesson," Blaze said.

"It was when I brought those reindeer cupcakes," she said. "Maybe he wants to learn how to bake." She started walking again, and Blaze fell into step with her.

"Will you hate me if I say I don't want to learn how to bake?" he asked.

She giggled now, the flirtatious side of her returning. "No, cowboy," she said. "I can't even imagine these big hands in the kitchen."

"Are you makin' fun of my hands?"

She simply kept laughing as she shook her head. They had to wait a couple of minutes in the frigid temperatures before his parents arrived, and Momma seemed to be in quite the mood.

"Sorry, sorry," she said, bustling past them all to unlock the condo. "That church needs a new parking lot. Getting out of there after a meeting is insane." She shot him a disgruntled look before she went inside. Daddy waited for everyone to go ahead of him, saying nothing.

Blaze wisely kept his mouth shut too. Once they'd all entered the condo and sealed out the winter weather, he helped Faith with her coat and then took her hand in his again. Momma had left the living room and kitchen, presumably to go change her clothes, and Blaze figured he could introduce Faith to Daddy first.

"Dad," he said. "This is Faith Cromwell." He squeezed her hand. "She owns Hole in One, and she's my girlfriend." The words rolled out of his mouth pretty easily, and Blaze couldn't remember the last woman he'd considered a girlfriend.

"It's wonderful to meet you." Dad wore a big smile as he reached to shake Faith's hand.

"My daddy," Blaze said as Cash started playing music on the old record player his father had. He gave his son a look, but Cash wasn't paying any attention. "Jerry."

Faith shook his hand, her smile etched across her lips. She was gorgeous, and Blaze couldn't help thinking it. She wore a black pencil skirt that swelled around her hips and then narrowed at the waist of her pale blue blouse. She made his mouth water in every single way, and Blaze schooled his thoughts before Momma returned.

After all, she'd always been able to read him like an open book, and the last thing he needed was a scolding in front of Faith.

Dad moved into the living room to help Cash with the record player, and Blaze's gaze skimmed Faith's. She seemed comfortable, but Daddy wouldn't be the one to say anything embarrassing. Momma usually didn't either, but Blaze suspected there was a reason she'd invited him and Faith for lunch today when she wasn't cooking for anyone else.

She returned to the kitchen in a pair of black slacks and the same blouse she'd been wearing at church. She sighed as a smile formed on her face. "Sorry about that. That skirt was killing me."

Faith grinned. "They can do that sometimes."

"Yours is lovely," Momma said, actually reaching out to brush her fingers along the fabric. "Just beautiful." She looked back into Faith's eyes. "It's been a long, long time since Blaze had anyone special in his life."

"Here we go," he said right out loud. "Momma, we're leaving if you start this."

"How long?" Faith asked.

He gaped at her. "Faith."

She grinned and patted his chest. "Just kidding. I know all about Blaze's past romances."

Momma's eyebrows couldn't have gotten higher on her face without them falling right off. "You do?"

"Sure," Faith said easily. She released his hand and moved with Momma into the kitchen.

"I didn't even introduce you." He followed along like a lost puppy. "Momma, this is Faith Cromwell." He muscled his way between them and glared at her. "I like her a lot, okay? Can you not say anything that will drive her away?"

"I thought you invited her to the family New Year's Eve party," Momma said.

"I did," he said at the same time Faith said, "He did."

"Then she'll see it all then." Momma turned and opened the fridge, completely unworried about Blaze. He'd never scared her the way he had some of his brothers, and he really wished that were different right now.

"We're great," Blaze said in his family's defense. "A little big. A little loud. That's all."

"A lot big and a lot loud," Daddy said.

"Hey." Momma faced him with a package of ground beef in her hands. "You're the one who wanted all the kids."

"*I'm* the one who wanted all the kids?" Daddy seemed made of shock. "That is so not true. *You* wanted a girl, and we kept trying for one until we had to give up."

"Oh, brother," Blaze muttered under his breath. He'd heard this argument before. "Can we not do this now? You wanted a girl. He wanted you to be happy. You didn't get a girl, so you decided to pray for granddaughters."

He looked at Faith, who did seem a bit worried now. "Took her a while to get one of those too. She got Bryce, Harry, and Cash before Otis finally gave her Joey. He's been her favorite ever since."

"That is *not* true," Momma said, slapping the meat against his chest. Blaze covered it with his hand so it wouldn't fall to the floor.

He chuckled and nodded. "It's true. Otis is a total Mommas-boy."

"No more than Mav," Momma said. "At least he keeps me updated." She peered past Blaze to Faith. "Did you know he's the one who told me about you two?" She zeroed in on Blaze again, her eyes sharp as knives. "Not Blaze himself, and I didn't even know until Thursday night, when I called him to make sure he was okay during the blackout."

"You didn't call me to make sure I was okay," Blaze said. "Because I'm not the favorite."

Momma stepped closer to him, and in a condo-sized kitchen, it felt menacing. She certainly didn't have the room to do it.

"Cecily," Daddy said.

"I didn't call you," Momma said slowly. "Because Mav told me you were sleeping over at Faith's. And I was like, 'Faith? Faith who?'"

"Cecily," Daddy said again. "Enough. The man's not a boy."

Blaze's heartbeat bumped against his breastbone the same way it had when he'd seen this glare of his mother's in the past. A shiver skipped down his spine, and he cleared his throat. "Nothing happened, Momma, if that's what you're worried about."

Faith shook her head in agreement. "Just sleeping. Your son has a bad back. It was cold; the power was out for hours."

"She has a fireplace in her bedroom," Blaze said. "And owns about fifteen hundred pillows."

"Oh, come on," Faith said. "I think it's only fourteen hundred."

He looked at her, glad she was on his side in this. "I might be able to agree that there were only fourteen hundred pillows between us." They faced his mother together. "See? And now she's here, and you're acting like I broke the law or something."

Momma softened, and Blaze grinned at her. "Besides, we all know *I'm* the favorite son." He wrapped his momma in a hug, because he knew keenly he wasn't the favorite. Trace beat him by a mile, and Tex had the lead over all of them. No matter what she said, Momma did love Otis a little more because he'd given her the first female Young in decades, but Blaze wasn't going to argue about it today.

"Momma." He stepped back and indicated his beautiful girlfriend. "This is Faith, my precious dove. Faith, my momma, Cecily. I'm sure you can see where I get some of my fire."

"Just some of it," she said.

"Blaze is the best of me and Jerry," Momma said. "Trust me when I say, you do *not* want to see that man angry." She gave him a smile, which he returned, though she'd ignored his warnings twice.

"I can attest to that," Blaze said, shooting his dad a smile so he'd know he was kidding. He'd been a ruthless taskmaster on the ranch where they'd lived as Blaze had grown up. But he'd been a very, very good father.

He never said more than he needed to, and Blaze appreciated not getting lectured. Momma could do that for hours, so they complimented each other well.

"It's my pleasure to meet you both," Faith said.

"Is your family in the area?" Momma asked. She took the ground beef from Blaze, and he edged out of the kitchen. He didn't think he should take up room where he wasn't wanted, and Momma wouldn't ask Faith anything she couldn't handle.

He glanced over to Cash, who sat on the couch with his phone. Blaze joined him and covered the screen with his hand. "I want a couple of minutes," he said.

Cash looked up. "What?"

Oh, so he had some attitude today. Blaze raised his eyebrows, and Cash deflated. "Sorry. What can I help you with, dear father?"

Blaze grinned at him, but this conversation wouldn't be easy or full of rainbows. "You told Faith you didn't know how you felt about us dating?"

Cash's face turned white. "No. Sort of. No."

"What did you say?"

His son's eyes moved between both of Blaze's. "I don't know."

"Mm, yeah, try again."

"She was whispering during church," Cash said like such a thing should be a crime. "She asked me if I liked going to church. I said I did. She said you didn't, and that she could bring me if I wanted to go."

"Okay," Blaze said. "And?"

"I don't want to go with her," Cash said. "If you're not going to go, then I'll go with Grandma and Grandpa." He looked over to the kitchen and back at his device. "I don't know what I said after that. Something about you liking her maybe. And she said she liked you, and...I think that's when she asked me if that bothered me."

"And does it?"

"I don't know."

Blaze tried not to sigh, but he couldn't hold all of it back. "We talked about why I'm dating."

"I'm fine with you dating."

"So you don't like her." Blaze frowned. What would he do if his son didn't like Faith? He was steadily falling in love with her.

"I'm sure she's fine, Dad," Cash said. "I don't know." He mumbled the last sentence and practically pinned his chin to his chest. "Can I play my game, please? As soon as lunch is ready, Grandma won't let me, and Bryson is online right now."

Blaze pulled his hand back to his own lap. "All right," he said. "But maybe you just need to spend more time with Faith."

"Sure," Cash said, but Blaze recognized the tone of disinterest. He wouldn't argue, because then Blaze couldn't be upset and the conversation would end. Irritation spiked through him, but Blaze got to his feet and left his son to his video game.

In the kitchen, Faith cooked with Momma, and even Daddy laughed and talked with them. It was impossible not to like Faith; she charmed everyone she came in contact with.

Except, apparently, his son.

"If someone rings the doorbell one more time...." Blaze said later that night. "Just come the heck in already." Four of his brothers had already arrived—Gabe, Morris, Luke, and Jem. The last one was a cop-out, because Jem lived there, but Blaze counted him anyway.

There were nine boys in the Young family, and if Blaze didn't count them, he wouldn't know if they'd all arrived or not.

Tex and Otis were both up in the air, but Trace walked in with two grocery bags in his hands, Everly at his side, and Harry right behind them. "Hot chicken dip," he said. Everly slid the baking dish onto the counter, and Trace put the bags of crackers and chips beside it. "Looks like you already have a feast."

"Was there any doubt about that?" Blaze asked. He watched his brother for his reaction, but Trace didn't give him one. He'd always been smooth, calm water while Blaze had been one of those massive, violent whirlpools, pulling everyone and everything down under the surface.

He tamped against the urge to say something about how his siblings couldn't show up to a party without something, though Blaze had not asked anyone to bring anything. Gabe and Morris had shown up together, and they'd brought a fruit and cheese platter and a veggie tray.

Luke had entered with his daughter's hand in one of his and two cases of soda pop in the other. Easy, but still something.

Blaze and Jem had purchased catering for tonight—a series of heavy appetizers. An apricot-glazed meatball, miniature beef wellingtons, goat cheese and fig sliders, and cream of potato soup.

The catering company had come and set it all up in his house, and the island practically groaned under the weight of the food.

"Where's Faith?" Trace asked.

"She hasn't arrived yet."

"No wonder you're in a bad mood." Trace grinned at him.

Everly shot Blaze a nervous look. "Trace, baby. You left your guitar in the truck. Go get it and leave your brother alone."

"Yeah," Blaze barked at Trace, a completely juvenile thing to do. His nerves had frayed twenty minutes ago when Cash had gotten in an argument with Cole over something stupid.

He tossed a dark look at his son, then refocused it on Trace as his brother chuckled and said, "He's a big boy, Ev. He doesn't need you to protect him." He still left to go get his guitar, and

Blaze watched him until the arched doorway leading into the foyer swallowed him.

"He might need you to protect him," Blaze grumbled. "If he's going to act like that."

"What's eating you?" Everly picked up a baby carrot and put it on a plate. She glanced up after a few grape tomatoes joined the party on the plastic plate.

"Nothing," he said.

She cocked her head and appraised him.

"Don't." He stepped around her so he wouldn't have to bear the weight of her gaze. He liked Trace's fiancé a lot, but that didn't mean he had to answer to her. He wasn't even sure why he didn't want to be at this party tonight.

"We're here," Mav called, and he had the good sense not to ring the doorbell. He herded his kids inside, and Dani entered behind them all—with Faith.

"Faith." Blaze was aware of how her name fell from his mouth, almost in awe. Almost like he was shocked she'd shown up. He moved toward her, the sight of her soothing his ragged soul in ways no one else could.

Mav didn't have anything in his hands, but Dani carried a tin of shortbread cookies. She smiled at Blaze and lifted them. "Your favorite. Should I put them in the office?"

"I can take them," he said. "Thank you, Dani." He swept a kiss along her cheek. She'd been the first woman to come into their lives after all of the divorce and sadness in their family. She'd been nothing but kind and accepting to him and Jem, the outcasts of the family, and they both loved her.

He took hold of Faith's hand and detoured her into the

office too. She giggled as she stumbled after him. "What are you doing?"

"If these go out on the counter," he said, ignoring the loud round of laughter from the other room. "Luke will eat them all in a couple of hours." He put the tin of cookies on his desk. "He loves them more than me."

He turned and took Faith into his arms. "I missed you."

"It's been three hours," she said, smiling up at him.

"Yeah, and I missed you in those three hours." He leaned down and touched his lips to hers. He'd told her he wanted to go really slow, and he did. But that was during the scary things, like sleeping in her bed when they weren't married. That was when he had to think about telling her about the things he'd been repenting of. That was when he wasn't kissing her.

When he kissed her...Blaze wanted nothing more than to speed things up. He minded his manners, however, and he pulled away after only a minute.

"Mm." Faith leaned against him, her eyes still closed. "I don't know if I'll make it to midnight, Mister Young."

"No?"

"I have to get up early to get up to the lodge. The Whittakers want breakfast doughnuts at nine-thirty."

It took her over two hours to make her doughnuts from start to finish. "Do you want me to come help you unload?"

"Absolutely," she said. "If you can."

"I can." He could, and he wanted to. He loved the merging of those two things, because then it didn't feel like work.

"You'll have people here late." She twisted as the front door opened again, letting in a blast of cold air, along with Momma and Daddy. Daddy carried Melissa in his arms, which meant Tex and Abby wouldn't be far behind.

They entered too, but none of them turned to look into the dark office where Blaze stood with Faith. "This can be our hiding place," he whispered against her ear.

She turned back to him, and Blaze took the opportunity to kiss her one more time. If she wasn't going to be here when the clock struck midnight, this might be what he got.

"Happy New Year," he whispered against her lips.

"Happy New Year, cowboy."

22

J em kept his smile on his face and a red plastic cup of Christmas cheer in his hand for the first hour after his brothers started arriving. Blaze disappeared into his office with Faith for several long minutes after Trace had come in, and for whatever reason, that annoyed Jem.

The moment Blaze reappeared, his hand secured in Faith's and her lip gloss all over his mouth, Jem knew why.

He'd felt abandoned by his brother for those several minutes. He'd found a corner of Blaze's massive living room, and he'd barricaded himself there by putting his kids and Gabe between him and everyone else.

Morris, Gabe, Luke, and Jem were the four youngest boys, and they'd shared a bond once the older boys—Blaze included—started leaving home. Of course, then Luke had joined Country Quad, and Jem had gone off to join Blaze in Las Vegas, and the family had splintered.

Jem still felt those splinters from time to time. For one, Luke didn't ever get too close to Gabe. They'd made up after Gabe had literally called Luke's ex-wife a cheater and implied that his daughter might not be his, but just because they could stand to be in the same room with each other didn't mean they liked one another.

Jem knew that, as Chanel had kept their marriage together for months after she couldn't stand to be in the same room as him—and that had come long after she'd stopped liking him.

He pushed his ex-wife out of his head. This was the first New Year's Eve without her, and he'd survive. Blaze hadn't wanted to have this party, but he seemed to know Jem needed it.

It would be better with a lot of booze, but Jem never, ever wanted to go through the alcohol withdrawals again, so he'd vowed never to touch the stuff again.

If someone made it past his kids, they wouldn't make it past Gabe. The man put off some serious *don't-mess-with-me-tonight* vibes, which was just fine with Jem.

Leigh, Morris's wife, had brought the punch, and she kept bringing around trays with refills, the smile on her face making it seem like she was really enjoying herself. Her brother sat next to Jem as well, and Denzel was an added barrier Jem needed.

He wasn't even sure why. He didn't want Momma's questions, though her eyes had found him the moment she'd entered. He didn't want to deal with Tex, who rightly needed a lot of support right now too. Jem felt like a poor excuse for a man, but he needed his own time to heal before he could be someone else's source for strength.

Tex had Trace, anyway, and neither of them had ever needed Jem much.

"Daddy," Cole drawled, and Jem lowered his plastic cup. "Grandma has cake pops. Can me and Rosie have one?"

"Sure thing, little man." Jem would probably regret saying yes to Cole and Rosie all the time, but since he'd moved back into Blaze's basement, it was the only word Jem seemed to be able to say to his kids.

The guilt he carried for the three months he'd attempted to live on his own assaulted him every day, every minute. He couldn't imagine telling them no or inflicting any more unhappiness on them, so he simply said yes. All the time.

"Daddy," Liesl said, toddling over too.

Gabe gave her a frown. "One, Liesl," he said. "Just one, okay?" He twisted to look at their mother. "Momma, she can have one."

Liesl didn't seem upset by this limitation, and she happily ran back over to the kitchen counter. She tugged on Dani's pants, and the woman bent to pick her up. Jem had to look away, because he didn't like the jealousy that rose through his whole body.

Mav, of course, was a far better man than Jem, and he absolutely deserved a woman like Dani in his life. Someone good and kind and who wanted to be a mother. In the beginning, Chanel had been that person.

Life had changed them. Two small children had changed them. Jem's success in the rodeo had changed him.

"You hidin' over here?" Blaze asked, leaning over the back of the couch where Gabe sat.

"I'm right here," Gabe griped at him as he leaned forward.

"I'm not even touching you," Blaze fired back. His eyes left Jem's for a moment, but they came right back.

"I'm not hiding," Jem said, his voice a touch cool. "I just don't want to be in the center of the room." He nodded to Faith, who gave him a kind smile. How Blaze had gotten her to go out with him, Jem did not know. He didn't want to ask, in case he caught Blaze at a bad time or implied that Faith was too good for him.

Blaze already felt like that about himself, and Jem couldn't understand why. His older brother had a heart of gold and always had. Sure, he'd done a few things here and there that would make their mother blush and scold, but he'd never really done anything *cruel*. Not on purpose, at least.

"Fair enough." Blaze faced the rest of the house. "I don't either."

"It's your party, cowboy," Faith said. "Come on. We can go around one time, and then come back over here." She gave Jem a quick, knowing look and tugged on Blaze's arm. "Good to see you too, Gabe. Denzel."

"Ma'am," Denzel said, tipping his hat at her. Gabe merely grunted.

"What is with you?" Jem asked. "She's nice." He glared at Gabe, because while Blaze hadn't expressly told Jem of his feelings for Faith, he also wore everything on his sleeve for those who knew how to look.

And Jem knew how—and Blaze liked Faith a whole heckuva lot, and there would be more punches thrown if he thought for even a second that Gabe wasn't being nice to Faith. One single second.

Gabe just glared back at him, but Jem had traveled with Blaze for years. He could handle anyone's glare, for as long as they glared it.

GABRIEL YOUNG TOLD HIMSELF FOR THE FIFTIETH TIME that day that he should've taken Liesl home that afternoon. He'd been in Coral Canyon for a couple of weeks now, and he wasn't sure it was healthy for him.

No, he told himself. *You're fine here. You just need your own place.*

He owned and operated a father's rights firm in Jackson Hole, but over the course of this past year, he'd picked up over a dozen clients right here in Coral Canyon. Not just his brothers either.

He'd closed his firm in Jackson Hole for the holidays, and he'd come to stay with Morris and Leigh for a couple of weeks to sniff out the possibility of opening a second office here. Even if he had somewhere to work twice a week, it would be better than the back and forth he'd been doing.

Liesl wasn't in school yet, and if he could get one of the new townhomes going in just south of Main Street, he'd have an office on the first floor and living quarters on the second and third. He could easily work with her there, as she was a good little girl and did almost anything he said.

If that didn't work, his parents lived here, and surely

Momma could help with babysitting, a luxury Gabe had never enjoyed in Jackson. Four of his brothers also had wives now, and they all had kids they stayed home to take care of.

Kind of. Georgia hadn't until she and Otis had adopted OJ only a week ago, and Gabe didn't really know what she was planning to do with her bookshop now that she had a newborn. He wasn't besties with Otis by any means, but he could at least talk to him without feeling like his skin might flake off from the withering gaze of his brother.

Whenever Luke looked his way, Gabe thought he might dry to dust on the spot. That was entirely his fault, and he'd talked to Morris about apologizing to Luke again. Morris had said to give it some time. Luke was still maturing, and being Corrine's full-time caregiver and parent had done a world of good for him.

He still possessed the hottest temper out of all of them, in Gabe's opinion, and he only lost to Blaze by a fraction of a point.

"Do you not like Faith?" Jem asked, refusing to drop the subject.

Gabe got to his feet with a hefty sigh. "Of course I like Faith. I like Faith a whole lot." He walked away then, knowing Jem wouldn't like it. He *had* been hiding in the corner, despite what he'd told Blaze, and he'd been using Gabe as a shield.

He joined the fray at Blaze's twelve-foot-long island, and Morris easily made room for him. Since his twin had become the manager for Country Quad, he'd gotten his light back. Perhaps that honor belonged to Leigh and Eric. No matter what, Gabe felt like he existed in shades of gray and black while Morris poured white light from every pore in his body.

"You're not having enough fun." Morris grinned at him. "Tex brought the dice."

"Oh, brother." Gabe watched as the oldest of them all—Tex —tossed the dice onto the granite.

"Nine," Mav yelled. A cheer went up, at least among the Youngs. An odd number above six meant Tex got to have another dessert, and as a ten-year-old, that was a coveted slice of his momma's chocolate rolled cake. An even number above six meant he had to skip his turn, and anything six or below meant he had to give a treat back.

The Youngs hadn't had much money growing up, but they'd always had a pair of dice and a mother who could bake. Now, the Young family had men who could buy whatever they wanted, Gabe included, and multiple women who could bake. Out of all of the brothers, Gabe would label himself the best cook, because he actually did it.

The band members never had, and that included Mav. Morris had learned a few things in the past couple of years since Eric had come into his life, and Gabe would say the same for Luke. The rodeo brothers lived out of trailers, driver's seats, and hotels. No cooking necessary.

Since he'd been taking care of his daughter since the day she'd been born, and he actually liked putting together meals, he was definitely the best at it.

He found Liesl perched on Dani's hip, and he couldn't stop the smile that came to his face at the sight of his little girl. He loved her with everything he had inside him, and he always had. He worked the way he did so he could go home earlier at night to her. So that they could have the kind of life he wanted to provide for her.

So that he could show her that she didn't need a mother and a father—he could do and be both.

That last reason stood on shaky legs, however, and Gabe knew it. He knew Liesl needed a mother. Simply the way she'd been glowing around Leigh and Dani in the past couple of weeks told him that.

He was terribly lonely too, isolated as he was in Jackson Hole. He'd be lying if he ever told anyone that wasn't a reason he was looking to open a second office here. If he moved here, he'd have a host of family to spend time with, literally at the drop of a text.

Sure, the band was going on tour again this summer, but Momma and Daddy would still be here. Blaze and Jem too. Mav and Dani weren't going anywhere.

No, it only felt like Gabe was drifting out at sea, watching from a dinghy while the rest of his brothers found their tropical islands and set sail toward happily-ever-after.

"Otis is here," someone said, and the dice game came to an abrupt halt. All talking and laughing silenced almost instantly, and Gabe looked toward the front door.

He couldn't see it from here, but he definitely saw Otis and Georgia standing up on the step, not having committed to coming completely into the house from the foyer. She carried the baby, and Otis held Joey's hand.

No one else moved. Not even the house breathed, and Gabe's heart went out to both Tex and Otis simultaneously.

OTIS HAD THE DISTINCT FEELING THAT HE AND GEORGIA should've stayed home. They'd hemmed and hawed over coming to this party, and this stare-fest in near silence was the reason why.

"I shaved, right?" He leaned toward Georgia, who'd commented on the way here that it felt strange to be out of the house as a family of four.

"Daddy, can I go see what Beth and Boston are doing?" Joey tugged her hand free, and Otis let her go without giving her a verbal *yes*. She didn't need to ask to play with her cousins anyway. He couldn't even see Boston or Beth at the moment.

Only Tex.

"Hey, brother." Blaze came out of nowhere and up the single step to where Otis and Georgia stood. He grinned down at baby OJ and then at Georgia. "He's lookin' so good." He kissed the baby real quick, then Georgia's cheek, and then he took Otis into a big, rodeo-champion hug. "It's good to see you. You're both still alive." He laughed and stepped back.

With Blaze at his side, Otis felt like less of a pariah. "All right," he called to the house. "I think you'll want to line up to see this baby. He's that cute, and y'all are gonna smother him if you don't." He stepped down into the house, and Georgia went with him.

Abby took her straight into her arms, and Otis's emotions wavered. Georgia had worried that this baby would change her friendship and bond with Abby, but it sure didn't look like it had. Tex stood at the counter, and Otis went over to him.

"Hey." He hugged Tex, who embraced him back. "I missed the dice game?"

"We just started," Tex said. He'd been over to the house since OJ's birth. Both he and Abby had, with Melissa. Bryce had not come, and Otis didn't see him here tonight either.

He pulled away from his brother. "Where's Bryce tonight?" He refrained from teasing about the young man having a hot date with someone.

Tex cleared his throat, and that wasn't good. Otis swept his gaze past Daddy, whose jaw clenched, and Luke, who wore a stone-faced look. So they all knew something he didn't.

Trace stepped between him and Tex. "Bryce left Coral Canyon," he said. "A few days ago." He hugged Otis too.

"He's in Nashville," Tex said.

"What?" Otis backed away from Trace again, though his brother wasn't done hugging him. "Is he going to do a solo album?"

"I doubt it," Tex said. "He just said that's where he was."

Children's laughter sounded at the table behind him, and Otis adjusted his stance so he could see the kids. He did love the kids in this family so very much, and he hadn't anticipated the rift that would come with him and Georgia adopting Bryce's baby. Had he, he wouldn't have done it. He and Georgia would've found a different way to become parents together.

"What's he doing there?" Otis asked.

"I'm not really sure," Tex said evasively, and whether he didn't really know or he didn't want to say, Otis couldn't tell.

"How's fatherhood?" Daddy asked.

"I've been a father before," Otis said, immediately regretting it. Daddy didn't let any emotion show on his face. In fact, he picked up another chip and dunked it in a creamy, white dip. "I mean, it's great." He reached up and scrubbed his hand down his face.

"You shaved," Luke said.

"Don't make it sound like a crime," Otis said. "There's plenty of time for it to regrow before tour."

"It has to regrow before tour," Morris said, ever the manager.

Coming here had definitely been a mistake, but Otis couldn't just walk out now. He and Georgia had agreed to come for an hour and then go home. No one would expect them to stay until midnight, not with a newborn and a ten-year-old.

"I'm aware of the tour contract we signed," Otis said coolly. He was also aware of Gabe's eyes on him, and he walked away from the band circle and toward the other end of the island. He picked up a plate as he went, hoping that told his brothers he simply wanted some food that wasn't by them.

Problem was, the only thing down by Gabe was the veggie tray, and Otis would never gravitate toward that. "Howdy, Gabe," he said anyway.

"Heya, Otis." He'd also been over to the house with Morris and their families, and Otis had appreciated all of the support he and Georgia had gotten.

"Are they still staring?" Otis kept loading carrots and cauliflower onto his plate.

"Yeah," Gabe said. "Yep." He started to laugh. "I think it might be from how many veggies you're taking, though."

Otis finally stopped. "I didn't want this to be a thing."

"It's new," Gabe said. "Of course it's going to be a thing."

He looked at the brother who'd helped him make sure every I was dotted and every T crossed when it came to the adoption. "When is it not going to be new?"

"Never," Gabe said. "Because that little boy is going to grow up, and every step of the way, Tex is going to see Bryce in him."

Pure misery flowed through Otis. "Not helping, Gabe."

"It'll get easier," Gabe said without missing a beat. "But it's always going to be new—at least for him."

"Go see Uncle Otis," Dani said, and he barely managed to drop his plate before she slid Liesl into his arms.

"Uncle Otis." She squished his cheeks together and grinned at him. The four-year-old radiated innocence and goodness, and Otis smiled at her.

"Hi, baby Liesl." He grinned over to Gabe too. "When are you and your daddy goin' home?"

"Tomorrow," they said together, and Otis got the impression that for Gabe, the day couldn't come fast enough.

"Otis, this baby is perfection," Abby said as she squeezed her way between him and Gabe. "Look at him, Gabe. Isn't he so beautiful?"

"He's amazing," Gabe said, and Otis caught a hint of wistfulness in his younger brother's voice—and his eyes. When Gabe lifted his again, that all disappeared. "Come on, girlie," he said, taking Liesl from Otis. "It's time to go potty."

"I don't need to go," she complained, but Gabe took her and left anyway.

Otis tucked his hands into his pockets, just in case he thought putting one of the veggies he'd taken in his mouth was a good idea. "How's Bryce for real?" he asked almost under his breath.

Abby didn't look away from the baby. "He's hurting, Otis, but he's fine."

Otis pressed his teeth together, like maybe if he did that hard enough, he could squeeze all the injustices out of the world. "And Tex?"

"Tex is amazing." She looked up at him then. "Aren't you, baby?"

"Aren't I what?" Tex asked. He stepped to Otis's other side and put his arm around his shoulders. "You and Georgia seem real happy." He smiled over to OJ, and Otis didn't detect any malice or unrest in his older brother. Maybe it really would just be awkward for a minute or two, and then things would blow over.

"We are," Otis said. He drew in a big breath. He had to tour with Tex in only six short months, and in the past, Bryce had always come with him. "I asked Abby how you were doing for real. That's why she said you were amazing." He glanced at her, noting the sharpness in her eyes now. "So I guess I just want to know if that's really true."

TRACE YOUNG WATCHED TEX AND OTIS AT THE OPPOSITE end of the counter. He didn't like the situation, not one little bit. Tex had asked him to act as a bit of a buffer between him and Otis, and because Trace had the grace of an ox, he'd done it poorly.

Still, he wanted to be useful to Tex if he needed him. Right now, it didn't look like he did.

"Dad," Harry said, but Trace didn't look away from Otis and Tex.

"Mm?"

"Sarah's almost here. I'm going to go wait for her outside, okay?"

"Okay." He was honestly surprised Otis and Georgia had come. He'd been over to Otis's once since Christmas Eve, and they hadn't left the house since they'd brought their baby home. They had no reason to, as Georgia had employees running her bookshop, and Otis could work out from a treadmill in his house.

Trace loved the freedom to do whatever he wanted when they weren't working on an album, and he mourned the day school would start again. Ev's teaching schedule would go back to normal next week. Harry would be back at school on Thursday. Life marched on, whether he wanted it to or not.

Right now, he did, because every day brought him closer to the day when Everly Avery would stand across the aisle from him and become his wife.

"You're staring at them," she said now, and that broke Trace's concentration

"Yeah."

"Your son just went outside in the sub-arctic temperatures."

Trace's gaze flew to the front door. "What? Why would he do that?"

"He said you said it was okay if he waited for Sarah outside." Her eyebrows went up, then her smile curved her mouth. Around them, the party had carried on, thankfully. Georgia stood insulated in a group with Leigh, Dani, Faith, and Blaze.

"That boy," Trace said. "He waited until I was preoccupied."

"He's not stupid." Ev tucked her arm through his. "It doesn't matter if Sarah's here. Look around. Who's missing Harry right now?" She actually gestured to the room, and Trace followed her hand.

No one. No one was missing Harry right now, because Bryce wasn't here. "Cash," he said anyway. The boy sat at the dining room table with Joey, Boston, and Beth, and he didn't seem to be unhappy about it. As Trace's eyes landed on the kids there, they all burst out laughing.

"Sure looks like it," Ev said dryly.

"If you have all the answers, why'd you ask me?" He gave her a dark look. "It's a *family* party."

"Faith is here, and she's not family."

"She's dating Blaze."

"And Sarah is dating Harry," Ev said. "No one will care."

Trace knew that, and he didn't want to say *he* cared. Sarah had come over for Christmas Day pie, and that was all, but Harry had texted her an astronomical amount that day. They'd spent time together every day over the winter break. In that regard, Trace couldn't wait for school to start up again.

"Come dance with me," she said, and she led him out of the kitchen. He didn't protest, but they couldn't have a private lesson the way they had in the past. Blaze's house was big, but that meant it was one huge room.

She led him over to the mouth of the hallway that led back to bedrooms, turned, and stepped easily into his arms. A touch of nervousness sat in her gaze as she looked at him, and then she eased herself into his chest. The anxiety inside Trace melted away, and while Ev normally let him lead, tonight, she kept him swaying back and forth, back and forth, never turning him so he could see the rest of the party.

Holiday music started to play, and Trace twisted his head to look around him. Morris and Leigh now danced nearby, as did Momma and Daddy.

"You started something, Miss Everly," he drawled.

She only smiled at him, and Trace couldn't imagine a better year than one with her in it. He leaned down and touched his nose to hers. "I love you, my Ev."

"I love you too, Trace." She drew in a big breath. "But I'm going to have to cut this short, because there's a few other men here who need a dance partner."

Before he could protest, she stepped out of his arms and over to the back of one of the couches. She extended her hand toward Jem, who looked at her like she'd turned into a frightening monster.

"Come on, Mister Young," she insisted in that playful way she had. "I see you lurking in the corner here, and I won't stand for it."

"Ev," Trace started when he saw Jem's face.

"I'll dance with you," Denzel said, and he labored to get to his feet.

"Perfect," Everly said. "And get yourself ready, Jem. I'm comin' back for you."

288

"He'll dance with me," Faith said, and Trace marveled at these women who'd come to this family. "Won't you, Jem?"

Blaze hovered a step behind her, pure stoicism on his face. Jem looked at him, and then Faith. He swallowed. "Yes, ma'am," he said as he got to his feet. "I'll dance with you."

Trace looked at Blaze. "That leaves me and you, buddy." He patted Blaze's chest, glad his brother had started to smile.

"I don't think I can, Trace," Blaze said. "I have to dance with Miss Rosie here." He swept Rosie up off her feet, and the little girl squealed in delight.

Trace grinned and got out of the way of everyone dancing, including Ev and Denzel, who were both laughing as he passed them. He joined Tex in the kitchen, but Abby had gone to stand beside Gabe.

Luke danced with his daughter, both of them smiling. Mav danced with Dani, and Otis had Georgia in his arms, both of them with their eyes closed and barely moving.

"You don't want to dance with Abby?" Trace asked.

"I'm kind of enjoying this from here," Tex said, his smile soft and genuine as he took in the couples dancing before him.

Trace looked again, and suddenly, a door in his mind opened. A sense of family and camaraderie existed here that didn't anywhere else in the world. There were men and women dancing who didn't love one another, those who did, and uncles and nieces. No matter who swayed with who, they belonged here.

Trace wished with everything inside him that Bryce could be here right now to see this. To feel it. *Lord, bless him to be safe*

289

this year, he prayed. *Bless him to know how much we miss him and love him. Bless him.*

He ended the last sentence there, because he couldn't think of anything more than that.

Abby turned back and brought OJ to Tex. "I'm going to dance with Gabe." She stretched up and kissed Tex's cheek, and then left him with his grandson.

Tex gazed down at the baby, and Trace had never seen such a look of wonder on his brother's face. Trace patted his shoulder and faded into the background, because it was clear Tex needed a moment to himself.

TEX HADN'T HELD HIS GRANDSON UNTIL NOW. WHEN HE and Abby went to visit Otis and Georgia, *she* held the baby. He loved the boy from afar.

Now, there was no afar. He didn't want to see his son's features in the little boy's nose or the way his eyes tracked something only he could see. Tex wanted to absorb the child for who he was, and as he did, the fractures and fissures in his chest widened.

Tears pressed behind his eyes, and then out of them. He didn't care. He held a choice spirit straight from heaven, and he loved this baby with every fiber of his heart. Just like he loved Melissa, he loved OJ. They did come from him, after all.

He didn't dare look up and take in his brothers dancing with their loved ones. That seemed to be happening in another world now, a completely different universe. Still, he knew enough people would be looking his way as soon as the song ended, so he slowly rotated, turning his back on the party.

Now, it really was him and OJ in their own pocket of reality. "Hey, buddy," he murmured to the baby, and the boy's eyes took a moment to come to his. "Hey. It's Uncle Tex." He didn't stutter or stroke over those words. They were simply true.

This was Otis's baby, and Tex knew it deep in his core.

Wailing started in his gut, because if Bryce had stayed in town, he'd know it too. He'd know that Tex was going to be okay with Otis raising the child. He'd know that he'd heal from having to give him up. He'd just *know* so much more, because he'd be able to *live it* instead of agonize over what-ifs.

Nothing Tex had said to Bryce had convinced him to return to Coral Canyon or Montana. In fact, in the past day or so, Tex had the very real feeling that his texts and calls and conversations with Bryce were pushing him further away, not bringing him closer.

"You're such a good boy," Tex cooed to the baby. "Aren't you? Yes, you are." He smiled so hard at OJ, he felt sure his face would crack. If Abby had noticed he never held OJ, she hadn't mentioned it to him. Neither had Otis or Georgia.

Someone opened the fridge on his left, and Tex looked over to Trace. "Take my picture with him, would you?"

Only a smidge of surprise crossed Trace's face, and then he took out his phone. Tex lifted baby OJ, pressing his face against the tiny boy's.

"Smile," Trace said, as if Tex could stop. He tapped and a false clicking sound filled the air. He grinned at his phone and said, "Got it. You two are cute together."

"That's because I'm already his favorite uncle." Tex settled the baby back into his arms properly and leaned down to kiss him. OJ's eyelids fluttered as Tex got close, and it took him an extra beat to get them open again. He was only a week old, so still very much a newborn, and his tiny mouth turned into a perfect oval as he yawned.

Tex chuckled, so much love filling him. Love washed out all the bad that had been lingering inside Tex. Love erased hurt. Love made hard things easier to bear.

He'd been afraid to love this baby, but he wasn't anymore. No, love made the situation less tense, not more.

"All right," Momma said, and Tex looked up. "Can I have a turn with him?"

"Of course." Tex eased the infant into her arms, being careful with his head as he did. When he turned around again, he found the couples on the dance floor had split up and moved on. He had no idea when that had happened, and no one looked his way.

Until Abby did.

She wore her love for him openly, as it was colored with concern. He gestured for her to come over to him, and she wrapped up her conversation with Leigh and Dani and headed his way.

He drew in a deep breath of her hair as she moved into his arms, and Tex started to dance with her right there in their corner of the kitchen.

"Are you okay?" she whispered.

"Yes." He let his eyes drift closed. "With you, I'm always okay."

His phone chimed, and he tugged it out of his back pocket, unable to just leave it for now. It could be Bryce, though Tex didn't hold much hope his son would be the first to contact him for a while.

The message came from Trace, and it bore the picture of him and OJ. "Look." He stepped back and opened the picture fully, studied it for a moment, and then turned his device to Abby.

She sucked in a breath and took his phone. "Tex, this is gorgeous. Look at how happy you are."

"Yeah." He hadn't been allowing himself to feel that happiness. "Look at how happy I am."

Her eyes met his, and he kissed her quickly. "I'm sorry I've been so absent this year."

"You haven't been," she said.

"I have," he said. "Since Bryce told me about Bailey, I have been, and it's not okay. We have a daughter to raise, and I have to take care of those four horses now, and apparently, I don't work out enough."

Abby started to giggle, and Tex let her joy infuse into him too. "I love you, Abs. I'll do better this year."

"I love you too, Tex," she said. "We all love you."

He nodded and looked past her to the rest of his family. He loved them all too, and he better get around to each of them and make sure they knew it, the way Mav always did. Abby joined him at his side, the two of them observing the others at the party.

"Look at them." Abby nodded toward the hallway where Trace and Everly had first started dancing. Blaze and Faith ducked down it, almost like thieves in the night. "They sure like each other, don't they?"

"Seem to," Tex said.

"I think they're sweet together."

Tex thought they couldn't be more opposite, but then again, he and Abby sometimes mixed like oil and water too, and he loved her fiercely.

"Now," she said. "What are we going to do about Gabe?"

"Nothing," Tex said instantly. "Abby, I forbid you to do anything about Gabe."

She grinned up at him. "You're no fun." She started to walk away from him, and Tex let her go.

"I'm tons of fun," he said to himself. He didn't care if he wasn't anyway. He reached into his pocket and found the dice there. His wife wanted to see him be fun?

He'd show her.

23

L uke Young pulled up to Tea's house, his chest already full of bees. "Today," he told himself. He had to break up with her *today*.

He hadn't been enjoying himself since before Thanksgiving, but he hadn't wanted to break up with the pretty doctor during the holidays.

"They're over," he told himself. "Two weeks ago, they ended."

It was time.

He unbuckled his seat belt and got out of the truck. His lungs immediately chastised him for taking such a deep breath of such cold air. The ultra-blue sky was so misleading, and Luke growled at it before turned toward Tea's house.

The small, quaint, white home fit her to a T. She kept it neatly decorated and perfectly clean all the time. It was the anal-retentive ways she operated that drove him nuts. Nothing about his life lined up, at least not the way hers did.

He continued up the walk to the door and knocked a couple of times. He had no doubt Tea was ready, for she never ran late. She had no pets, no kids, no pressures outside of work, and no personality.

When he'd first met her in the hospital, he'd thought she did. She'd been fun and flirty, even as she discharged him. Their first couple of dates had been exciting and fun, but despite Tea being a doctor, she had no depth.

Luke wanted more than giggling and flirting, and his daughter definitely deserved someone who could love her, raise her, and be her mother.

Mandi wasn't coming back to Coral Canyon, and Luke had to face facts. She'd gotten pregnant again. Married again. In Canada. She didn't care about him or Corrine, and he had to move on.

If only moving on didn't cost so much or drag him down so far.

He waited, his impatience with Tea growing by the second. When she opened the door, she wore a completely inappropriate outfit for the weather, and he scanned her down to the pinpoint heels. "You realize it's twenty below zero," he said.

Her glow didn't dim at all. "We'll be inside," she said as she reached for her purse, which always sat on the side table next to the door. He'd thought about telling her that wasn't a great place for it. A thief wouldn't even have to enter her house to grab it. *He* could do it right now and run.

Luke said nothing. He'd gotten better at holding his tongue, at least when it came to things like this. With his brothers, he still struggled, and most of the time, he opted not to show up rather than risk saying something that could cause another Young Family War.

"Tea," he said, but he didn't want to have this conversation in the cold. He stepped into her house, which caused a blip of surprise to cross her features. "I wanted to talk to you about something."

"What?" She turned toward the coat closet and pulled out a bright green coat that would fall to her knees, same as the skirt she wore. It was black, so the green complimented it perfectly.

Luke didn't know how to do this. Breaking up with Mandi had been easy—she'd been sleeping around on him. This wasn't —there wasn't necessarily anything wrong with Tea. She just wasn't for him.

"I have a daughter," he blurted out. Tea spun to face him, shock coursing through her bright blue eyes now. "She just turned six this past fall, and she loves school, horses, and her cousins."

His chest heaved, and he didn't know why he'd told her what Corrine liked. He thought of his daughter and where she was right now—with Morris and Leigh. She loved playing with Eric, as the little boy had a ton of energy, and Corrine could boss him around a little and not get in trouble.

With her in his head, he calmed. "This isn't working between us," he said. "I'm sure you can feel it."

Tea said nothing, and he wasn't sure how to read her now. "I know you don't want kids, and well, Corrine is my whole world.

I love being her dad, and I...." He couldn't say he found her boring. That would be so rude.

"I don't feel what I need to feel to keep seein' you," he said. "I'm real sorry."

Tea nodded then, her bottom lip trembling slightly. "I'm sorry you feel that way, Luke."

"Yeah," he said. "Me too." He dropped his chin toward his chest and used his cowboy hat to hide his face. "So, uh, the dress looks great." He looked up. "Do you still want to go to the gallery?"

She shook her head, and relief flooded him. "Okay. Uh, sorry." He reached for the doorknob and opened the door. He backed out, his eyes stuck on hers. "Really, Tea. Sorry."

"It's okay," she whispered. "Just go on home."

He let go of the door, and she eased it closed, the look of sadness on her face punching Luke in the chest over and over and over.

Staring at the closed door with the blue, white, and silver snowman wreath on it, Luke felt like the biggest jerk in the whole world.

He turned away and walked to his truck. Once buckled in, he backed out, took one last look at Tea's house, and drove away.

Every new breath expanded his chest a little bit more. Every second brought a new sense of release, of relief.

He arrived at home, and the house he shared with his darling daughter sat quiet and empty. Luke looked around, trying to make sense of everything that had happened in the past few months.

"You started dating," he whispered to the walls.

And he had. It hadn't gone well, but he'd done it. Which meant he could do it again. Not right away, or anything, but if the opportunity came up, Luke now knew he could ask out a woman, take her on a date, and break up with her.

He wasn't as broken as he'd thought.

He looked at his phone, wanting to celebrate with someone. Mav would be happy for him, and so would every brother in the band. Heck, Blaze and Jem would congratulate him too.

"Probably even Gabe," Luke muttered. That particular brother had been grumpier and nastier than usual lately, but Luke didn't know why. He didn't talk to Gabe on a personal level, and he didn't ask Morris questions about his twin.

If he needed legal help with Corrine, he called Gabe. That was it.

The dark part of his heart where Gabe should live shouted at him to do something about that fractured relationship, but once again, Luke found himself at a loss.

He also wanted to celebrate with a certain woman who rubbed all of the tension from his body. But there was no way he could text Sterling Boyd out of the blue and tell her he'd broken up with his girlfriend. She probably didn't even know he had one, because they didn't talk about too many personal things while he lay on her table.

In the end, he tapped out a message to the brothers and sent it. *Broke up with Tea. Feels good. Do not set me up with anyone.*

He expected messages to fly in, because that was what seemed to happen when any of them did more than lift a finger.

About time, Blaze said, and Luke knew he meant it in the kindest way possible.

Sounds like it was easy, Tex said. *And that you're happy about it.*

Luke was, but he felt no need to respond. Tex said nothing of Sterling, thankfully, and he walked over to the couch and sat down, simply enjoying that fact that he was single again, the house was silent, and he had a slew of family surrounding him.

LUKE WAITED OUTSIDE MAV'S HOUSE, WITH MORRIS IN THE front seat. They said nothing, because there wasn't anything to say.

He was nothing if not regimented, and he loved getting Corrine to school and then going to the gym. Morris and Mav had joined his routine at the beginning of the year, and together, they'd been getting their workouts in between school drop-off and lunchtime.

Mav finally opened his front door and came outside. He wore a hooded sweatshirt with his gym shorts, and he flipped up the hood and jogged down the steps and toward the truck.

"Whoo-ee," he said as he launched himself into the back seat. "That weather woman lied. It is *not* warmer this week."

Luke only grinned at him in the rear-view mirror. "Dani must've taken Boston to school this morning."

Mav did a lot with his kids, but today, he nodded. "Yeah, and then she and Lars went to their mommy-baby swimming class."

Sometimes Morris drove, and sometimes Mav, but this morning, Luke put the truck in reverse and backed away from the edge of the driveway so he could turn around. Morris and Mav were two of the calmer Youngs, and they dialed down Luke a couple of notches. Maybe that was why he enjoyed spending time with them so much.

At the gym, they scanned their cards and entered, and Luke headed for the treadmill. He'd warm up first, then lift weights, then end on the treadmill again. That was his routine, and he liked it.

"Luke," Morris said. "That trainer is here." He nodded toward the petite blonde coming out of an employees-only door. She wore spandex from knee to shoulder, and she might have more muscles than Luke himself.

Her blonde hair had been gathered into a high ponytail, and those blue eyes zeroed in on him. She was definitely his type, and his heartbeat hammered a couple of times at him.

Then he turned away. "I'm not interested," he mumbled to Morris.

"She could help you," Morris said.

"In more ways than one," Mav added.

"Stop staring at her," Luke barked, glad he'd turned his back. "It looks like you're salivating over her."

"Oh, she's coming over," Morris said, and his voice sounded half hopeful and half terrified.

Luke's pulse began beating erratically again, but he had no choice in turning to greet the woman when she said, "Hello, cowboys."

"Hey," Mav said easily. "We've heard you do great things for people."

Oh, my word, Luke thought. *That could be taken so wrong.*

But the woman smiled as she surveyed them. "I think a couple of you are here for support." Her eyes landed on him. "For one of you."

"He's Luke Young," Morris said, and Luke wanted to punch him in the throat so he couldn't keep talking. "Country Quad goes on tour in a few months, and he's trying to be in the best shape of his life."

The woman scanned him down to his gym shoes, which were surely lacking. The look on her face when she raised her gaze to his said so. "I could help you," she said.

"You think I need help?" he asked, unsure as to why.

"You do," Mav said. "You were talkin' last week about how you should hire a trainer to get that definition in your biceps." He nodded around the gym, indicating the whole space. "Then we saw her working with that guy you were admiring."

Luke's face flamed, and he wished his brothers had one ounce of tact. Just one. "First," he said. "I wasn't admiring a man."

"It was Jonas, right?" the woman asked.

Luke frowned at her. "I don't know his name. Or yours."

"Oh, I'm Willette." She touched her palm to her chest. "You can call me Wills or Willie or any variation of it. I answer to it all."

That didn't help Luke. He wasn't just going to call her whatever.

"And Jonas...." She twisted and turned in a full circle, looking for him. "Yeah, he's over on the rowing machine." She pointed in his direction. "Was it him?"

"Totally," Morris said, which made Luke glare at him. He

turned his attention back to Luke and saw his face. Luke had no idea what he was putting out there, but Morris flinched. "I mean...maybe we don't have time today."

"Don't have time?" Mav asked, and he finally looked at Morris and Luke too. "Oh."

Awkwardness descended on the four of them, and Willette faced them. Her smile lit the whole gym. "I have a waiting list for clients here," she said, either not seeing his face or not caring what she saw. "If you want to be on it, I can add your name. Then I'll call you when I have an opening, and if you're still interested, we can go from there."

Luke folded his arms, something that always built his confidence and made him seem bigger. Willette didn't care at all.

"Might as well get on the waiting list," Mav muttered. "It's no commitment."

Luke sighed. "All right," he said. "How do I get on the waiting list?"

She took his name and number, and then looked up as someone called her name. "Oh, there's my next client. It was wonderful to meet you boys." She moved away, and yes, Luke watched her go. She was pretty, and personable, and why shouldn't he go out with her?

Willette joined another cowboy, and he was absolutely huge. He had to be on steroids to be that muscular, and the three of them stood there and gaped.

"I don't want to look like that," Luke said. "I just want to be able to take my shirt off on stage and look good."

"I think she can help with that," Morris said, his voice nearly a monotone.

"You don't have to go out with her," Mav said. "Just work with her here."

"Who says I want to go out with her?" Luke glared at Mav.

Mav rolled his head. "Your attitude." He bent and plucked a headband from his bag. "Now, come on. I have a PTA meeting at one, so I need to get this done and get home to shower."

Only he would have a PTA meeting, which Luke actually admired. He didn't volunteer at the elementary school; he donated money. He figured that was just as good, and then he didn't have to try to fit into a room of mostly moms, all of them eyeing him like they were lionesses, and he was fresh meat.

He stretched and put his fifteen-minute warm up on the treadmill. As he got off to head over to the weights, his phone chimed, and it came through the earbuds he wore. He tapped to play the message, and it said, "From Sterling masseuse. Good news, Luke! I'm opening my own massage therapy studio, and I'm taking on clients outside of the spa. I have space in my home where you can come, or I have a mobile massage table, and I can come to you. If you want to book a session, please let me know!"

He wasn't sure of all the exclamation points, and his phone had read him the message in a horribly robotic voice.

But he knew Sterling, and he could hear her excitement in the text. He really shouldn't text, as his muscles would grow cold, but he bent his head and let his fingers fly.

That's great, Sterling. Of course I want to book with you. I'd love to come to your place. Tell me when, and I'll be there.

He read the last sentence and then deleted it. He didn't need her to know he worked out and then...didn't have much else to do until Corrine got home. He took care of the house and yard, but it was winter, and the grass didn't need to be clipped.

He amended his text to say he was available most days from eleven to two-thirty, and then he shoved his phone back in the arm holder and headed for the weights.

With every rep he did, he thought of Sterling, and he didn't even know why. She had a way of burrowing into his mind, and he couldn't get her out, no matter how hard he tried.

24

Gabe opened the door to the furniture store ahead of Morris and Leigh. "This won't take long," he said. "I swear."

Leigh just gave him a dry look and entered, and Morris grinned at him. That was about their relationship, and Gabe had to say that Leigh was absolutely perfect for Morris. He'd always thought so, and he found their second chance romance charming and whimsical.

He'd been thinking about it too much lately, because fantasies of getting back together with his ex-wife had started to play in his mind.

That *so* wasn't happening, as Kendra was currently serving time in the Wyoming State Penitentiary. She'd been dealing drugs while pregnant with Liesl, and Gabe took his daughter to the doctor every few months just to check on her growth, her progress with her speech, and to monitor her health.

She hadn't been born addicted to drugs, but it had been a concern. A possibility.

That was when Gabe had realized that he needed to be concerned about raising his daughter alone. That was the first time he'd realized that might be a possibility.

How he'd missed what Kendra was doing, Gabe would never understand. Thus, he was hyper-vigilant now, and he spent far more time observing people than he used to.

Kendra had been arrested in the hospital on the second day of Liesl's life, and Gabe had filed for divorce the next day. He'd loved Kendra—at least a version of the woman she'd become— but he had a child to protect.

That was literally what he did for a living—he protected children.

"Good afternoon," a brunette said, and she tickled Gabe's attraction. She was dark from head to toe, her hair clipped back on the sides to reveal high cheekbones and then those dark, delicious eyes.

"Hey, Hilde," Leigh said as she stepped into the woman and gave her a quick hug. "Gabe's just looking for a desk." She looked at him, as did Morris, and Gabe felt very on-the-spot.

Hilde's eyes moved to him. "What kind of desk?"

"Just something simple," he said. "I mean, I don't want cheap. Not a student desk. But the office isn't huge. I don't need huge." He told himself to stop talking, and thankfully, he did.

Hilde smiled at him, her straight, white teeth only adding to her charm and beauty. "I've got loads of desks. You look like a man who wants something new."

"Do you sell used furniture here?" he asked.

"Sometimes," she said over her shoulder. "This way."

Gabe started to follow her, but Morris said, "We're gonna go look at lamps, okay? Maybe get one for Joey's birthday."

"All right," Gabe said, though he didn't want to be alone with Hilde. Did he?

Maybe he did.

Her hips swayed as she walked, and he noted that she wore a professional pair of black slacks and a black and white dotted blouse. She oozed all the right things, but Gabe knew that appearances could be false.

Housewives could deal drugs, after all, and no one knew until officers showed up in the maternity ward.

"This is our office section," Hilde said, her voice smooth and cool.

Without an audience, Gabe's confidence returned, and he picked out a desk for his new Coral Canyon home office within a few minutes.

"Great," Hilde said. "I'll get one of my girls to ring you up, okay? I have a phone call I need to take." She flashed him that gorgeous smile, and Gabe found himself lunging toward her.

"Can I get your card?" he asked.

Her eyebrows went up, but she said, "Sure. I own the store. If you have a problem, you let me know." She extracted a card from her pocket and handed it to him.

Gabe took it and looked at it, sure the number on it was for business only. Not pleasure. He told himself that was okay. The door stood open, and he could walk through it or not now.

The lovely Hilde O'Dell glided away from him, and Gabe simply watched her go, almost like he'd fallen into a trance.

"Sir?" someone asked, and he blinked.

"Yes."

"You're getting the Houser Collection desk?"

Gabe turned back to it. "I suppose. Is that this one?"

The younger woman smiled. "Yes, sir. I can ring you out up here, and then we'll look at the delivery schedule."

Gabe went with her to pay for his desk. That done, he found Leigh and Morris waiting for him at the front entrance. "Good news," he said. "It's in stock, so they'll deliver it on Saturday when I'm back in town."

"That's great." Morris held up the pinkest, sparkliest lamp Gabe had ever seen. "Look what we found for Joey."

Gabe smiled, because Liesl would love that lamp. "That's incredible." He looked past Morris and Leigh. "Is there another one?"

"We don't have time," Leigh said. "We have to meet Blaze in literally fifteen minutes, and Faith's truck is clear down at the big red barn." She grabbed onto Gabe's arm and hauled him toward the exit. "Come on."

"Blaze won't care if we're late," he said, stumbling after his twin's wife.

"Yes, he will." Morris gave Gabe a look, and they communicated without any words at all. He was right, of course. Blaze had a surprise for Faith, and he was relying on Gabe, Morris, and Leigh to be on time.

Precisely fifteen minutes later, Morris pulled up beside Blaze, and their brother looked over from where he sat behind the wheel. He did not look happy, but Gabe wasn't fazed. Blaze had the dark horse, tortured billionaire act down perfectly.

Gabe didn't judge, because he'd been building walls and perfecting his glare for a great many months too. Blaze was simply sharper than Gabe, so his gaze could scald a person in less than a second—as he was currently doing to Morris, who unbuckled and jumped from the truck like an eager puppy, ready to please his master.

Blaze got out of his truck too, and he glanced over to Gabe, who joined his brothers in a much slower fashion. "You two ready for this?"

"You're the one with the surprise," Gabe said. He looked over to the bright pink truck that bore sprinkles like a kid's doughnut.

Blaze switched his gaze to Gabe, and ouch. It was piercing and sharp, and even Gabe retreated from the fierceness of it. "You should take that stare down a notch." He looked to Morris for help. "I think my skin is blistering and falling off my face."

"She's leaving for a party soon," Blaze said in a calm, even tone.

"Then let's do this," Gabe said.

Blaze reached up and adjusted his cowboy hat. "You guys are ready?"

"Totally ready." Morris zipped up his jacket and led the way out of the space between the two trucks. Blaze went next, and Gabe went last.

He moved to Blaze's right side while Morris flanked his left, and the three of them approached the doughnut truck. Whatever surprise Blaze had brought, it fit in a pocket, because he carried nothing.

"Well, well, well." Faith grinned and leaned onto her

elbows on the counter inside the truck. She stood several feet higher than them, but her enthusiasm and cheer were contagious, even from a distance. "What are you three doing here?"

"Just lookin' for doughnuts," Blaze said.

Faith looked at Gabe, who stared right back, and Morris. She shook her head. "That one gave you away." She straightened and turned to her co-worker in the truck. "I know what these boys want, Joe. Salty cowboy, red velvet, and cookies and cream."

She faced them again. "Did I get it right?"

"Sort of." Blaze inched forward and put something on the counter in front of her. "My brothers want those doughnuts, but I have this coupon."

"I thought you were out of coupons." Faith frowned as she picked it up. Her eyes blitzed back and forth, left to right, as she read. When she looked up, Gabe and his brothers might as well have transformed into aliens.

"I can't leave the truck."

"Yes, you can," Morris and Leigh said at the same time. Gabe glanced over to his twin's wife. He hadn't realized she'd gotten out of the truck.

"I'm a professional baker," Leigh said. "I can take orders, I swear."

"I'm here to help," Morris said.

"Me too," Gabe said.

"I brought three people to do what you do, Faith," Blaze said. "Please."

She looked helplessly at the coupon again, and Gabe saw the moment she cracked. His heart fissured a bit more too, because he wanted a woman to look at him with soft doe eyes like that.

He glanced over to Blaze, but his brother still stood in front of hm, and Gabe couldn't see his face. Faith twined her fingers with his and said, "You're very hard to say no to, Mister Young."

"I'm going to take that as a yes."

Gabe couldn't believe he'd agreed to work a doughnut truck in the middle of the winter—in Wyoming—but he couldn't say no to Blaze either. Faith came flying out of the end of the truck, and she squealed as Blaze wrapped her in his arms and picked her right up off her feet.

"I can go in these clothes?" she asked. "Or do I have time to change?"

"You look amazing," Blaze said, linking his fingers with hers. He paused and looked over to Gabe and Morris. "Thank you." He hurried to them and took Gabe and Morris into a hug at the same time. "Thank you," he whispered again.

"Of course," Morris and Gabe said together, and Blaze grinned at them before he left with Faith. Leigh had already gone into the truck, and she was getting a tutorial from Joe.

Gabe watched Blaze and Faith until he'd helped her into his truck and then backed out of the parking space.

"If you'd let me set you up with our neighbor," Morris started.

"No," Gabe said. At least it wasn't a bark. "I can get my own dates, Morris." He met his twin's eye, and again they had an entire conversation without words. Of course Morris would know how lonely Gabe was. He'd known without having to ask what was in Gabe's head as he watched Blaze leave with Faith.

They had identical genes, and yet, Morris had learned to tame some of the harsher parts of himself. Gabe hadn't—yet—and he wondered that if he could just do that, maybe he'd have a chance with a woman.

Who? he wondered. His clients were single or about-to-be-single dads, and his partner at the firm was a man. He could maybe hire a part-time secretary here in Coral Canyon....

He dismissed the idea, and the gorgeous furniture store owner paraded through his mind.

Yeah, he pushed her out too. Hilde wasn't an option in his eyes, even if his heartbeat picked up speed just thinking about her.

GABE MADE THE TURN ONTO OTIS'S STREET, ALL THE PICK-up trucks in front of the house at the end of the street putting Gabe in an even worse mood. He'd lost his buffer, and the air in Coral Canyon was slowly suffocating him.

He hadn't seen any way out of attending this joint birthday party for Cash and Joey, and Otis had planned it specifically to coincide with his first four-day week in Coral Canyon. He'd worked his first two days out of the bottom floor of the town-home he'd closed on last week, and he'd spent the morning unpacking more boxes for him and Liesl to live in his hometown for half of every week.

He'd return to his home in Jackson Hole on Sunday after-noon, and he'd work out of the office there on Mondays, Tuesdays, and Wednesdays. Sometimes Thursdays, depending on his court schedule and other commitments.

Gabe had the flexibility to do whatever he needed to do for his clients, as he'd brought on other lawyers in the past year and a half. The three of them had plenty of work to do, and Gabe had been taking on the Coral Canyon clients.

Next week, he had to be in court here for a client, so he'd be back. His mother was thrilled, as was Morris. Gabe, on the other hand...he came to a stop a little bit down the block, due to all the other family members who'd arrived ahead of him.

Liesl didn't say anything, as she usually didn't have a lot to talk about.

"We're here, bug," he said. "You want to see your cousins?"

"Yes, yes, yes!" She grinned in the back seat and bounced in her seat.

Gabe grinned, as she was his one shining light in his life. He loved his firm too, and even though they annoyed him, he appreciated and loved his family. But there was nothing like snuggling up with Liesl and dozing while she watched her favorite cartoons and they both ate cold cereal right from the box.

He collected Liesl from the backseat, making sure she had both presents clutched in her hands before he faced the house. They'd surely be last to the party, and honestly, he was fine in that position. He'd arrived late or last to everything over the past few years anyway.

The front door wasn't locked, and Gabe and Liesl went right in. He set his daughter on her feet and said, "Go find out where to put the presents, okay?"

She ran off, her dark, bobbed hair swinging as she did. He'd just finished potty training her, and yes, that was late for a little girl her age. She'd be four in six months, and Gabe had decided he didn't care. He worked a lot, and he could only do what he could do.

"Hey," Georgia said as he entered the house-proper from the foyer. She handed him a basket with a handle. "This is for you. I know how much you love your popcorn and movie nights."

He stared at the simple gift, marveling at how thoughtful it was. "Thank you, Georgia," he murmured.

"This is for Liesl," she said. "She's so fast, I couldn't catch her as she came in." She smiled as she faced the rest of the party. "Oh, Harry is helping her put the gifts on the table."

Georgia handed him a furry, pink notebook. The pen looked like a fuchsia bear paw, and he once again stood in awe of her ability to have the perfect thing for his daughter. "Georgia, this party is for Joey. You know we bring *her* the gifts, right?"

"Hey, brother." Otis arrived with his baby in his arms, and he slung one around Gabe. "Got your gifts, I see. Put them in the office, okay? There's so much going on in here." He released Gabe, and he backtracked to the dark office off the front of the house.

He flipped on a light, and he saw instantly that Georgia hadn't put together bags of popcorn, blu-ray discs, and drink mixes for everyone. Just him. Every gift was different and unique, and some of them he'd bet good money on who they belonged to.

The front door opened again, and Jem said, "Go on. Go find

Grandma," before he turned to face Gabe. So he wasn't last to arrive.

Blaze and Cash were surely here already, as this was partly Cash's birthday party.

"What's goin' on in here?" Jem asked.

"Georgia," Gabe said. He followed Jem back into the house, where Georgia did descend on Jem. Gabe eased past them, letting his fingers skate down her forearm so she'd know how thankful he was.

He found Morris and Mav camped out in the kitchen, and he went that way. They were his safe zone, and he saw no reason to operate outside of that tonight. Once he had a drink and had said hello, he soaked in the rest of the party.

Whoever had decorated had done an amazing job. Joey loved pink and frills and glitter with her entire being—much the same way Liesl did—but Cash was turning twelve. The pink banners seamlessly switched to cream with light blue and then gold and orange halfway across the room.

Clusters of balloons in pink, cream, and gold lifted from every lamp, and others held blue, white, and orange in them. The colors shouldn't have gone together, but they did.

Faith had obviously brought the doughnuts, and a tray bore pink and purple-frosted red velvet ones, and another held long Johns with cream frosting and blue accents.

"This is incredible," he said out loud before he could censor himself.

Mav looked over to him. "Which part?"

"The part where Faith fits with everyone?" Morris asked. "I mean, look at her."

She stood with Leigh, Everly, and Abby—who held baby OJ now. They laughed and talked, and Faith welcomed every child into her side who went by and wanted to tell her something about a doughnut or a balloon.

"He's a lucky guy," Gabe said, finding Blaze seated on the couch close to where Faith stood. Tex and Trace sat with him, and Gabe's first thought was *Of course*.

The three oldest boys. It didn't matter that Blaze wasn't in Country Quad. He was a rockstar of his own. A champion. A billionaire.

Gabe wasn't any of those things, and yet, as he stood there with his brothers, surrounded by his eclectic and loud family, he had the very, very real feeling that he belonged.

His chest buzzed as if he'd suddenly discovered an active hive behind his lungs. He wasn't sure he'd ever felt like this before, and he didn't know what to do with it.

Lord, he thought, but he couldn't go anywhere else. God was already talking to him, and Gabe knew he needed to start mending bridges in his family, start thinking about moving back to Coral Canyon for good, and start acting like he was a Young.

Because he was.

A WEEK LATER, GABE FOUND HIMSELF RUNNING LATE. FOR a lawyer, that wasn't uncommon. For him, it was. He hated the harried, hurried feeling in his stomach, and he dashed up the steps to the courthouse in Coral Canyon.

Going through security always took way too long, and Coral

Canyon didn't have the express lanes for known lawyers and police officers the way Jackson Hole did.

By the time he made it to the fourth floor, where the family law courtroom was, Gabe was sure the doors would be closed.

Thankfully and mercifully, they weren't.

He ducked inside, finding the courtroom nearly full but the judge not there yet. Today's hearing should be fairly easy. He simply needed to get full custody for his client, whom he saw and nodded to as he searched for a place to sit.

He'd taken two steps when his eyes landed on someone else he knew—Hilde.

The goddess who'd sold him his desk and delivered it precisely when she said she would.

He tried to stop moving, but his feet got the message late. He stumbled, which caused him to reach out for something, anything, to grab onto.

That happened to be the back of a bench. Another miracle and mercy.

His briefcase still went sliding along the tile floor, and he still went down on one knee. The people in the near vicinity gasped or said, "oh," and two women—*women*—got up to help him.

"I'm fine," he said out loud, which drew even more attention to him. It wasn't like he couldn't talk in here. People just weren't. Maybe they'd been told the judge was coming already. Gabe had no idea.

His shoulder socket ached from how he'd twisted it, and he quickly got back to his feet, his face on fire.

He brushed his hands down the front of his jacket and

tugged everything back into the proper place. Cuffs. Tie. Hair. All good.

"All rise," the bailiff called, and Gabe needed to find a seat, fast.

He also needed his briefcase, and he glanced around for it.

Hilde O'Dell held it in her lap, and she nodded to the bench beside her.

She'd made room for him, and Gabe didn't want to be rude, so he hurried to take his seat before the judge had him thrown out.

25

Hilde O'Dell had never been as nervous as she was sitting next to Gabe Young. Not all of that anxiety was because of him, but he'd definitely kicked it up a notch. Fine, ten notches. A lot of notches.

He was as handsome as the day was long, for one. For another, his cologne would get any woman to pick up his briefcase and hold it hostage, hoping they could get him to come a little bit closer to them.

As it was, Hilde couldn't make a scene in court, because that was where most of her panic originated from. Her ex-husband had re-opened the custody case, and he wanted their daughter full-time.

She saw no reason for that, after five years of Hilde raising Lynnie by herself. But Ethan said Hilde spent too much time at the store, and Lynnie needed more parental involvement now that she was a teenager.

That logic made no sense whatsoever. Now that Lynnie was older, she could come home in quaint, quiet Coral Canyon alone and do her homework before Hilde returned from the store with dinner. Or, Lynnie sometimes came to the store after school and worked—and Hilde paid her.

They'd gotten only about half of the required child support and alimony over the past five years, and he only wanted Lynnie to live with him more so he didn't have to have his checks garnished for as much, as she'd won in the last hearing she'd attended.

She'd attended, and he hadn't, so she'd won. Hilde took a big breath and held it. She shouldn't have gone after his money. She had plenty of money from the store, and it had been a petty thing to do. Now, he wanted to take Lynnie from her completely.

A storm raged in her soul, and Hilde told herself to exhale first. Then inhale again. She'd been to hearings like this before, and her lawyer knew what to do. She didn't have to do any of it.

One by one, the cases went before the judge, and then the bailiff called, "O'Dell and Thompson, custody hearing."

She got to her feet, surprised when both men on either side of her did too. Her lawyer she understood. Gabe, she did not.

She watched in horror as he stared first at her, his eyes as wide as hers felt, and then at her ex as he approached.

Hilde turned on the heel of her shoe and marched away from both of them, her back feeling like someone had just stabbed knives into it. That made no sense. She wasn't Gabe's girlfriend. He hadn't been concealing the fact that he repre-sented her ex-husband. They weren't even friends.

She'd sold him a desk last week, nothing more.

Hilde knew the "more" only existed inside her fantasies, and she quickly shut those down as she arrived at the podium on her side of the courtroom and faced the judge.

Gabe and Ethan went to the other podium, and Hilde told herself she would not look at or speak to either of them. She simply had to be here to defend herself; she didn't have to say anything. Lynnie was still at school, and Hilde had worn her professional attire—complete with heels—to court.

"You're asking for full custody, Mister Thompson?"

"Yes," Gabe said. "The fourteen-year-old is often left alone in the afternoons, Your Honor, due to Miss O'Dell's work schedule."

"That's not true," her lawyer said. "Out of the past sixty days, the minor child has been home alone four times, as documented by the doorbell camera. I have the logs here." Henry extracted something from his folder and handed it to the bailiff. "Miss O'Dell runs a busy furniture store, yes. But she is not negligent to her daughter. It is Mister Thompson who owes the pair of them a sum totaling more than fifty thousand dollars, and his custody claim is an attempt to get out of paying the alimony and child support for which Miss O'Dell is due."

"His wages are being garnished," Gabe said in a deadpan, as if everyone in the courtroom except for him was an idiot. "He pays."

"The wages only started getting garnished on January first," Henry said. "Because Miss O'Dell filed for the garnishment. That's also why Mister Thompson re-opened this case. He's angry about the garnishment, because he doesn't want to pay for his child."

"My client can easily pay what he's expected to," Gabe said. "The garnishment has nothing to do with it. He simply wants his daughter to be well-cared for."

She is well-cared for, Hilde screamed in her head. She wanted to poke her finger into Gabe's chest and tell him that too.

"Mister Thompson works from very early in the morning," Henry said. "Until three p.m. in the afternoon. Won't his four-teen-year-old be expected to be alone and get up and get ready for school herself? And how will she get there?"

"My client lives with his brother," Gabe said. "The girl will never come home alone or be unattended, as his sister-in-law is a stay-at-home mom and will be there."

"The woman in question works as well." Henry shuffled some papers and plucked one out. "She makes bath bombs from home and sells them online. She's not attending to children all the time."

"She'll still be home," Gabe said.

Hilde broke her promise and looked over to him. He was like dark lightning in a bottle. Gorgeous and glorious and full of power. If someone unstopped the bottle, they'd get shocked and burned, and she wanted to do both.

She glanced up to the judge as Gabe looked at her, their eyes not truly meeting. Thankfully. Hilde wasn't sure what would explode if they did.

Judge Fonsbeck frowned at the papers handed to him. "I see

no reason why Lynnie should be removed from her mother's care." He looked up. "Miss O'Dell?"

"Your Honor?" she managed to say.

"I believe you want what's right for your daughter."

"I do."

"Mister Thompson?" He looked over to Gabe and his client, and once again, Hilde couldn't stop herself. Henry busied himself with items in his briefcase, almost like he didn't care what the judge said.

"Yes, Your Honor."

"If you want to see your daughter more, keep paying your child support. Then file for partial custody. Don't try to take your daughter from the only parent she's known for five years, especially without cause."

"Your Honor," Gabe said. "There is cause."

"Not for full custody, Mister Young."

"Then partial," he said, but it wasn't rushed, and it didn't sound desperate. "Half and half."

"Miss O'Dell objects to shared custody," Henry said, finally looking up. "Lynnie has finally started to excel and heal after the divorce, and she doesn't want to be shipped back and forth twice each week."

"I agree," Judge Fonsbeck said. "The custody agreement stands without changes." He handed the papers back to his bailiff and looked up. "Call the next case."

Hilde turned to Henry, who gave her a curt smile, and she turned her back on the courthouse. She walked as fluidly as her stiff, wooden legs would allow, and once she reached the hall, she paused and took a long, deep breath. The air out here didn't seem so full of panic, and her lungs welcomed it.

Then she got quite the nose full of that sexy, heady cologne she'd breathed in while she waited for her case to be called. "No," she actually said aloud. Yet her body turned toward the sexy cowboy lawyer she really wished wasn't representing her ex-husband.

Gabe Young stood there, a look of utmost disgust on his face. It cleared instantly when he looked at Henry. "Good to see you again, Henry."

"You too, Gabe. Did you move here?"

"I'm just here a couple of days a week." He looked at her out of the corner of his eye. "Thursdays and Fridays."

Ethan joined them, and Hilde quickly moved to the side of the hall, out of the way. She didn't need to stay and debrief with her lawyer, and she held her head high and walked toward the elevator.

It seemed like another court had just gotten out, and she had to wait for two cars before she could get on. She barely made it and had just turned around to face the front when Gabe said, "Hold it, please." He put his hand over the doors. "Room for one more?"

He didn't wait for an answer. He just crowded his way onto the elevator and stood immediately next to her.

Against her better judgment, she looked up at him. Oh, those eyes—they reminded her of milk chocolate. His suit coat hung precisely right on his broad shoulders, and every stitch of him sat in exactly the right place, despite his near fall only thirty minutes ago.

He kicked up one side of his mouth. "Hello, Hilde." His voice came out smooth, the way melted chocolate came together when stirred.

"How's the desk?" she said. "I presume you put it in your new office here in town?"

"Yes," he said. "It's fantastic. Great piece of furniture."

Hilde rolled her eyes and faced the silver doors of the elevator again. Just because she stood near him didn't mean she had to speak to him. She wasn't talking to any of the other ten strangers in this car.

And he was a stranger, despite him coming into the store last week, and despite knowing several of his brothers. "Knowing" was a stretch too. She knew Everly, and she'd gone to dinner with her and Trace once. She knew Abigail Ingalls too, but she hadn't spent time with her or Tex since they'd been married.

Dani Young had practically furnished her whole home from Hilde's store, and out of all the Youngs, she knew Mav the best.

They reached the bottom floor, and Gabe gestured for her to go first. He held back all the other traffic to do it, and he didn't care one whit. Well, Hilde did, and she scoffed and strode off the elevator ahead of him.

The man had long legs, though, and he kept up with her easily. So easily that he opened the door to leave the courthouse too. She glared at him. "I can open my own doors."

"I know that." He still waited for her to walk outside, which Hilde did. She stuffed her hands into her coat pockets and hurried down the steps. She didn't wear heels very often, but she could walk in them when she had to.

"Hilde," Gabe said from behind her.

"Go home, Gabe," she said. "You did your job." She knew men like him, and she wasn't interested. Perhaps she had been last week when he'd come into the store with his twin. She knew he was single, and she'd even gossiped with Everly about him a little bit. Five or six texts.

But he was representing Ethan, and that meant they'd forever be on opposite sides of the table.

"Are you going back to the store?"

She spun back to him. "Why do you care?"

He stopped, clearly within arm's reach of her though he made no move to touch her. "I...don't."

"You're not going to gather any evidence on me for how terrible of a mother I am," she said. "School is almost out, so I'm going home." She looked down to his shiny shoes and back to that stunningly gorgeous face. "I heard you have a daughter. I wonder who takes care of her while *you're* working."

His jaw clenched, and his eyes turned a shade darker. "I don't always agree with my clients, but I do what they pay me to do."

"Have a great day, Mister Young." She turned and walked away, glad when he didn't call after her or come with her. Once she sat behind the wheel of her car, she scanned the parking lot for him and didn't see him. He probably had a driver come pick him up after his court appearances, and Hilde shook the thought out of her head.

This was a small town in Wyoming, not a big city. Gabe didn't have a driver here; no one did.

Hilde smoothed her hair off her forehead and gathered it all into a ponytail at the base of her neck. She exhaled and made the drive home, relief filling her with every minute between her and that hearing.

Lynnie wouldn't be home for another forty-five minutes, and while Hilde wasn't like Faith and loved to bake, she could put together a decent batch of chocolate chip cookies. The measuring and blending helped soothe her, and the house filled with the scent of warm chocolate by the time her teenage daughter pushed through the back door and said, "Hey, Mom."

"Hello, my girl." She smiled at her gorgeous daughter, who had more of her ex's red hair than she'd like to admit. Lynnie was auburn through and through, with Hilde's high cheekbones and big eyes, thick eyelashes and kind smile in other places on her face.

"How was the hearing?" Lynnie dropped her backpack. "Do I have to go live with Dad?"

"No, dear." Hilde opened her arms and folded Lynnie into her chest. "The judge threw it all out, just like I said he would."

Lynnie exhaled, but she didn't say anything negative about her father. Hilde worked very hard not to as well. "Good," she said as she stepped out of her mother's arms. Her face glowed now, and Hilde couldn't tell if it was from the cold or if her daughter was blushing. "I have some exciting news too."

"Do tell." Hilde grinned at her and picked up the plate of cookies. She offered one to Lynnie, who took one and then bent to get something out of her bag.

When she straightened, she held a miniature bouquet of red roses. "Gavin Henderson finally asked me to Sweethearts!" She bounced on the balls of her feet as she squealed. "Please, can I go, Mom? Please? We talked about it, but you said if I didn't get asked, I couldn't go with friends, but I got asked." Her eyes turned to those of a puppy dog, and Hilde couldn't say no to that.

"When is it?" she asked anyway.

"It's on the eleventh," Lynnie said, as if they hadn't talked about this dance before. "Because Valentine's Day is a Tuesday. I'm babysitting for the Malcolm's that night, so if you got a date...."

Hilde scoffed, though a particular lawyer eased his way into her mind. She tried shoving Gabe out, but he was resistant to go. She beamed at her daughter and took her face in both of her hands. "When do you want to go shopping for a dress? This boy waited until the last possible minute, didn't he?"

Lynnie squealed again. More jumping up and down happened. "We can go tomorrow," she said. "I mean, if you can."

"What about today?" Hilde asked. She'd already taken the day off from the store. "You have this weekend, and then the dance is next Saturday."

"Let me call Mya and change our plans." She hurried off to do that, leaving Hilde to look at the cookies she'd made. No one here would eat them, and she'd take them to work tomorrow for her employees.

While Lynnie spoke at the speed of sound to her best friend, Hilde picked up her phone. She saw she'd missed two calls and a handful of texts, and her heart leaped into the back of her throat. She'd forgotten she'd silenced her phone to be in court.

Hopefully nothing was wrong at the store. A few questions she could answer via text, and two calls from an unknown number. Probably a scammer.

The last text was from the same number, however, and it said, *Hello, Hilde, this is Gabriel Young. I was wondering if you had a few minutes to chat. Nothing about the case.*

She stared at the letters, trying to get them to make sense. "If it's not about the case, then what could it be about?" she wondered aloud. She could just hear him saying, "Hello, Hilde," in that suave, sultry voice he possessed.

If it's not business, it's personal, she thought, and then Lynnie said, "Ready, Mom?"

She jerked her attention away from her phone, nearly dropping it. "Yes," she said, painting a smile over her confusion, hope, desire, and disbelief. She shoved her phone into her purse and picked it up. "I'm ready."

26

Blaze laughed with Jem as they pushed open the doors to leave the mall. He'd wanted to get his kids a little gift for Valentine's Day, which was tomorrow, and Blaze had been glad for something to get him out of the house.

Now that his Stocking Stuffer project had ended, and Cash had settled back into school, Blaze didn't have much taking up his time. He could work out with his brothers in the morning, but he didn't want to disrupt their bro-club, and he'd never been one to join up with others and go to the gym.

He worked out on his own just fine, thanks. He didn't even go with Jem, who had Rosie with him a few days a week still. He'd been getting up with the kids since he'd moved back in with Blaze, and he got them dressed, fed, and ready for the day. Rosie had preschool twice a week, and that happened to be this morning.

"Jem Young?" a woman asked, and both he and Blaze turned back to her.

Blaze knew her instantly, and the way Jem whooped told him he did too. "Oh, boy," Blaze muttered as Jem slammed the bag of candy and toys he'd bought for his kids into Blaze's chest.

He managed not to drop the bag as his younger brother practically steamrolled the woman. Thankfully, they hadn't made it all the way outside yet. They'd left the mall, but there was a foyer between two sets of doors. It wasn't heated, but the wind and snow couldn't get to them.

"Jem!" She squealed, and Blaze had the good sense to put a smile on his face for Sunny Samuelson before Jem set her back on her feet.

"What in the world are you doin' here?" he asked.

"What am *I* doing here?" She swatted at his chest, and he acted like she had the strength of ten men by falling back three steps. They laughed together, and Blaze's mood started to brighten.

Maybe Sunny would be a good addition to Jem's life.

"I'm Blaze," he said. "Remember me?"

Sunny's pretty eyes moved to him, and she sobered slightly. "Yeah, sure, Blaze. It's good to see you too."

"Sure it is." He kept his voice friendly, and he looked at Jem. "I'm going to go wait in the truck, okay? Remember, we're on a clock."

Jem's eyes turned panicked. "You don't need to go wait in the truck." Everything in his expression transformed when he looked at Sunny again. "We're retired. Blaze and me. Me and

Blaze. From the rodeo. So we moved back up here with our kids."

"Oh, you have kids," she said, her voice much higher than it had been a moment ago.

"Yeah," Jem said. "Two of 'em. We have to go get my daughter from preschool. That's our clock." He grinned at her. "What are you doin' here?"

"Oh, uh, my dad." She shifted her purse over her shoulder. "He fell, and I'm the oldest, so I'm here to help him for a while."

"That's too bad," Jem said, and he sounded like he meant it. Blaze was sure he did. Jem and Sunny had been inseparable in high school, at least if Momma was to be believed. She'd thought Jem was being naughty with Sunny, but Blaze was six years older than him and had been long gone by then.

He still knew the Samuelsons, as they were long-time Coral Canyon residents, and he distinctly remembered a summer when he'd come home to visit and all Jem did was talk about Sunny. Or hang out with Sunny. He'd even dragged Blaze along to some of the events, so he definitely remembered her.

She'd matured, obviously, and she had reddish-blonde hair with sort of blue and sort of green eyes. She stood a good six inches shorter than Jem, and she looked so dang happy as she said, "He'll be okay. He just needs some rehab and someone to watch after him." She nodded like she was just so happy to be that someone. "I was able to transfer to the hospital here, so it's all good."

Blaze hated that saying, but he kept his lips turned up. "You work at the hospital?" he asked.

She switched her gaze to him again. "Yeah. Yep. I'm a nurse

there."

"A nurse," Jem said, patting Blaze on the chest. "What do you know, Blaze?"

"Not a lot," Blaze said back, not really sure where Jem was going with this. He wasn't exactly flirting, but he wasn't exactly not, and Blaze really wished he'd been able to leave his brother to do his thing.

"Give me your number," Sunny said. "I can't *be*-lieve you're here. We need to hang out."

"Well, he's not fifteen anymore," Blaze said.

"Blaze," Jem barked, his dark eyes flashing.

"What?" Blaze let his smile drift away. "You don't 'hang out' in your thirties. You date." He looked at her and then Jem. "Do you want to go out with her?"

Jem stared at him like he'd lost his mind. Blaze sort of felt like he had, but he couldn't stand the banter. He didn't understand it, and he never had.

"Yeah," Jem said as he pulled his phone from his back pocket. "I do want to go out with her." He looked at Sunny. "So give me your number, and once I'm away from my grouchy brother who thinks he's my keeper, I'll call you."

"Jem," Blaze warned.

"I'm kidding." Jem sent him a semi-sharp, semi-nervous look. Blaze wasn't sure what was going on, but something told him to stay where he was instead of going to the truck. So he stayed while Sunny and Jem exchanged numbers. He hugged her again, and she practically bounced into the mall.

"Not a word," Jem growled as he left the mall completely.

"Not a word?" Blaze hurried after him. "Come on. I get to

ask all kinds of questions."

"Not until we're in the truck." Jem glanced left and right like he might get mowed down in the mall parking lot before noon on a Monday. There wasn't a moving car in sight, and Blaze let him have his silence all the way back to the truck.

The moment the engine turned over and they had their seatbelts on, he said, "You seemed nervous there."

"I was nervous there."

"You didn't want me to leave."

"No." Jem stared out the side window, which only fueled Blaze's impatience.

"Jem."

"I don't know, Blaze. I'm only a few months sober, and I'm living with you, for crying out loud." He swung his head toward Blaze. "And you were right. I don't *hang out* with women anymore, especially not her."

Blaze eased the truck out of the parking lot and set his sights for the preschool. "Why not her?" he asked as gently as he could.

"We had a thing in high school," Jem said.

"So what?" Blaze asked. "So did Abby and Tex." He glanced over to Jem and immediately saw the difference. "She ended things with you."

"She did," Jem said. "On prom night, because she said I was flirting with all the other girls."

Blaze refrained from asking Jem if he was. Jem had always been happy-go-lucky, and he'd never hurt for female attention. He was quick to laugh, the life of the party—at least he had been until he'd turned to the bottle.

He was slowly coming back, and Blaze wasn't sure why he didn't want to start something with Sunny. "She seemed excited to see you," Blaze offered. "She wanted your number."

"Yeah, and I'm not fifteen anymore."

"I didn't mean to put pressure on you."

"I know." Jem knew Blaze, and he didn't have to explain the things he disliked about the conversation Jem and Sunny had had.

"Follow your gut," he said. "You have good instincts, brother."

Jem looked at him, pure vulnerability in his eyes. "Do I?"

Blaze nodded, feeling the Lord with him once again. "You do, Jem. You absolutely do."

His brother nodded, his jaw set, and that was the conversation. Blaze didn't need to beat anything to death, and he texted with Faith while Jem ran in to pick up Rosie.

He wanted to trust his instincts when it came to Faith, and everything inside him told him things were going very, very well.

Don't go too fast, he warned himself, and they certainly hadn't been. He'd meet her sister for the first time tomorrow night when he went to pick her up for their Valentine's Day date, and Blaze had ordered almost an entirely new wardrobe so he had something clean and fancy to wear.

He had a beautiful necklace for Faith, as well as her very favorite treat. He'd made a phone call this morning, and he expected to hear from Faith regarding her food truck before too much longer.

But for now, he drove Jem and Rosie home, ate leftovers his

Momma had sent him home from yesterday's lunch, and started trying on his clothes so he'd have what he wanted to wear ready for tomorrow night.

He heard crying behind the door at Trinity Wilson's house, but he'd already reached for the doorbell, and he couldn't stop now. The ringing sounded faintly through the door too, and at least two dogs started to bark.

Blaze reached up and smoothed down the collar of his jacket, his nerves off the charts. Faith's mother and father didn't live here, but she was ultra-close with her sister. Meeting her was a big deal, and if Trinity didn't like him, he might as well kiss Faith goodbye tonight.

The door opened, and a woman who definitely came from the same gene pool as Faith stood there. Trinity smiled despite the chaos around her and held back a black lab by the collar as she yelled at the smaller dog she couldn't reach.

Blaze bent and scooped the pup into his arms, smiling at the chihuahua mix. "Heya, buddy. You tryin' to escape?" He looked up at Trinity, who seemed a bit surprised.

"Come in," she said. "It's freezing out there tonight."

"I can't wait for spring." Blaze stepped into the house and closed the door behind him. "What's this dog's name?"

"Esther," Trinity said. "And this is Bull. He thinks you came to see him."

"Well, I did." Blaze crouched down and let Bull lick his hand and face for a moment. Then he chuckled and pushed the dog's head away from him. "No licking, bud." He scrubbed Bull along the jaw and up behind his ears. "You're a good dog."

The little one in his arms whined, and Blaze turned his attention to her. "Yes, you're special too."

"Oh, you let him meet the dogs."

He looked up at Faith's voice, and he dang near fell backward. That would've been terrible for his back, as Trinity's floor didn't have a stitch of carpet on it.

She smiled down at him, and she wore a bright pink dress that hugged all those curves that kept him up at night.

He put down Esther and got to his feet. The dogs continued to adore him, but he ignored them. "Sorry. I'm Blaze Young." He stuck out his hand, and Trinity took it.

"My sister, Trinity," Faith said needlessly, as she talked about her all the time. "Her husband Marc." She looked at him as he entered this front, formal living room. "And my non-crying nephew, Ty." She took the boy from his father, and the three-year-old had definitely been crying. "Guys, this is Blaze."

Ty only cowered into her collarbone, but Marc stepped forward and shook his hand too. "Great to meet you," he said. "Faith talks about you all the time."

"Does she now?" he teased as he looked at her. She rolled her eyes and set her nephew on his feet.

"Go give him what we made for him." She didn't wear any shoes right now, and Blaze found her absolutely beautiful in that party dress, her hair pinned back, and just the right amount of makeup on her face.

He couldn't wait to be alone with her, and he couldn't wait to see what footwear she'd put on to do that.

Blaze crouched down again and looked at the little boy. "You made something for me?"

Ty clung to his father's leg, and Faith heaved a big sigh. "Fine," she said. "I'll do it." She stepped forward as Blaze stood. "Ty drew a card for you."

"Wow, really?" Blaze took the card, which was a piece of light blue construction paper folded in half. No envelope, so all he had to do was flip it open, which he did. Inside, a little boy had drawn a cowboy and a horse. A smile sprang to Blaze's face, and he drank in the words that Ty had clearly not penned himself.

Faith had written: *To Blaze, I hope you have fun with Auntie Faith tonight.*

The child had used a purple crayon to put the two letters of his name below that, and Blaze looked up, pure joy streaming from him. "This is so great," he said. "Thank you, Ty."

The boy looked at him, and Blaze smiled as wide as he ever had.

"Let me get my shoes," Faith said. "And we can go."

"That coat is on my bed," Trinity said after her, and Faith called, "Okay," as she disappeared.

Blaze looked at Trinity. "I'm fairly sure you have another child. A little girl, if I'm remembering right."

Trinity smiled. "Yes, Tabitha. She's eating, and if you get her out of the highchair before she's done, the house becomes a war zone." On cue, a baby squabbled from the other room.

"I'll get her," Marc said, and he left too.

Blaze met Trinity's eye, and he didn't know what to say. He'd been praying for a solid week that this introduction would go well, and now he felt like someone had tied his tongue into a knot.

Lord, he prayed again, and something popped into his mind. "Faith says you were the one to give her the name for Hole in One."

Trinity's face broke into a smile. "I did. We'd gone miniature golfing, and she'd just hit one, and as she turned back to me, I told her—that's it, Faithy. You should name your doughnut truck Hole in One. And she did."

"Yes, she did." Blaze glanced down the hall toward the rest of the house. "Did she say anything about her third truck?"

Trinity's eyebrows went up, and hers were just as sculpted as Faith's. She had the same green eyes, though hers were darker. Her hair had more brown than Faith's auburn, but their noses sloped the same, and the surprise in her expression mirrored what Blaze had seen in Faith's many times.

"Why would she say anything about her third truck?" Trinity asked.

Blaze swallowed, his question answered. "I'm a little surprised she didn't call me about it yesterday."

Trinity checked for Faith too and then zeroed in on Blaze again. "Again, why would that surprise you?"

"Did she pick up her truck yesterday?"

"Why won't you answer any of my questions?" Trinity folded her arms and leaned away from him, and Blaze saw that fire he'd seen in Faith a time or two.

"She must not have picked it up," Blaze said. "Because if she had, she'd probably have canceled this date."

Trinity searched his face. "You paid for the paint job on the truck."

"It's Valentine's Day."

Her eyes narrowed. "You realize my sister has a card her nephew made and a funny T-shirt we found at the mall this morning."

"She had this morning off?" Blaze asked. "That little liar. She said she had to work." He looked down the hall again, wondering how long it took to get a pair of shoes.

"She *was* working," Trinity said. "Trying to find something for you."

Blaze met her eye again. "I don't need anything."

"Are you saying you didn't bring her a gift? For your first Valentine's Day together?" She bent and picked up her toddler when he whined. "You paid for her paint job, for goodness sake."

"What?" Faith asked.

Both Blaze and Trinity turned toward her. She'd put on a pair of white wedged sandals that made Blaze's mouth a little drier, but nothing she wore outweighed the edge in her eyes.

"Nothing," he said, shooting Trinity a look. "Aren't you the most beautiful woman in the whole world?" He didn't care that her sister heard. He didn't care if she watched him kiss her. He wanted to tell her how pretty she was, and he wanted to kiss her on their first Valentine's Day together.

He took her into his arms and kissed her gently. "That card was exceptional," he whispered after only a couple of moments of his lips against hers. "Do you have a coat to go with this stunning dress?"

"I'm holding it." She handed the white, puffy, bomber jacket to him, and he helped her put it on.

"Gorgeous," he murmured.

She stepped over to her sister and gave her a quick hug. "Okey dokey, Ty," she said brightly. "You be good for your momma and daddy tonight, or we can't do our sleepover this weekend, okay?" She booped his nose, which couldn't have hurt him, but he started crying again.

"Go," Trinity said over him. "He'll be fine."

Faith nodded, reached for Blaze, and they escaped the house. "Why's he upset?" Blaze asked.

"I usually babysit when Trin and Marc go out," Faith said. "He thought I was there for that, and he's quite upset that *I'm* the one going out tonight." She gave him a smile over her shoulder, and Blaze returned it.

He helped her into his truck, and then he leaned into her. "I need a better kiss than what happened inside."

"Do you now?" She mimicked him, and he chuckled. She leaned down and kissed him, and Blaze wove his fingers through her hair and held her face close to his. He'd just started to get hot under his collar when she pulled away and grabbed that collar with both of her hands.

"Blaze," she said evenly. "Did I hear my sister correctly in there? You paid for my paint job?"

Blaze couldn't lie to her, and the only reason they hadn't had this conversation yesterday was because she hadn't picked up her truck on time.

"Happy Valentine's Day, dove," he whispered, but the fire in Faith's eyes didn't dim. Not even a little bit.

27

Faith didn't want to make a big deal out of something that wasn't a big deal to Blaze. The problem was, him paying for the paint job on her doughnut truck was a big deal to *her*.

He sighed, backed out of the doorway where she'd just kissed him, and closed her door. He walked around the truck, but instead of going in front of it so she could watch him, he went behind.

Faith's stomach stormed at her, but she had to say something. If she didn't, she'd be mad at herself for the rest of the evening—and beyond. So the moment he sat down, she said, "Blaze, you're the sweetest man in the world. Really. But I don't need or want you to pay for things for me. It makes me feel weak, and I know that's dumb, but that's how I feel."

"It was a gift, Faith," he said. "You said it was okay to do gifts for Valentine's Day."

She looked away from her hands, which twisted around one another. She'd taken today off from the trucks—a luxury he'd already given her when he'd written that check almost four months ago now—and she'd gone shopping this morning and then gotten a manicure. She'd been so excited for him to meet Trin and Marc, and of course they loved him.

She'd never *seen* Esther let a stranger pick her up before, and she knew Trinity would have plenty to say about that.

"You already changed my life with the check from Thanksgiving," she said, desperate for him to understand. "I took today off, because of that."

"And now, because of this, you'll have even more freedom." He pulled away from the curb. "I know what that paint job costs, Faith. Why can't you just take it like you took the check in November? What's the difference?"

"The difference is that anyone could've drawn your check," she said. "Not anyone can get you to pay for their business expenses."

He could probably pay off any business debt and expense for any business in Coral Canyon, big or small. But he said nothing.

She didn't know what else to say either, and she looked out the windshield at the neighborhood lights going by. She'd felt glamorous and fancy in her sister's jacket and shoes. The new dress she'd gotten last week brought out the color in her face and lips and made her feel ten years younger.

Now, she simply felt like she wanted to go home and put on sweats, then get her hands dirty in a bowl of dough that she'd fry into deliciousness.

"Blaze," she said, containing the wobble in her soul so it didn't show in her voice.

"Yeah?"

"Why aren't you saying anything?"

"What do you want me to say?" he asked. "I don't want to apologize, because I don't think I did anything wrong. And I'm not going to call Ruda up tomorrow and say, 'Just kidding, can I have my money back?' It makes no sense."

He took a left turn and continued with, "I don't see how me doing something nice for you makes you feel weak. And secondly, Faith, if this is going to work out long-term, you have to come to terms with the fact that I have a ton of money. I'm going to be buying you things and doing things I think will make you happy for the rest of your life. If you don't want that, then maybe—"

He didn't go on, and Faith didn't want him to. She knew what came after those words anyway.

"I can't even say it," he said, his voice full of disgust. "I don't want to break up, Faith, okay? Not now, and not ever, but I don't know how to *not* spend money on you."

"Blaze, maybe you—"

"I feel like God has blessed me with this money. Why can't I use it to help you? Or someone else here in town? They're not complaining, and yet, my own girlfriend gets mad every time I try to do anything nice."

"That's not what I said," she said.

"I know, you're right." He sighed and stopped talking, but the silence in the cab was far worse than anything he'd said.

Faith's body trembled, and she wasn't sure if it was because her feet were lumps of ice, or because she'd brought up a hard topic with Blaze, or because he'd said, *I don't want to break up, okay? Not now, and not ever.*

She let him drive past Main Street, past all the restaurants, and out toward the southern edge of town. She didn't ask him where he was taking her, though she normally would have. She simply let some time go by, hoping it would settle her stomach enough so she could sit across from him, eat, and continue to talk.

Once he turned into a driveway that led back to a big, red barn with lights all along the roof, she said, "There's a lot of things we need to talk about in what you just said."

"Good things or bad things?" he asked.

"Both."

He brought the truck to a stop in one of the only remaining parking spots in front of the barn. The night felt magical out here, away from civilization and with those warm, twinkling lights. He looked over to her and picked up her hand. He brought it to his lips and kissed the back of it, then turned it over and kissed the inside of her wrist.

"Okay, but can we do the bad stuff another day? It's Valentine's Day, and I just want to spoil you." He gave her a quick grin and went back to kissing her fingers one by one.

He wasn't playing fair now, but Faith didn't call him on it. Instead, she said, "You said a lot of things about...marriage. Long-term, buying me stuff for the rest of my life. You don't want to break up, not now and not ever."

He lifted his eyes to hers, and she lifted her eyebrows. "What's your long-term plan, dove? Keep dating forever?"

"No," she said, but she didn't have much more. "We just haven't talked about marriage. Not really."

"Maybe we should."

Faith's throat turned dry. "Yeah, maybe."

Blaze's smile turned up two degrees. Then ten. "Okay, but we have to go in now, so we don't miss our reservation. I'll come get your door."

The moment he opened the door, Faith spilled into his arms. She didn't know what to say to him, not with his dark eyes devouring her and asking questions at the same time.

"C'mon," he said gruffly, and he led her into the barn. The most magical restaurant known to mankind spread before her, with tea lights draped in the rafters, and hand-hewn tables and chairs taking up the open space.

The kitchen sat at the back of the restaurant, and it was open for all to see what the chefs and cooks were up to. As she stood there, she watched a couple of waiters light a tomahawk steak on fire with herbs resting on top of it.

"My goodness," she said.

"It's a steakhouse," he said, his hand lightly resting on her hip. "They're only open sometimes."

"I had no idea this existed here."

"They move around," he said. "They're in Coral Canyon for a few weeks, and then I think I saw that they were moving on to an abandoned restaurant in Yellowstone for a while."

"They all travel?" Faith asked, still watching the fire. "The wait staff and the chefs? All of them?"

"Yes," Blaze said. "It's like a touring company for Broadway, but this is a restaurant."

The scent of meat and butter and rosemary hung in the air, and Faith honestly felt like her feet had come off the ground and she was floating. It was Valentine's Day, and this was the most magical place on earth, and she did not want to ruin it with hard conversations about what Blaze could and couldn't pay for.

Because this restaurant wasn't cheap. She knew just by what the wait staff wore, and the people who'd come here tonight. She saw an Everett sister with her husband, and Graham Whittaker with his wife. He owned and operated the biggest energy company in the state, which meant he had money coming out his ears.

Just like Blaze.

All of the men and women here were just like him. Refined, even while wearing a cowboy hat. Polished, right down to the tips of their boots. Wealthy, with so much money that the menu didn't need prices. They could pay whatever it cost.

Or connected, like the mayor and her husband. The hospital administrator and his wife. The man who owned a horse racing facility up in Dog Valley.

Everywhere Faith looked, she saw importance and wealth.

Sure enough, once Faith and Blaze had been seated, the waitress opened her menu for her and handed it to her—no prices existed. "Our specialty drink tonight is called The Heart-buster." She grinned. "It can be made with or without alcohol, and it's got real strawberry, raspberry, and lime in it." Her smile came from years of professionalism in this industry. "Your server will be Jacques, and he'll be here in just a moment."

"Thank you," Faith murmured. Blaze said it loud enough for the woman to hear, and she walked away. Everything on the menu looked like steakhouse fare, but there was a high-class twist that reminded Faith of where she sat.

They got through ordering—wherein they both got The Heartbuster; her with vodka and him without—and then Blaze settled his hands in his lap and looked at her. A glint rode in his expression, and his lips curved upward slightly.

"I did get you something else," he said, his voice almost a whisper. "Dare I present you with it?"

"You do not dare...to talk like that." She smiled at him. "Can't we just be normal? I mean, I know we're at this super-fancy restaurant, but I'm not a super-fancy person."

"Have you seen yourself in that dress and jacket?" He looked down, but most of her body was tucked under the table. "Because you look like a movie star." Glancing around, he leaned forward and added, "In fact, I think people will start coming over to ask for your autograph."

"Stop it," she said, though a tingly feeling had started to burst through her. "They will not."

"They won't know why," he said. "They just know that a woman as stunning as you must be *somebody*, and they'll want a signature."

She rolled her eyes and reached for the glass of water Jacques had brought ahead of their specialty drinks. "You're the one who gets stopped on the street and asked for his autograph."

"That happened one time," Blaze said. "And only because those kids were down here from Dog Valley. Everyone in Coral Canyon knows to leave me alone."

"Mm." Faith had barely set down her glass when someone said, "Blaze."

They both looked up at Todd Christopherson, a fellow former bull riding champion. He'd married Violet Everett, one of the famous sisters, and she had her arm linked through his. She wore a gown in purple, but not the bright, ghastly color. A wealthy, rich color meant for royalty. Her white gloves didn't hold a spot, and she also beamed at the pair of them.

"Todd." Blaze got to his feet and hugged the other cowboy. "It's great to see you. Vi." He nodded at her and glanced over to Faith. "You two remember Faith Cromwell." It wasn't a question, and Faith hoped she smiled with as much dignity as Vi did. "Are you coming? Going? Need a table? We could combine, I bet."

"We're going," Vi said. "Todd here likes to get to bed early." She grinned at her husband, who only gave her half a smile in return.

"Vi's the one who's asleep the moment the clock strikes nine."

"Wow," Blaze said with a chuckle. "You better get going then."

Todd smiled at Faith. "Didn't mean to interrupt. Good to see you again, Faith."

"You too," she said, and she held very still while Vi ran her hand along her shoulder

"I love this jacket," she said. "Nice to see you, Faith."

"You too," she said again, hating herself for only having those two words to say to someone. They left, and Faith practically sagged into the back of her chair.

Blaze re-took his seat, and as he settled his napkin across his lap, he said, "That doesn't count. We're friends."

"He's a bull riding champion and she's a country music singer."

"Yeah, so? My brothers are all country music famous. You don't have an issue with them."

Faith's mind buzzed, and she shook her head. That was Blaze's cue to let this go. He would too, and Faith appreciated him very much for allowing her to shake the topic away until she was ready to talk about it.

"I'm going for it," he said, and he placed a long, dark blue, velvet box on the table between them. "I love buying jewelry for you." He gave her the kindest smile she'd ever seen him wear. "If you hate it, I'll take you to the store and let you pick out a replacement, but when I was there, I saw this, and it screamed at me to buy it for you."

Faith reached for the box, awe filling her. With it in her hand, she felt the weight of it, and she paused. "Blaze." She looked at him, shame and humiliation crowding into her core. "My gift for you is really, really sub-par compared to this."

"Dove." He reached across the table and took her free hand in his. "*You're* my gift tonight. I don't need anything else." He squeezed her fingers and let go. Nodding, he added, "Open it."

Faith took in a slow breath through her nose. She had to find a place where she could exist where it was okay for Blaze to buy expensive jewelry, pay for all the maintenance and upgrades on her trucks, and spoil her rotten.

She'd never had a boyfriend like him before, and she looked up at him as she started to open the box.

28

Blaze couldn't get a full breath while he waited for the top part of the box to be separated from the bottom. Faith finally did it, and the gems in the necklace glittered in the lights hanging from the rafters.

Faith sucked in a breath and said, "Oh," in a voice that had gone up an octave from her normal pitch. She looked at him with wide eyes. "Blaze, this is stunning."

"It's Wyoming jade," he said. "The green stones. The white and black ones are Buffalo turquoise."

Faith lifted the piece from the box, and Blaze couldn't help smiling at it. "It's black and white and green," he said as if she couldn't see it. "All your favorite colors."

"I love this." Faith stood up and moved the few feet to his side of the table. "Put it on for me, would you?"

He stood, took the necklace, and waited while she gathered

her hair out of the way. He fitted the clasp together, and she turned. He couldn't look away from her, but he knew he stood —*stood*—in a crowded restaurant, and he couldn't kiss her too passionately right now.

Leaning down, Blaze did touch his lips to hers briefly. That was almost as erotic as something more, and he gave her a shy smile. "Sit with me."

He sat back down, and he took her onto his lap despite her noise of surprise. "Blaze," she said, glancing around.

"Dove," he said back. "It's fine. I just want to see this necklace up close." The gems alternated with one another, none of them exactly alike. He touched the biggest piece of jade, right in the deepest curve of the necklace. "Do you really like it?"

"I love it," she whispered. She wrapped her arms around him now, apparently satisfied that they could sit like this and not get in trouble.

Blaze looked up at her, the words *I love you* sitting in the back of his throat. Faith wore warmth and joy in her face, and if Blaze still lived in Vegas and went to the casinos to gamble, he'd bet one of the emotions on her face was love.

He could simply *feel* it, and that was such a gift to him. He hadn't been able to feel much before coming to Coral Canyon. He lived life in black and white; no color. There was working out and training; nothing more.

Now, he held on his lap his entire future, and it scared the three words he wanted to say way back down into his stomach.

"Happy Valentine's Day," he whispered instead, and Faith tipped his cowboy hat back so she had a better angle to kiss him.

Hours later, after the best steak and creamy, mashed potatoes he'd ever eaten, after the most beautiful dessert he'd ever laid eyes on, and after the most magical of wagon rides around the property where the barn stood, Blaze finally pulled up to Faith's house.

His adrenaline had kept him going this late at night, as had the gorgeous woman at his side. He looked over to her, and she looked at him. "That wasn't so bad, right?"

She giggled and shook her head. "Come in for a minute. Can you?"

Blaze's eyebrows went up. "You want me to come in?" He always walked her to the door, but she didn't invite him in. She didn't make coffee, and they didn't sip it on her couch while the date lingered.

He thought of sleeping in that bed with her, and his skin immediately heated.

"I have a gift for you too," she said. "Just one minute. I know it's late." She opened her door, and Blaze hurried so he could meet her at the front corner of the truck. He took her hand and walked with her toward the door.

She unlocked it and led him inside, and Blaze felt like he'd just taken a step from familiar to unfamiliar. Faith reached over the back of the loveseat in the front, formal living room and picked up a package.

The paper crinkled under her grip, which did seem to be more of a strangle. He looked up in time to catch her swallowing. "It's so dumb, I almost don't want to give it to you."

He shook his head. "Dove."

"What do you buy a billionaire?"

He wanted to tell her this would be a problem for their entire relationship, as he had earlier tonight. But he was tired, and he didn't want to end the evening on anything but a high. So he tamped down his frustration that this topic had come up again, and he simply smiled.

"I'll take that before you squish it to death," he teased. She released the package then, and Blaze tore off the glittering red paper. A dark brown T-shirt emerged, and it had burnt gold lettering across the front of it, spelling out CHAMPION.

He grinned at it and then Faith. "Thank you, dove."

"It's a T-shirt."

"Yeah." He looked down at it again, noting some smaller letters above the main word. "She's my champion." His heart swooped through his chest before settling back where it belonged. "Do you mean that?"

Blaze met her eyes again, and the strong, confident Faith Cromwell who'd told him off from inside her smoking food truck had fled. He really liked that woman and wanted her back. He also liked the softer side of Faith, and the passionate side. The side who served her friends and family and community, and the side who'd invited Cash to come make doughnuts with her.

"Why are you nervous?" he asked.

"I want to be your champion," she said. Her lower lip trembled, and Blaze wanted to make that stop. He had to erase all of the negativity in her life. "But I'm afraid I don't know how."

Blaze wrapped her in his arms, the T-shirt pressed between their bodies. "My dove. My beautiful Faith. You *are* my champion, and how you can't see that is beyond me."

She clung to him, and Blaze simply held her close, breathed her in, and prayed they could find a way past this issue that kept coming between them.

"You champion me by letting me take you to any restaurant I want, no questions asked." He swayed slightly with her and let his eyes drift closed. "You champion me by introducing me to your sister as your boyfriend. You champion me by putting up with my family."

"I love your family," she whispered.

Blaze did too, even though it had taken him a while to realize how very important family was. Or what that word even meant.

"You champion me by spending time with my son. By wanting to get to know him."

Blaze could go on, but he fell silent again. Faith said nothing either, and after a few, tension-filled minutes, he stepped back a half-pace. "Are we okay?"

She nodded, only her eyelashes glistening with tears.

"Faith." He put two fingers under her chin and raised her face, so she'd look at him. "We can work through this, okay? Together. Because I think I'm in love with you, and I don't want...."

"What?" she prompted, her voice barely there. "What don't you want?"

"I don't want *me* to be the reason we can't be together."

"It's not you."

"It is," he insisted. "It's me *being me*. Me having money and wanting to spoil you with it. Me buying you things you don't want."

"I want the necklace," she said.

He paused, searching her face. Trying to find what she meant by that when she'd been so upset about the truck earlier. His brain fuzzed, partly because of the late hour, and partly because Faith brought out every emotion Blaze had ever felt in his life.

He couldn't make sense of anything right now, and he knew in his heart he better get on home. Nothing good would come from this conversation tonight, and Blaze touched his lips to Faith's and kissed her.

The passion exploded between them, and Blaze kissed her deeper and longer than he'd initially intended. By the time he finally gained his senses and pulled away, his breath came in short spurts and his pulse rocketed through his veins.

"I need to go," he said. "I'll call you in the morning, okay?"

She nodded, and Blaze stooped to pick up the T-shirt from where it had fallen to the floor. He left, the cold early-morning air clearing his mind slightly. He still wasn't sure why Faith could accept some gifts and not others, and now that he was alone, he was glad he hadn't told Faith he loved her.

Maybe he did, and maybe he didn't. He wasn't sure, and words as important as those three shouldn't be said until he was absolutely sure.

~

February faded into March, and the sun started to show its face more and more often. He came out of the master bedroom and into the kitchen, where Cash had just taken something out of the microwave.

"We have to get going, bud," he said.

"I can take this in the truck." His son stirred the scrambled egg cup before putting it down and then grabbing his backpack.

"Remember, Faith is picking you up after school." They'd been spending more time with Cash, the three of them, and he seemed to like Faith. He hadn't wanted to go to church with her, and Blaze could see that. Sitting by Momma was more fun, as she had treats and snacks in her purse that Faith did not.

"Yeah, I remember." Cash smiled at Blaze. "Do you really think she'll let me work on the truck this summer?"

Blaze tousled his son's hair. "I think you'll have to earn that right, my friend. And it won't be a cake walk. Faith means business when she's making and selling doughnuts."

"I can't wait," he said. "I did good in that cooking class at the community center, right?"

"Yeah." Blaze herded him toward the door. "You did, which is why I'm finally letting you go to Faith's. But you needed some experience first." He'd had no idea that his son cared about learning to cook and bake. But he did, and once Blaze had found out, he'd put Cash in an after-school cooking class for beginners at the community center. It had gone for eight weeks, and he'd learned a lot of valuable skills, like how to read a recipe and how to do basic measurements.

Honestly, Blaze could use the class, but he hadn't seen one come up for adults yet.

He got Cash off to school, and then he made the drive out to Tex's farm. The band hadn't been using the white barn recording studio, and while Tex had a baby about to turn a year old, he found himself with some extra time on his hands too.

Trace had agreed to separate himself from Everly for a morning, and the three of them were going horseback riding with Bryce's horses.

Blaze hadn't been on a horse in a long time, and a quiet excitement built inside him. He arrived at his brother's house at the same time Wade Ingalls came down his side steps. He waved to Blaze, who held up one hand in return.

Hollis hung his head over the seat, and Blaze chuckled. "Yep, we're here, buddy."

They'd arrived last, as Harry went to the junior high, which had an earlier start time than Cash's school. Wade paused and waited for Blaze to drop to the ground and let his dog out, and then he said, "They're in the barn, waitin' for us."

"Are you coming too?" Blaze asked, keeping one eye on Hollis as the dog started running through the snow Franny had already tamped down.

Wade smiled and nodded. "Yep. Bryce has four horses, and I figure I haven't ridden for fun in a while."

"Same." Blaze indicated that Wade should go first down the sidewalk that led to the stables, and he did. His gait with the prosthetic legs he wore was long and bouncy, but Blaze was used to it.

"How's the baby?"

"Good," Wade said. "Cheryl's got him at her mother's today. I guess some old friends are in town."

Old friends. Blaze didn't want to run into any of those, and so far, he hadn't. It helped living up the canyon in a ritzy community where most of the owners were only summer residents. Still, he couldn't imagine getting together with anyone from high school.

A dog barked, and Hollis answered. Blaze's whole countenance lit up. Wade opened the door to the stable, and Franny came bolting out, another bark coming out of her mouth. She loved to speak when she got excited, and she wound a circle around Wade twice before setting her sights on Blaze.

She barreled toward him, and Blaze laughed as the dog went in circles around him too. "Calm down, Franny," he told her, and the excitable dog finally did. He crouched down while Wade continued inside the stables and scratched along Franny's head and under her jowls. "Are you comin' riding with us too? Huh? Are you?"

Hollis arrived on the scene, and he and Franny started circling and sniffing the way dogs did.

"Blaze," someone called from inside, and he groaned as he straightened. The world tilted, and Blaze's sense of balance zoomed out. His perspective of himself became a tiny dot, and he had no idea where he existed in time and space.

Everything zoomed back in as he landed on his right hip, a shock of pain moving through his back and shoulder, as well as down his leg. He grunted, then groaned again as he continued toward the ground.

It had to be over in a matter of a breath, and Blaze found himself lying on his back, looking up into the blue sky. He panted, trying to get his bearings.

Franny loomed over him, and Blaze closed his eyes. He drifted, the pain in the right half of his body floating away as he did the exact same thing.

29

Faith handed Cash an apron. "Baking can be very messy," she said. "Loads of flour."

Cash grinned like a cat in a canary cage as he took the apron and put it on. "We got to keep the aprons from the cooking class," he said. He'd told her about those when they'd first started, and she got a recap every week.

"You can keep that one too," she said. "I bought it just for you."

"Really?"

"Or you can leave it here," she said with the shrug of one shoulder. "And use it when you come bake with me." She smiled at him and patted the bright blue binder on the counter. "Now, Cash, you're about to see something no one else has ever laid eyes on."

His eyes got big, and she loved how animated he was. Blaze seemed to hold everything behind an imaginary and invisible barrier, but Cash wore everything on the surface. His joy. His enthusiasm. His pain. His confusion.

"What is it?"

"This is my recipe binder," she said. "All of the doughnuts I serve at Hole in One are in this binder. Some ideas I have are in here, for doughnuts I haven't made yet. Some are retired flavors."

"Retired flavors?"

"Stuff I used to make and don't anymore."

"Why would you stop making a type of doughnut?" He looked at her, a dry sponge, ready to soak up whatever she said.

"Lots of reasons. Because they weren't very popular," she said. "Because the flavor wasn't quite right. Because it really wasn't a good doughnut."

"I'm sure they're all good." Cash finished tying his apron and looked at her.

"Not everything is good," she said. "That's baking lesson number one. Sometimes you think something will work, but it doesn't. The important thing is that you don't quit trying and experimenting."

Cash nodded, listening to every word. "But on the way here, you said the first lesson of baking was to follow the recipe exactly. Weigh it all." He cocked his head. "That doesn't mesh with experimenting, Miss Faith."

She laughed, because maybe Cash didn't do well in school, but he wasn't dumb. "You're right," she said. "We always follow the recipe when it comes to the dough. Even then, sometimes I put in a flavoring or a fruit to the dough, and it doesn't work out. So the recipe has to be adjusted."

"Adjusted," Cash repeated.

"Right." Faith tapped the flour container. "Should we make some dough?"

"Yes." Cash stepped up to the counter too, and while Faith hadn't taught a lot of baking lessons, a sense of goodness filled the kitchen. She smiled at Cash, her emotions wavering. Putting together a really good batch of doughnuts had always alleviated that for her, so she opened the binder.

"What do you want to make?" She flipped the plastic sleeves, which protected and held her recipes. "Plain glazed doughnuts? We don't want to start with something too hard."

"I'm good with whatever," Cash said. "You can do chocolate on the ring doughnut, right?" He peered at her book too, though Faith didn't expect him to understand what he was looking at.

"Yes, sir," she said. "We can do half plain and half chocolate. Your daddy will like the chocolate ones."

"He likes anything with chocolate," Cash said.

"Me too."

"Me three." They laughed together, and then Faith set him to measuring and building the dough.

"The first thing we do is bloom the yeast." Faith loved the smell of it, how it came across as slightly off, but also called to a deep sense of her taste buds. "That takes about ten or fifteen minutes, and we want to make sure the milk isn't too hot. If it is, it kills the yeast."

She told him how much milk to measure, and he heated it in the microwave before adding the yeast. "See how it sort of froths a little? That will get bigger, but only if we feed it."

"Feed it?"

"Yeast needs to grow," she said. "Just like you. So we feed you, and you grow up big and strong. Same thing here." She slid the sugar canister toward him. "One tablespoon in the milk. Stir it up and set it aside."

He did that while she lined up their next ingredients. "How's Hollis?" she asked. "Your dad said he'd gotten into some burrs down by the lake."

"Yeah," Cash said as he measured out the sugar. "Daddy had to shave his paws to get them all out."

"You still like having him?"

"Yeah, Hollis is great." Cash turned to her. "Fed and mixed."

She smiled at him. "Okay, now we get the rest of the milk ready, along with another thing yeast really likes—eggs." Faith hadn't spent much time with Cash alone. In fact, the only other time had been when he'd sat next to her at church a few months ago.

She knew him; the three of them had been doing more and more together. But she hadn't done anything like this with him before. "What's your dad doing this afternoon?"

"He went riding this morning," Cash said. "Out at Uncle Tex's. That's all I know."

Faith had known he'd spend the morning with his brothers, and she realized he hadn't called her or texted her to make sure she'd picked up Cash. Blaze didn't need to check in, but he did it anyway. He always did.

"Wet ingredients first," she said. "We want those to coat the flour and really hydrate there."

"Hydrate?"

"Yeah, it means it's wet. We don't want dry flour in the dough. It won't rise properly, and the doughnuts will be tough." She glanced over to him. "You never want tough bread. It should always be tender and light."

She showed him the recipe, and Cash kept measuring the flour.

"Now," she said. "We let the mixer do the kneading."

"I've kneaded," he said. "We practiced on some play dough in the classes."

She grinned at his boyish enthusiasm. "I used to knead by hand, but I don't anymore. The mixer does a really good job, and I can always give it a final turn."

Then the dough went into its first proofing stage, and Faith told Cash, "This is where you think about your icings and frostings, glazes, and decorations. Or you go take a nap." She started cleaning up the canisters and ingredients while Cash took the dishes and measuring spoons and cups they'd used to the sink.

"Miss Faith?"

"Yes, sir."

"Do you think you'll marry my dad?" He kept his back to her, seemingly focused on his task in the sink. She had no idea of his skills in the kitchen, and she didn't much care. She could always re-wash something later.

"Cash, I think...maybe." She didn't know how to say yes to that question, but she also couldn't say no. "We're dating. That's what adults do. They spend time together. They talk about nothing and everything. Important things and just fun things. And you decide along the way if you want to spend the rest of your life with that person."

"Do you fight with him?"

"Not very often," Faith said slowly. "But everyone disagrees about things sometimes, buddy."

"Yeah," he said. "Like how me and my dad don't agree on me bein' old enough to ride my bike to town with my friends this summer."

Faith wasn't going to weigh in on that. Blaze had griped to her about how Cash thought he was older than he was. "Right," she said. "No one agrees with everyone all the time."

"But you don't fight-fight?" He turned from the sink and reached for a dish towel hanging from the handle of the stove.

"No." Faith shook her head.

"He and my mom did, for a while. Now that I'm living with him, they don't at all."

Faith nodded, unsure of where to take the conversation. She just wanted to get to know him, and he was a bright kid, with a head-full of dark brown hair and eyes that yearned to find somewhere to belong.

She realized as she watched him dry his hands that he was just like her. Born into this great family of brothers, where some of them—almost all of them—were famous in their own spheres. Where he wasn't sure where he fit. Where he just wanted to have a safe space to belong.

She knew, because she wanted someone to pull out a chair for her and say, *Sit right here, Faith. I'll get you whatever you need.*

"Do you like living with your dad?" she asked.

"Yeah," he said. "I have friends here, and all of my cousins and aunts and uncles, and it's...better than Utah."

Faith smiled and started wiping the counter. "I'm glad, Cash."

He joined her at the counter. "I think there's room for you in our house," he said. "I think if you married my dad, it would be...nice."

Faith smiled, her focus still on her granite. "Thank you, Cash. I guess we'll see what the future holds when it becomes the present." She tossed the dishcloth into the sink, surprised at herself for repeating something her mother had always said. "Now, let's talk about cutting the dough. You want to make sure you have a really sharp cutter...."

"I'M ALMOST THERE," FAITH SAID, HER PULSE POUNDING through every vein in her body. "I'm so sorry, Trin. He's an amazing kid, and he won't be any trouble for you." She glanced over to Cash, who rode in the front seat of her car.

He nodded once, the way his father did when he wasn't happy about something. He said nothing, because he'd already protested about Faith taking him to her sister's house.

But Blaze was in the hospital, and she didn't know why. He hadn't called to tell her. She'd finally called him, and he hadn't answered. She didn't have anyone's number besides Everly's, and it was then that she'd learned that Blaze had gone to the hospital earlier that morning.

Everly hadn't known much either, other than Trace was on his way home, and Harry had been texting him. She'd said she'd learn what she could and call back, but Faith had made the executive decision to go right to the source.

Blaze. In the hospital.

Her emotions surged, and she made the last turn onto her sister's street as Trinity said, "We'll be fine. I know what to do with twelve-year-old boys." Her sister came outside as Faith rounded into the driveway, her phone stuck to her ear and a smile on her face.

Faith put the car in park and turned toward Cash. "Cash, baby, I'm going to call you the moment I see him, okay?"

The boy looked at her with wide, round, scared eyes. Faith grabbed onto him and pulled him into her chest for a hug. "Hey, he's okay," she said. "If he wasn't okay, someone would've called us." She took a deep breath, trying to steady herself too. "They would've come to get you from school or my house."

"Then why didn't he call or text?"

"My guess?" She released him and let him wipe his eyes. "He thought he'd be released by now, and it wouldn't be a big deal." She forced a smile to her face. "I have your number. This is my sister. I trust her more than anyone in the whole world." She leaned toward him. "Okay? She will take good care of you until your daddy or I can come get you."

He nodded, a brave mask sliding into place. It cracked and fissured, because he was only twelve and didn't ride bulls for a living. "Okay, Faith." He took a breath. "I'll be okay."

"You'll be more than okay," Faith promised. "I will call you in less than thirty minutes, I promise." Trinity lived only a few minutes from the hospital, and surely Faith could get some kind of report on Blaze very soon after that.

She nodded and got out of the car. Cash met her at the front corner, and she passed the boy to Trinity. Her sister held her eyes for a long, long moment, and then Faith had to turn away from all the concern, all the questions.

"I'll call you both soon," she promised, and then she watched them walk up the sidewalk and into the house.

Ten minutes later, she found herself walking down a hall toward a bank of rooms, one of which still housed Blaze Young. He'd been admitted earlier that morning for "a fall," but she didn't know much more than that.

She drew in breath after breath, using the oxygen to clear her mind. She recited a list of things in her head to keep her focus, and before she knew it, she stood outside the appointed room.

Anything could be behind that door, and Faith told herself she possessed enough bravery to face whatever it was. Blaze included, for he hadn't called or texted for a reason.

After knocking lightly, she pushed open the door. It swung on a wide arc, and the hospital bed came into view. Blaze sat in it, and when he saw her, his nearly black eyes widened and then filled with fire.

"What are you doin' here?"

No one else lingered in the room with him, and Faith turned to close the door before she spoke. "You were supposed to pick up your son a half-hour ago," she said. "We both expected you at my place to do a taste-test on the doughnuts."

Blaze shook his head. "I sent Tex to get Cash."

"He didn't show up then."

"That's impossible," Blaze said. "Tex always shows up."

Faith wasn't going to argue with him. "I took Cash to my sister's after I called Everly to find out what was going on."

"Nothing's going on."

Faith folded her arms and cocked her hip, her heartbeat practically flying through her body now. "You're lying in a hospital bed, Mister Young. It's very, *very* clear something is going on. Your son is upset. Heck, *I'm* upset that you fell and then thought you didn't have to tell me."

"I'm fine."

"Then why are you still here?"

A muscle in his jaw jumped, and he looked away. The fire inside Faith only roared brighter. She wasn't going to let this go the way she had other things. He didn't just get to charm his way out of *falling down* and then trying to cover it up.

"They don't like something in my blood work," he said. "They won't release me until it's where they want it."

Faith took a step closer to him, wanting to comfort him but also needing him to know that his behavior wasn't okay with her.

"How are you feeling?"

"Fine," he said.

"I'm going to text Cash," she said. "He wants to know you're okay."

"I fell this morning before the horseback ride," he mumbled. "It was so stupid, and I'm fine."

Faith raised her eyebrows at him, but he wasn't looking at her. "I couldn't get up, and Tex and Trace insisted I come to the ER. They had to do x-rays and they wanted to get my back surgeon in here. The whole day has been a circus."

"And you hate monkeys."

His eyes came back to hers. "With a passion."

"And?"

"And what?"

She let out a heavy sigh, pressing it on for longer than normal to make sure he knew how difficult he was being. "What did the back surgeon say? What did the x-rays show? Anything?"

"Nothing is broken," he said. "They think the fall just sort of shocked my body into a non-responsive mode, and these blasted nurses come in every few minutes to make me walk around. The surgeon ordered a physical therapist for me. I did some exercises to help my hip understand it's just fine."

She nodded, something swirling inside her. "And you were going to tell me when? Or Cash when?"

He glared at her. "When it was important for you to know."

"It was important for me to know the moment you came to the hospital," she said.

"I didn't need you to come," he said. "You and Cash were baking this afternoon."

Faith took another step toward him, and in the small hospital room, it felt menacing. "*You* might not have needed me to come, but *I* needed to know. I can't make good decisions if I don't know everything."

"I'm sure I'll be done any minute now."

"That's not the point, Blaze."

"Then what's the point?"

Faith wanted to roll her eyes, but she refrained. "The point is...the point is...."

He raised his eyebrows, clearly challenging her. Everything that had been shifting and broken between them landed in place, and the fire inside Faith surged.

"The point is, Mister Young, that you don't get to decide what I need. Not anymore. It's completely unfair of you to choose for me what I should care about and what I shouldn't."

"I don't do that."

"You do," she insisted. "You do, and you have been for months. The twenty-five grand is no big deal, Faith." She lowered her voice to speak like him on the last sentence. "Stop telling me thank you for it."

"I don't need to hear that."

"*You* don't," she said. "But *I* need to say it. I *need* to say it as many times as I need to say it, and you being grumpy and condescending about it doesn't help."

He folded his arms and lowered his chin slightly, but he didn't look away from her.

"I didn't want or need you to pay for the paint job on truck three. You did it anyway, and you told me I better get used to you spending your money on me. Because that's what *you* need. So I do the only thing I can think of that fulfills my needs—and that's thanking you for it."

"It was a gift. One thank you is enough."

"For you," she cried. "For *you*, Blaze. Don't you get it? This whole relationship is about what you need and don't need! None of it is about me and what I need to feel like I'm worthy of you, or an equal partner in the relationship."

Her chest heaved. "I need to know you're okay, and you decided for me that I didn't. That's not fair. I need to be able to express my thanks when you do something for me, and you decide for me that I don't need that. It's condescending. I need to feel like I'm in control of my business, that I know what I'm doing and I'm managing my time and money wisely. Then here you come, paying for things and making me feel out of control and weak. I accepted the gift—graciously, I might add—and then you decide I can't thank you for it. It's just...wrong."

She shook her head. "It's wrong," she repeated. "You don't get to decide how I should feel or what I need, and you don't get to negate how I feel or what I need."

"Maybe you don't know sometimes," he said.

"Are you serious right now?" She looked at the IV bag hanging from the pole next to him. He wasn't wearing the IV. "What did they give you in that thing?"

"Nothing." He glared at her as she backed away from the bed. "But you were kind of a mess last year, Faith. Your business was dying, and your trucks were on fire. I fixed that."

Her heart pinched. He thought she was a mess? "I didn't *ask* you to do that. Any of it." Her instinct told her to run, get out of this room, but she couldn't do it.

"I have been nothing but kind to you," he said. "Paying for things, bringing you to my family functions, letting you into my son's life."

And? she thought. That was what people did when they were dating and talking about marriage, the way she and Blaze were.

"So I paid for a thing you didn't want," he continued. "It's one thing. Get over it."

"I *did* get over it," she said. "But you still made me feel like a

377

loser for saying thank you." Tears pressed behind her eyes, but she would not cry in front of him. The stubborn streak inside her burst out of the cage she'd kept it in, and she gave his glare right back to him. "You have to admit you were wrong. About the truck and about not calling me—or your son—today."

His jaw clenched again, and he said, "I did what I thought I needed to do."

"Yep." She nodded, her stomach rolling and free-falling through her body. "You did. You always do what *you* think you need to. It's never about what someone else needs." She turned away from him to leave.

"Faith."

"When you feel like I *need* to know something, call me." She opened the heavy door, wishing she were stronger physically, and walked out.

"Faith!" he called after her.

She turned back, holding the door open with her hip. "I'll call Everly and deliver Cash to Trace. Then, I'm sure you Youngs will figure out where he should go and with whom. Good luck, Blaze."

"Faith, come on."

She would not, and she gave him one final withering glare before she walked out.

30

Morris Young pushed his truck to fifteen over the speed limit. "I'm still six minutes out," he said. His wife, Leighann, had called to say she'd had a contraction. Country Quad had started practicing in the studio again, as their tour was only two months away now.

They'd had a nice break, but the music and lyrics had to be perfectly memorized. Their show had to be choreographed and set. They'd brought in their usual producer, and Barb had whipped all of the band members—including Morris, who was orchestrating his first-ever tour for the band—into shape.

But Leigh was in labor with their second child, and every moment Morris wasn't there was a moment he missed. Since he'd missed so much with the birth of their son, Eric, he was determined to be present for as much as possible with this baby.

They were having a girl, and they'd still not decided on a

name. They had a short list of three, and Leigh had assured him that the moment he saw their baby, he'd know her name.

"Are you there?"

"Yes," Leigh panted. "I just had another one, Morris. They're coming closer and closer together."

"You can't drive yourself, Leigh," he said, more forcefully this time. "I will be there in less than five minutes. Where's Eric?"

"Judy took him next door," she said, her voice more even now. "Hurry, Morris."

"I'm almost there." He pressed harder on the accelerator, though he had some corners coming up. "Was Eric early like this?" Their baby wasn't due for another eighteen days, the little stinker.

Suddenly, Morris didn't feel ready to be a father of two. And a daddy to a little girl? He couldn't do it. He didn't know how to take care of a newborn, as Eric had come into his life when the boy was three years old.

He swallowed against his fears and listened to Leigh tell him that Eric was only two days early, which was nothing like this. They'd both learned that each pregnancy was different from another, as Leigh had had different cravings with this baby, and different pains, and had gained way more weight.

"And you just knew his name should be Eric?" Morris asked, though he'd heard this story before.

"When I saw him," she said. "Yes. I can't wait to meet her, Morris."

"Me either," he whispered. "Two more turns, Leigh." He

took one on nearly two wheels, and then jammed on the gas pedal again. He didn't need to keep her talking; just being on the line with her was enough for both of them, and two minutes later, he arrived at his house.

He jumped from the truck, not bothering to close his door, and ran inside. "Leigh."

She was just standing from the couch, one hand on the top of her very pregnant belly and one beneath it. "Here."

He jogged to her, turned, and started escorting her outside. "Almost there," he kept saying, though they still had to make the drive to the hospital.

"What if we don't make it?" Leigh asked, true fear in her voice.

"We'll make it," he said. "You haven't had a contraction in four minutes."

"I feel like she's coming any second now."

"Not any second," Morris said. "Not until we're at the hospital." He helped Leigh into the truck and ran to get behind the wheel. "Call the hospital," he told the truck, and it started dialing.

"Morris, they're not going to do anything."

"Yes, they will." He cut a glance over to Leigh, because he hadn't told her that he'd called the hospital in a non-emergency moment and asked them if he could call in when he was on the way with his wife in labor. They'd told him he could, if he felt like he couldn't help her get up to the maternity wing alone.

And he didn't feel like he could.

Leigh didn't answer, and he looked over to find her eyes

pressed into tiny slits. His pulse bobbed against the back of this throat. "Leigh."

She didn't move, both hands pressing on the top of her belly now.

"Breathe," he told her, feeling like a complete mansplainer. But she wasn't breathing. "Come on, Leigh," he said in a calmer voice. "Breathe."

"Coral Canyon Hospital," a woman said. "How may I—?"

"My wife is having contractions about four minutes apart," Morris said. "I'm going to need help getting her up to Maternity. We're still about ten minutes away."

"Has her water broken?" the woman asked.

Morris looked over to Leigh, who nodded with her eyes still closed.

"Yes," he said.

"I'll have some nurses meet you at the delivery entrance. Do you know where that is?"

Morris did not, and the woman explained it to him. Leigh's contraction passed, and she started to soften in the passenger seat.

Morris reached over and took her hand in his. "Hold on, baby," he said, meaning both her and the little girl she carried.

He found the delivery entrance easily, and two nurses stood there, one behind a wheelchair. He pulled up and jumped out. One had the door open ahead of him, and together, they helped Leigh down and into the chair.

"You can't park here, sir," the male nurse said. "Come up to Maternity, and we'll give you her room number." With that, they took her from him, and all Morris could think was that he was missing things.

Still, he couldn't just defy the rules, and he wanted to have a truck to take his wife and daughter home in, so he got behind the wheel again and went to park. It took him far too long to get up to Maternity, in his opinion, but was probably only seven minutes.

Time enough for one contraction, he thought, and when he entered Leigh's room, she was being helped into a blue hospital gown. So he hadn't missed much.

Relief painted through him and over him. They were here now, and no matter what happened, they had the help of doctors and nurses who knew what they were doing.

Once Leigh had managed to get into the bed, Morris leaned down and pressed a kiss to her forehead. "We made it, honey."

She smiled up at him. "For the first part."

He wanted to ask her what was next, but the nurses converged on them, and Leigh got an IV, her blood pressure checked, and other vitals noted. Another contraction started, and another heartbeat appeared on the monitor.

"Baby's heartbeat is tolerating the contractions okay," one nurse said. "Doctor Plymouth is on his way up."

Morris stayed out of the way and yet nearby, listening to every monitor and every word the nurses said. Leigh didn't ask many questions, and he reminded himself that she'd been here before.

The doctor arrived, and Morris had gone to a few of Leigh's appointments, so he knew the gentleman. He'd delivered almost eight hundred babies, and Morris liked him. "Let's see where we are, okay?"

He grinned at Morris and Leigh and checked Leigh. "Oh, we're progressing nicely. You're doing an epidural?"

"Yes," Leigh said, her voice breathless. "It's not too late, is it?"

"No, ma'am, but it's time. You're up to a six." He smiled at them again and started giving instructions to the nurses. He came to Leigh's side and said, "The anesthesiologist is on his way. Then we'll get this baby delivered."

"Thank you," she said.

"Thank you," Morris added.

"You're staying for the epidural?" Doctor Plymouth asked.

Morris nodded, his throat tight. He reminded himself to breathe this time, and when the doctor came to give Leigh her epidural, he didn't ask Morris if he was staying or not. The nurses helped Leigh roll onto her side, and Morris sat in front of her, holding both of her hands.

He made the mistake of looking up right when the doctor raised the needle, and the whole world spun. He was going to put that in his wife's back?

Morris pressed his eyes closed as all the sound in the room blurred and whirred together. *Don't pass out*, he coached himself. *Do not pass out.*

Thankfully, he didn't, but he definitely drifted. When someone said, "Okay, done," he opened his eyes to find Leigh had already been rolled onto her back. She seemed much happier now, and while Morris had had surgeries in his life and he felt like he knew pain, he didn't know what Leigh had to go through in order to bring a child into the world.

It was awe-inspiring and awesome to him, and Morris leaned over and kissed his wife again. From there, everything accelerated, and before Morris knew it, the wails of a newborn baby filled the air.

The nurses whisked his daughter away before he could truly glimpse her, and Doctor Plymouth kept working with Leigh to deliver her placenta. Morris stayed with Leigh, and he watched in pure wonder as she finished and the nurses brought her the baby girl almost in the next breath.

"Oh," Leigh said.

Morris couldn't say anything. Tears filled his eyes and splashed down his face. He didn't care who saw him crying, but he wiped his face, because his vision had blurred, and he couldn't see his baby girl properly.

"What do you think?" Leigh looked up at him.

Morris gently took the baby from her and gazed down at the tiny, tiny human he'd had some part in creating. He didn't know the official weight of her, but she had to be one of the smaller babies he'd ever seen.

She had her eyes closed, but she belonged to the Youngs, what with her long, sloped nose. A shock of dark hair poked up on her head, and Morris stroked it softly back. He'd never felt this instant love for another human being before, but he did now.

He loved her with a love that knew no bounds, and he didn't even know her yet. But she was his, and she belonged to him, and Morris had never known this kind of foundational love before.

"Rachelle," he murmured. "Her name is Rachelle."

"Rachelle Anne," Leigh said.

"Yes," Morris agreed. "Rachelle Anne Young." His daughter.

31

Abigail Young shushed the baby as Rachelle started to fuss. Leigh was sleeping, and Morris was out in the white barn, and Abby loved, loved, loved these soft afternoons with a newborn in her arms and her own baby asleep in her crib.

Her phone had chimed, startling her and Rachelle, and Abby got to her feet. She shot a look down the hall to the bedroom where Leigh slept—Bryce's old room—and then moved into the kitchen to see who'd texted her.

Speak of the devil—Bryce himself.

I am coming for the wedding, but I'm staying at Gabe's townhome in town. Do you think my dad will be upset about that?

"Yes," Abby murmured, still bouncing the baby as she read her step-son's text. All Tex wanted was for Bryce to come home. Home, home. Here to the ranch and recording studio, so he could see how very loved he was. So he could feel the binding power of the Youngs, something that everyone felt when they came to the ranch and farmhouse.

She'd broken some news to Tex over the course of the past three months, but this? She didn't feel like this was her job. She could play the middleman if that meant Bryce would keep talking to one of them, but Bryce also needed to grow up and talk to his father.

Abby hated texting with one hand, and she figured she could talk and hold a baby a lot better. So she called Bryce and prayed, "Lord, let him pick up. It'll be a fast conversation, but it needs to be said in words, not letters."

The Lord did answer prayers, because her step-son picked up with, "Heya, Abs." If she hadn't been the one to dial her phone, she'd think her husband had answered.

"Baby," she said, sighing. "It's so good to hear your voice."

Bryce said nothing, and while Abby hadn't spoken to him much since he'd left town, on the few occasions she had, when he didn't speak it was because he couldn't. His emotions had tied his vocal cords in knots, and Abby had filled the silence between them.

"Baby," she said. "I think you have to talk to your daddy on this one."

"Abby, I just can't stay there."

"Explain it to me," she said. Bryce didn't like questions, and Abby and Tex had found a way for him to talk to them—they told him to "explain more" or "tell me why you think that." And Bryce did—usually.

"For one, Uncle Gabe won't ask me any questions. He has a

spare bedroom that's ready to go, and I know you and Dad will have to get mine cleaned up."

"The basement is ready for guests any time."

"But I'm not a guest at the farmhouse," he said, his voice tight. "Abby, if I come back there, I'll want to stay."

"And that's bad, because...?" She cringed when she heard the question in her own voice. "I'm holding Morris's new baby," she whispered. "She's beautiful, Bryce. Everyone loves her so much, just like they love you, and Melissa, and OJ."

Abby never knew what to say to Bryce, but God had made it clear to her that he needed to be reassured that he was loved. That love could bring him back home one day, something she wanted and she knew Tex desperately wanted.

He'd spent years away from his son, only touring with him in the summer or having him live in Nashville with him when he wasn't in school. Then, right when he'd gotten his son back, he'd lost him again. Her husband was strong and powerful, the lead singer of a popular country music band—a true shining star in the universe of men.

Yet, losing Bryce had brought him to his knees more than anything else Abby had seen, and she'd listened to her husband weep more in the past three months than she had in the man's whole life.

"At the risk of pressuring you," Abby said, looking up and out the window again. "It might be a good time to tell your daddy your plans for the summer. He wants you to tour with the band, and...yeah. I know he's invited you, and you haven't RSVP'ed."

"I'm working out some details with my job," he said.

Abby nodded, though this wasn't a video call. Rachelle had settled back to sleep, and Abby rocked her gently. She searched for the words to say. The young man didn't need a lecture. He felt like he got one even when he didn't. Both she and Tex had been careful about what they said to him, and really, Bryce was doing plenty of self-loathing without Abby offering him advice he didn't want.

"I love you," she said to him, her throat now the one tight and narrow and full of knots. "Tell me something you've done lately. I just want to hear your voice."

Bryce didn't start talking right away, but then he took a breath and said, "I went and saw another horse this past week. I think she'd do so well with the ones up there, but I had to leave her where she is."

"Mm." Abby turned away from the window and leaned into the countertop now behind her. She adjusted Rachelle's blanket, so it was tighter across her top arm and listened to Bryce talk horses.

The boy loved them with everything in his heart, but he was currently working in a sports bar, waiting tables and charming giggling twenty-somethings and more reserved tourists who left big tips.

He'd mentioned guitar lessons to Tex a month or so ago, but Abby didn't ask how those were going. Bryce had talent in spades, and he could be building his horse rescue ranch or laying the foundation for his country music career.

She didn't want to tell him he was wasting his time and energy at the sports bar, because she was sure he already knew it.

Bryce finished with the horses and cleared his throat.

"I'll have to let you go," Abby said. "Thank you for taking my call, and...let me know if you want to bounce some ideas off me for talking to your daddy."

"The wedding is in four days," Bryce said. "I don't have time to bounce ideas. I'm just going to tell him the same thing I told you."

"Okay," Abby said. "He's in the studio right now. They usually finish about seven, and Morris ordered pizza for everyone afterward." She wasn't sure why she told him that, but sometimes Abby's mouth got away from her.

The doorbell rang, and she straightened from leaning against the counter. "Oh, someone's here. I love you, buddy. I can't wait to see you and give you a giant hug."

"I love you too, Abs."

The call ended, and Abby left her phone on the counter to go answer the door. She wasn't sure who to expect on the porch, because the ranch sat on the west side of town, and pretty far north too.

It had to be a neighbor, but not her brother or sister-in-law. They would've just walked in the side door and called for her.

She opened the door, her greeting dying in her throat. Shock coursed through her as she stared at Faith Cromwell. The auburn-haired beauty reminded Abby so much of herself, especially the wide, fearful edge in her eyes.

Faith carried a huge tray of doughnuts—the cutest, most adorable and most delicious-looking doughnuts Abby had ever seen. The long Johns were only half of their normal length, and they'd been coated with white frosting, then topped with doughnut holes glazed in pink sugar, rolled in it, and then a small plastic piece that looked like a rattle handle.

"Faith." Abby didn't know what else to say.

"Leigh asked me to bring doughnuts for your—" She cleared her throat. "Family party tonight. I came early, so...the doughnuts are here." She lifted the tray as if Abby couldn't see it.

"Come in." She backed out of the way, and Faith stepped up and into the house. "The kitchen is straight back."

Faith continued through the house, and Abby closed the door and patted baby Rachelle's bottom. She wasn't exactly sure how long ago Blaze and Faith had broken up, because Blaze kept everything close to his heart. He shared very little, and what he did share came after lots of questions—which annoyed Blaze to the point that everything spilled out of him.

He came out to the ranch to ride horses a few times a week, always in the morning, and Abby appreciated him including Wade and giving Tex something to focus on besides the band or his son. She spoke to him often, and it had been at least three weeks since he'd glared at her as he went out to the stables.

"Four," she murmured. "Maybe five."

She had a source right in front of her as Faith came out of the kitchen, trayless. "Well," she said.

"Faith," Abby said. "Are you still seeing Blaze?"

Faith's eyes got big and round, then they settled with a heat in them that Abby often felt raging in her soul. Becoming a mother had tamed some of that. Marrying Tex had definitely smothered some of the raging flames inside her. But she still recognized the passion of another woman who had hopes, dreams, goals, and wanted to be her own person.

"No," Faith barked out. "We broke up the day he fell." She started toward Abby, her eyes hooked on hers. "And no one—not even you—called to tell me."

Abby watched her go by, another round of shock coursing through her. "I—I didn't know I needed to call you, or I would've."

Faith reached the door and opened it, and Abby thought she'd simply leave. She paused, her shoulders boxy and rising and falling in quick succession. "I didn't mean to blame you," she said without turning to face Abby.

"You miss Blaze."

Faith spun toward her then, the fire angry now.

Abby patted the baby as she started to squirm and squeak. "I miss seeing you at our family parties," she said quietly. "I know Blaze misses you like crazy. You should see him; he lurks in the corner, glaring and growling at anyone who comes too close to him."

"That's his choice." Faith's fingers fisted and unfisted. "He knows where to find me, and he knows what he needs to do to make things right between us."

"I'm sure he does."

"He just won't do it, because it's his way or the highway." She shook her head. "Forget it. I'm sorry I said anything." She softened and added, "I really didn't mean to blame you."

Abby shook her head. "I'm sorry if I should've done something and didn't. It's a big family, and Blaze is a bit of a...dark horse."

Faith nodded once, and she turned to leave again. "It's good to see you, Abby."

"You too, Faith." She moved to the door and watched Faith trek back to her car. She backed out of the driveway and drove away, and still Abby watched her. Her heart rate had increased, and she didn't know how to make it settle back to normal.

The baby monitor fuzzed, and Abby backed into the house and closed the door as her daughter woke and started to cry. "Come on, Rachelle," she said to the baby in her arms. "Let's go get cousin Mel out of bed. Then we can feed everyone before the boys come in from the barn."

32

Blaze pushed the button on the remote control, and the channel flipped. Another push. Another channel. He didn't care what ran in front of him, because nothing could take his mind off Faith.

Today was just another day without her, and he couldn't remember the last time he'd showered, or what he'd feed Cash tonight.

Since he didn't drink, he was very aware of every painful minute of every blasted day, and his chest started to squeeze. It constricted and tightened until Blaze was sure his lungs would collapse.

They didn't, but he didn't know how he kept breathing through this pain. A person couldn't do it, and yet Blaze pushed the button, and the channel flipped.

He didn't die, and he kept breathing and blinking, and his

heart kept beating despite this emotional agony tearing through him.

Faith walked through his mind, and he closed his eyes to really see her. Everything she'd said to him at the hospital had sunk deep into his gray matter, and he hadn't been able to get it out. He didn't even recognize himself, because he'd never really cared what anyone said to him. Their harsh words about him or something he'd done went in one ear and out the other.

But Faith....

He had to get her back.

He opened his eyes, and the TV still blared the same thing at him. Some sport he didn't care about. Baseball. Spring training.

Blaze sat up straight. "Is the wedding today?" Panic tore through him as he reached for his phone to check the date. As soon as he picked it up, his mind caught up with his adrenaline. Of course Trace's wedding wasn't today. Cash had gone to school, and the wedding was on a Sunday afternoon.

So not today. Blaze checked his phone, just in case Faith had texted or called. Of course she hadn't. She'd laid everything at his feet, and he knew he had to pick up the pieces and somehow make them fit together.

He simply didn't know how. He'd never been in this place before, and he'd never cared this much before, and he simply didn't know how to navigate his feelings for Faith.

His relationship with her had crumbled, and Blaze hung his head and let his eyes close. "Lord," he whispered. "I think I love her. Please, please help me get her back. I'm standing here in the dark, Lord, and I just need a tiny light to point me in the direction I should go. I'll take that step, I promise. I just don't know what the first step *is*."

"Front door, open," the security system said, and Blaze lifted his head and turned toward the front door.

Jem walked in, and Blaze got to his feet. "Hey," he said.

"Goin' shirtless today." Jem grinned at him and continued into the kitchen. He lifted the bags of groceries he'd brought in to the countertop and turned back to Blaze. "Or have you just not gotten dressed? Because it's not exactly no-clothes weather out there."

"I'm dressed," Blazed said.

"Gym shorts is not dressed."

"True. I've got to get ready to pick up Cash and then we're headed over to Trace's to help with...something."

"The thing at Trace's is dinner and then we're tying bows around vases for the centerpieces."

"Wedding in two days," he said, wishing it was over and he didn't have to attend it. He immediately recalled the thought, because it was mean and of course he wanted Trace and Everly to have an amazing wedding. The start of an amazing life together.

"He has the hats too," Jem said as he started to unpack his groceries. "And Tex is bringing the ties."

"I hate wearing matching things." Blaze growled afterward and rolled his eyes.

Jem looked over to him, and the moment went on and on. "You know she's going to be there."

"Who?" Blaze asked, though he knew very well who.

"Everly wants you two to walk down the aisle together."

All of Blaze's bravado fled. His mouth dropped open. "What?"

"She's put Hilde with Gabe," he said. "Leigh and Morris, of course. Tex and Abby. Otis and Georgia. Dani and Mav." He started counting them off on his fingers. "Luke is walking with Ev's friend, Lucy. She's a dog trainer that Ev has known for years. I'm walking with some woman named Charlotte. Ev texted me and said she's 'super sweet and I should compliment her hair no matter what I think of it.'"

He grinned but it went away quickly. "And you're walking with...Faith."

"I can't," Blaze said.

"You should get dressed and head over there right now," Jem said.

"Front door, open," the house said again, and Blaze looked toward it again.

"How everyone just walks into my house is infuriating," he said to Mav.

Mav only smiled, his little boy toddling in after him. "Hey, brother." He didn't comment on Blaze's bare torso as he hugged him, slapping him on the back. "I brought those meals you asked Dani for."

Blaze caged the angry tiger inside him, wishing he still lived in Vegas. Then he could find something to drink, and some bar to hide in, and some woman—or two or three—to go home with.

He didn't want any of that, but he couldn't face the pain. He went outside with Mav, and Jem was right. It wasn't warm enough to go shirtless, even though the calendar had flipped to April and the sun shone more hours in the day than it didn't.

Still, he continued to the back of Mav's oversized SUV and picked up the basket of pre-portioned meals Dani had made for him and Jem and their kids. Blaze paid her a hefty sum for food like this, and he found himself staring at the disposable plastic containers, unable to move.

"Blaze?" Mav asked, and he jerked back to focus.

He turned toward his younger brother. "Yeah?"

"Are you okay?"

"No." Blaze shook his head and looked back into the basket. "No, I'm not okay, Mav." His eyes burned, and he didn't try to force the tears back. "I've been working so hard to find the version of myself I'm supposed to be."

"Blaze, you're a good man and a good brother."

"I miss her so much." Blaze wiped at his face, glad his tears hadn't slid down his cheeks. He couldn't remember the last time he'd cried. "I feel like this breath will be my last, because it hurts so much."

He lifted the basket an inch or two and set it back down. "I need her, and I don't know how to get her back."

Mav put his arm around Blaze, and suddenly Jem was there too. "What's going on?" he said. "The front door doesn't like that it's standing open." He seemed to clue in that Blaze was one breath away from either going postal or breaking down completely.

He put his arm around Blaze too, and he suddenly felt like he might make it through the next moment. And then another one. None of them said anything, and Blaze closed his eyes.

"You're okay," Jem said quietly. "It's okay."

"I can't walk down the aisle with her," Blaze said. "Not with us how we are."

"Then you have to change how you are," Mav said.

Blaze shook his head, anger flooding him. "I've been working to change who I am for almost two years now, and it's not who she wants. I'm not good enough for her." He drew in a breath, feasting on the anger, and lifted the basket. "I'll text Dani thank you for the meals." He stepped away from the back of the SUV, and Mav and Jem parted for him.

"Blaze," Jem said, but Blaze kept walking the way Faith had. She'd walked right out of his hospital room, and he hadn't seen her since.

Five weeks. It had been five weeks of misery, emotional torture, and agony. Sometimes, he'd scroll through their past messages, which made him smile. But then her words from the hospital would land in his ears.

You always do what you think you need to. It's never about what someone else needs.

He'd told her before that he liked to think of himself as confident. She'd laughed the last time he'd said it, but he knew he could be bossy and overbearing. He didn't know how to *not* be like that, though he'd been slowly taming that part of himself.

Not enough, apparently, because Faith still found him arrogant and cocky. He could admit he'd never given much thought to what someone else wanted or needed. He knew how to feed his son, and he'd learned how to listen to his son and how to help him with his homework.

They got along great, and he managed to get along with his brothers, though they irritated him sometimes. Those relationships were easier, because Blaze could leave their houses or kick them out of his, and he had his distance and sanctuary again.

Nothing felt like a home or a sanctuary without Faith.

"Blaze," Mav said. "Let us help you."

Blaze buried himself in putting the food in the fridge and said nothing. As he slid the last container on top of the stack, he paused. His mind opened, as if the bright light in the fridge was a beam from heaven.

He needed help, and his brothers could give it. He should listen to them and take their suggestions into consideration. Maybe he didn't know everything. Maybe they had a need that he could help them with.

Blaze closed the fridge and turned to face Jem and Mav. "Okay," he said, the word grinding through his throat. "Anything will be better than living another day without her."

Jem and Mav exchanged a look, which annoyed Blaze to no end. He caught himself rolling his eyes, and he quickly stopped.

"I need help," he said slowly. "I'm willing to listen."

Mav's eyebrows went up. But he said, "Okay," smoothly. "Jem?"

"It might help if you told us the real reason she broke up with you."

Blaze's face heated. "How did you know she broke up with me?"

"Because if you'd broken up with her, you'd be furious," Jem said matter-of-factly. "I've seen you break up with women in the past. You're angry for a few days, and then you move on. This... you're in utter misery—this is how I was with Chanel. You love Faith, and she left you for some reason."

Blaze hung his head and looked at his bare feet. He suddenly felt naked from head to toe, and he didn't mean physically. "A lot of reasons, actually," he muttered.

"Start with the biggest one," Mav said. The scraping of a barstool against tile filled the house, and then Mav sat down. Jem took the spot beside him, and with both of them facing Blaze, he couldn't hide any longer.

So he looked them in the eyes and started with, "She thinks I don't consider what she needs—and you know what? She's right."

Mav and Jem sat there for a moment, and then Mav nodded. "All right. What specific instance happened that made her think that?"

Blaze sighed and rolled his neck from side to side. But he had to do this. He couldn't attend Trace's wedding without Faith, and it would be the cruelest form of torture to walk her down the aisle if she wasn't his.

So he started at the beginning, all the while praying that Mav and Jem would have some suggestions for him.

Later that night, Everly sidled up to him and handed him a tumbler with Sprite in it. She'd put in several good spritzes of cherry flavoring, as well as a lime wedge. "So," she said.

"I can't do it, Everly." Blaze lifted the glass to his lips and took a sip. Pure joy slid across his tongue and down his throat. "I love this drink."

"Thank you." Everly folded her arms, and as Blaze stood on the edge of the party, so did she. "I can switch you and Luke if that will ease your mind."

"It would," he murmured.

Everly sighed like Blaze was making her life hard on purpose. Maybe he was, but he didn't know how to change a fundamental part of himself in such a short time. It would require so much more from him than a few weeks staring at the television and one talk with his brothers.

"You should know she's miserable without you too," Everly said.

"I don't want to hear that."

"I don't care if you don't want to hear it," Everly said. She gave him a dry look. "I don't know everything that happened between the two of you. She won't say exactly. But Blaze, she called me when you were in the hospital, and I know she was really scared and then really mad. I've never seen her so passionate, actually."

"Everly, please." He reached up and wiped his hand down his face. "I don't want to hear this."

"Go apologize to her," Everly said. "She's open to it."

Blaze finally turned toward her. He'd been standing for a while, and he needed to switch to sitting. "Did she tell you that?"

"No," Everly said. "I just know it. I was so open to Trace coming to talk to me. Any woman who's in love with the man knocking on the door will open it." She gave Blaze a smile and added, "I'll switch you and Luke for now," before she walked away.

Blaze gaped after her. "Any woman who's in love with the man knocking on the door...will open it."

Could Faith be in love with him?

They had been talking about marriage. He could admit—only to himself—that he loved Faith. He wanted to change for her, but he couldn't just take off one pair of boots and switch them out for another.

Changing a person was really hard, really long work, and Blaze was tired. He'd been working so hard—and he still wasn't good enough for a woman like Faith.

He left the fringes of the party and picked up a pretzel dog before joining Gabe and Morris in the living room. Morris held his two-week-old baby and laughed with his twin.

Gabe turned his attention to Blaze, his smile fading slightly. "I heard you switched who you're escorting."

"Everly is kind to me," Blaze said. "Can we talk about something else, please?" He glanced over to Morris, and Blaze hated that everyone in his family was talking about him.

"I'm just wondering if she'll switch me," Gabe said, his eyes now roaming the party. He found Everly and watched her.

"Who are you walking with?" Blaze asked. "We could just switch, but she said she'd give me Luke's lady."

"Hilde O'Dell," Gabe murmured, and Blaze observed the way his voice softened though his eyes hardened.

Blaze gave him a moment by taking a sip of his drink. "What's your story with her?" Gabe had one, that was for sure. He liked this Hilde O'Dell, Blaze could tell.

"She owns the furniture store," Morris said.

"Morris," Gabe warned.

"Then tell him," Morris bickered back. "You brought it up." He took the empty bottle out of his daughter's mouth and moved the baby to his shoulder. She grunted and groaned, and Blaze grinned at the baby sounds that were so cute.

"We had this...chemistry when I bought my desk," Gabe said. "Or at least I thought so. Then I represented her ex-husband in a custody case that was ridiculous."

"Mm." Blaze finished his drink and set the glass on the table next to him.

"And I have her number from buying the desk, so I texted her," Gabe said. "Said I just wanted to chat. Something casual. Not related to the case." He threw back his drink, which was something stronger than Sprite.

Gabe never had more than one drink, and he usually sipped it slowly throughout the evening, so surprise shot through Blaze when he saw his brother throw back the last half of his drink all at once. "Wow," he said. "She's under your skin. The date was bad?"

"There was no date," Morris said.

"She hasn't answered me," Gabe said, almost like he and Morris had rehearsed this. They were twins, and they sometimes did some freaky things Blaze didn't understand.

He flipped his gaze to Morris, who wore concern in his eyes. Gabe hadn't been shy about the fact that he was ready to date again. Blaze hadn't realized he needed to send texts and make announcements about his love life, but he wasn't Gabe.

And he didn't need to be.

He needed to be Blaze Young, but better. He'd already transformed himself from Blaze 1.0 to Blaze 2.0.

Now he needed to level up again, and a glimmer of light flickered in his mind.

"I told him to just text her again," Morris said. "It was right after court, and she was probably really busy."

"Mm," Blaze said. He had gone after Faith again and then again. Her words had hurt him, but the more he ruminated on them, the more he realized what he'd done to her.

He had to fix it, and if that meant he got down on his knees and begged her to forgive him, he'd do it.

Then he'd work on reinventing himself...again.

33

Faith stepped into Trinity's heels, knowing they were the shoes she'd wear to Everly's wedding tomorrow. "I hate them," she said, though she felt like Cinderella and she'd finally been reunited with her glass slipper.

Trinity looked up at her from her spot on the floor. They'd been going through shoes for twenty minutes now, and Trin had found these in the box, in the back of the closet. "You do not," she said.

Tears pressed into Faith's eyes, and she started to weep. "I can't go to the wedding." Her voice came out pinched and nasally. "I know we're friends, but maybe I can just call Ev in the morning and tell her I'm violently ill."

Trinity sighed and clapped her hands on her thighs. "Faith, you need to talk to him."

She shook her head, willing to be stubborn about this thing. "No," she said firmly. "I'm not bending to him again. I'm *not*."

She stepped out of the shoes. "Those are the ones. Can I please borrow them tomorrow?"

"Of course."

She helped Trinity to her feet, and they left the shoe mess to clean up later. Marc had taken the kids to his mother's for a movie afternoon, giving Trinity the house to herself for a while. She craved time alone, without any noise, and that was all Faith had at her house.

She hated it, and she wished she had a reason to have Cash over to her house to make doughnuts, or for her doorbell to be ringing, a stunningly handsome cowboy on the other side of the front door, ready to take her to some secret billionaire restaurant only the rich and famous could find out about.

In the kitchen, Faith sagged onto a barstool while Trinity continued to the coffee pot. They'd baked cookies with the kids this morning, and Faith picked up one of the white chocolate macadamia nut ones and bit off a piece.

"You even make eating cookies seem like a miserable thing to do." Trinity put a mug of steaming coffee in front of Faith, her eyebrows up.

Faith simply chewed as she reached for the sugar bowl. Trinity put a carton of cream on the counter, and Faith poured in a little bit of that too. She stirred, anticipating a great sip, because Trinity made great coffee.

"Faith."

"I already told you I'm not going to him first," Faith said. She could think about Blaze without crying now, but she had to force him out of her thoughts after only a few moments or the tears would come.

"You're going to see him tomorrow." Trinity sat beside her. "What's your plan for that?"

Faith had been thinking about Everly's marriage to Trace Young for a couple of weeks now. Originally, Blaze would've escorted Faith down the aisle to his brother's altar, and Faith would've been dreaming about her own wedding with a handsome Young cowboy the whole time.

Now, she'd been crying at night about the loss of that wedding that had never been on the schedule to begin with.

"I'm not sure," she said. "Trace's family is big. I'm sure I can find somewhere to blend into the background."

"Yeah, because Blaze is the type to let you do that."

"He hasn't come over, has he?" She gave Trinity a glare and lifted her coffee mug to her lips. "Can we please talk about something else?"

"You know you can't cancel on Ev." Trinity broke off a piece of a chocolate chunk cookie. "You'll never do that to her, so I'm just saying you need a better plan than 'I'm going to try to hide from Blaze.'"

"That's not what I said at all."

"That's so what you said."

Faith didn't argue with her again, because her plan wasn't great. "What would your plan be?"

"I'd text the man I'm in love with."

Faith sighed and turned toward her sister. "Did you and Marc ever have a time like this? Did you ever break up? I don't remember."

"We didn't break up per se," Trinity said slowly. "I was ready to talk marriage before him, and after months and months where I felt like I'd been extremely patient with him, I told him we *would* break up if he didn't propose." She smiled as she popped the bite of cookie into her mouth.

"Trinity." Faith enunciated all three syllables of her sister's name with precision. "What if he wasn't ready?"

"He was," Trinity said. "I told him if he wasn't, he should break up with me. But if he didn't want to do that, then he was ready. He proposed three days later." Trinity grinned and grinned. "And we're happily married, and I just *know* you and Blaze could be too."

"He has to get out of his own way," Faith said firmly. "He didn't want to be the reason we broke up, but he is." She met her sister's eye. "I don't want to talk about this anymore."

"You haven't said what he did."

It was what he *hadn't* done, but Faith kept her mouth shut. She didn't want Trinity to judge Blaze too harshly, and she hadn't known about Marc's reticence to get married. Trinity was her best friend, but they obviously kept important relationship details to themselves.

"How's Tabby's teething coming?" Faith asked, clearly closing the conversation.

"I get it," Trinity said. "Well, I can't wait to hear how the wedding goes."

"Yeah," Faith said faintly. "Me either."

BRYCE LOOPED HIS TIE AROUND ITSELF, HIS FOCUS ON THE forming knot in the mirror. If he didn't concentrate on the thing right in front of him, his mind moved in directions he didn't like.

Being back in Coral Canyon brought up things he didn't like, and he expected his father to arrive at Uncle Gabe's town-home in the next five minutes. Bryce had been tempted to text his daddy and tell him that he'd meet everyone at the wedding, but he'd agreed to getting picked up after hearing the disappointment in his father's voice that Bryce wasn't staying at the farmhouse.

He'd rolled into town last night about ten-thirty, and Uncle Gabe hadn't asked any questions. His daughter had been in bed already, and Uncle Gabe had met Bryce at the door in a pair of sweats and a T-shirt and a quick, one-armed hug.

Once he'd been shown his room, Bryce hadn't come out of it until this morning. He'd showered while the scent of bacon filled the house, but he hadn't had a bite of breakfast. The wedding was scheduled for three-thirty, and Bryce had agreed to a lunch with his family before they all went to the wedding.

He was packed and ready to go, because he wasn't staying another night in Coral Canyon. He was sure Dad would try to get him to stay, and Bryce had been working on his reasons for getting out of town for the past twenty-four hours.

"Speak of the devil," he muttered to himself as the doorbell in the townhome rang. Uncle Gabe's place was three levels, with the doorbell down on the ground. He could buzz people up past the business storefront, where he ran his law office a couple of days each week, but he'd been gone for a bit now. His family knew just to come in, and he waited to hear their voices.

He stood in the third-floor bathroom with the door open to the loft, which hovered above the second level below it. His father's voice filled the townhome, and Bryce's heartbeat jumped and leaped. He loved his dad, and being faced with him would be really hard. He'd want to come home. Have his daddy take care of him until he was completely healed. Let Abby feed him and hug him and treat him like he wasn't fragile.

Bryce finished with his tie, sighed, and exited the bathroom to get his bag off the bed, which he'd already made. He didn't want Uncle Gabe to have to do any work at all, and he hoped he'd done enough.

He went downstairs, seeking his father's eyes even as his dad looked his way. "Daddy," he said before he could stop himself.

Dad's face broke into a smile that reached right up into his eyes instantly. "My boy." He met Bryce at the bottom of the steps, and Bryce dropped his bag and let his daddy wrap him tightly in his arms.

"Ooh, it's so good to see you." Dad didn't add the word *finally*, though he could've. Bryce heard it, but he closed his eyes and drew in a breath of his dad's cologne, the scent of the cotton of his white shirt, his strength and wisdom.

He held his father tightly in return, and only the squabbling of his half-sister made him step back. Melissa reminded him that he wasn't alone with his father, and he'd planned it this way for a reason. He couldn't break down now.

He wasn't staying.

He wasn't.

"Look at you," Abby said with plenty of fondness, and she ran her hand along his beard, which he kept clean, trim, and neat. Her smile radiated warmth, and she switched Melissa to her other hip before she leaned in to hug Bryce. "I love seeing you, Bryce."

"Thanks, Abs." He hugged her as well, and then he took Melissa from her. "Hey, sissy. Do you remember me?"

Melissa squawked and flapped her arms, which only made Bryce smile. Her hair had grown in a lot more in the past few months, and it shone like wispy, red gold. Her cheeks had been puffy as a nine-month-old, and she still carried the chub there.

She was a gorgeous baby, with Dad's eyes and Abby's hair and the pointed shape of her chin, with a spitfire personality who would surely lead everyone in her family one day, the way both Dad and Abby did.

"We better get goin'," Dad said. "Where's your uncle?"

"He went over to Uncle Morris's about a half-hour ago," Bryce said, switching his smile from Melissa to his father. "Can you grab my bag?"

Dad eyed it, then bent to pick it up without saying anything. Together, they left Uncle Gabe's townhome, and Bryce made sure he twisted the lock behind him, because Gabe ran his business here, and he'd had to wait for him to unlock the door when he'd arrived last night.

"We thought Angelo's." Abby linked her arm through his. "Does pizza sound good?"

"Have I ever said no to pizza?" Bryce grinned at her, because while he didn't want to admit it out loud, it sure was good to see her, be in her presence, and let her be in charge. He'd never realized how hard it was to be an adult—to always have to be the one in charge of his life.

He had to pay the bills. He had to get or know where his

next meal was coming from. He had to fill his truck with gas. No one would do it for him, and he didn't have to check with anyone. He had to manage it all, and every once in a while, that fact overwhelmed him, and he wanted someone else to be in charge for even a few minutes.

This lunch would accomplish that, and Bryce passed Melissa to Dad and said, "I'm going to follow you over." He took his duffle from his dad. "Then I can leave right from the wedding." He swallowed, sure he'd be challenged here.

Dad's eyes darkened, and his eyebrows drew in. He looked from Bryce to Abby and back. "Can I ride with you?"

Bryce hadn't expected that, but he nodded as Dad passed the baby to Abby and asked her, "Can you drive, love? Meet us at Angelo's?"

"Of course," she said, her eyes filled with concern as she turned away from the two of them and moved to buckle Melissa into her car seat in the back.

Bryce dug his keys out of his pocket, checked for his phone and wallet, had both, and started for the driver's seat. By the time he got behind the wheel, Dad sat in his passenger seat, his seatbelt clicking as he buckled it. He looked over to Bryce, his face a picture of happiness and joy.

"It's really so, *so* good to see you, son."

Bryce started the truck and reached to buckle his seatbelt too. "I know, Dad. It's good to see you too." He offered a small smile. "I know you want me to stay. I know you want me to call more. I know you worry about me."

"All true," Dad said. "I'm not going to deny it. I miss you. You're my son, and I feel like I didn't get enough time with you before you left for college. And now this...." He sighed. "I do worry about you. Both Abby and I do. You won't let me send money, and I'm not convinced you have enough to live in Nashville."

"I have two roommates," Bryce said. "I know how to eat really cheaply, and besides, I get tons of free food from the bar."

"I'm surprised they let you work in a bar."

Bryce shifted in his seat, because his daddy wouldn't like this answer. "Uh, yeah."

"You're not twenty-one," Dad said. "Don't you have to be twenty-one to work in a bar?"

"I don't work in the bar-bar," Bryce said. "I wait tables."

"You serve alcohol." So he wasn't going to let this go. Bryce had known he wouldn't, because Dad could be a bear about some things.

"I don't, actually," Bryce said. "If someone at one of my tables orders alcohol, a bar runner takes it for me. I only carry non-alcoholic drinks. That's how they get around my age."

Dad nodded, and Bryce had barely backed out of the parking spot when he said, "I feel like there's an 'and' to this story."

"And my boss knows me," he said simply.

"He's not telling the truth on his liquor license, is what you mean."

"It's his business, Dad." Bryce shot him a look, but Dad's mouth remained a firm, thin line. "It's a great job," Bryce said. "I need the money it provides, and I can't get better in Nashville without being twenty-one. It's only a few more months anyway."

"You know how many a few is, right?"

"Dad, come on."

Dad said nothing, and Bryce hated the tension and awkwardness in the truck. But they might as well get it all out now. "I just can't stay here, Dad."

"You're going to see OJ at the wedding."

Bryce's jaw and mouth tightened this time, and he imagined it to look taut and thin, just like his father's. "I know. I've prepared myself. I love that baby, as weird as that may sound. I barely know him, but Dad, it's not him that I don't want to run into here in Coral Canyon."

"Who is it then?"

"Bailey," Bryce said honestly. "Any of the Whittakers. Her parents, her uncles, any and all of them. It's the people I went to high school with, who might know something. And of course they'll know something, because this town is small enough for people to still know everyone's business."

"You lived here for a year," Dad said.

"It's Harry," Bryce continued. "Who I made a huge mess of things with. It's not you and Abby, but it's you and Abby too, Dad. You're always asking me how I am and looking at me with big, sad, puppy dog eyes."

"I love you and care about you."

"I know that." He cut a glance over to his father. "I'd love it if we could call and text just...normal things. Things that happened or that you want to tell me. No questions about how I am or if I need money. If I'm not okay, I'll call you. If I need money, I'll call you."

"Will you really?" he asked. "Because I talked to your

mother just last week, and she said she didn't even know you weren't living here."

Bryce's chest pinched again. "My relationship with Mom is my own, Dad." He looked at his father. "I didn't talk to her when I went to college either. You really think she's the one I'm calling and pouring my heart out to?"

"No," Dad said quietly. "I just wish...."

Bryce looked at his phone, which navigated him toward the pizza parlor. "What, Dad? What do you wish?"

"Who *are* you pouring your heart out to?"

Bryce's muscles tightened again, and he worked to release the tension there. "I'm seeing a...counselor," he said. "A grief counselor, okay?" He looked over to his father as he rolled to a stop at a stop sign. "I talk to him."

Dad blinked a couple of times, clearly surprised. "How do you pay for that?"

"He's the uncle of one of my roommates, and he gives me a discount," Bryce said. "He's helped me a lot already, Dad."

"I'm glad, son," he whispered. "I'm so sorry you have to go through this."

"You didn't make my choices for me, Dad," Bryce said. "Tell me you're not blaming yourself." He got the truck going again, moving through the four-way stop and continuing to follow Abby in the truck in front of him.

"Maybe I need to see a counselor too," Dad said, immediately clearing his throat afterward. "I know you're going to hate me, but I figure we'll do all the hard talking now, and then we can enjoy lunch and the wedding."

Bryce let a tiny smile curve his lips for a moment. "You want to know about the tour."

"You're still playing the guitar, and you're so, *so* good, Bryce. You could do a number or two with us."

"Not without being here to practice, and practice, and practice."

"We could include you via video."

His father had an answer for everything, and Bryce had been working through the schedule for Country Quad. "Here's what I can do: You'll be in Nashville for two shows. I can do those. I can do the ten shows you're doing in the South, from Tennessee to Alabama to East Texas. But once Country Quad heads to Houston, I have to return to Nashville."

Only a beat of time went by before Dad said, "Tell me you're not kidding."

Bryce grinned and even added a chuckle. "I'm not kidding."

Dad whooped and laughed, and Bryce had to join him. He loved his father, and he did want to perform with Country Quad. He hadn't made up his mind for his future, and as his therapist said, he didn't have to know everything right now.

He was twenty years old, and he didn't have to have every week, month, or year of his life mapped out. Not yet. Not ever, if his counselor was to be believed.

They arrived at the restaurant, and Bryce managed to find a spot not too far from where Abby parked. He and Dad caught up to her, and Bryce looked at her as she dropped from the truck. "I love you guys," he said. He took her into one arm and opened the other for his dad to join him.

He did, and Bryce let them both engulf him. He let them love him, and he let them hold him up for those few moments.

He allowed the tears to prick his eyes, and he allowed their whispered words of "I love you, son," and "I love you so much, my beautiful boy," enter his ears and ring true in his heart.

Then he stepped back, drew in a deep breath, and wiped his eyes. "I'm really sorry for all the pain and unrest I've caused," he said. "And will probably continue to cause by not coming back here." He looked at Dad and tilted his head slightly. "For making you take care of my horses. For being so undecided about what I want to do with my life. For just all of it."

"Don't you dare," Abby said. "You don't need to apologize to us." She looked at Dad and said, "Right, Tex?"

He shook his head. "Nothing to be sorry about here."

"I did leave town and not tell you where I was going," Bryce said. "That deserves an apology, and I'd appreciate it if you'd just accept it." He frowned at his dad and step-mom, praying they'd say okay, and then they could all go eat.

"Fair enough," Dad said. "I accept your apology."

Abby still looked like she could throw fire with her eyes, but as Bryce gazed evenly back at her, she softened. "Fine," she said, finally turning away to open the back door of the truck. "I accept your apology."

She muttered something else as she leaned into the truck to get Melissa out, and Bryce said, "What, Abby?"

"Nothing," she said sweetly, emerging with the little girl in her arms. "Let's go eat."

His parents flanked him, and Bryce let them, because he loved them, and he was ready to eat, and he was beyond ready to talk about something that wasn't quite so serious.

34

Trace stood in the groom's room and let his brothers dress him. Everly wanted the whole Young show, while Trace would rather sneak away with her and get married at City Hall. As it happened, he and his brothers wore matching bow ties, though only he wore a tuxedo.

They all had the same hat, and it wasn't one he'd worn to another wedding. Oh, no. They all needed new cowboy hats for this wedding. Trace wasn't truly upset by that, as he loved cowboy hats and owned at least two dozen of them.

His son did too, and Trace glanced over to Harry. He also wore a tuxedo—yes, it was the same one as Trace's, just a smaller size—and he looked over to Trace too. Hatless, Trace could see his dark hair, which swept to the side in a handsome way. His dark eyes glinted with happiness, and Trace gave him a smile.

"Ready?" he asked his son, who would be walking Everly down the aisle in less than thirty minutes.

"It's walking, Dad." Harry grinned back at him. "And no, I'm not ready." He looked down to his boots, where Luke currently ran a polishing brush over them. "Uncle Luke is fixin' up my boots."

As if the brand new footwear needed to be fixed up at all.

"You're next," Luke said. "So hang tight there."

"I don't even have my jacket on," Trace said. "I'm not goin' anywhere."

"We need Harry in ten minutes," a woman said, and Trace followed everyone's gaze to the door of the groom's room. The wedding planner stood there, a woman named Ondy Larsen, who was a friend of Ev's.

Ev knew everyone in town, it seemed. She ran a dance studio in small-town Coral Canyon, and she hosted a few dances every year in the parking lot of her building. Of course she knew the other small business owners, consultants, and women trying to support themselves or their families.

She attended the small business commerce meetings in town, which is how she and Faith Cromwell were such good friends.

Trace nodded to Ondy and said, "He'll be ready," and then looked for Blaze. His brother had brought Trace a new pair of cufflinks that morning, and Trace reached for them as he thought of him. He'd been nearly silent these past few weeks, both in person and via text.

Trace and the band had started up regular practices six days a week again, as they had to memorize their set for their new album, as well as mix in bestselling songs from previous records.

That, combined with a rigorous workout schedule, and Trace found his days full again. Then Harry came home from school and Trace turned into a father who needed to monitor his hormonal teenager who happened to have a very pretty girlfriend.

Harry had two guitar lessons per week, and he practiced almost as much as Country Quad. He loved coming out to Tex's farm and the white barn recording studio, but he often wandered over to the stables and took care of Bryce's horses in the evening for Tex, so he could maintain his focus on the band.

Trace loved his son with a ferocity he couldn't explain. His mother hadn't caused any more trouble since last year, and Trace had told her he was getting married again. She hadn't responded, and Harry saw a counselor to deal with whatever feelings, emotions, or issues came up with his mother being so absent.

"Your turn," Luke said, and he switched his polishing station to Trace. "Harry, you're done. Go get your hat from Uncle Morris, and don't make Miss Everly wait for you."

"Yes, sir," Harry said, and he walked away.

"Hey," Trace said, and his son turned back to him. "Hug me first." He didn't move his feet, but he opened his arms to his son.

Harry grinned and did what Trace asked, holding him tightly before he pounded him on the back just once. "I love you, Dad."

"Love you too, bud." He cleared his throat and stuffed his emotions away. He was getting married very, very soon, and he'd vowed he would not cry before he even stood at the altar. Not crying at all was preferable, but he didn't want to stifle how he felt either.

He released Harry, and his son walked over to Morris. He got outfitted with his hat and then got passed to Tex, who took the boy out of the groom's room. Harry glanced back to Trace before he left, and Trace lifted his hand in a *you-got-this* wave.

His son smiled and ducked out into the hall. Tex nodded to Trace too, and then he followed Harry.

Trace's pulse bumped in his neck, and he took a deep breath to try to calm it.

"Jacket," Gabe said, and Trace lifted his right hand to let his brother help him into his jacket. "Other hand." Trace once again obeyed, and he let Gabe pull the jacket up and over his shoulders.

"It's perfect," Gabe said. "Nice tailoring job. Maybe I should move my clothes over to Reggie."

"They do good work," Trace agreed. "We're getting our jackets for the tour done there."

"Perfect." Gabe smiled, though some tension pulled behind it.

Trace knew Morris had invited Gabe and Liesl on tour that summer, but Gabe had declined, saying he had too many clients who needed him to be gone so long. Trace would have Harry all summer long, and his son had never complained about the travel during his off-school months. This year, though, he'd asked about going for only part of it so he could be in Coral Canyon to spend time with his friends.

Trace knew that meant Sarah, his girlfriend, but he did

want his son to have friends. He had four years of school left here—his entire high school career—and Trace didn't want to make Harry's life any more difficult than it needed to be.

His parents lived here permanently. Blaze and Jem would be in Coral Canyon all summer, as would Mav. Any of them would take Harry in a heartbeat, but Trace had told Harry he needed time to think about the idea and make arrangements if necessary.

"Boutonniere," Jem said, and Trace lifted his chin so his brother could pin it in place. "When Luke's done, Daddy wants to circle up."

"Two minutes," Luke said, his brush moving in *swish-swish-swish* motions. The sound comforted Trace, and he took another breath in, slowly expanding his lungs and letting them collect as much oxygen as possible. Like loading a brush with paint, he wanted every cell to be fully saturated before he exhaled anything out.

Then, he'd have as much color in his life as possible with every new breath. Each new moment.

Live in this moment, he told himself. He didn't want to be thinking about something that had already happened or what might come. He wanted to live in this moment, right now.

"All right," Luke said. "Done." He got to his feet and studied his handiwork before lifting his eyes to Trace's.

"Thanks, brother." Trace pulled Luke into a hug, and they pounded one another heartily on the back.

"Boys," Daddy said, which caused Trace and Luke to turn toward him. "Let's circle up."

Trace couldn't imagine raising nine boys the way Momma

and Daddy had, especially as the nine of them came along in fifteen years. Harry was almost that old himself, and Trace didn't have eight kids following him the way Momma and Daddy had.

His father had always had the boys "circle up" when he had something he wanted to tell them. They hadn't had much money growing up, but when they did go on family vacations, Daddy would tell them to circle up so he could give the boys a stern warning about how to act at Yellowstone National Park or some famous museum.

This didn't feel like it would be a lecture, because Trace had circled up with his brothers at a few weddings previous to this one. Funnily enough, for his marriage to Val, Daddy hadn't called them all together. The family had been so splintered back then, and Trace marveled at how far they'd all come.

He lifted his arm over Luke's shoulders, and then did the same on his left for Mav. He'd brought blue handkerchiefs for each brother that morning, and they all poked just a triangle out of their jacket pockets.

They circled quickly, with Tex sneaking in at the last moment. "Harry's with Ev."

"Thanks," Trace murmured, bowing his head.

"All right," Daddy said. "This is Trace's wedding day, and I've never seen him the way he is with Everly." He smiled briefly at Trace, and he only really ever softened for Momma or one of the grandkids. He'd been a good father, but strict, and Trace had never wanted to nor dared to defy him.

Blaze and Luke did, and Daddy still loved them, so it could be done. Trace knew his father loved him. Of course he knew.

426

He'd gotten more and more touchy-feely over the years, and Trace never left his father's presence without getting a hug goodbye.

"I know some of us are feelin' things that could cause some issues this afternoon, and I'm asking you to set them aside for a few hours." His gaze lingered on Blaze, who finally lifted his eyebrows.

"What?" he asked.

"This is Trace's wedding day," Daddy said again. "Your mother wants it to go off without a hitch. Miss Everly has worked hard. None of us will ruin it for either of them."

"No, sir," most of them chorused to him. Blaze said nothing, Trace noticed. He didn't worry about Blaze at all. If he had something going on with Faith, he'd keep it as private as possible. If he disappeared from the dinner party for a while, Trace wouldn't care at all if it meant he could get Faith back into his life.

Blaze obviously loved her, but he'd been extremely tight-lipped about why they'd broken up or why he hadn't done anything to get her back. Trace didn't even know if she'd ended things with him or he'd broken up with her, and he wasn't one to pry or ask questions—especially of Blaze. He was even less tolerant of being bothered with personal questions than Trace himself.

"All right," Daddy said, only a slight frown between his eyes. "Trace asked me to pray, so I'm gonna do that, and then we better get in place."

They dropped their arms and removed their matching cowboy hats, almost as a single unit. Daddy gave them several long seconds to get ready and settled, and Trace bent his head and closed his eyes after only one or two.

Not all of his brothers were religious, but they didn't cause a problem during family prayers. They'd all been brought up going to church and praying, so they knew the drill.

"Lord," Daddy said, and Trace absolutely loved listening to his father pray. Every muscle relaxed as he waited for the next word. "We gather as thy sons, humble and willing to do Thy will. We're grateful for each other, first and foremost. We know Thou has put us into families so that we always have the help, strength, and support we might require. For that, we are so grateful, and we're grateful that we belong to each other, and to Thee."

He paused, and Trace heard at least one man sniffle. He pulled back on his emotions, reining them in the best he could, simply because he hadn't even made it out of the groom's room yet.

"Father, we're grateful Trace has found Everly, and that she has agreed to be his wife and join our family. Bless her today, that she will not miss her parents too badly, and that she can rely on her brothers as well as all of us to buoy her up in case she does."

Trace's eyes filled with tears then, his mouth and nose turning hot as that happened. Everly had loved her parents so much, and he knew she missed them powerfully at times like these.

"Bless us to act as good men today, and always. Bless us with Thy spirit and the ability to hear Thy will and then follow it."

Another pause, and Trace took the opportunity to quickly wipe his eyes while maybe not everyone was looking.

"We love Thee, Lord. Amen."

"Amen," Trace said with his brothers, their voices combining into glorious notes of harmony. The tension increased and then broke as the brothers stepped back from one another. Tex wiped his eyes and grinned at Otis, who did the same.

Morris had always been sensitive, and he grabbed onto Gabe and hugged him. The twins had always either gotten along splendidly well or not at all, and Trace had heard of some tension between them. Maybe not anymore, as they stayed fused together while they whispered to one another.

He hugged Mav, then moved around the circle, getting an embrace and a whispered word of love and encouragement from every brother. Then he hugged his father and said, "You're the best daddy in the whole world. If I'm half of what you are, I'll be lucky and blessed."

"You're a good man, Trace," Daddy said, the highest compliment he could give. They separated and Daddy kissed his cheek. "Let's get married, yeah?"

"Yeah." Trace stood next to his father and let Tex lead the way outside. He'd go last, only to be placed at the front of the line once they arrived at the double doors that led into the banquet hall where he and Everly would be married. "I'm ready," he whispered once Morris, the youngest of the Youngs, left.

"I'm so ready for this."

EVERLY AVERY SMOOTHED HER HANDS DOWN THE FRONT OF her body, her wedding dress very nearly stuck to her skin. She'd chosen to do things a little...less traditional than maybe some other brides would've done.

The tutu around her waist spoke of that. A leotard covered the upper half of her body, with hundreds of silver and clear gems and sequins stuck to it. She also wore snowy, white leggings, those without any sequins or gems at all. The tutu sparkled in the light, only because that was what tutus did.

She wore ballet flats on her feet, because she hadn't danced en pointe in many years, and she saw no reason to torture herself on her wedding day. She'd gone far enough with the dance outfit that doubled as a wedding dress.

Without a mother or sisters to help her get ready, she'd called on the women in the Young family, as well as a few other friends.

"Nervous?" Faith asked, and Everly nodded.

"Do I look like I am?"

"You keep smoothing your stomach," Faith said with a smile. She adjusted a strap over Everly's shoulder. "It's almost time. Harry's here, and if Trace looks anything like his son, you'll need the three men walking you down the aisle to hold you up when you see him." She smiled, and Everly knew what it cost her to be here.

"Faith," she said, love for the woman nearly overcoming her. Their eyes met, and Everly's filled with tears.

"Don't." Faith shook her head, her smile wobbling on her face. "Really, Everly. You're gorgeous, and *he's* the lucky one."

Everly sniffed and pulled everything back into the box where she needed to keep it. For now. She'd cry once she saw Trace. Once she kissed him as his wife. Until then...she'd save her tears.

"Thank you for being here," she whispered.

"Thank you for switching me to Luke." Faith's voice barely registered in Everly's ears, but she nodded.

"Ev," Shawn said, getting to his feet. "It's time." He nodded to the door, which now stood open. She hadn't heard Ondy come in, but the woman stood there now, waving her forward.

Her brother came to her side and wrapped one arm around her shoulders. "You're amazing," he said.

Reggie joined them, and Everly took in the three of them in the mirror. It had only been the three of them for several years now, and Everly pressed a kiss to Shawn's cheek and then Reggie's. "I love you both." Her voice broke, and she didn't care that tears filled her eyes this time.

"I'm so glad you found him, Ev," Shawn said. "And if he doesn't treat you like a queen for even one second, you'll—"

"He will," Everly assured him. Their eyes met in the mirror. "Okay? I know you'll be there if he doesn't, though."

"I will too, Ev." Reggie squeezed her waist. "Now, come on. Harry's ready. The word is everyone's ready. We're all waiting on you."

She sniffled and wiped her eyes. "I'm ready, I swear." She turned into Shawn and held him tightly until her chest felt like it wouldn't collapse. Then she spun to Reggie and gripped him too. They said nothing, because they didn't need to say anything.

A tear ran down her face, and Everly pulled away and wiped at it. "My makeup." Her voice hardly sounded like her own, and she would not say "I do" to Trace sounding so nasally.

To do that, she took a deep breath and contained her emotions. She stepped quickly over to the mirror and swiped at her face to make sure she didn't look streaky or have black makeup around her eyes.

Satisfied that she looked like the bride she wanted to be, she turned toward the door. Ondy had left it open, but she didn't stand in the doorway any longer. Harry did, and he nodded at her smartly, that impish smile just below the surface.

He let it out as she approached, and she opened her arms to the boy. He stood taller than her, and he drew her into his chest and then lifted her right up off her feet.

"Oh, I love you," she said. "I'm going to do my best, I swear."

"I love you too, Miss Everly." He set her back on her feet and held out his elbow. Everly linked her left arm through his, and they went into the hall together. Shawn came to her right side, and Reggie took his place in front of her.

She'd booked the Old Stratham House for her wedding, and they had a gorgeous, stone banquet room covered in vines and flowers and fancy Cupid lights. She'd brought in vases tied with bows for the dinner party following the ceremony, and Ondy had made sure every other detail sat in place for the wedding.

They were just waiting for their bride, and Everly took the first step down the hall, ready to become Mrs. Trace Young.

35

G abe's skin itched along his collar, and he reached to adjust it again. Perhaps for the fifth or sixth time, and he couldn't help cutting his eyes down the row of men. His only saving grace was that Morris had been born six minutes after him, or he'd be at the very end of the line.

"Ladies," Ondy said, her back to the line of men waiting outside the banquet hall. "Find your groomsman, please. Flowers held in the left hand. Your right should go through your cowboy's arm. We didn't practice, but it's walking."

She stepped out of the way, and Abby beamed at Morris and then Gabe as she passed. She touched his forearm, and a swell of affection for the woman filled him. She led the family exceedingly well, the same way Tex did, and Gabe's next reaction was one of wanting.

He wanted a woman like Abby.

Or maybe Georgia, who went past him next. She brought

trinkets and books to Liesl without any reason at all, and Gabe adored that about her.

He wanted a woman like Georgia.

Faith then nodded to him, and mercifully, she only went to the man directly in front of him, Luke. Then she didn't have to pass Blaze, who stood second in line, as Trace had to lead them all down the aisle.

She smiled at him, and Luke must've been bitten by some nice bug, because he returned the grin and offered his arm. Gabe could love a woman like Faith too, and while he hadn't involved himself too much in the drama between her and Blaze, he prayed now that they'd find their way back to one another.

Dani smiled at him as she passed on her way to Mav, and Gabe wanted a woman like her. She wore a bright blue party dress, the same as all the other women Gabe had seen, and she stretched up and kissed Mav before she linked her arm through his.

Leigh appeared, but she didn't have to pass Gabe. She smiled and smiled at Morris, then Gabe, and she kissed him and then reached to squeeze Gabe's hand before settling back into her spot in line.

Gabe wanted a woman like Leigh.

He couldn't believe Hilde had never responded to his text, and he shifted his feet. He'd never asked Everly to switch him for someone else, because she had enough work to do.

In the next moment, Hilde came to his side, her head held high. Gabe's mouth turned instantly dry, and his mind blanked.

"Hello, Gabe," she said, her voice filled with diplomacy.

No one had made him as tongue-tied as this woman in

years. Not even the woman he'd married. His pulse boomed at him to *say something!* and he cleared his throat to give himself another few seconds to think.

Hilde was a stunningly gorgeous woman, and Gabe couldn't even see past her as another woman went by. One of Everly's friends to hang on Blaze's arm, and then another for Jem. Gabe didn't know who they were, and he didn't want to know.

He only wanted to get to know Hilde.

His professional side emerged, and he reminded himself he could talk to anyone, about anything. He was a lawyer after all. "Hello, Hilde," he said, his voice thankfully and mercifully smooth and hitch-free.

He offered his arm, and she slid hers through it seamlessly. Gabe hadn't dated much until the past several months, but he'd been out with enough women in that timeframe to know what attraction felt like. To know how the electricity between him and her lit his veins on fire.

The wedding party hadn't started to move yet, and Gabe had time to chat with her. Maybe this could be their casual conversation he'd wanted a couple of months ago.

"Did you get a new phone number?" he asked.

She looked at him with those gorgeous eyes, blinked her long lashes, and said, "No, why?"

"I texted you," he said. "I never heard back."

Panic crossed her face. Gabe knew, because he'd seen it plenty of times on a client's face, or the man's ex-wife's face. Sometimes another lawyer's face, but there weren't many surprises in family court.

"I—" she started, but then her mouth snapped shut.

"I was hoping for coffee," he said. "Something casual to start with."

"To start with?"

"Everyone ready?" the wedding planner called. "We're headed down the aisle in one minute. Ladies, flowers on the left side, right at the hip, please. Gentleman, right hand in your pocket, elbow out."

"Yeah," Gabe said as he tucked his right hand in his pocket. "To start with. Most people start with something light and casual when they're getting to know each other."

"You want to get to know me?"

Gabe looked fully at her now, despite the fact that Ondy continued to call instructions. Walk down the aisle. Gabe understood.

He smiled at her surprise. "Yes, Hilde." He leaned a little closer, aware of his height, his dark good looks, and the effect his cologne could have on a woman. The question was, would it work on Hilde?

Hilde's whole body tensed as Gabe Young leaned closer and closer to her. Her body wanted to slant into his too, and by sheer will, she managed to stay completely upright. His lips still grazed the side of her face as he whispered, "I want to get to know you better."

She shivered at the nearness of him, the crisp, cedarwood scent of his skin or cologne, the stunning handsomeness he possessed. He was a god of a man, and Hilde's stomach danced with glee at the idea of sipping coffee with him.

"All right." The words scraped her throat as she said them.

"Hmm?" He straightened as the wedding planner approached.

"Gabe," she barked. "No thumb out. All fingers in your pocket."

"Yes, ma'am," he said, turning his charming smile on her. The moment she went by to check his brother, Gabe's smile changed. He looked at Hilde, and a new light entered his eyes. "I didn't hear what you said."

In front of them, his brother took his first step. Hilde's time was running out. She looked right at Gabe, straight into those deep, chocolatey eyes, and said, "All right, Gabe. I'll meet you for coffee sometime."

His smile could make the earth stop spinning, and Hilde felt her world tilt on its axis.

"Great," he said easily. "I'll text you again." He faced the front and added, "Come on, sweetheart. Let's not ruin this for Everly, okay?"

"Okay." She murmured the word, her feet moving in sync with Gabe's. They entered the banquet hall precisely on time, on the right step, and Hilde took in all the fabulous people who'd come to celebrate with Trace and Everly.

The walk down the aisle happened in the blink of an eye, and Gabe paused at the altar, where Trace stood alone. He squeezed his elbow against his side, then released Hilde's arm from his. He stepped up to his brother, and Hilde moved left to join the other bridesmaids on that side of the altar.

She took in the white and blue roses, the sprigs of greenery, and the lights hanging along the arches, the backs of the chairs, and around every window. The building had old masonry and ancient charm, and a sense of relaxation and joy filled Hilde.

Her first wedding had felt this way too. A spirit of magic, almost, that rode in the air. All the happiness in the world. She'd really thought she'd achieved the ultimate dream.

It was amazing how many lies a person could weave inside their lives, and how once they were exposed, they could web out and touch so many other people.

She glanced to the other women arched around the altar, surprised that she knew them all. She and Ev shared a lot of the same friends, and she let the fact that her small-town friends—a librarian, a bookshop owner, a woman who'd once been a florist, and someone who'd owned a bakery in another small town—had gotten these gorgeous cowboys to fall in love with them.

When she looked behind the altar, where Trace still stood as he waited for Everly, and met Gabe's eyes, she wondered if her own fairy tale could start over coffee.

No, she thought. It had started in her store, when she'd helped him with that desk. It had continued when he'd stumbled in court, and she'd picked up his briefcase. The crackling energy between them arced from where he stood, thirty feet away, and Hilde suddenly wanted much more than coffee.

Then an image of her daughter entered her mind, and Hilde told herself that she'd go slow. Coffee. And if the fire between them burned as hotly as it had in the hall, then maybe they could try dinner.

36

Blaze growled under his breath as Luke appeared in the doorway, with Faith on his arm. There was so much wrong with that picture, and Blaze's blood buzzed with live wasps through his veins. His muscles hadn't relaxed since he'd walked into the building a couple of hours ago, and standing at the corner of this altar and watching another man touch his Faith was pure torture.

Her eyes found his, and Blaze couldn't let go. She didn't look away from him either, and she wore challenge in her eyes, something that only drove his attraction to her higher and higher. She'd looked like that the first time he'd met her and snuffed out her fryers.

She'd barked at him not to touch them, and he'd done it anyway. He'd told her the truck was on fire, when really it had been every cell in his body that had been burning.

Luke and Faith stopped in front of Trace, and he gave her a

cursory glance before they separated. Luke gripped Trace like he was losing one of his limbs, and maybe he was. Luke and Trace were really close, because of their work in Country Quad, and when they separated, Luke actually wore emotion on his face.

Blaze hadn't seen Luke show many feelings other than anger. He only got upset when anyone talked about dating, marriage, or his first wife. He'd broken up with Tea months ago, and he hadn't started seeing anyone else, at least to Blaze's knowledge.

Gabe and Hilde came down the aisle, then Morris and Leigh. Once all the players were in place, every eye turned back to the door, anticipating Everly's arrival. She didn't immediately fill the double doorway, and Blaze's heartbeat did flips and cartwheels and back handsprings through his chest.

He had to talk to Faith today. He had to hold her in his arms, sway with her, whisper all the deepest secrets in his soul, and touch his lips to hers. He had to.

He would die if he didn't.

Seeing her on Luke's arm.... It was wrong. She belonged with him.

Everly appeared at the top of the aisle, and the crowd said, "Ahhh," all at the same time. Even Blaze got momentarily distracted from Faith by Miss Everly Avery.

She wore white from shoulder to ankle, but not in the traditional sense at all.

A few feet away, Trace chuckled and lifted his right hand to his heart, as if pledging to Everly right now. Blaze yearned for that, and he tore his gaze from Everly's tutu and the white leggings that stretched down her long, dancer legs, and refocused on Faith.

She had all of her concentration on Everly, and she reached up to wipe her face more than once as Everly advanced down the aisle with her three bodyguards.

Blaze forced himself to watch as her brothers and Harry brought her to Trace, and each one of them hugged him, with her oldest brother leaning in to say something to Trace before he moved away. Shawn and Reggie didn't go far, instead adding themselves to the arc of groomsmen as they took spots next to Tex and nearly behind Trace.

Then Everly stepped up to Trace, and he pressed a kiss to her cheekbone.

Blaze couldn't breathe, and his pulse raced as if attached to a racecar going two hundred miles per hour around a track.

Daddy's words circled in his head, but Blaze had to say something. Right now.

"Dearly beloved," the pastor said, starting the ceremony.

His toes curled in his cowboy boots, and Blaze reached up to adjust his hat. He had to do something. Would Everly forgive him? Would Faith?

He had to try, and it had to be now.

Blaze took a step forward. "I'm so sorry," he said, his voice rusty in his throat. The weight of too many eyes settled on him, including Trace's and Everly's. "I'm dying, and I have to say something."

"Right now?" Tex growled from his left.

"Yes." Blaze gave him a wicked look that caused his brother

to fall back to his spot in the groomsman line. "Right now." He looked past the altar and the pastor to Faith.

Her eyes had gone as wide as they could go, and she stared openly at him. Blaze took another step forward, his belt buckle almost touching the altar where Trace and Everly stood. "Faith, I can't do this. I can't stand here without you."

Trace sighed, but it was quiet and short, and Blaze didn't look at him.

"I'm in love with you," Blaze said, increasing the volume of his voice so the whole hall could hear. "I hate not talking to you every day, all day long, and I am the most miserable man in the world without you. I know I messed up, and I will do anything and everything I can to fix it. Please."

His voice broke, and he drew in a breath to strengthen himself. No one said a thing, not a single thing, including Faith.

Blaze had found himself standing there watching Luke escort the woman he loved down the aisle, and he stepped between Tex and Trace and then past Shawn and Reggie, who likewise gaped at him.

"I love Faith Cromwell," he said. "Most of you probably know her. She owns the pink doughnut trucks with all the sprinkles on them? Great doughnuts, by the way."

"Blaze," Everly said quietly, and he did drop his chin and look at her. "This is my wedding. You have five more minutes."

He nodded and some of his courage failed him when he took in the shocked look on his momma's face. Daddy wore his stoic mask and shook his head, but Blaze was used to disappointing his father. He had tried hard not to do it in the past few years, but this had to be said. Now.

442

"She broke up with me," he said. "Weeks ago, because I do what I need to do, and I don't consider what she needs to do. How she needs to communicate with me, or how she needs to feel about certain things. I've been thinking a lot about that, and I fear I'm doing it again, right now. Because I have to say this. I *need* to, because I wanted to start punching something when I saw her on my brother's arm."

He turned his back on the crowd, ready to wrap this up. He started toward her, his eyes not leaving hers with every step he took. "I love you. I can't stand seeing you with anyone else. I'm not perfect, but I can change, Faith. I can. I've proved over and over that I can, and I will consider each and every one of your needs before my own."

Blaze reached her, noting that her eyes weren't nearly as round as before. "Blaze," she whispered.

"I love you," he said again, his voice much quieter. "Please forgive me, Faith. I will try to do better."

"You don't try," a woman said, and Blaze glanced down the line of bridesmaids. Abby stood out from the rest, her hands on her hips. "You *will* do better, Blaze."

"I *will* do better," he said, looking back to Faith. "I will. I promise I will. But I need you. I can't go another day without using your phone number. Without hearing your voice. Without kissing you. I can't."

"All right," Faith said. She shot a look toward the altar, toward Everly and Trace. "All right, we can try again." A tiny smile curved her lips, and then Faith looked at Leigh, who nodded.

"Go on," she whispered.

She checked with every woman in the bridal party, and finally Everly. She grinned and nodded, and then Faith's eyes came back to his.

"I'm sorry," Blaze said. "I'm so, so sorry. I will do anything and everything needed to get you back into my life. Anything." He drew a breath, and it finally felt like the air went into his lungs the right way. "Everything. Whatever you need, I will do."

"I just need you," she said.

Blaze blinked, sure those hadn't been the words she said. "What now?"

She giggled and then launched herself into his arms. "I love you, too, cowboy."

He wrapped her in his arms and spun her around as the crowd started to clap and cheer. He wanted to kiss her senseless, but this wasn't the time or the place, and he quickly put her back on her feet and leaned in close. "I have ruined this wedding. Let's let them finish, okay?"

"Or start," she whispered back.

He ran his lips down the side of her face in a false kiss and stepped back. "Okay." He walked around the front of the altar again, avoiding his parents' gazes. "Thank you, everyone. Sorry. Sorry." He retook his place between Tex and Otis, both of whom smiled like they didn't know how to arrange their faces any other way. Tex was still clapping, for crying out loud.

"Carry on," he said to the pastor, as if the man needed his permission. "Sorry, Everly. Sorry, Trace."

She grinned like the Cheshire Cat too, and Trace lifted his hand in an *it-doesn't-matter* gesture.

Blaze knew it did, but he didn't feel like ripping down every flower, vine, and light in this place. He didn't feel like upending the altar and bellowing like a beast.

I love you, too, cowboy.

Faith's voice rang in his ears, and as the pastor started the wedding ceremony again, he only had eyes for her. The good news was, she didn't look away from him either.

37

Tex loved nothing more than a wedding, and he felt very much like his father as he watched and listened to Everly say, "I do," to being Trace's wife.

"Trace Joseph Young," the pastor said. "Do you pledge yourself to Everly Noel Avery, to be her legally and lawfully wedded husband, to honor her, cherish her, and support her in daily life, in tough times and in rosy, in things that are easy and things that are hard, as long as you shall live?"

"I do," Trace said, and the pastor smiled at the pair of them. Tex wished he stood a little closer to Abby, so he could squeeze her hand and whisper to her that he loved her. So much love attended a wedding, and it wove through and around Tex, making his heart grow and expand with so much love for his family.

Bryce hadn't been in the wedding party, but he sat next to

447

Momma, and she had her gloved hand in his, and once the pastor said, "I now pronounce you husband and wife. You may kiss your bride," they both started to clap.

Tex joined them, adding his big, boisterous voice to the cheering lifting up toward the ceiling, the very heavens, to celebrate the joining of these two people into one family.

Everly's brothers engulfed the couple, leaving Tex to turn toward Blaze. "You couldn't wait until after the wedding?"

Blaze laughed outright, something he hadn't done in weeks. "No," he said. "I couldn't. Excuse me." He stepped out of the line and went behind the altar, only pausing long enough to shake the pastor's hand briefly before continuing toward Faith.

He hugged her again, lifting her right up off her feet, and Tex lost sight of them after that. He was happy for Blaze, and he and Otis closed ranks. "Leave it to Blaze," Otis yelled so Tex could hear him. "Always making a scene."

"He loves the spotlight," Tex said.

"He did," Otis said. "I don't think he does anymore."

Trace turned toward him, and Tex opened his arms wide. He laughed as Trace stepped into him, and he didn't care at all that he might be crushing their flowers as he gripped his brother in an embrace.

"Incredible," he said. "Just incredible." He stepped back. "You and Ev. You're both incredible."

"Just following your example, once again." Trace grinned as he pulled back, and then he stepped into Otis. Tex retreated to Abby's side, and together, they fell back to join Bryce. Abby bent to pick up Melissa from where she sat on the bench beside her brother, and Tex had never felt more complete in his family than he did right now.

He linked his arm through Bryce's, glad when his son pressed his elbow against his body and didn't try to move away. Tex wasn't going to bring up staying in Coral Canyon. Not again.

Bryce didn't want to, and Tex had to let him fly. It felt like the hardest thing he'd ever had to do, and he couldn't quite get himself to let go. Still, he had to figure out a way, and as he smiled and watched Everly's brothers hug her as one unit, he let their love wash over him in wave after powerful wave.

She let tears run down her face, though her smile was as bright as the sun, the moon, and all the stars put together. When Shawn and Reggie set her on her feet, she stayed close to them and wiped her eyes, using them as a shield against the rest of the patrons gathered together for the wedding.

"Uncle Blaze knows how to bring people to their feet," Bryce said.

"That man," Momma said, and Tex looked around to find him and Faith. "I'm going to give him a piece of my mind. Disrupting the wedding like that." She reached up and patted her hat, which was pinned precisely in place. Her white curls bobbed out from beneath it, and she added, "Come on, Jerry. Let's give them our congratulations and then go help with the food."

Tex only continued to grin as his parents moved away. Everly had hired a caterer and an event planner; they didn't need Momma's help with the food. "I'd give a kidney to be in the room when she gives Blaze a piece of her mind."

Abby burst out laughing, and Bryce turned to gape at Tex before he did too. "Me too, Dad," he said. "Can you imagine?"

"Blaze will bear hug her into silence," Abby said between giggles.

"Ma Ma Ma Ma!" Melissa babbled, and Tex swept his darling daughter away from his wife.

"No, you say, 'Da-Da-Da-Da!'" He nuzzled his nose against Melissa and leaned back, chuckling, as her baby arms started to flail. He met his son's eyes, and so many things were said then. Tex had the very, very real feeling of time stopping. In that moment, the Lord allowed him to see his son so plainly that Tex could never deny what he felt moving through him.

Pure love. Joy. A bond that he would never be able to share with anyone else. Not Abby. Not one of his brothers. No one. Bryce was his child—he carried his DNA in his veins—and Tex could *see* him.

The moment broke, and what Bryce had experienced, Tex couldn't know. "So," he said as he settled the baby on his hip. "When are you takin' off?"

"After dinner," Bryce said casually. "No reason to leave a free meal behind, right?"

"You'd get lots of free meals here," Abby said just as casually. "Tex, baby, there's Lorelai. I'll be right back." She bustled off to talk to one of her friends from the library, and Tex knew there would be no "right back" for her.

"Don't set her up with Jem," he called after his wife, but Abby didn't hear him. He sighed, and Bryce heard that.

"Is she really trying to set up Uncle Jem?"

"Discreetly," Tex said. "Because she knows he's like a wolverine right now. If anyone gets too close, he'll claw off their face." He grinned at his son, who blinked at him with wide eyes.

"You miss a lot not bein' here," Bryce said. "I'll say that."

"Yeah," Tex said. He curved his free arm around his son's shoulders. "Let's go scope out the shadiest spot outside, and you can tell me what songs you want to play while on tour with Country Quad this summer."

Bryce, to his credit, didn't roll his eyes or sigh. "I don't know, Dad."

Tex nodded him toward the door, where a rush of early spring air had hit the banquet hall. "Country Quad will pay you to tour with us."

His son walked away, a scoff riding the air behind him. "Sure," he said. "That's fair."

"It is," Tex insisted. "You'll be working, son. It's no free ride on tour." Bryce had come on tour with him before, and it had been a free ride then. But Tex would work those fingers and his guitar-playing skills this summer if he came. Abby and Melissa were coming too, and it was already going to be a very different type of tour than Tex had ever been on before.

Nerves rode in his stomach over it, and as he followed his son outside, he suddenly had another reason to call the therapist Abby had found for him. He hadn't been able to pull the trigger yet, because he didn't want every conversation to rotate around OJ or Bryce or both of them.

Now, it wouldn't have to.

"I need to see a contract," Bryce said. "From King Country,

Dad." He faced Tex. "I don't want this to be you and Abby paying me, just so I'll come."

Tex nodded, hoping the swallow moving down his throat wasn't too pronounced. "Okay. I'll call Marv in the morning."

"You do that." Bryce looked around and pulled a pair of sunglasses from his inside jacket pocket. "Now, let's see if I can get through this wedding without seeing anyone else I know."

"Stick with us," Mav said, joining them with his family. "We'll insulate you." He grinned at Bryce and then he took him with him toward a table where Leigh and Morris had settled with their two kids too.

Another dose of love filled Tex. Mav always knew what to say and how to say it. He always came in at the right moment, and Tex quickly pulled out his phone to text his brother. If he wanted Bryce on tour with him this summer, he needed all the help he could get.

A couple of weeks later, Tex sat in his truck and looked at the ordinary office building standing in front of him. Abby and Melissa hadn't come with him, and he'd wanted it that way. Now, however, he wondered if he should've relied on the strength of his wife to get him out of the vehicle and inside the office.

Doctor Dalton Michaels' secretary had been amazingly bright. She'd found an appointment for Tex he hadn't had to wait months to get. His pulse rattled at him, and Tex reached to unbuckle and push himself out of the truck.

He'd worked out at the gym that morning and showered there, so he hadn't been back to the farm yet. Things were coming along nicely for the summer tour, at least according to Morris. Tex had never concerned himself with tour details—that was why Country Quad had a manager.

Trace had gone on his honeymoon and returned already. The four of them, plus Morris, were leaving Coral Canyon for their first scheduled arena concert in Nashville in only six weeks.

It felt impossibly far away and yet so close at the same time. All of his brothers except for him and Morris had to wait for school to get out for the summer, and they were all bringing their wives and children.

Luke had started to disappear inside himself a little bit, and worry gnawed at Tex over him. Out of the five of them going on tour, only Luke wouldn't have a significant other. He already felt left out, and Tex had talked to both Trace and Morris about him privately.

He'd not brought up Sterling Boyd again, because Tex valued having both ears attached to his body, thank you very much. That thought alone got him to crack a smile, and that got him to keep walking toward the building.

Inside, he scanned the directory quickly, though he knew he needed to go up to the third floor. Once off the elevator, a bolt of panic hit him, and he nearly turned around and ran for the stairs. Instead, he kept going.

Into the office. He gave the woman sitting there his name. She looked up at him with a hint of wonder in her eyes, and Tex only pushed his cowboy hat down lower over his eyebrows. He did not need the world to know he was here today.

He pushed the thought away. So what if he was here today? Plenty of people saw counselors and therapists. It wasn't shameful, and he lifted his head and gave the receptionist a smile.

"He's right on time today," she said easily, all traces of awe gone. "So I can take you back right now."

"Great." Tex followed her down the hall and into a room. He had no idea what to expect, but it was less doctory and more homey than he'd imagined a therapist's office to be. A brown leather couch took up the wall beside the door, and a man turned from the wall of windows where he stood.

"This is Tex Young," the woman said. She didn't enter the office but indicated that Tex should. "Tex, this is Doctor Michaels."

"Thank you," he and Dr. Michaels said at the same time. Tex relaxed as he entered the office. He could talk to this man; he talked to strangers and people all the time. He'd literally made a living off of it.

"Tex," he said when he met the counselor in the middle of the room.

"Dalton." He smiled at him. "It's your first time here. Where would you like to sit?" He indicated the couch. "You can sit there, and I can take the chair. Or some clients would rather be by the windows, and I can sit at my desk."

Tex gauged the two areas, and he decided the windows sounded nice too. "It overlooks the wildlife refuge," he said. "So let's do the windows."

Dr. Michaels smiled, and they settled into their spots. Tex

wasn't sure what he was supposed to do next, and thankfully, Dr. Michaels didn't have a notebook or anything else to distract him. "So, Tex," he said. "Why don't you tell me what's on your mind."

Tex drew in a breath, his mind suddenly a frenzied mess. "Well, I'm worried about my son," he said. "And my brothers. And my band. See, I'm the lead singer for Country Quad, and we go on tour in only a few weeks—oh, and my wife and daughter are coming for the first time, so I'm worried about that too."

Dr. Michaels smiled and held up one hand in a universal gesture of *slow down, buddy*.

"Okay," he said. "We're not going to solve all of this today." He possessed a good air about him, and Tex relaxed further. "We may never *solve* all of it. *Solve* isn't the right word. But let's start with one thing. The *biggest* thing you'd like to talk through."

Tex took a moment, and shockingly, when he spoke, it was to say, "My brother, Luke," and not anything about Bryce. "I'm worried about my brother, Luke, and my brother Otis." Especially if Bryce came on tour, Tex would need to add some prayers about Otis, OJ, and Bryce to the time he spent on his knees.

"All right," Dr. Michaels said. "Brothers. How many do you have?"

"Eight," Tex said.

Dr. Michaels's eyebrows flew up. "*Eight* brothers?"

"Yes, sir."

"Wow." He chuckled. "I thought I had a lot with five."

"I wish I only had five," Tex said dryly. "And I can tell you which ones." They laughed together, and then Tex wiped his palms down the front of his jeans. "See, Luke isn't married or dating anyone, and everyone else on tour is. He feels left out, and he's already got some issues with that, so I'd like to help him if I can...."

38

Faith stepped out of the sundress and into her plain, everyday clothes. She gathered everything in her arms and left the dressing room to find Trinity there, her gaze locked on her phone. She looked up, the glazed look in her eyes disappearing instantly. "So? The dress? The shorts?"

Faith's stomach buzzed at her. "I don't know," she said. "I don't see when I'm going to wear any of this."

"You're going to wear it to your parties and catering events," Trinity said. "Come on. Marc and I are buying you the dress for sure."

"I don't need you to do that."

"It's for your birthday." Her sister took the sundress from her anyway, and protesting would be like trying to get a river to run in the opposite direction. Trinity left the dressing room area, her voice floating back to Faith, "She's almost ready."

Faith followed her, curiosity pricking at her. Who was she talking to? She and Trinity had come shopping alone.

She stepped out into the department store and came to a severe halt. "Blaze Young," she said.

"Oh, and she's feisty." He grinned at her, his hands all tucked neatly in his front pockets, and nodded to the clothes in her hands. "Did you find something you wanted?"

"You're not buying it for me."

He rocked back on his heels. "No, ma'am. I wouldn't dream of it." He wore the look of a tomcat who'd just eaten a canary, and Faith narrowed her eyes as she looked from him to Trin. "What's going on?"

"I'd love to steal you away from your shopping," Blaze said, his smile slipping away. "But only if you're done." He cut a look over to Trinity too. "I know you love hanging out with your sister."

"I have to get back to the kids," Trinity said, and that was true. "Faith, get the shorts, okay? And that blue blouse. It looked so good with your hair."

She let Blaze take all of the clothes from her as she moved over to hug her sister. "You called him, didn't you?"

"No," Trinity whispered back. "It was a text, and I think he's adorable. So be nice to him."

Faith stepped back, somewhat surprised at Trinity's chastisement. "I am nice to him."

Trinity grinned at him. "I know you are." She gave Blaze a look. "You be good to her."

"Always," Blaze said, and Trinity held up the dress as she turned to leave. "I'll give this to you next time I see you."

Faith didn't want to say that she was going to wear it for Blaze's birthday, which was the following day. She simply let her sister take it toward the checkout counter, and then she looked at her handsome cowboy boyfriend.

"I didn't mean to interrupt," he said. "She texted me and said you were done." He'd been nothing but kind and courteous and respectful since his brother's wedding. He checked with her about everything, and he didn't do anything she told him she didn't want him to do.

Of course, Faith wanted him to do everything now that she knew he loved her and that she'd admitted she loved him. She adored seeing him walk up to her doughnut truck while she was working, and she couldn't wait to text him back when he sent her a message.

They spent every evening together, and every spare moment where she wasn't working or he wasn't busy with his son.

"I am done," she said. "I am going to get the shorts and the blouse." She plucked the articles of clothing from his arms. "You can leave the rest in the dressing room."

He did, and she watched him as he came back to her. "It's your birthday tomorrow."

"So my momma keeps telling me." He sighed, his smile right behind it. "She's still not very happy with me about the wedding thing." He laced his fingers through hers, and everything inside Faith quieted and settled.

"So I made a deal with the devil," he said.

Faith tried to navigate the racks of clothes and look at Blaze, but that didn't work very well. He kept his gaze forward as she asked, "What does that mean?"

"It means we're having dinner over there tonight," he said. "For my birthday. That way, tomorrow is all mine." He reached the main walkway in the department store and looked at her. "Me and you. Cash has school, and then we'll do something with him in the afternoon and evening. But he even said if I want to go out with you, he's cool with it. He just wants to do the cake and candles with me." The lines around his eyes crinkled as he smiled, and Faith loved everything about him.

"Yes, we're doing the cake together tomorrow," she said coolly. "Remember, you'll have a couple of hours to yourself after school? Trace told me he'd babysit you."

"Babysit me?" Blaze growled, and Faith giggled as she bumped him with her hip.

"He said you could go horseback riding with him and Harry and Tex."

"Mm hm."

Faith wasn't one to put on public displays of affection, but she did stop near a rail-thin mannequin and tip up onto her toes in front of Blaze. "Or you can come to my house and watch us bake for you. It's up to you. He wants it to be a surprise, but if you want to crush your son's dreams...." She grinned at him and let her eyes drift closed. "It's been ten minutes since I saw you, and you haven't kissed me yet."

"Tragedy," he murmured just before touching his mouth to hers.

Any moment where he wasn't kissing her was a tragedy, and Faith sucked in a breath through her nose and kissed him back.

"Come on," he said under his breath. "Let's get out of here, so I don't feel like the world is watching."

Faith hurried through checking out, and since she'd arrived with Trinity, it was easy for her to swing up into Blaze's truck and put her shopping bag on the floor beside her feet. Blaze's hand slid along her hip, and she faced him.

"Faith." He didn't say anything else, and he didn't have to. He wore a soft, loving look on his face, making his harsher, darker features lighter and more rounded.

"You just want to kiss me again." She leaned down and kissed him this time, enjoying the slow way he slid his fingers through her hair and the passionate but careful way he kissed her back.

"I love you," he breathed against her lips. "Thank you for giving me another chance."

Faith put her hands on either side of his face and held him in place. "Blaze, baby, I don't need you to keep telling me thank you for giving you another chance." Her eyes met his and searched. "Do you need to keep saying it?"

He shook his head slowly. "Not if you don't need to hear it."

"I don't."

"Feels like we needed a lot of chances." He sighed and stepped back. "I hate that I let so long go by before just coming over and talking to you."

"Yeah," she said. "Me too, but you know, I could've shown up at your place."

He shook his head, and Faith didn't want to repeat this conversation anyway. They'd had it a couple of times now.

"Listen," she said. "We're going to have an amazing pre-dinner dessert somewhere. Then dinner with your parents. Tomorrow is all about you, and it's going to be the *best* thirty-ninth birthday anyone has *ever* had."

His gaze came back to hers. "All about me?"

"Yes," she said simply, the heat in his gaze making her stomach drop. "It's your birthday. That means it's all about you."

"What if I just want you for my birthday?" He stepped closer to her again, something Faith really liked.

She leaned closer to him, feeling dangerous and a little reckless. "Then you better put a ring on my finger, Mister Young."

"So it's not all about me." He grinned.

"Within reason," she said. "I know you don't want to get engaged super fast. I'm okay with that. But...then, some...perks can't happen."

Blaze started to laugh, and he shook his head as he backed out of the doorway. "Maybe I can pray down a blizzard or something. Get all the power shut off, and then I'll have to sleep over at your place again." He looked just crazy enough to do it too.

"Please." Faith scoffed. "It's May. There aren't blizzards in May."

"Sometimes there are," he said with a devilish grin. "Sometimes there are."

THE FOLLOWING DAY DAWNED BRIGHT AND BLUE, WITHOUT any storm clouds in sight. So whatever Blaze had or hadn't prayed for hadn't impacted Mother Nature all that much. Faith had taken the entire day off from her doughnuts, and she'd be picking up Cash from school that afternoon so they could make his father's birthday cake together.

The twelve-year-old possessed skills in the kitchen, and he could put together a basic doughnut dough now without a recipe at all. Faith liked baking with him, and she liked having a connection to him that wasn't through his daddy.

She'd barely poured her morning coffee when her doorbell sang. Blaze's voice followed it, and she called, "In the kitchen," as the sound of his footsteps came closer.

He appeared, and he was carrying a gift in a snowy white box and a bright red ribbon around it. "It's not my birthday," she said, eyeing the present.

"This is for me," he said.

Faith raised her eyebrows. "Is it from me?"

"Not exactly." He wore mischief in his eyes as he entered the kitchen. "Can I have some coffee?"

"Yes, you may." She stepped back so he could have free rein in her kitchen, and he made himself a cup of coffee as he chatted about what he wanted to do that day. Breakfast at some new place in town only the rich and famous knew about, of course.

A movie he'd been dying to see. Lunch with Tex and Otis and Trace, who would then take him out to the ranch for horseback riding.

"Then we'll meet back up about five?" He looked at her and lifted his mug to his lips. He'd placed the bowed box on the corner of the countertop and hadn't looked at it again. "Do the cake and candles and song and dance, and then, it's dinner here."

"I'm not cooking," Faith said. She'd also planned very little of this birthday experience for him. "This isn't at all what we're doing today."

"No?" His eyebrows went up. "You sure?"

"Blaze." She swatted at his chest. "We're having breakfast at Sliders, not whatever fancy schmancy thing you said. The movie is literally in the Old Main theater, and it's *Being Human* from the nineties. You'll probably fall asleep."

"Mm." He lowered his mug, his smile only halfway on his face.

"Then we are having lunch with your brothers, and they are taking you horseback riding. We are meeting up *at your place*, not here, for cake and candles with Jem and the kids. Then, I promised you an amazing dinner, and I booked a private pod at the Sanderson Estate."

"Did you now?"

She rolled her eyes and turned to leave the kitchen. "I'm going to go get dressed. Is it blizzarding?" She made an overdramatic pause in front of her living room windows, which faced her backyard and only showed her sunshine and blue sky. "Nope. Looks like I'm safe to wear the sundress."

"It's not safe for me," he muttered, but Faith went to change without replying. She took a few minutes to blow out her hair and swipe on some makeup. It was her boyfriend's birthday, after all, and while Blaze tried hard not to attract attention, he did. Everywhere he went, he did. Everyone in town knew who he was, that he had a lot of money, and that he had connections with other celebrities.

On the rare occasion that they went out to fancier places, she felt like a plastic doll on his arm, her face arranged in a never-ending smile. Thus, the private pod at Sanderson's tonight.

As she walked down the hall, she called, "Sorry, that took an extra minute. I couldn't find my earrings."

Blaze didn't answer, and it took Faith a moment to find him when she re-entered the living room and kitchen area of her house. For he had gotten down on both knees.

"Blaze Young," she said. "Get up right now."

He held the white box in front of him. "This is a gift for me," he said. "I know it's fast. I know I said I didn't want to get engaged quickly. I know it's my birthday."

Faith opened her mouth to say all of those things, each of them registering a little bit late. She snapped her mouth closed.

"I don't care about any of that," he said. "I need you in my life permanently, Faith. I can't do that without a diamond ring, so I'd love to give this to myself today, on my birthday." He untied the ribbon and let it fall to the floor. "I love you. I know I'm not perfect at it yet, and I may never be. But I love you in the way I know how right now, and I promise I will continue to change and adapt to love you in the way *you* need me to."

He looked up at her, so much hope burning brightly in those dark, dark eyes. "I want you in my life and my son's life. I want you in my home. I want you in my bed. I want you all the time. What's important to you is important to me."

He stopped talking, but he hadn't asked her any questions

yet. A look of confusion ran across his face. "I've never done this. The first time was...rushed." He cleared his throat. "I'm carrying on a little, aren't I?"

Faith smiled softly at him and took a couple of steps closer to him. "Your knees have to be hurting by now."

"A little," he admitted, that joy back in his expression. "Faith Cromwell, will you marry me?" He flipped open the box, and Faith should've expected to be utterly blinded by the strength and size of the diamond inside. It sat nestled in light blue—no, teal—silk, the kind she knew came from expensive designer jewelry stores in major cities.

"Blaze," she breathed out. Her eyes moved from the gem to his. "Honey, I can't wear this ring here. People will follow me home and do anything to get it." She closed the lid on the box. "Baby, we don't live in Vegas."

A frown appeared between his eyes as he said, "Todd said Vi loves jewelry from Vincent's."

Faith was sure she did. The country music star probably had occasion to wear a diamond this big. Faith dropped to her knees too. "Blaze, I love you." She ran her hands down the sides of his face, stroking his beard. "I do. I want to marry you. I'm going to say yes, because who would tell a man on his knees with a diamond like that—on his birthday—no?"

She smiled at him and touched her mouth to his in a quick, chaste kiss. "But, baby, we're going to need to modify our plans a little today."

"We are?"

"Yes." She nodded and kissed him again, a little longer and a little less chaste this time. "Because we need to go by a regular jewelry store and get a regular diamond ring." She beamed at him. "Okay?"

"You don't like the diamond ring?"

"I love it," she whispered. "But really, Blaze. It's...not typical small-town Wyoming jewelry. I really do think it'll cause a huge uproar everywhere I go."

"And you hate that."

"*You* hate that too," she pointed out. "You retired to small-town Wyoming to get away from that."

He looked down at the closed box. "So we'll make it into something else."

"Like a paperweight?" She giggled, the sound gaining strength the longer it went on. "I know. It can hold down the receipts in the truck, so the wind doesn't snatch them away."

Blaze laughed too, and together, they quieted. "I love you," he whispered. "I don't want to be on this journey with anyone but you."

"I love you too," she said. "Now, let me help you up so you can kiss me properly." She took the box with the enormous diamond in it, really feeling the weight of it, and got to her feet. Blaze groaned as he did, and Faith gave him a sharp look.

"I'm okay," he said. A smile graced his face, widening with each passing moment. "Am I crazy, or did you just say you'll marry me?"

She wrapped her arms around his neck. "You're not crazy, cowboy." Faith gave her eyes a half-roll. "Well, about this."

He chuckled and gathered her close, close, closer. "Mm, I'm going to kiss my fiancé now." And he did.

467

Read on for a sneak peek at **GABRIEL**, featuring Gabe Young, the next brother in the Young Family who's STILL waiting for that date with Hilde...turn the page to get to the bonus chapters!

Sneak Peek! GABRIEL Chapter One:

G abriel Young sat on the piano bench and resisted the urge to look at his phone. He knew what time it was—time to teach Liesl her lesson. His darling daughter came skipping into the living room with both hands wrapped around a Winnie the Pooh cup with a straw poking out the top.

"Come on, baby," he said to her, patting the bench beside him. "It's time to practice."

She wasn't quite old enough to protest yet, to know that practicing the piano would be something they'd fight over, to give him the stink-eye before she huffed and then did what he asked. Not that he'd ever done any of those things. A smile spread through him internally before appearing on his face, because his momma had tried to teach all of the boys how to play the piano.

Only Gabe had truly enjoyed it, and he'd still argued with

her over practicing, glared when she wouldn't pass off his pages, and gave her the silent treatment if she insisted he play in church when he'd rather not.

Liesl set her cup on the floor and climbed onto the bench beside him. "Twinkle, Twinkle?" She looked at him with pure light in her face, and Gabe's love for her tripled, expanded, and grew until it had no end.

"Yep," he said before leaning down and pressing a quick kiss to the top of her head. "But first, we do the warm-up. Remember that?"

They'd just started lessons a couple of weeks ago, and Gabe had only done it so Momma wouldn't. Gabe did everything he could to be both mother and father for Liesl, and he already hated having to drop her off for someone else to take care of, even his mother.

As Liesl put her tiny fingers on the keys, and Gabe prompted her through how to move them up and down the ivory in a scale, he wondered—not for the first time—if he should move his office to Coral Canyon completely.

He'd been operating out of Jackson Hole for the past five years, and he'd gotten a lot of high-profile clients who liked to keep things on the down-low when it came to their personal lives by being the one and only firm that focused on father's rights. There were only two lawyers at the firm now, but everyone knew Young Family Law was the place to come to get a dadvocate. No, he hadn't named his firm something cutesy and punny.

He wasn't cutesy or punny. He was a no-nonsense, single father lawyer who fought for the rights of other single fathers who wanted to be involved in their children's lives. He lived the life. Walked the walk. Knew the law better than anyone.

As Coral Canyon had expanded, and as his brothers had returned and brought with them the family name, Gabe had picked up more clients here, in his hometown about an hour from his office in Jackson.

He'd taken on another lawyer last year, the first at his firm. It was just the two of them, and an office manager, and he loved providing the personal attention and utmost privacy his clients wanted and needed.

Can't leave Jackson, he told himself as Liesl finished the warm-up and looked up to him again. His firm had roots there. He had a partner there. His *life* was there.

He nodded at her and watched as Liesl opened the book. She was such a tiny waif of a child, and the book dwarfed her as she brought it to her lap.

"This is a C," she said, pointing to the note. Her high-pitched voice, so proper and so perfect, made him smile again.

"Play it," he said.

She did, and then she proceeded to name all the notes and play them on the piano, one finger at a time. "Let's write them in today," he said. His optimism remained cautious, because while Liesl attended a private daycare that had preschool built into it, she hadn't advanced much in the way of writing.

Most children her age could write their names and knew their ABCs. Liesl could sing the song, sure. She could scrawl her name, but the curvy S still gave her a trouble or two. Her fingers, small as they were, couldn't seem to hold the pencil right.

He gave it to her anyway, his thoughts drifting to the next problem on his list as Liesl got down and put the book on the bench. She knelt in front of it, and Gabe watched as she drew a clunky C in the line below the note.

Hilde O'Dell ran through his mind. Trace and Everly's wedding had aged a month now, and they still hadn't gotten together for dinner. Heck, he'd take coffee at this point. Of course, he'd promptly left Coral Canyon and returned to his work in Jackson, and when he'd come back to this three-level townhome that doubled as his office space here, Hilde had had an emergency at her furniture store.

Every date they set up got spoiled by something until Gabe had stopped putting things on his calendar.

As Liesl sang *Twinkle, Twinkle Little Star* Gabe pulled out his phone and texted the beautiful brunette who hadn't left his mind for longer than five minutes in the past several months. He wasn't even sure how or why she'd infected him so strongly, only that she had.

How's the store? he asked, quickly following it with. *I'm just finishing with something, and then we could grab a bite to eat if you're not busy.*

He'd dated very little since his divorce, because anyone he started to get to know had lots of questions for him about his ex-wife. Hilde already knew he had a daughter, though Gabe hadn't introduced the two of them formally. He wouldn't do that until very deep into the relationship, because he held Liesl very close to his heart. She was the last door for him, and if he unlocked and then opened that to let a woman in, he might as well drop to both knees and propose.

Hilde had a daughter too, Gabe knew, because he'd represented her ex-husband in a hearing a month or two back. The man had not won the hearing, and Gabe had passed his case to Brian, his partner in Jackson. Not that Hilde's ex had any reason to want something different than his custody documents gave him, and Gabe didn't expect to hear from him again.

"I play, Daddy?"

"Yes." He twisted and groaned as he lifted his four-year-old back to the bench. He swiped the book out from under her quickly and set it on the piano. "Sing with it, okay?"

She grinned, her joy filling the whole living room, then seeping into the kitchen. All of the living accommodations sat on this second floor above his office space, with the three bedrooms in this townhome all on the third floor.

His phone buzzed as Liesl's pitch-perfect voice filled the air, and Gabe ignored it. This moment filled his life with beauty, and for half a breath, he wished Kendra was here to see their daughter. The girl had his ex-wife's nose, and the slope of her chin. She'd been an excellent singer too, and Liesl had surely gotten that from her mother.

A mother she'd literally never met.

Gabe's heart sagged in his chest, because he had loved Kendra once-upon-a-time. For a brief hour or two after she'd been arrested, he'd even thought he'd stay with her. They'd work through things. Then he'd looked at his precious newborn, and he'd known he couldn't do that to one of God's choicest children.

So he'd left. He'd filed for divorce. He'd made sure the law was on his side, protecting Liesl—and him—from Kendra's reach.

And now, he sat listening to his daughter sing a nursery rhyme while he thought about going out with someone else. She finished the song, and Gabe beamed down at her. "Amazing," he murmured, placing another tender kiss to her head. "Do it again, okay? I'll record it for Gramma."

He stood from the bench, so it was just Liesl taming the huge piano as she played and sang. Momma and Daddy would love that, and Gabe even had the fleeting thought to put the video on the brothers' text. His eight brothers shared about their families and lives constantly, but Gabe usually only hearted their pictures or congratulated them on something. He rarely contributed anything of his own.

Morris, his twin, had been encouraging him to attend more family functions, and if Mav texted any more, Gabe might have to start billing him for the time it took Gabe to go through the messages. Even so, he loved that he had a lifeline to his brothers.

For now, he thought, because five of his brothers—including Morris—would be leaving for the summer tour of Country Quad in another month. Gabe tried not to be bitter, but the back of his throat narrowed slightly. He pushed himself to swallow over and over, and it finally subsided as Liesl finished her song.

He stopped recording and started clapping for her. She got to her feet right there on the bench and launched herself into his arms. The two of them laughed, and Gabe held her close to his chest. "You're so good," he told her. "Always be good, okay, baby?"

"Okay, Daddy." She squirmed to get down, and he lowered her to her feet. "I go swing?"

"Sure." He watched her grab her cup of Winnie the Pooh water and skip out of the living room. She pulled hard on the sliding glass door and went out onto the balcony, letting in a blast of brisk spring air, to the swing he'd installed for her there. With her toeing herself back and forth, Gabe extracted his phone from his pocket.

Hilde had texted and said, *The store is drying. There are fans everywhere, and the noise is going to drive me mad. I'd love to get out of here. I need to check on a couple of things, and then I'll let you know.*

That had come in ten minutes ago, and Gabe hadn't answered. He started tapping, and another message popped up. *I'm good anytime now,* Hilde said. *If you still are, I think I'm close to your place.*

Gabe looked up and toward the door that led down the stairs to the first floor, as if Hilde would be there. Of course she wasn't, and Gabe still needed to text his mother and ask if she could take Liesl for a couple of hours.

I'm good now, he said. *I've got to take my daughter to my momma's, though. So maybe like 20 minutes?*

You live in the new townhomes off Beaver Dam, right?

Gabe had multiple conversations with multiple people regularly, so he said, *Yep, I'm on the end.*

I see your truck.

Gabe's heartbeat started pounding through his body like a big steel drum. Hilde was here. He was really doing this—whatever this was.

"It's starting to get to know a woman," he told himself. He was only twenty-seven years old, but he'd been married before. He and Morris had dated a lot in high school, often pretending to be each other just for kicks. He'd dated a lot in college too, and all through law school. He'd graduated and started his firm as the youngest lawyer in the state of Wyoming to have ever done so.

He could go grab dinner with Hilde. It would be fine. Just fine.

"You need to tame your inner grump," he told himself as his fingers flew to get a call going with Momma. Her line rang, and his impatience grew in the time it took her to answer.

"Hey, baby," she drawled. "How are you?"

"Good," he bit out. "I need you to take Liesl for a little bit. Can you?"

Momma didn't answer right away, and Gabe pressed back another sigh. "I just...there's this woman I've been trying to meet up with, and she's actually here now."

"Daddy and I are on our way to get ice cream," Momma said. "We'll swing by and get Liesl."

"Two hours, tops," Gabe promised. "Sorry I was a little barky there."

"You're going out with someone new," Momma said. "I should've known when you called and didn't text." She laughed lightly, but Gabe couldn't join in. He strode toward the steps, then doubled back. "We'll be there in ten minutes," she said.

"Okay." He practically threw the phone as he opened the sliding door. "Liesl, Gramma and Gramps are on their way to take you for ice cream, okay? Come inside and get your shoes on."

"Ice cream!" She cheered and left her cup on the ground as she came running inside. Gabe fought the urge to tell her to get it. They had very little time, and he suddenly wanted to shower.

He didn't, but he sent a quick text to Hilde to keep her updated on what was going on, and then he changed out of his white shirt and tie and into a light blue button-up. He brushed his teeth, and helped Liesl sweep her hair up into a ponytail.

They barely had that done before the doorbell rang and his mother's voice called from down the steps. "Go on," he said to his daughter. "Be careful on the steps. You walk, not skip."

"Okay, Daddy," she said, already running away from him. She barely broke stride to open the door, and Gabe grabbed it to keep it from crashing into the wall.

"Come on, my precious pretty," Momma said at the bottom of the steps, her arms outstretched for Liesl. The girl launched herself from the third step, and Momma laughed as she caught her. Daddy looked up the steps as Gabe came down them, and he too grinned like having Liesl was the best thing that could happen to them.

"Thanks, Daddy," Gabe said, giving him a quick hug.

"Of course," Daddy said. "We love having her." He leaned closer. "Plus, now Momma will let us go to The Real Cow, and I love their butter pecan." He practically glowed, and Gabe wished he got that excited about a treat.

His parents left with Liesl, and Gabe stood on the sidewalk in front of his townhome and waved them down the street. Only then did he turn toward the navy blue sedan that he'd not seen parked on this road before.

The tall, dark, gorgeous Hilde O'Dell rose from it, the breeze clawing at her long skirt enough to revel a knee-high pair of black leather boots. Gabe's throat went dry at the sight of those, and his eyes snapped back to Hilde's.

A smile curved her lips, and her hips swayed left-right, left-right as she walked toward him. His pulse increased, and Gabe tried to remind himself of who he was and why he was worthy of going out with a goddess like her with every hammering beat of his heart.

Sneak Peek! GABRIEL Chapter Two:

Hilde O'Dell couldn't stop smiling as she approached the mysterious cowboy in front of her. Gabriel Young. He didn't wear a cowboy hat like the multitude of other men in this town, but Hilde could picture one perched on his head just-so. After all, she'd seen it there at his brother's wedding.

He tipped his head as if he wore one, and his hand even rose as if to touch the brim. His mouth curved ever-so-slightly, like he was trying to fight the smile. He won, of course, because a man like Gabe didn't lose. "Ma'am," he said. "Thanks for waiting."

His breath rode the air, and Hilde caught mint with the whiff of his cologne. The man could bring a woman to her knees, that was for certain. Hilde locked her legs and kept her smile in place as she paused about an arm's length from him. "Finally," she said, immediately regretting it.

Her smile faltered, but Gabe closed the distance between them and brushed his fingers along hers. "It's good to see you again," he said as if she hadn't spoken at all. He pulled his hand away, leaving hers cold though the spring weather had already started to warm considerably.

Wyoming weather could be fickle, and Hilde wouldn't be surprised if it snowed again before summer truly set in, as it was barely May.

May.

Her birthday month. Hilde was turning thirty-seven this year, and her gut gnawed at her. She'd been lying awake at night, thinking about this very man. "Gabe, I wanted to ask you something," she said at the same time he said, "Should we go?"

He unleashed the smile now and gestured for her to go back to her car. "You drive," he said. "I'm not as familiar with the city as I once was. Then you can ask me whatever you want."

She had not anticipated being the one to drive, but she didn't let her step hitch as she turned and went back to her car. Gabe opened her door for her, and Hilde sank into the driver's seat. An exhaustion pulled deep in her bones, and she wasn't even sure why.

Lynnie had been sick this week, and that always tore at her mother's heart. The store had been getting new shipments every day as they anticipated their pre-summer sale, and then the Memorial Day sale Hilde hosted every single year.

This year, she'd coordinated a sort of Market Faire too, and other vendors, food trucks, and local artists were coming to set up booths in her parking lot over the long, Memorial Day weekend.

She hitched her smile back into place as Gabe slid gracefully into the passenger seat. For once, she'd like to see a single hair out of place on him. He glanced over to her and paused. "You don't want to go."

"I'm just a little tired," she said.

He didn't pull his seatbelt across himself. "Then let's not go."

She leaned her head back against the rest. "What were you finishing up?"

"Excuse me?"

"You said you were finishing something up, and then we could go to dinner."

He looked away, as if he needed to study the seatbelt system to get it right. "Yeah," he said. "Something with my daughter."

A flash of irritation bolted through Hilde. "Yeah, I've got a million things with mine too." She put the car in drive and perhaps pressed on the gas pedal a bit too hard.

Gabe yelped—actually yelped—and threw his hand up to grab onto the handle there. "Whoa, where's the fire?"

"Nowhere," she said as casually as she could. She came to a stop at the end of his street and looked at him again. "How old are you?"

He blinked at her, clearly confused. "I'm sorry?"

"How old are you?" She said each word crisply.

"Uh, twenty-seven." He looked out the windshield and to the rearview mirror. He lived on a street with plenty of other people, but there wasn't another car in sight at the moment.

Just as Hilde had feared. A decade. He was a *decade*

younger than her. The image of a cougar prowled through her mind.

"Why?" he asked.

"How old do you think I am?"

More blinking, as if he'd never thought of it before.

"I can't believe you're only twenty-seven," she said. "Did you graduate from college when you were eighteen?" She looked down to his lap and back to his face. "You're a lawyer, for crying out loud. Doesn't that take years and years of schooling?"

She eased onto the gas pedal more carefully this time, and Gabe lowered his hand from the bar above the window.

"Yes." He straightened his jacket—a lightweight windbreaker. Sensible. Not too brightly colored. Nothing flashy, but definitely well-made. His daughter had been wearing the cutest flowery jacket too. "I took an...accelerated course of study." He cleared his throat and said nothing more.

Of course. Gabe wasn't exactly verbose, and Hilde's mind suddenly blanked on what they could talk about. That wasn't entirely true; she had plenty to talk to him about, she simply didn't want to.

You're sabotaging, she told herself, and she'd have to report to Mindie and Rhea in the morning. Heck, maybe even tonight. The fans at the store did drive her crazy, and she could've left for any reason this afternoon. Lynnie was home sick. It was almost time for her to leave anyway. She wanted to swing by the grocery store.

Instead, she'd told two of her best employees that she'd gotten a text from Gabe and was going to dinner with him. Mindie had even made her switch shoes with her, saying she'd gotten asked out on more dates wearing these ridiculous boots than any other piece of footwear.

Hilde wasn't twenty-five like her front-end manager, but she'd put on the boots. She wasn't trying to get a date with just anyone. She was trying to get another one with Gabe.

Then say something!

She wanted to spend a couple of hours with him, lazily ordering five courses from a delectable menu. Instead, with Lynnie home, she needed to choose somewhere fast and casual. "Italian okay?" she asked.

"Yes, ma'am," he said quietly.

She glanced over to him and found his attention out the window. Hilde nearly rolled her eyes, and she wondered if this would take off. If it did, would a relationship with him work? It didn't feel like it would; they didn't even have anything to talk about.

"How was work today?" she asked, finally bringing his attention back to her.

"Good," he said. "I just had client meetings this morning."

"So you must've been finishing...dinner with your daughter."

He shook his head, those milk chocolate eyes so mesmer-izing she nearly drove into the curb. Thankfully, she managed to save the turn into a fast-casual place with the best pasta carbonara in town. He still didn't say what he'd been doing, and for some reason, that annoyed Hilde to no end.

She pulled into a parking space, put the car in park, and faced him. "Listen," she said. "I know you're really protective of your daughter. In the texts we've exchanged, you've said that, oh, fifteen times. I know you don't want me to meet her right away. That's fine. I'm like that too."

Gabe nodded a couple of times, and she wanted to reach out and grab his chin. Make it go up and down as she mimicked talking.

She drew in a breath. "I'm thirty-seven, Gabe. Or I will be, in a few weeks. That's a whole decade older than you." The extra air in her lungs whooshed out. "And this is never going to work if you're just going to sit in the passenger seat, silent. You have to at least *talk* about your daughter. You have to talk about your life."

"I know," he said, the words filled with a defensive bite.

"Then why did you even ask me out tonight?" she asked. "So we could sit in awkward silence while you refuse to answer my very simple questions?"

Those eyes fired at her, and she'd swear in a court of law they darkened by one degree. "Piano lessons," he finally said. "I was giving Liesl piano lessons."

Surprise caught Hilde completely off-guard. "Oh," she said. "I—you play the piano?"

"Yes," he said. "Do you?"

"A little," she said. "I made Lynnie take lessons up until a couple of years ago. She's pretty good."

He nodded again, and said, "I don't care about the age difference."

"It's weird," she said.

"Is it? Why?"

"I think it technically qualifies us as an age-gap couple. Society looks down on those."

Gabe scoffed. "You've got to be kidding."

She shook her head, her mouth as straight as her hair. "I'm not kidding. I don't normally date men younger than me at all."

"Ever?"

Hilde hadn't dated in a while, but Gabe didn't need to know that within the first fifteen minutes of their first date, when he wouldn't even say he'd been giving his daughter piano lessons. Honestly, the way he held back information, she could assume he was doing much more nefarious things inside that brand-new townhome.

"Ever," she confirmed. "Given our tense ride over here, and how hard it was for you to tell me you play the piano, I'm not convinced we should even go in."

Gabe folded his arms, and that made his presence in her car twice as big. "What do I have to do to convince you?"

Hilde allowed a small smile to curve her mouth. "You can drop the Mister Grumpy attitude, for one. Smile when you see me. Say hello and act like you're glad to see me."

"I *am* glad to see you," he said. "I said it right out loud." His brow furrowed. "Didn't I? I swear I did."

"Actions speak louder than words, Mister Young."

"I really don't want you to call me that," he said, back to his dark, dangerous persona. "We're not in the courtroom. We're on a date."

"Almost," she said.

He sighed, the sound of it hissing through her whole car. "I may have certain protections in place, Hilde, that's all."

"Protections? From what?"

"With a woman like you?" He cocked his eyebrows, and

Hilde had no idea what he meant. A woman like her? She wondered what he saw when he looked at her. He leaned closer, the lightning that seemed to zip around his person so electric and so, so hot. "From falling completely on the first date."

With that, he got out of her car, the resulting slam of the door closing loud enough to jolt her back to her senses. She'd been leaning toward him too, and she hadn't even realized it. She hadn't even seen him go around the hood of the car before he was opening her door.

He took her hand, and while she still wasn't sure she should go inside and continue this date with him, she had no other choice but to stand. He pressed her into the small space between his body and the car, and Hilde's pulse jumped into the back of her throat.

"I don't want you to call me Mister Young," he said.

"Okay," she whispered.

"I don't care about the age difference."

"Okay."

"I think you're gorgeous and smart, and maybe I was nervous when you first showed up. I was rushed getting ready, and I hate that. But I'm *thrilled* to see you. I can't wait to tell you more about myself, and Liesl, and whatever else you want to know." His hand moved up her back to her neck, where he slipped his hand, his long fingers curling around to her ears.

She nodded, her throat too dry to even enunciate a two-syllable word, as she fought an entire rainstorm of shivers.

"Your turn," he said.

"My turn?"

"What do you want?" he asked. "And what don't you want?"

Hilde came back to her senses. She was a tall woman, but Gabe still towered over her. He had both hands on her body, and Hilde let her eyes drift closed so she could really feel where they connected.

His hand along the skin of her neck. His hand on her waist, appropriately high, but with enough pressure to keep her right where he wanted her.

"I want you to talk to me," she said, opening her eyes. "I've been in relationships where I'm digging and digging for conversation or how you feel. I hate it."

He swallowed. But he said, "Okay," without a hitch in his voice.

"I'm busy. You're busy. I get that. We both have children and very demanding jobs. But if we do this—*if* we really are going to do this—we have to find a way to make time for one another. I have to come first sometimes."

He nodded. "I can do that."

"Not all the time," she said. "I get it. Sometimes my store comes first. Sometimes you'll have a case that comes first. Our daughters are both important to us. But how long did it take us to get here?"

"Well, someone wouldn't text or call me back," he said. "So a while."

Hilde lifted her hand, quelled the shaking in her fingers, and ran them up the front of his shirt. "I've apologized for that. Are you going to hold it against me forever?"

"No," he said simply. His pulse beat against her fingertips, and it did seem a bit frenzied.

"Do I really make you nervous?"

"One hundred percent," he whispered as he leaned in. "And I will deny that to my dying breath if you tell anyone until we're ready for them to know it."

She couldn't help the very girly giggle that came out of her mouth. "Deal," she whispered back, because she believed Gabe wholeheartedly. The man didn't do anything halfway, so he wasn't testing her out. But he was cautious, and he would go slow. He wouldn't be texting anyone about this date, despite the fact that he had eight brothers and his parents had just taken his daughter for him.

"Anything else?" he asked. "Have I convinced you to go inside yet?"

"Almost," she said, enjoying this game.

He pulled back, and his eyes searched hers. "Name it," he said. "And if I can do it, I will."

Hilde smiled at him, feeling brave and completely out of control at the same time. "Gabe, this won't be for a while, but I expect a really, really, *really* amazing first kiss. If you can't deliver that...maybe we shouldn't even start this journey."

His eyes widened and his eyebrows nearly shot off his face. The pulse beneath her fingers accelerated for a couple of seconds, and then it quieted again. "I have a couple of follow-up questions for that," he said.

"Mm." Hilde stepped to the side, her hand falling naturally to meet his. She laced her fingers through his. "Ask away."

"How long is 'a while' in Hilde-time?"

"It's more than physical," she said. "It's emotional too. A man has to really earn the right to kiss a woman, don't you think?" She looked over to him, not sure what she'd find. It wasn't to see him nodding. "She—I—have to feel cared for. It's not something cheap, not when you're my age."

"Okay," he said. "So I'm hearing that's an undetermined amount of time."

"Correct."

"Is there a scale or rubric for first kisses you can provide me?" He smiled at her, and oh, he kept that thing hidden for a reason. The glory of it rivaled the sun, and Hilde wanted to bask in the light and joy of it. "A man would like to be prepared as much as possible if he's expected to get all the way to 'amazing' on the first try."

Hilde laughed and shook her head. "It's subjective."

"I don't like that answer." He reached for the door of the restaurant and opened it. "I feel like you're setting me up for failure."

Hilde let herself look at his mouth for only a moment, because any longer would have her knees weakening and a sigh to course through her lips. "Gabe, I don't think a man like you knows how to fail." She squeezed his hand and tugged him inside. "See? You got me into the restaurant when I was sure we'd end the date after fifteen minutes."

They joined the line, and Gabe leaned into her again. Hilde definitely pressed back into him too, though she told herself not to be so obvious. The man addled her brain, and she couldn't think properly around him. She knew this honeymoon phase of her hormones would wear off, but it felt exciting and fun to be here now.

"Do I get a second chance if I mess up the first time?"

"I can allow for a do-over," she said with a smile. She scanned the menu, though she'd been here scads of times and knew exactly what she wanted.

"Good," Gabe said. "Because I'm really good at do-overs."

Hilde was sure that was true, and she found a ribbon of anticipation running through her. Not for her first kiss with this man...but the second.

Well, the date isn't over yet! That's good news for Gabe, right? Look for Gabe in paperback by scanning the QR code below.

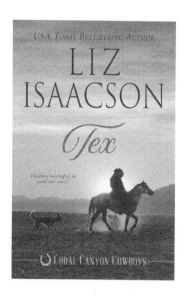

Tex (Book 1): He's back in town after a successful country music career. She owns a bordering farm to the family land he wants to buy...and she outbids him at the auction. Can Tex and Abigail rekindle their old flame, or will the issue of land ownership come between them?

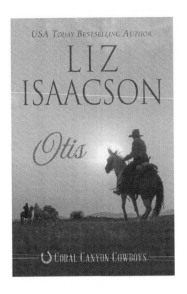

Otis (Book 2): He's finished with his last album and looking for a soft place to fall after a devastating break-up. She runs the small town bookshop in Coral Canyon and needs a new boyfriend to get her old one out of her life for good. Can Georgia convince Otis to take another shot at real love when their first kiss was fake?

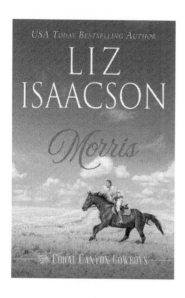

Morris **(Book** **3):** Morris Young is just settling into his new life as the manager of Country Quad when he attends a wedding. He sees his ex-wife there—apparently Leighann is back in Coral Canyon—along with a little boy who can't be more or less than five years old... Could he be Morris's? And why is his heart hoping for that, and for a reconciliation with the woman who left him because he traveled too much?

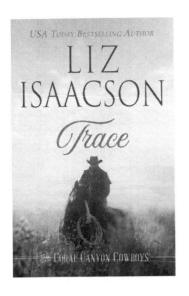

Trace (Book 4): He's been accused of only dating celebrities. She's a simple line dance instructor in small town Coral Canyon, with a soft spot for kids...and cowboys. Trace could use some dance lessons to go along with his love lessons... Can he and Everly fall in love with the beat, or will she dance her way right out of his arms?

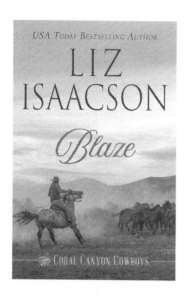

Blaze (Book 5): He's dark as night, a single dad, and a retired bull riding champion. With all his money, his rugged good looks, and his ability to say all the right things, Faith has no chance against Blaze Young's charms. But she's his complete opposite, and she just doesn't see how they can be together...

...so she ends things with him.

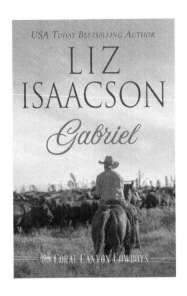

Gabe (Book 6): He's a father's rights advocate lawyer with a sweet little girl. She's fighting for her own daughter. Can Gabe and Hilde find happily-ever-after when they're at such odds with one another?

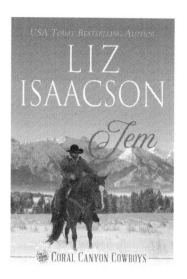

Jem (Book 7): He's still healing from his vices, and Jem has dedicated everything he has to his two kids. At least he's not mourning his divorce anymore, and in fact, he might be ready to move on. She's his former best friend, and once he breaks his wrist, his nurse. Can Sunny somehow rope this cowboy's heart?

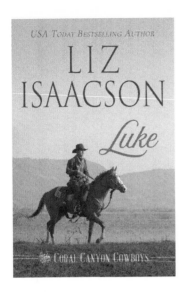

Luke (Book 8): He swore off women when his ex told him he might not be their daughter's father. But a paternity test confirmed he is, and Luke Young has dedicated his life to his little girl and his brothers' band. There hasn't been time for a girlfriend anyway. He's tried here and there, and the women in small-town Coral Canyon are certainly interested in him.

Books in the Christmas at Whiskey Mountain Lodge Romance series

Her Cowboy Billionaire Birthday Wish (Book 1): All the maid at Whiskey Mountain Lodge wants for her birthday is a handsome cowboy billionaire. And Colton can make that wish come true—if only he hadn't escaped to Coral Canyon after being left at the altar...

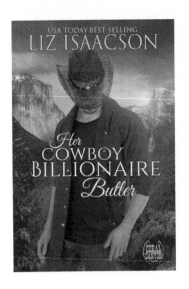

Her Cowboy Billionaire Butler (Book 2): She broke up with him to date another man...who broke her heart. He's a former CEO with nothing to do who can't get her out of his head. Can Wes and Bree find a way toward happily-ever-after at Whiskey Mountain Lodge?

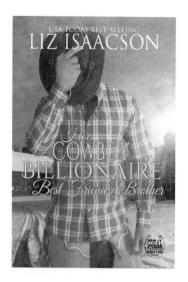

Her Cowboy Billionaire Best Friend's Brother (Book 3): She's best friends with the single dad cowboy's brother and has watched two friends find love with the sexy new cowboys in town. When Gray Hammond comes to Whiskey Mountain Lodge with his son, will Elise finally get her own happily-ever-after with one of the Hammond brothers?

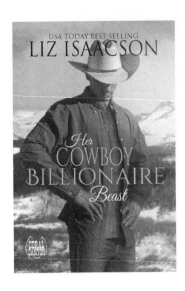

Her Cowboy Billionaire Beast (Book 4): A cowboy billionaire beast, his new manager, and the Christmas traditions that soften his heart and bring them together.

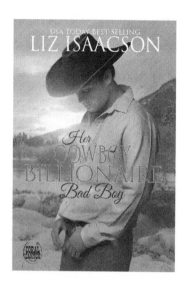

Her Cowboy Billionaire Bad Boy (Book 5): A cowboy billionaire cop who's a stickler for rules, the woman he pulls over when he's not even on duty, and the personal mandates he has to break to keep her in his life...

Books in the Christmas in Coral Canyon Romance series

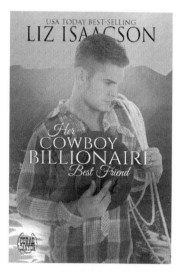

Her Cowboy Billionaire Best Friend (Book 1): Graham Whittaker returns to Coral Canyon a few days after Christmas—after the death of his father. He takes over the energy company his dad built from the ground up and buys a high-end lodge to live in—only a mile from the home of his once-best friend, Laney McAllister. They were best friends once, but Laney's always entertained feelings for him, and spending so much time with him while they make Christmas memories puts her heart in danger of getting broken again...

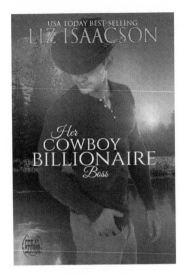

Her Cowboy Billionaire Boss (Book 2): Since the death of his wife a few years ago, Eli Whittaker has been running from one job to another, unable to find somewhere for him and his son to settle. Meg Palmer is Stockton's nanny, and she comes with her boss, Eli, to the lodge, her long-time crush on the man no different in Wyoming than it was on the beach. When she confesses her feelings for him and gets nothing in return, she's crushed, embarrassed, and unsure if she can stay in Coral Canyon for Christmas. Then Eli starts to show some feelings for her too...

Her Cowboy Billionaire Boyfriend (Book 3): Andrew Whittaker is the public face for the Whittaker Brothers' family energy company, and with his older brother's robot about to be announced, he needs a press secretary to help him get everything ready and tour the state to make the announcements. When he's hit by a protest sign being carried by the company's biggest opponent, Rebecca Collings, he learns with a few clicks that she has the background they need. He offers her the job of press secretary when she thought she was going to be arrested, and not only because the spark between them in so hot Andrew can't see straight.

Can Becca and Andrew work together and keep their relationship a secret? Or will hearts break in this classic romance retelling reminiscent of *Two Weeks Notice*?

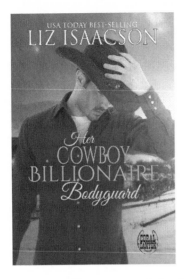

Her Cowboy Billionaire Bodyguard (Book 4): Beau Whittaker has watched his brothers find love one by one, but every attempt he's made has ended in disaster. Lily Everett has been in the spotlight since childhood and has half a dozen platinum records with her two sisters. She's taking a break from the brutal music industry and hiding out in Wyoming while her ex-husband continues to cause trouble for her. When she hears of Beau Whittaker and what he offers his clients, she wants to meet him. Beau is instantly attracted to Lily, but he tried a relationship with his last client that left a scar that still hasn't healed...

Can Lily use the spirit of Christmas to discover what matters most? Will Beau open his heart to the possibility of love with someone so different from him?

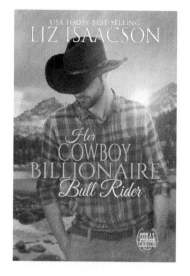

Her Cowboy Billionaire Bull Rider (Book 5): Todd Christopherson has just retired from the professional rodeo circuit and returned to his hometown of Coral Canyon. Problem is, he's got no family there anymore, no land, and no job. Not that he needs a job--he's got plenty of money from his illustrious career riding bulls.

Then Todd gets thrown during a routine horseback ride up the canyon, and his only support as he recovers physically is the beautiful Violet Everett. She's no nurse, but she does the best she can for the handsome cowboy. **Will she lose her heart to the billionaire bull rider? Can Todd trust that God led him to Coral Canyon...and Vi?**

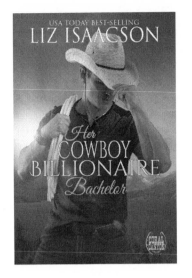

Her Cowboy Billionaire Bachelor (Book 6): Rose Everett isn't sure what to do with her life now that her country music career is on hold. After all, with both of her sisters in Coral Canyon, and one about to have a baby, they're not making albums anymore.

Liam Murphy has been working for Doctors Without Borders, but he's back in the US now, and looking to start a new clinic in Coral Canyon, where he spent his summers.

When Rose wins a date with Liam in a bachelor auction, their relationship blooms and grows quickly. **Can Liam and Rose find a solution to their problems that doesn't involve one of them leaving Coral Canyon with a broken heart?**

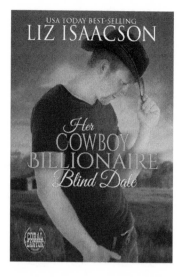

Her Cowboy Billionaire Blind Date (Book 7): Her sons want her to be happy, but she's too old to be set up on a blind date...isn't she?

Amanda Whittaker has been looking for a second chance at love since the death of her husband several years ago. Finley Barber is a cowboy in every sense of the word. Born and raised on a race-horse farm in Kentucky, he's since moved to Dog Valley and started his own breeding stable for champion horses. He hasn't dated in years, and everything about Amanda makes him nervous.

Will Amanda take the leap of faith required to be with Finn? Or will he become just another boyfriend who doesn't make the cut?

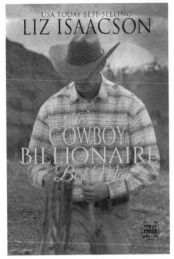

Her Cowboy Billionaire Best Man (Book 8): When Celia Abbott-Armstrong runs into a gorgeous cowboy at her best friend's wedding, she decides she's ready to start dating again.

But the cowboy is Zach Zuckerman, and the Zuckermans and Abbotts have been at war for generations.

Can Zach and Celia find a way to reconcile their family's differences so they can have a future together?

About Liz

Liz Isaacson writes inspirational romance, usually set in Texas, or Wyoming, or anywhere else horses and cowboys exist. She lives in Utah, where she writes full-time, takes her two dogs to the park everyday, and eats a lot of veggies while writing. Find her on her website at www.feelgoodfictionbooks.com.

Made in the USA
Monee, IL
21 June 2023

36498793R00300